LOST CHILDREN

Also by Maggie Gee

DYING, IN OTHER WORDS
THE BURNING BOOK
LIGHT YEARS
GRACE
WHERE ARE THE SNOWS

MAGGIE GEE

LOST CHILDREN

Flamingo
An Imprint of HarperCollinsPublishers

Flamingo
an imprint of
HarperCollins*Publishers*
77–85 Fulham Palace Road,
Hammersmith, London W6 8JB

Published by HarperCollins*Publishers* 1994

1 3 5 7 9 8 6 4 2

Copyright © Maggie Gee 1994

Maggie Gee asserts the moral right to
be identified as the author of this work

A catalogue record for this book is
available from the British Library

ISBN 0 00 224132 3

Photoset in Linotron Bembo by
Rowland Phototypesetting Ltd
Bury St Edmunds, Suffolk

Printed in Great Britain by
HarperCollinsManufacturing Glasgow

This book is dedicated to my beloved mother,
Aileen Gee,
in whose house it was largely written,
and who died before it was finally completed.

1

WHAT IF NOTHING IS LOST, nor can ever be lost?

What if all of time is still happening?

What if we are the kind of creature we dream of being, finding the grey defeated sister (so badly married, so beaten down) a child again, straight and slim, doing handstands in the dandelions down the green back garden?

If only we could slip from the room for a second. Maybe we could wake with the French windows flung wide and walk out into the landscape we have just dreamed, stretching away in every direction, perspectiveless, dazzling, unbounded, peopled.

What if the children are there already? Millions of them. The uncountable lost ones. Loud as life, running, laughing. Sun on the black, the ash-blonde, the auburn.

Myself, yourself, my mother, my father. Still young, still potential. All the lost children.

One day, Alma found Zoe had gone. Gone, one morning, her beautiful daughter. She had left a note at the top of the stairs. Alma picked it up absently, tidying in her sleep, glanced at it as she threw it in the bin. Picked it out. Started reading. Couldn't breathe.

She ran into Zoe's room, which was empty.

Impossible, but Zoe had gone. She was sixteen, and the note said nothing.

'Paul. Help me! Help me! *Paul!*'

Still half-asleep, Paul stumbled in and stared at her as she stood open-mouthed in the brilliant room, her ash-white hair pouring over her shoulders, startled eyes like polished coals, both hands clutching her bird-thin clavicles as if they would wrench her bones from her body, tear herself apart to find the pain.

Dear Mum and Dad, I have to go away for a bit. I know you wouldn't understand. Don't try to find me. Don't worry about me. I've taken the money from my Post Office book. I'll be all right. Give my love to Adam. I know you'll be upset. I do love you. Zoe.
PS I can't help it, I have to go.

'Help me! Help me!' Alma screamed to no one, turned away from Paul, turned inward, sobbing.

2

BUT ALMA HAD ALWAYS been hard to help. Because she was always helping other people. Putting them first. I don't want to be selfish, she always said. I mustn't be selfish. I really don't mind. I like to help. Whatever you want. Doesn't matter to me. It's not important.

And underneath, another voice whispered, nibbled: I'd like to be selfish, but I don't know how. I do mind what happens. I don't want to help. Why can't someone help me for a change? How about what *I* want? Doesn't that matter? There's something important I keep on missing. I can't be myself. I've lost it, somewhere.

One day when Zoe was thirteen or fourteen Alma heard the voice shouting furiously at her husband, who stood in his over-coat, white with shock. 'I am a person, you know. I'm not a fixture. I do have feelings. You don't notice I'm here.'

Her hand clapped over her lips at once; she felt herself reddening; she started to cry. Paul was looking at her as if she'd gone mad.

'I'm sorry,' she whispered. 'I'm not myself.'

'You're the most important person in this house,' he fussed, stroking her arm, giving her a hanky. 'Without you this house just wouldn't function. None of us could cope without you, Alma. Never think I'm not grateful, darling.'

He paused. She said nothing. Nothing came. The window behind him was a heavenly blue, the stupid blue of eternity, where the word that mattered would never be spoken, the thing that was lost could never be found.

She patted at him vaguely. Reassuring. 'Doesn't matter,' she attempted. 'I don't know why . . .' Trailing off, running down. He stayed there frozen a minute, staring at her, then looked at his watch, sighed, brightened.

'Cheer up,' he said. 'You need a holiday. We should go and spend some time with the family.'

Your family, the little voice hissed. *Your* sodding parents, it said quite distinctly, but Alma smiled at her husband, stood up. 'Have a good day,' she said. 'Don't be too late. I love you.'

She always said the same things. But now the little voice had started talking on its own.

There were four in the family. A family of four. 'Four's a good number,' said Paul. He often said the same things too, because they were a comfort, and held time together. Things you could go on believing through time.

'What's so good about it?' Alma asked, very loudly and suddenly, one day soon after the other voice was born.

'What do you mean, darling?' He was anxious.

'Oh . . . nothing . . . of course it is.'

Families aren't so great, the little voice grumbled. And this family isn't so wonderful either. Four is too many, but also too few. Trapped. For ever. For ever four.

There were Mummy and Daddy, of course. Adam, the eldest son, a trainee barrister. Zoe, the daughter, adored, adorable, fourteen, fifteen, growing up now, come back, I'll miss you, please don't go . . .

But of course Alma always encouraged her to go. 'University is marvellous, whatever you decide to do.'

'What's so marvellous about it?'

'You have . . . time. To . . . develop yourself.'

'Were you really happy at university, Mum?'

'Of course I was.'

The little voice nipped at her sharply. You liar. You were lonely the first year. Unhappy with your boyfriend the second year. Terrified of exams the third year. There were flashes of happiness, true, and life was *interesting* . . . at least life was interesting, then. And time went slowly. There was so much of it.

'*Really* happy,' she repeated emphatically. 'Work hard and you'll have no trouble getting in. You're very bright. Everyone says so.'

(Zoe had also been called a dreamer. Lazy. Happy-go-lucky. 'Not as *motivated* as some of our girls.' 'Only does what she wants to.')

'I might have a baby instead.'

Alma smiled a tolerant smile. 'When I said that to *my* mother, she went through the roof. I didn't really mean it.'

'*I* might mean it . . . did you say that to Gran? I might – I don't know – just want to have fun. You don't know everything about me, Mum.'

'Of course I don't, darling.'

'I have my own life . . . I *have* to have my own life.'

'Yes. Sorry. I didn't mean to push you, but . . . everything's so competitive these days.'

'You sound like Dad. He says that. You sound like a tape of Dad.'

Alma's other voice raged in her skull. I don't care if you have a sodding baby. Go on then, have one. Have fun. Do what you want to do. *I* never did.

They both chewed noisily on their salads. Zoe's thick dark curls hung over her forehead, her hair was getting darker, Alma couldn't see her eyes, becoming a stranger, a mystery . . .

'Great salad, Mum,' said Zoe. 'Thanks.'

Something a bit fishy here. Zoe sounded remarkably meek.

'Thank you for saying thank you.'

'Mum . . . I'm going out in half an hour.'

'Fine. Don't be too late.'

You're always saying that to people, whined the little voice, discontented. But *you're* the one who's left it too late. Too late for everything.

'I was wondering . . .'

'Oh God, don't ask.'

'Please please please could you give me a lift?'

'It's the other side of London, isn't it?'

'Well it's Highgate, actually. It's not too bad . . .'

'Not too bad for *whom*? Can't you take the tube . . . ?'

'. . . so I wondered if you could pick me up, as well. There are so many attacks on the tube these days. But you don't want to, do you? You think I'm a nuisance, don't you?'

'No.'

'I could get a lift home from some horrible drunken boy, I suppose . . . Or stay in someone's house and be late for school tomorrow.'

'Right. I'll drive you there. And pick you up.'

'Oh thanks, Mum . . . haven't you got a deadline to meet on that china book?' Alma was a freelance editor.

'It doesn't matter.' You know I have.

'Sure?'

'Look, it's fine. I can manage.'

'You're a saint, Mum.'

That's the trouble. 'It's OK.'

Outside Annie's house, Zoe said goodbye. 'Bye.'

'Always say goodbye nicely.'

'Why do you always say that?'

'It's a good idea, that's all. You never know what might happen.'

'Goodbye, Mum. Thanks for the lift. See you later.'

'Goodbye, Zoe. Take care. I love you.' And shouting, through the window: 'Don't be too late.'

It was a forty-minute drive through the traffic, it would be a forty-minute drive back. By which time, Paul would be home from work, and hungry. He would offer to cook, only half meaning it. She would refuse, and cook herself. They would eat together, and wash up together. He would say, 'I'm going to watch *San Francisco Specials*.' She would say, 'Fine.' He would say, 'You don't want to watch, do you?' She would sigh, and say, 'OK, but at ten I must go and work.' At ten she would go and work. Paul would say, 'Good girl, work hard.' At eleven-thirty, which would seem like only five minutes later, Zoe would ring and ask to be picked up. 'It's a crappy horrible party. It's not too early for you is it? You're not working are you?' 'It's fine.' 'Are you sure?' 'I really don't mind, I'm on my way.' Paul would say, as she went down the hall, 'I'll go if you'd rather,' not stirring from his chair. She would say, 'It's all right,' thinking *He should go*. He would say, 'Alma, you're an angel . . . drive safely.' 'Goodbye.' 'Are you going to give me a kiss?' he would ask, lightly aggrieved, lazy, loving. 'Good girl. I love you.' A slight pause,

12

then she would say, because she knew he expected it, 'I love you too.'

And she did, didn't she? She did love him. Her family had become her life, replacing whatever had nearly been born when she managed to escape from her first family. It was too frightening to be alone.

Yet something was lost, something was stifled too long ago to be sure of its face. Now the new secret anger filled up the absence.

'Good girl. I love you.' That frozen pause. And then she sighed, 'I love you too.'

These conversations, while actually in progress, had an eternal quality, unstoppable, circular, inching their way down the same narrow channel, pulling Alma with them, making pre-arranged moves. They were the medium through which the skinny silver minnow of her real life darted, struggling to survive in the thick half-light. His move, her move, my move, his move. Adam, Zoe, Alma, Paul. Ever more. Ever after. Until we all die, the little voice nagged. Until we are all bloody dead.

They had running jokes. Running quarrels. They ate their food. They cleared away. Adam ate too little, Zoe too much. Alma shopped and cooked, cooked and shopped. They watched each other growing older.

But it wasn't eternal. It wasn't unstoppable. The four-strong family wasn't, as it seemed, a four-legged table, well-built, light oak, on which endless meals advanced and retreated.

One morning, Alma found Zoe had gone.

Gone, one morning. With her sleeping-bag. And her water-proofs.

– And time broke down.

3

THIS WAS THE CHILD she had taught to swim. She was three when they started, not so young for London, where parents start competing when their babies leave hospital. Alma was aware they were already too late for the 'Waterbabies' class and the 'Toddlers' Splash', but her work had been demanding in those first years. She worked at home, for inadequate money, editing manuscripts for Sutton and Ford, which hardly paid for the part-time nanny who also picked Adam up from school.

When Zoe was three, Paul moved jobs, got a better job at another school and was put on another salary scale. Alma had just finished six months of working flat out on a series of books called *The Growing Child*. Suddenly there was more money. Alma decided she could spend more time with Zoe.

'With Adam too, of course,' said Paul. 'She sometimes upstages him, you know.'

'Of course with Adam as well,' said Alma. 'He was my first-born. I haven't forgotten him.' And yet, she had never taken Adam swimming, and now it was too late, because he'd learned at school.

She taught Zoe to trust the water. It was heated, balmy, like the waters of the womb. Ripples from the pool moved across the ceiling like watered silk; it was warm and quiet, for the big children were all locked up in school.

'Lie on your back,' she said. 'Make a star. A shape like a kiss. Just rest on the water. You're safe. I'm holding you. Good. Good girl. Now let your head slip backwards. The water will hold you. I can let go . . . you're floating! You're floating!'

'Naaah!' screamed Zoe, and went bubbling under. 'You let go of me! Horrible Mummy!'

'I said I would. You were *fine*,' said Alma. 'Now try again.'

'No. I'm paddlin'.'

'In a minute, then.'

'Trust the water . . . trust the water. Lovely warm water . . . see, it's your bed. Make a star, Zoe. Go on. Be a star . . .'

'No,' said Zoe crossly. 'I'm makin' a kiss.'

And it wasn't too long before Zoe was floating.

'My water-baby,' Alma said. 'Good girl, Zoe, I'm proud of you.' She was, and proud of herself as well. They were very happy, floating together, side by side on the amniotic water, Zoe's heavy blonde hair reduced to a fine dark fan of weed spread out round her head, the islands of her round solemn cheeks, her elfin nose, the blue-green eyes in a watery dream, sandy lashes fluttering, her round child's belly almost breaking the water, the two pale dumplings of her knees.

Helping her to float, without being held. Helping her trust herself and her body.

As a teenager Zoe still remembered it. 'Do you remember, Mum,' she said one day when they were drinking tea together after a quarrel about whether or not she should give up her music. 'When you first took me swimming. You taught me to float. It was my favourite thing. Just . . . hanging there suspended. Just doing nothing.'

'You learned very fast. And then when you started lessons, your teacher said you were a natural. You'd swum your first length before you were six. You were diving by seven.'

'It's the floating I remember. You and me together. It was warm, wasn't it. So . . . easy . . . it sort of seemed to go on for ever.'

'You kept up your swimming till you were really good. Don't you see, it's worth going on with things? No point in *half*-learning to play the piano . . .'

'I don't like Mrs Ramm. She's narrow-minded. She doesn't want me to play anything pop.'

'Of course not, because you are taking an exam. Time enough later to play for pleasure.'

'I don't agree,' said Zoe, mildly. 'I don't want to wait for everything good.'

'But you could be a brilliant pianist, darling!'

'I think I just want to play for myself.'

'Ah well, my sweet, I can't make you . . .' (In fact, she had made her for nearly nine years, and Zoe had the certificates to prove it.) 'It's just that I sometimes feel you're wasting your talents . . . Have some more cake. I love you, Zoe. Never forget I love you, darling.'

The baby stage passed quickly away, vanished into a dim warm limbo, a state of suspension where time had been slow, where life had been gentler, more physical. Where Zoe would sit still in Alma's lap when the nanny wasn't there and be stroked and read to, where she would fall asleep with her cheek on Alma's shoulder, where they could float together on the dreaming water.

The stage of Swimming Lessons was utterly different. Zoe was five, just starting school, her legs got longer, her chin was stronger. Her life had become very busy, suddenly, and Alma wasn't sure she had chosen it all.

There was school, and swimming, and French Club on Wednesdays, though how could a five-year-old belong to a club? – and piano lessons, and visits to friends, and educational trips with the school, for which they required lunch and a parent. Adam did football, and went to Gym Club, and belonged to the school orchestra, though Alma had forgotten to get him music lessons. Instead, he had joined the group lessons after school and could play the violin quite creditably. Paul had suggested they get him private tuition, but she said 'I think he's quite happy where he is. Let sleeping dogs lie, don't you think, darling?' Adam too had his educational visits, for which he prepared his own packed lunch, and was surely too old to need a parent. In any case, his outings often clashed with Zoe's swimming lessons.

The swimming lessons were 'excellent', as Alma pointed out to her fellow-mothers who hadn't yet discovered them. But also exhausting, which she didn't tell them. The grim battle through the rush-hour traffic, with Zoe struggling to obey instructions and put on her swimsuit in the back of the car without removing her safety belt. The sprint from the car park, trailing towels, swimsuits, clean pairs of pants. They would burst into the brand-new Sports Complex and find they had left their season ticket behind. Routine humiliations would be imposed before they were grudgingly let through the turnstile. By then they would both be drenched in sweat, since the temperature inside the Sports Complex was geared to the needs of naked bodies. Then the skate through the slippery, crowded changing-rooms, frantically searching for the one empty locker . . . Always that five minutes later than the others, Alma afraid that Zoe would lose out, that the race of life had already started, that the vanished minutes could never be caught up.

Calming down, slowly, in the first-floor balcony from which the mothers watched the lessons, clamped over the wall like limpets, watching their offspring thrash about in the water, trying to restrain themselves from shouting instructions, discussing avidly among themselves the little derelictions of the teachers – 'Tony doesn't notice when they *do* do it right' – trying not to sound too competitive – 'Julian had private lessons in the holidays. But look, your Sandra is doing really well, come on, Sandra, well *done* . . . Oh dear!'

It was weeks before Alma relaxed enough to notice that the keen, articulate two- and three-piece sets of mothers-and-children were just a determined minority there. The Sports Complex harboured other tribes.

There were the Youth; jewel-bright, be-lycraed adolescents, wearing wonderful clothes which had come with the eighties and clung to their sculptured thighs and buttocks, sweatbands, wristbands, fluorescent watches, chronometers, pedometers, saddlebags, hipbags, talking to each other in athletic code, way up front, on the edge of the future.

The Youth were newly in love with themselves. The Youth were fast, and fresh, and fun, birds of paradise who moved in flocks, flowers which in the moment of perfection knew they were going to be young for ever. They could wait for the show in the world outside where their beautiful bodies would be praised and applauded.

– Which is to be doubted, Alma thought, just a little sourly because she had children, she was over thirty, a different kind of being; and she knew the world had grown older, meaner, less hopeful, less welcoming to the young. But the place needed stars, and the youth supplied them.

How didn't I notice them at first, she wondered?

There's something about parenthood that makes you purblind. The world becomes a very narrow mirror. When you're pregnant, the world is full of pregnant women. When the baby's born, you see mothers and babies . . .

This curious myopia fell away in stages.

Alma began to notice other figures, smaller than the Youth, less certain, less vibrant. They were in the café when she took Zoe up for crisps or ice-cream after the swimming lesson. There were a few in the changing-rooms, slender forms between the bossy, hurrying bodies of the mothers, trying to manage their own wet clothes. They were in the lobby, scrabbling in their satchels, she supposed for the coins to come inside. They were by the vending machines, looking wistful, waiting, but the parent with money never came. They were in the viewing gallery, chewing gum, looking curiously down on the pampered water-babies whose mothers leaned above them, miming strokes.

They were children. Half a dozen, she thought at first, or a dozen. Nine- or ten-year-olds, she thought. Come after school, for a lesson, perhaps, though most of them didn't seem to have any kit. They weren't together, though they nodded to each other, recognizing each other, not often smiling.

They watched the grownups, it seemed to Alma. That was the puzzle; they watched the grownups. She supposed they came to see the glamorous Youth. That must be why they came here. Role models, she thought. It was a new phrase then, and she rather liked it.

Quite soon she realized there were dozens of them. Seven- or eight-year-olds. Sixes or sevens. Even five-year-olds, clutching the hands of bigger brothers or sisters, bigger, but nevertheless much too small to be there on their own. But there was no one with them.

She realized they didn't watch the Youth. It was mothers they watched. Mothers and children. They sat in the café and watched the mothers, watched them buying sandwiches and cakes for their children, stroking their faces, towelling their hair. They watched the mothers talking to the children. They slowly moved closer to the ones they were watching, big eyes serious, saying nothing.

Mostly the mothers didn't notice them, blinded by love for their own babies, blinded by thoughts about the round of activities that middle-class parenthood demanded. Longing for a rest, longing for bed, longing for their husbands to be home by children's bedtime. Planning, with one decimal point of their brain, to have another baby and do it all better, to have a proper nanny, to afford private school . . .

The children didn't know about any of this. They just saw a mother gazing at her toddler, patting his curls, feeding him chips, patiently retrieving the straw from his carton when for the hundredth time he lost it inside. They were like wild animals, slowly edging closer as it became clear they would not be challenged, would not be shouted at or hurt or rejected. Sometimes they would actually sit down at the table, still staring mutely at the browsing pair.

Then the mother might notice, and register 'hungry' – for those steady eyes were certainly hungry – and, slightly flustered, offer them a chip, or occasionally fish out a coin for them to buy themselves something at the vending machine. Which they sometimes accepted, but always came back, and sat there observing the mysteriously fascinating scene of a parent looking after children. Not eating much, but hoping to be fed. Hoping to be less hungry, one day. Hoping to catch normality.

Alma began to watch out for the children every week when she went with Zoe. There was something she recognized about these children. Something she knew, but couldn't name. Alma's looks must have intimated sympathy; it didn't take much; someone had seen they were there.

They would come like a flock of homing pigeons to the table where she sat and cradled Zoe, wet from her swim. Alma would ask them if they had eaten. They had never eaten. She would offer them food. Some of them whose parents had warned them of strangers before they sent them into a place full of strangers were wary of accepting; others accepted, some of them half-laughing as they took the money, amazed or amused, as if she might be simple, or not know the rules, as if they ought to be protecting her.

But they ate, gratefully. And started to talk.

'How old is she?'

'Five.'

'Has she got any brothers or sisters?'

'I've got a brother,' Zoe said. 'He's bigger than you. He can swim on his own. This is my Mummy.' Jealously.

'What school does she go to? Can she swim? Who's the boss of your house? Has she got a daddy? Where do you live? Have you got a car? Have you got stairs? Have you got a garden? Do you like Michael Jackson?'

The questions came in an endless stream. Alma answered, and replied with her own. The answers, when they came, were harrowing, though delivered with factual simplicity and an occasional desire to reassure, as if the child knew its life was sad but did not want to upset this new friend.

'I haven't seen him since I was six . . . I'm going to meet him this year in Jamaica . . . I live with my mum's sister. She works . . . I go to school most days, when my mum can drive me . . . I'd like to learn to swim one day, but my uncle says it costs too much . . . I like it here. People leave you alone, only sometimes you feel . . . I dunno. But I like it here. It's like my home. My mum says I haven't got to eat bad food. She cooks me good things. What . . . ? Beefburgers. Sausages . . . My mum said we was to go down the playground but there's someone there who bullies my sister . . . When it gets dark, I've got to go home. Oh yeah, you can walk, it's not too far. One day I got lost, and my dad whopped me.'

Zoe would be interested at first, then become restive as Alma ignored her, gripped and appalled by these stunted stories. 'Mum,' she'd say. 'I want to go home. I want to see Adam. Let's go home.'

In the end Alma would gather their things together. 'You going, then,' they'd say, expecting it, as if everyone was always leaving them. 'Will you come back tomorrow?' 'No,' she'd say. 'But we often come here. We'll see you again.' They would usually say nothing, not believing her, not believing, she thought grimly, that life went on, that people made plans and grew and survived, or that anyone did what they promised to. 'Are you all right?' she would ask them. 'Is someone going to come and collect you?'

Sometimes they would say there was someone coming 'before bedtime', a vague relation, or 'my dad's friend'; more often they would make their own way home when it was late enough for them to be let in, late enough, perhaps, for them to be forgiven for the mysterious sin which kept them here.

Alma began to dream about them. For years, those children were in her dreams, travelling the night with the quiet adroitness that came from surviving on their own, hundreds of them, thousands, too many to help, too many to count or feed or talk to. They would simply come, and want to sit near.

They came nearer and nearer to the heart of the dream, trying to hear what she was saying to Zoe, trying to learn from Zoe's lessons, watching her like a strange form of life – the nurtured baby, the nourished baby. The girls would try to mother Zoe, trying to give her what they hadn't been given, but they'd soon get bored and put her down and start watching Alma again for clues. Sometimes these legions would get on her nerves, their terrible quietness, their patience. And sometimes Adam came with them too, and she would call to him, but he stared at her gravely and stayed with the others.

When Zoe was twelve, she gave up her swimming lessons.

'But Zoe, you're brilliant. You're competition standard. Every single teacher has said the same thing.'

'I know. I'm fine. I don't need more lessons. I can come on my own now. I'll come with Rochelle.'

'But you won't get anywhere if you don't *train*!'

'I don't want to get anywhere. I just want to enjoy it. I enjoy swimming. Just – *being* in the water.'

And although every fibre of Alma's body resisted, she couldn't help remembering the way they'd begun, the small kiss-shaped body that once floated on the water, the stillness, the warmth; *you're safe, it will hold you.*

'You're just being difficult.'

'No I'm not.'

'And I'll miss going with you. I love you, Zoe.'

'You could go on your own. You could go with Adam. He loves swimming.'

'It's not the same, darling . . . never mind.'

The dreams carried on for a month or two after Alma stopped going to the Sports Complex, unwilling to go without Zoe, because it would prove that part of her life was over, that she was being pushed forward into the future.

– Soon they'll have gone, and I shan't be a mother. I'll be left with my own abortive little life, I'll have to think, I'll have to make changes . . . I'm not ready, yet. I'm not ready to move on. I want to stay with the mothers and babies.

She had a guilty feeling of abandonment. She had left those children without a word. They would think she had died, or moved away. They would think she'd forgotten them. As if she could. They streamed in their hundreds over the long sheets of Alma's bed, their faces blank in the August moonlight, fading only as she woke in a sweat, some essential word dying on her tongue. And then there were the other dreams, rare, unforgettable, leaving the print of their light on the day, when she sat with them in a clear new landscape, for the roof of the swimming pool had lifted away and only the clouds looked down on them, only the clouds, only the sky, and the water had risen to wash away the café, the ugly changing-rooms, the vending machines, and there was only water, calm warm water, and no one was excluded because they couldn't pay, they were all together, floating, dreaming, *it's lovely, Mummy, come with me*, that was Zoe, her fingers still short and pudgy, her belly still round, her hair still a mermaid's, floating past her, slowly, touching hands, touching fingers . . .

After a few months she did begin to forget, and the dreams stopped, as if the children had lost interest. She imagined them standing in the street outside, making one more visit just to make sure, one more time in case she looked out and saw them. They were used to the streets; they were cold, but not frightened. They shivered a little, but they were always patient. After a bit they nodded, and went away, and her mouth opened, but no sound came, and it was too late for her to look for them, too late for her to try and help them . . .

I can't help everybody, she thought. I can't love everybody . . . do I love myself? I do love Zoe.

I must love Paul.

– And Adam. A voice from the shadows reminded her, as if one of the children had suddenly returned, standing by the table, staring at her, silently begging to be asked inside.

4

ALMA HAD ALWAYS loved Zoe more than Adam. She never admitted it, she knew it with her body. There was no comparison. Zoe was the one. If Zoe wasn't there, the whole charade was pointless.

Zoe lost. Zoe gone for ever . . .

Her ghost squatted on the bedside table. A photograph, an icon for memory. Zoe was seven years old – 1983, Paul had scribbled on the back.

They had gone to Lavender Hill for the day. With Blotto, the spaniel who always looked drunk, one rakish red patch over his bloodshot eye. Zoe had loved him quite beyond reason.

Her hair in those days was golden brown, harvest gold, thickly plaited, the generous gold of plaited bread. In the photograph she was jumping towards the camera and the plaits flew up like great ears of corn, edged with sun against a dark blue sky. Below the hill was all bluebells; green and blue and blue and green, those drenching, youthful blues of April.

Her face was almost the cartoon child's face, broad at the brow and the gleaming cheeks, wide-set eyes, parted lips, smiling and shouting straight out of the picture, tapering to a pointed chin. Her heart-shaped face. Shining, shining.

Smiling at her parents, all those years ago, her sun-narrowed eyes staring straight into theirs (or the eyes of whoever holds the picture, now the bluebell hills have slipped away into the distance).

In the picture, you can't see those eyes are green. They were blue at first, baby-blue, the timeless blue in which babies seem to dream, as if they will never be different or older. As if she would always be Alma's baby. By the time she was six, they had a grey-green tinge, and a few years later they were truly green, quite startlingly bright, vivid, living.

And then they were only a photograph, shrunk under glass on the bedside table. Alma kept it in the bedroom where only she could see it, now Paul was gone, now everyone was gone.

Alma broke down. That was what they called it. 'She's having a breakdown. It's only natural.' And Alma broke out. The other voice broke out. The whispering voice began to shout and scream, to swear vilely, to tell home truths that meant home could never be home again.

Paul said, 'You've gone mad. I shan't take any notice. It's only natural.'

'You're a stupid bore. You're a dull little creep. You were a hopeless father . . .' It wasn't enough. She had to do more damage. 'You never loved her. I was the one who really loved her. She was the only thing I cared about.' The home truths; the home lies.

'You're saying terrible things. You're not yourself. Maybe you would like a cup of tea, Alma.'

'I'd like a sodding whisky! A sodding big whisky! And my dinner, on a tray! You fucking bastard! Don't you try being calm with me.' (It felt wonderful; it felt terrible. She had become huge, and terrifying. Yet part of her was sick with fear.)

'Don't shout at me, Alma, it doesn't suit you.'

'It does fucking suit me, it suits me very well. I should have been shouting for years and years.'

'Please, darling. Please. What's the point of being angry . . . I really need you. We need each other . . .' And horribly, grating, Paul started to cry, his shoulders jerking, big baby-heavy tears pouring under his glasses, one pink hand groping towards his wife.

Alma ignored him. 'Where's my fucking whisky? It's your turn, bastard. You look after me.'

'Alma, Alma . . . you're my beloved. We have to come through this thing together.'

The salmon-pink slab of her husband's hand flapped and fell, limp then convulsing, flapped at her shoulder, a barren rock. Flapped, fell, once, twice. Her hands stayed cold and inert by her side.

'I've got nothing left, Paul. I can't give you anything.'

25

'Please, hold me. Please, look at me.'

Alma would have died before meeting his eyes. Something awful, injured, thrashing and suffering, pleading with her to put him back in the pond, the safe waters where they'd lived together. She kept her eyes on the worn grey carpet, worn by the patterns of two decades of marriage, the two of them circling round each other, chewing on each other, eating each other.

'I'm sorry. I can't look at you.'

'I'll get you supper. Please, please let me.' He was sobbing again, jerking like a puppet.

'I'm sorry, Paul. I have to go out.'

Alma at weekends, waiting for rain. Alma waiting for Zoe to ring. Alma waiting for the knock on her door. Alma at fifty, frosted with need, possessed by Zoe's absence.

Absence makes the heart grow fonder. A soft lie, a sickening lie. Absence makes the heart grow hungry, angry, chewing on air for sustenance.

Absences are vacuums, sucking emotion into themselves, sucking and swallowing, gasping for more, anything more than this choking nothing.

None of Zoe's friends knew anything about it. None of their relatives. No one at school. No other mother. None of the teachers. Everyone seemed to use the same voice, shocked, concerned, then emptily comforting – 'Zoe is so *sensible*' – 'Zoe is so *bright*' – 'Lots of sixteen-year-olds manage alone.' Or 'Perhaps there's a boyfriend. Could she be with him?' 'I would *know*,' Alma protested, 'if there was a man.' (Paul had thought the same thing, but he knew nothing. Alma knew her daughter. There was no boyfriend.) 'We were very close. We're a close family . . .'

'You go or I go,' she had told Paul.

'Something like this should bring people together . . .'

He had the same air of stunned disbelief that he'd worn when she showed him Zoe's note. 'You're making things worse. This doesn't have to happen.'

'It has to happen. I'm sorry,' said Alma.

'It's the stress. You don't know what you want.'

'I know what I want. I want a separation.'

'So you've lost your daughter, now you lose your husband. I love you. I want to look after you—'

'Why haven't you then?'

'What do you mean?'

'It was always me, looking after you three. I'm tired of that. There's no point any more.'

'What about your son? You've still got a son. He'll be gutted to hear this – *nonsensical* thing . . .'

'I'm sorry about Adam, but he's twenty-one . . . I really am sorry. I dread telling him. But I have to think of myself as well. I'm fifty years old. Not a lot of time left.'

'The boy loves us both. He loves his home . . .'

'He comes home what, seven or eight times a year . . .'

'He phones every week.'

'So fucking what? I can't build a life around *phonecalls*, Paul.'

'We could . . . change things. Anything. Just say the word. Tell me what you want. I'd do . . . anything . . .' Everything repeated, helplessly, emptily.

'There's just no point without Zoe, Paul.'

'You always loved her more than Adam.'

'I do love him. But it's not the same . . . you can't *make* yourself love someone more. If I could, God knows I might still love you . . . I mean I do in a way, sorry, sorry, I'm not trying to make this harder, but everything's changed . . . you don't see it, do you . . . maybe I'll feel different in a year's time.'

'Remember all we've been through together . . .'

'I do remember, but it makes no difference.'

She said it partly to convince herself; it was still unthinkable, even to her, that everything could change, that the family could shatter, that the house would rise up and shake them out, doll-like bodies flung on to the pavement, tiny cries that died on the wind. Herself alone. Larger, stronger. Alma alone, in her empty house, her parents' house, the house of her childhood, the place where she'd learned what to expect from life: and later, that life didn't always

27

deliver, that being good didn't make you happy, that a surfeit of safety was dangerous, that nobody thanked you for giving your all, though she'd gone on giving till her world imploded. Alma alone, in her empty house, where only Adam still visited.

Adam came home much more often after the family fell apart. He saw Paul, too, when Alma couldn't bear to, and carried news between the two of them. Kind Adam, slightly pompous Adam. Boring Adam, who could never be Zoe.

'How are you coping, Mum?'

'Fine. Really.'

'No news, I suppose?'

'Of course not.' (Angrily.)

Another kind of news, in fact, had replaced the news she wanted to hear. She watched every news bulletin, every evening, every atrocity on every channel, but she didn't want her family to know about that. She knew they already thought she was crazy.

'How's the new job, Mum?'

'OK. Great . . . are you still working so horribly hard?'

'They have to have high standards. It is the Law. I've never been afraid of hard work.'

'Sod the Law,' said Alma absent-mindedly.

Adam was silent, reddening, hurt. 'That's not what you said when I was accepted. You were proud of me. You *said* you were.'

'Ignore me,' Alma apologized. 'You're a dear boy. A good boy.'

'You and Dad always *told* us to work hard. Especially Zoe. Zoe was lazy.'

'I was a different person then.'

'I don't believe you. You just *want* to be different.'

'Children don't like their parents to change.'

'Well it has upset me. Terribly. And Dad. He's lost weight, you know. I don't think he's eating.' His voice sounded thin and sanctimonious to Alma, but his cheeks looked jowly, heavily reproachful.

'I'm sorry I've upset you.'

'I do have exams at the end of the year.'

'Look, Zoe might be dead,' Alma shouted at him, 'and you expect me to worry about you and Dad. I won't, you know.

I've decided not to. I've spent my whole life worrying about my family –'

'You always worked. You were always working.'

'I worked at home. Part-time. To fit in with you children. Below my capacities.'

'Editing books is perfectly respectable.'

'Maybe I wanted to be brilliant, not respectable. You're the one who's keenest on being respectable.'

'Would you rather I took Ecstasy?'

'No, of course not. Let's not quarrel. But some of the manuscripts I did were crap. I did it for you two. It was . . . frustrating.'

'You had the job at the ICA.'

'Where I was a glorified hostess. And secretary.'

'We were always proud of you for working there. I thought you liked it.'

'It was *interesting*. The writers. Some of them. The ideas. But no one there was the slightest bit interested in me. I was a facility, not a person. And in any case, I gave it up. You got ill, remember. I looked after you.'

Alma had worked as a Talks Assistant at the Institute for Culture and the Arts. She was much too old for the job, in fact, which was usually filled by recent graduates, pretty young women with semi-shaven heads and bland, universally enthusiastic voices. And she had been grateful when Adam got ill. The burn-out rate in the job was high.

'I couldn't help getting glandular fever.'

'Of course you couldn't. Of course, darling.' She reached out across the angry space between them and patted the orange sleeve of his jumper.

'I'm still trying to find her, every spare moment.'

'You're a good son. A good brother.' (Why couldn't he say she was a good mother? She paused for a second, but nothing came.) 'Do you think she'll come back?' she said suddenly, helplessly, and to her annoyance began to cry.

His eyes softened; he touched her arm. His mother in tears was less strange and alarming than the new hard woman who lived alone.

Alma wept for the child she loved best who was gone, and let the less loved be her comforter.

29

5

BUT MOST OF THE TIME there was no one there.

Single.

Singular.

A singularity.

Back to the beginning of the universe, before anything happened, anything grew. Once she had been an only child, but surely that had slipped into the past . . .

'Is that for two, Madam? . . . Oh, just one.' That look of disappointment when she entered a restaurant. She would sit with her book, back to the room, reading about time and space again, taking some comfort from enormous numbers, where her loss might be lost, where her pain might lessen. She would go home later slightly dizzy with wine.

The house would be dark. It had never been dark. A dense black hole in the row of bright houses. She'd wonder how she had shrunk to this, after fifty years alive on earth. Completely alone in a four-bed house where four people had once slept together. As a child she had sworn not to be alone again, but somehow it had crept up and trapped her.

As she walked up the path she'd have a sudden conviction that the phone would be ringing when she got to the door, that Zoe would be there, ringing from a call-box, that the phone would stop ringing as she picked it up.

She would push her key in with desperate haste, irritated with her clumsy fingers. Light would flood down upon absolute silence. Maybe Zoe had phoned when Alma was out; perhaps she'd forgotten to switch the phone machine on. But the light on the phone machine would stare back steadily, no messages, no wink of hope.

She would vow to leave lights on the next time she went out, in case Zoe came back and thought they were dead, or had moved away, or some unspeakable disaster . . .

A more rational Alma looked on wearily.

She'll never come. She'll never phone.

Alma alone. Was it possible?

Would she be alone for the rest of her life?

Here in the house where she had lived as a child, where she had been an only child. It was sometimes comforting, sometimes a torment.

It had changed enormously, of course. When she was little it had always seemed dark, dark curtains over net curtains, dark carpets over layers of lino, dark drawers full of tidied secrets, things Alma wasn't allowed to ask about, places where little girls shouldn't go, where if they went they would get into trouble; places where Alma had been bad, had been punished . . . Forgotten sins, long folded away.

But when Alma and Paul took it over, in the seventies, all the dark layers were dispensed with; the walls and woodwork were painted white, the dark cupboards were stripped and varnished, the lino was torn out and lay in the garden, crude curling entrails, till the rubbish men came.

And a new history began in the house, new small footprints and fingerprints, new inscriptions shadowing the whiteness. Alma's new life, which now looked old. Her own children. Her own family. Who had grown up, who had gone away, and everything needed to be painted again . . .

She could have sold the house for a lot of money, but she couldn't leave without abandoning Zoe –

And she knew in her heart she wasn't ready to leave. She wanted to escape, but her feet were rooted. She was still looking backwards, looking for something, something which hid, which lay and waited; a child, maybe; something quiet, which hurt.

There were ghosts in this house who must have seen the little one. She still heard them talking, the old rhythms, the voices of her parents, nagging, roaring, the enormous voices which had made her small.

One day, she thought, she would really be free. If Zoe returned.

If the child were found . . . And at last she would be able to move away. But for now she remained, and so did the voices. So much louder, now that she was alone.

When she was the only child in this house, Alma had planned to fill her life with people. She had half-despised her mother, Gwen, for getting so tired with just one child. Other mothers seemed to manage three or four without complaining as much as her mother. Other mothers were younger and happier.

These wicked thoughts only emerged in her teens, and even then they were never spoken. Alma loved her mother with a locked, guilty love, guilty because her mother wasn't happy as a better daughter might have made her happy. It was a love that bound, but gave no pleasure, since Alma always felt in the wrong. Her love was the love of a debtor. She never gave enough, she was always behind.

Alma was selfish, her mother said. 'Try and think about others, Alma. You're a thoughtless child. You're a selfish child. You will have to learn to share, Alma. I'm afraid you're spoiled, being an only. Now give your friend that tricycle. Guests first, dear. Don't push. Don't shout. The universe doesn't revolve around you.'

Alma couldn't ever remember being selfish; she couldn't believe she was ever allowed to be selfish, as all small children are naturally selfish, as all good mothers allow them to be. She only remembered being told she was selfish, and constantly being urged to overcome it. Told it so often she believed it utterly, and lived thirty years of her adult life in a rearguard campaign against selfishness. 'Please, after you. I want to help. You go first, honestly, it doesn't matter . . .'

And her mother's voice intoned in the background: 'Kiss Mrs Phillips. *Give her a kiss.* Say thank you to Father. Say sorry to Father. You upset your friend with that cruel remark. You were rude in the shop. For goodness' sake *smile.* Why are you so awkward? Other children aren't . . . You embarrassed me, crying in front of everybody. Can't you ever think about anybody else? *I want, I want.* That's all we hear. Hasn't anyone told you, *I want* doesn't get.'

32

Gwen Thomas was so exquisitely attuned to the feelings of others that every outing was a minefield for the two of them. She made Alma feel big and clumsy and dangerous. All the child's movements became hesitant, careful, waiting and watching for people's reactions.

When she was good there were undoubted rewards. Alma was 'an angel', when she was good. Her mother would cuddle her and stroke her hair, and buy her gobstoppers or sweet cigarettes.

At home things were simpler but more restricting, for there only one person's feelings counted, those of her stepfather, black-browed Owen, difficult, furious, roaring his love. His wild white hair, the thick bars of those eyebrows. The world was black and white to him, and he raged against anything he didn't think right.

'Don't tell Father. Don't say a word.' If a plate got broken or a bill was unpaid or a neighbour came round complaining about something, the two women would keep it dark. At home they were conspirators, deferring yet controlling, deciding what Owen could bear to know. Family triumphs, weather forecasts, domestic trivia, the menu for their meals, though even then some ingredients could never be revealed, because Owen (wrongly) believed he did not like them.

Owen was 'Father' to distinguish him from Daddy, Alma's real father, Jack. She was only four when Daddy died. The older she got, the more she longed to remember him. But all she could recall was a warm dark tenderness, a yielding, something absolute and mysterious. He wasn't peppery or strict like Owen – she half knew that, and had often been told it. The years with Daddy were the Golden Age. Gwen had told her so, and Alma believed it.

He was very handsome, big and blond. Adam, Gwen said, took after him. 'Jack doted on you, Alma. Worshipped little girls. Loved them to death. And you – you would have died for him. You would have done anything for my Jack.' His face in the photos was a matinée hero's, with sand-pale hair that arched in a striking wave across his forehead.

He was excused from the Army because of short sight, and

became an Air Raid Warden. The story of his death had no rhyme or reason. 'It's no use quarrelling with God,' said Gwen, 'they say He moves in mysterious ways.'

Just before VE Day, Jack was on patrol when the sirens screamed. A woman called out to him from a window somewhere at the top of a bomb-damaged building. He ran upstairs to escort her down and as he pushed the door of her room she shot him in the face and chest. A passer-by heard her screaming that Jack was a spy, a peeping Tom, an obscene, perverted Nazi bastard. Her mind had gone, he told his wife when she came to see him in hospital. He had never seen the woman before, he said, he insisted; she must have been mad. He died three days later in hellish pain, a hero mourned by his wife and daughter.

It was only men that Gwen protected from the facts. Alma was her daughter, and she let her have it. 'I'll never forget what you said when he died. You were in one of your moods . . . I suppose we'd been ignoring you. I came out of the ward and you were with a nurse, helping her fill some glasses of water. "He's gone," I told you. "Is he dead?" you said. "He's at rest," I said, and burst out crying. "Serves him right," you suddenly said. You had that spiteful look you used to get. "Can we go home, just the two of us? Will he never come back again?" God forgive me, but I couldn't bear it. I slapped you so hard you spilled the water. The nurse looked at me as if I were a murderer.'

'I'm sorry,' said Alma, a pale ten-year-old when her mother gave her this information. 'I don't remember. I'm really sorry. I don't remember anything at all.' She saw her mother's face curdle with reproach. 'I mean, I remember I . . . adored him, of course.' (She had been told. She knew it was true.) 'I know he was marvellous. And . . . kind. I just don't remember anything . . . real.'

And it always bothered her, after that, that she could have said anything so vicious, on the day of her father's death. Maybe her mother had misheard. Maybe Gwen was mad, and had made it all up . . . But her mother was as sane as bread, or a stone.

When Owen retired from his job in the City, he and Gwen had moved back to his village in Wales. They let Paul and Alma buy their London house more cheaply than any of them realized, though Owen made a scene when he found out, and of course Alma and Paul never had any money to make good the deficit her stepfather imagined, which grew with time, like all grievances, till a stroke tied his tongue at sixty-nine, still roaring at life, righteous and loving.

So Gwen had outlived both her husbands. She lived on in the mountains in her crabbed grey cottage, clamped like a barnacle to the earth. Age had refined and concentrated the will-power which had always fuelled her, but she saved most of her dis-approval for others, for her sister Eileen, most notably, the eccen-tric, sweet-tempered younger sister who had made little Alma's life bearable. 'Your Aunty Eileen' was a reprobate; she drank beer and wore her blouses untucked.

Now Alma had become the perfect daughter, a transformation she could never quite believe. Mysteriously, Gwen still made her feel guilty, however much she sang her praises.

Perfection arrived at around eighteen, when Alma had apparently stopped being a brat. 'The age of reason,' Gwen told her one day as they sipped cups of tea in her tidy front garden with its acid-bright dahlias stunted by the wind, watching Zoe and Adam fight over a ball. 'You'll see, they arrive at the age of reason and they won't be difficult any more. You became a credit to your upbringing.'

Only as a mother, perversely enough, did Alma fall short of this acquired perfection. It seemed she nagged her children too much – *I wonder where I got the habit from?* Whereas Gwen adored them uncritically, completely. Sometimes Alma was seared with jealousy; *if only she could have loved me like that . . .*

Zoe fell on the flowerbed and Alma shouted. '*Zoe!* Those are your *Grandma's* flowers! Get up, for goodness' sake, and say sorry to Grandma!' Gwen let Zoe apologize, then hissed at Alma. 'Alma, you're always on at those children. Leave them alone, dear. Let them have their head. They have to think for themselves, you know.' Alma stared at her mother mutely. 'I thought you thought children have to be told?' Gwen just smiled a maddening smile, the wrinkles fanning out over rock-firm cheekbones. 'They're lovely children. You ought to be proud.'

Alma gazed at the bobbing heads of the dahlias, sunny, simple, jewel-bright. Was it possible she misremembered everything? She longed to speak, but her voice had died, locked in her throat by a swelling pain. She snipped off the dahlias with imaginary shears, one by one, very carefully and neatly.

One day, she thought, staring helplessly upwards – and the sky agreed, its towering freedom, its immense carelessness, billowing, growing, flowering worlds of water-bright cloud, unfurling upwards with glorious daring, flowing in light, in the realms of light – one day, she thought, I shall find my voice, I shall speak to her, I shall tell her I suffered, I shall make her give back whatever was lost, I shall make them give up what was taken from me. I could go back and find it. Be whole again. Tears filled her eyes; the light was dazzling. A moment's courage opened her lips –

But 'Maybe they need their tea,' said Gwen. 'You look tired, dear. I'll go and make sandwiches. It's lovely to have my family here. I wish that Daddy could see Zoe in that frock . . . He adored young children. So did Father, of course.'

'Thanks,' said Alma. 'I'm not hungry.'

'You *do* sound tired, dear. Early to bed.'

Paul never relished visits to Gwen. By mutual consent, Alma often went alone. But in bed, at night, she longed for him; his body, that proved she was no longer a child. For in that narrow bed, so near to the one where her mother lay wakeful in the black dark, there was nothing to prove that Alma had grown up, had made a life, was loved and needed. She was swept into the past, diminishing, diminished.

Alma lost.

Alma alone.

Alma shrinking towards the singularity.

But if she could find that bright point in the distance . . . ?

6

FOR REASONS WHICH WERE never made quite clear, since Gwen had only one child to cope with, and never had a job, in deference to her husbands, Alma was regularly, all through her childhood, sent away to Aunt Eileen's to stay, and somewhere in a background of whispered voices was the implication that Gwen couldn't cope. Alma knew she always went in mild disgrace, punished for making things too much for her mother. The feeling was disagreeable, but didn't stop her enjoying life with Aunt Eileen.

Certain things, however, were definitely queer.

First of all, the question of Eileen's age. She never seemed at all like a proper grownup, with her shiny black hair and unstockinged legs, sitting on the carpet or lying on the sofa, laughing a lot, eating chocolates, telling stories. They were curious stories which grew and grew, starting off true but becoming fantastic: there were racehorses, there were seahorses. Nothing remained as it began.

Alma's favourites were the ones about changelings.

'Do you think I might be a changeling, Aunt Eileen?'

'I am,' said Eileen, her big eyes serious, staring straight at her niece under her thickly sprouting fringe. 'So it's possible. At any rate, your father's kicked the bucket, so I don't see why you shouldn't think you are. Only don't mention it to your mother, Flower.'

Eileen always said thrilling, shocking things. At home no one would have said 'kicked the bucket'. No one even specified that Jack was dead. He floated in a permanent limbo of saintliness.

'How old are you, Aunt Eileen?'

'Young enough to know better,' said Eileen.

Ten-year-old Alma thought about that. It was the opposite of what her mother said. 'You mean, young enough to know better than my mother?' – for Eileen was certainly younger than Gwen.

'She wouldn't thank you for saying so,' Eileen hooted. 'But it could be true. So sharp you'll cut yourself, our Alma.' She didn't seem cross; she was smiling. Alma was tempted to further disloyalty.

'Why do children have to be seen and not heard?'

'I see you,' said Eileen. 'I hear you, dear.'

'They said it at school, and then Mum agreed.'

'She doesn't mean everything she says.'

'Was she always good, when she was your sister?'

'She's still my sister. Don't forget. I mustn't go telling you all her secrets.'

'Oh please, Aunt Eileen. When she was a child . . . ?'

Eileen looked away, out of the window which she'd curtained with an oddment of purple-striped towelling.

'When she was a child, of course she was childish. Does that answer your question . . . ? I suppose it doesn't . . . But she's grown up now. She had to grow up early. She was the eldest, and our parents were strict . . . It's not really fair. I had all the fun.'

'Mum says you're sad because you haven't got children.'

Eileen's nostrils flared with indignation, and she flung back her head on its elegant neck. 'That's all she knows,' she said proudly, and muttered something else that Alma didn't hear. For a moment Eileen looked different, taller, darker, more frightening, strong as a witch. 'I have her child for her, don't I?' And then she laughed, and her neck relaxed. 'I've thousands of babies,' she said. 'Babies your mother knows nothing about. All the village children come here, don't they?'

Alma nodded. 'But . . .' she said, and stopped. She thought, but they come here for jokes and stories and apples and chocolates and rides on the swing. They don't come here because they have to, like real children do. They don't come here because they're afraid. It was all very different from having real children.

'And my boyfriends,' Eileen went on, stretching and stroking her long black hair across her strong shoulders. 'My boyfriends are like my babies, dear. And your mother knows nothing about my boyfriends.'

38

Alma was silent, briefly, flattered to be told, blushing with pleasure but stiff with shock. Her mother, she was sure, had never had boyfriends. Husbands, yes, but no men like babies who would make her want to stroke her hair and stretch in the way that Eileen was, like a cat in the sun, unlike a grownup.

'Do you really have boyfriends?' she finally asked.

'And why not?'

'How old are you, Aunt Eileen?'

'Why?'

'I thought, you know, only seventeen- or eighteen-year-olds had boyfriends . . .' Alma was suddenly not quite sure if Eileen was too old or too young for it. But Aunts surely didn't have boyfriends. Aunts were people with nieces, or nephews, and husbands if they could get them – which Eileen evidently could not. Gwen always said spinsters 'couldn't get a husband'. Alma sometimes worried it would happen to her.

But another part of her wanted to be like Eileen, driving around in a van selling dresses and living in a house full of multicoloured rags. Eileen made jokes and danced around the garden. Eileen had a blue net petticoat. Eileen smoked. She wore big rings which drew your attention to her square brown nails, and the smoke had got into the cracks in her face, the smiling lines like a faint tattoo.

The question of age was never quite settled. One time when Alma came to stay, Eileen was pinning up her washing in the garden, wearing crimson corduroy trousers exactly like the ones the Tunnard twins wore at Alma's school, which drove all the other girls wild with envy. And she had her hair in a long thick plait, tied with a twist of crimson ribbon! Alma hugged her and was swung in the air, round and round till her heart pounded, and the wind blew, and the apple trees shook, and the blue-green hills snaked silently past them –

'Stop,' said Alma. She had to get it straight. 'Are you a girl or a woman, Aunt Eileen?'

'I'm myself, silly,' Aunt Eileen said.

Suddenly Alma had felt very unhappy.

'I don't know if I am,' she told the grass, but Eileen was back at the clothes-line, singing.

*   *   *

39

As Alma grew up, she asked harder questions. Many of them did not receive answers; Eileen was oblique, it was part of her charm; besides, there were things she wouldn't say about her sister.

Once, however, she was moved by pity to tell much more than she should have done.

Alma was fourteen years old. She had come for Easter. She had three spots, which felt like thirty. For the first time she had travelled on the train on her own, what seemed like endless hours on her own as the smoky train rattled on towards Wales, as her suitcase swung in the net of the rack and she shrank from every man who walked down the corridor.

There had been rows at home, between Owen and Gwen. As usual, it seemed to be Alma's fault: Gwen screamed at her; Owen sent her away. 'It's better if you go. Your mother needs a break.' For once Alma hadn't been keen to escape. She had friends at school; she had hoped to see them. There were plans to go to a coffee-bar, where there were boys with shadows on their cheeks and a juke-box and something exotic called a *Cappuccino*; where she might have smoked, where the future waited . . .

The evening she arrived it all spilled out, as Eileen cooked eggs and bacon in the kitchen.

'Mother hates me. She always did. That's why she never had another child . . . that's why I'm always on my own . . .'

'She doesn't hate you. Of course she doesn't.'

'She must have hated me as a baby . . . It's because I was selfish, it's all my fault . . . I hate myself . . . I wish I was *dead* . . . I'll kill myself, I will, I will –'

And Alma had burst into passionate sobs, pulling at her hair in its painful plait. She did want to die. To unmake herself. There was no worse fate than being herself, her horrible, difficult, unlovable self.

Eileen silently dished up the brown-laced eggs and slapped two pieces of toast on the plate.

'Now listen. This is important. I'm going to treat you like a grownup, I'm going to tell you something I've never told anyone. But no more talk of killing yourself. Please, Flower. You're too . . . *dear to me.*'

And as they ate, in her hot, kind kitchen, she told Alma why she was an only child.

Gwen had got pregnant again, this time by Owen, a year after they married, when Alma was six. Then the doctors found a faulty valve in her heart. 'She was thinking of you, as much as herself. The risk of leaving you an orphan . . . She had an abortion. D'you know what that is? Owen took it very badly.'

Alma did know. This news was momentous. Something fearful, dark and bloody. Imagining her steely mother pregnant. Imagining her mother feeling, suffering.

'I would have had a sister,' Alma burst out. 'I would have had someone to be on my side.'

'But you might have lost your mother,' Eileen said.

Alma was quiet. It was the child she missed. The lost child. The missing ally. (The horror of abortion would stay with her always, and she passed on the secret to her own daughter. 'It's horrible, abortion, not that I blame Grandma. But you might have had cousins. I'm sorry, Zoe.')

'– You see, you mustn't blame yourself,' Eileen concluded. 'You're a lovely girl. She's very proud of you.'

'She isn't, she hates me,' Alma said, darkly. The egg had cooled, and tasted of fat.

'You should hear the way she talks about you, child,' Eileen insisted. 'The pair of them are mad with pride.'

If you knew, Alma thought, what they say about *you* . . .

For they talked a great deal about Eileen at home. She was one of the topics Owen tolerated, because she was family, and because, Alma realized as she grew older and understood more, both of them enjoyed disapproving of her.

'She'll be very unhappy when she's an old woman,' Gwen asserted, with gloomy pleasure. 'It's all very well for now . . .'

'She won't have a pension,' Owen agreed.

'She won't have a family,' Gwen said.

'Aren't we her family?' Alma asked.

'It's not the same as getting married,' Gwen said. 'There were plenty of men would have been happy to have her,' she added. 'Notwithstanding her queerness, and . . . other things.'

'What things?' Alma asked, but Owen frowned a warning.

'Our family was always a good-looking family.' Gwen preened

herself. 'Including Eileen.' Alma could see no trace of beauty in her mother's tight features, but perhaps there had been once, before she was a mother. Could Gwen have been young? It was unimaginable.

'Old age will hit your sister hard,' said Owen, looking forward to his own well-ordered future. 'She is the sort of person who lives in the present.'

That sounded perfectly all right to Alma, but her parents, she knew, lived a different way, regretting the past, calculating the future, suspicious of the narrow strip in between, anxious always to hoard their pleasures for the distant day when they'd finally deserve them. 'Yes – old age will be a blow to Eileen.'

In fact, the blow fell first on Owen, tripped by the stroke which crumpled and disfigured him. Age slowly dried and hardened Gwen. Whereas Eileen had somehow slipped the leash. At seventy-nine, she still didn't seem old.

All the parts had aged, but the whole had not. She still had long hair, though the black had turned purplish like the new dark bottle on the bathroom sill. Her cheeks were the hectic shade of dried apples. Her eyes shone as she walked down the garden, moving quickly, then stiffly, then quickly again, more quickly than ever to make up for the stiffness and get her on the road in yet another battered van. They were like caddis shells, those vans; things that promised a new stage of life. One broke down and another one arrived, scarred but jaunty, a house for the soul.

She still drove round the steep hill roads with a collection of gaudy clothes in the back, some home-made, some bought at a discount, a few picked up at jumble sales, washed and mended. People these days, she sometimes complained, didn't seem to see the beauty of synthetics, how easily they washed, how you didn't need to iron them. 'These serious young people all ask me for cotton. You wouldn't see me dead in cotton! Sweet young faces in sacks of black cotton. Like Zoe, Alma. Are they all in mourning? It seems to be the mothers I sell to now. Even the grandmothers . . . Isn't it queer? I used to sell to my own generation.'

Whose generation was she, then? Was it the lack of children

that made her seem young? She still *acted* young. She still thought young. She still drank beer, and hooted with laughter; she still had brown fingers, and sat on the floor, and sometimes smelled of cigars and Indian scent.

Zoe had been close to her great-aunt, and went to stay with her as Alma once did. It was Eileen, not Gwen, who Alma rang first with the terrible news that Zoe had gone, and part of her hoped, when Eileen answered, that her aunt's deep voice, still laughing and youthful, would say 'Do you want to speak to Zoe, Alma? The wonder child is drinking beer in the garden . . .'

Instead Eileen gasped and wept on the phone, the first time Alma ever remembered her crying, and grief made her ordinary, grief made her old.

Time stopped, for all of them, when Zoe left. Time stopped, and broke, and they had to muddle on, though the future had grown dark, and today was endless, and now no one wanted to live in the present, everyone wanted to creep back into the past and curl up in the kindness of some unremembered moment, some moment they never knew they'd need to remember, when Zoe was there, chattering, yawning, sitting on the stairs with the sun on her cheek. When life was full, because the loved one was there, but it seemed so normal that no one noticed.

Only to understand too late. Looking back, Alma felt she had never understood anything until it was gone. Life had speeded up, since she was a child. Now it rushed her pell-mell into the future, unable to see forwards, staring at the past, never realizing what was to be left behind until the fingers had loosened and the moment was gone and the loved face dwindled, too small to console her.

7

ALMA'S LIFE WAS NOT EMPTY, however, as Gwen reminded her, energetically. Gwen made lists of all Alma's possessions, and enumerated them, on the phone.

– Good health.

– A perfect son.

– A mother 'who'd do anything for you, Alma.'

– A living husband. 'He still loves you. Paul's put up with *a lot.*'

Perhaps there was a hint that Gwen's own life was emptier, having lost the grandchild she adored, and two husbands through no fault of her own. And her only daughter had rejected her – for Alma, by the skin of her teeth, by indirection and delay, had succeeded in turning down Gwen's kind offer of coming to live with her 'until you feel better'. Gwen was thus restricted to the telephone, where her comfort killed by a thousand cuts.

'You know Zoe and I understood each other,' Gwen said more than once, during these endless phonecalls. 'If only she'd thought of talking to her grandma.'

'She talked to me, Mother. Frequently.'

'There are things that children can't say to their mothers.'

'There are things that children can't say to their grandmothers.'

'In any case, she wasn't a child. It's hard for a mother to realize that.'

Alma allowed her mother to triumph, as usual. It didn't matter. Nothing mattered.

'I'm glad you're getting on with your life,' Gwen said. Somehow it managed to sound disapproving.

'I am, Mother. Or else I'd die.'

'You have a lot to live for, Alma. That's no way to talk. I'll ring you tomorrow.'

Alma never managed the direct 'No,' never found in time the patch of firm ground she needed to stand on to confront her mother. Mysterious enemies had been there already, a lifetime ago, digging under the soil, leaving hollow places, an emptiness where the imagined words of courage echoed and died.

In any case, perhaps Gwen was merely being kind. 'You have a lot to live for, Alma.'

Alma's best friend Verity said the same thing. She asked Alma to supper, a delicious supper in the creamy comfort of her new house in Hampstead. There were florist's roses on the table, and a good bottle of red. She hugged Alma extra tenderly.

– *She's sorry for me*, thought Alma crossly, but she ate her *langoustines* with appetite; she couldn't be bothered to cook for herself.

Before all the giant prawns were dispatched, Verity was urging her to draw up a checklist, and some of it duplicated Gwen's. Alma had:

– A husband who wanted her back.

– A car, a Fiat Uno, three years old.

– A new job at the local estate agent's which was easier and more enjoyable than her old one at the ICA. More honest, too, since she knew what people wanted and did her best to sell it to them. People told lies, but they were honest lies, inspired by greed for precise amounts of money. Alma found money interesting, now Paul wasn't there to pay half the household bills. It was a safe emotion, greed for money. It helped suppress thoughts of Zoe for hours . . .

Alma had:

– A husband, a car, a job and a home she was freshly trained to appreciate, seeing how her clients longed for space and how they made do with shoeboxes. Her house was detached, good decorative order, four beds, three receps, good size kitchen/break-fast, five-year-old roof, large mature garden, double garage (now half-empty) . . . fitted cupboards, emptying . . . empty beds . . . emptiness . . .

– In fact, the house was too big for her, but if she left, how could Zoe ever come home?

– Husband, car, job, house . . .

45

– oh, and a son (remembering, guiltily).

'Your lovely son,' said Verity, indignant, serving the main course of chicken and ginger, filling up Alma's empty glass. 'Adam's an absolute sweetie. More ginger, or is that enough . . . ? How could you forget him?'

'I didn't, really. I just – took him for granted.'

'Precisely,' said Verity, beady-eyed.

Verity was a novelist, and when she was just starting, twenty-five years ago, and Alma was working at Winkworth Slope, Alma had picked her novel from the slush pile. A year later she was Alma's bridesmaid, and quite soon after, Adam's godmother. Everything happened to Alma, in those days. Verity never married, and success came slowly. But in the last five years she'd grown rich and famous, while Alma's life had crumbled.

'Sometimes I can't think where time has gone,' Alma said, staring across at her friend who in the soft light, with her slight, compact body and wide fawn's face, could still have been thirty. 'I mean, twenty-five years is practically a lifetime . . . but part of me still feels so young. And you really *look* young, Verity.'

'The single life is less harrowing,' said Verity. She didn't say *You look young too.* 'Motherhood takes it out of you. And – darling, things have been so awful for you.'

'Does it show so badly?'

'I know you too well . . . but you're still great-looking. My Ian fancies you.'

'Well that's no good. He *is* your Ian.' But Alma was touched and cheered to think so, warmed by the little gift of praise. I'm still not used to it. Gwen so rarely praised me. She shook her pale hair, pulled in her stomach.

'Are you . . . going to take Paul back?' Verity asked, tentative.

'He drives me crazy. I can't bear to look at him.'

'At least you're not indifferent, darling.'

'I'd always be thinking about Zoe, you see.'

'Do you blame him then?' Verity's groomed brows lifted, as if it would be utterly unfair to blame him.

'I bloody blame him,' Alma snapped, a little jet of energizing anger. She could show it with Verity; anger was allowed. 'For being alive, when Zoe might be dead. For going on working and walking around. For not understanding why we had to split up.

For treating me like a demented child. For not having spent more time with Zoe. For spending too much time at his bloody school . . . *I blame him for bloody everything. I blame him because we had her in the first place.'*

Verity said nothing, so the bitter speech hung there, spreading, echoing, shadowing the room. Verity waited till the stain had faded.

'Paul's miserable too. I saw him last night—'

'I can't stop you seeing him, but don't tell me about it.'

'– he doesn't look well. He still really loves you.'

'Don't you start, Verity, for heaven's sake!'

'I'm fond of both of you, you know.'

'Look, as far as I'm concerned, I'm single.'

'You can't just – wipe out time, Alma. You were with Paul for all those years.'

'I wish I could go back to before I met him.'

Verity cleared the plates, filled up the coffee-grinder, switched it on. The noise was an assault in the pretty golden room where everything was light, harmonious, blended with the silken touch of money. Alma watched her old friend's bell of dark hair swing and shake as she took cream from the refrigerator. Hennaed now, but still profuse and youthful. She had never had children, and now she never would. It was as if she had declined to move through life's stages, and Alma had often had to suppress feelings of pity or superiority. Now pity had been replaced by envy. If you never had children, you could never lose them.

'I wish I'd never had children,' she burst out.

'You're mad to say that. Your kids are wonderful. And she's not dead, for Christ's sake. At least you know that much.'

There had been a message through the organization 'Alive and Well', which told parents their runaways were still alive. Still alive, but not where, not how . . . the relief and torture of getting that message, a month after she left . . . so long ago. Since that, only an uncertain sighting. A voluntary worker at an East London day centre for the homeless had been almost sure she recognized Zoe's photo. Almost sure that someone just like Zoe had come in every day for a week or so, and then vanished, when they started to talk to her. Dark curly hair, 'well-spoken', she said. Plumper than the photo Alma showed her . . . 'I can't be sure. We

47

see so many faces.' But the woman did remember a sleeping-bag. 'Clutched it to her all the time, like a baby.' And Zoe had taken her sleeping-bag with her . . . almost the only thing she had taken. This was in August. Since that, nothing . . . nothing but the hell of imagining their daughter on the streets with all the crazy people.

Verity broke in on Alma's grim thoughts. 'You've still got two kids. Don't wish them away. She will come back, I know she will.'

'I'm angry with her . . . I'm really angry . . . I almost hate her . . . but I miss her so desperately . . .' Alma could hear how confused she sounded, and very faintly slurred, with an edge of tears. She didn't want to feel like this. Verity waited, holding the coffee-cups. Her calm, concerned face was a mute reproach. 'You don't understand,' Alma burst out. 'How *can* you understand, when you don't have . . . you don't have . . .' Her voice trailed away, but the unspoken words hung like a blade in the air between them; *how can you understand, when you don't have kids?*

Verity passed the thick dark green cups too quickly so the dark liquid slopped over the gilded rims. Alma could see that she had annoyed her. Verity looked up, then down, then looked again, cheeks bright, and suddenly said it. 'Look, I met Ian too late for kids. My other men never inspired confidence. And I was too poor to do it on my own. Too poor, or too scared, it's the same thing. So I missed my chance. And I really regret it.'

'I always thought . . . I thought you wanted your freedom. You were, what, forty-two when you met Ian?'

'We tried for three years, but nothing happened.'

'You never said. I can't believe it.'

'Even now, I feel the odd pang of hope, when I read about fifty-year-olds having babies. Maybe I'd have been a terrible mother, but I wouldn't have minded the chance, let's say.'

'I wish you'd told me . . .'

'It was too painful.'

'But your work, Verity. You love your work. And it's the last half-dozen years when you've become so successful. Maybe with young kids you couldn't have done that.'

'I expect I would have managed somehow.' And her lowered eyes said *So what, in any case. If I'd had kids, I wouldn't have cared.*

'I'm sorry,' said Alma. She stirred her coffee. Verity wouldn't look at her. 'I'm sorry I said that you don't understand . . . And I'm sorry to sound so beastly about my children. It's just that once you've got them, they can really hurt you, just like you once hurt them, I suppose. Like my bloody awful mother hurt me. And then it's so primal, you forget you love them. Thank God I'm with you, and can say what I feel. And you're being so nice. Real coffee. You're spoiling me.'

Verity managed to look up and smile. 'I hope it won't keep you awake all night.'

'I'm awake all night in any case. Any little noise, I think Zoe might be back. Then I tell myself I'm crazy. And then I begin to think it's burglars . . . I suppose I've forgotten how to be alone.'

'I lived alone for fifteen years.' Then Verity laid her small hand on Alma's arm, her pale strong hand with the ruby Ian gave her. 'I'm sorry you're not sleeping. You can always come and stay.'

'Am I one of those women whose husbands leave them and then go and weep all over their friends who never had a husband in the first place? I was never sure that you wanted kids . . .'

'Don't worry, Alma, nor was I. Is anyone? And I didn't mean to go on about Paul. Anything I can do—'

'You're doing it, Verity. I do need company. Paul and the children were just *always there* . . . And now they're not. I can't quite believe it. Everything seemed so . . . permanent. Like the way you look in the mirror. Nothing seems to change –'

'– And then one day you wake up ancient!'

Alma wasn't quite sure who the 'you' was meant to be. 'Have you got a brandy, Verity?' she asked.

'I was just thinking a brandy would be nice.'

Alma had things she hadn't managed to say. The wine in her bloodstream urged her to attempt it. 'I keep trying to make sense of life. Things slipping away. I feel everything is slipping away. I keep reading about time. Till my brain aches. I can't sleep at night, and my mind goes in circles. Why do we have to keep pressing forwards? I mean – I want to go back. And find things.'

'Like . . . ?'

'Zoe. Being happy. And . . . childhood. I seem to remember almost *nothing*.'

'You can't go back.'

'I know, but I want to.'

49

Verity wasn't one for abstract conversations; she was hugely curious about specifics. She looked distracted as she sorted through bottles.

'Armagnac, Courvoisier, Rémy Martin?'

'Do you remember how poor we once were?'

'I'm glad we're not now. Some things improve. I'm going to have a Rémy Martin.'

'Me too,' said Alma, with a small surge of cheer. 'Oh God, I hope Zoe isn't drinking—'

'She didn't drink, did she? Enjoy your brandy.'

'She was drunk a few times. Once. Twice.'

'*All* teenagers get drunk a few times . . . Look, there's something I promised Paul I'd say.' Verity took a deep swig of her brandy. 'He wants you to go to counselling with him.'

'*Counselling*? About Zoe? How could counselling help?'

'No. Couple counselling. You know, Relate.'

'I hope you told him there was no chance. There is zero chance we shall get back together.'

'They don't only see people who are going to stay together.'

'You're not on his side, are you?' Alma stared at her friend accusingly. 'You don't actually think I should go?'

'As a matter of fact, I think you should.'

'I've got friends, why should I need a counsellor?'

'Do you think you're too good for counselling, then?'

'Put like that, no . . . well yes, I do. I don't want strangers to know my secrets—'

'– I don't want my *friends* to know all my secrets,' said Verity, with her expensive smile. Whiter, more regular now she was successful.

'I suppose you work things out in your books,' said Alma. 'Recently I've wished that I could write . . .' It was hard to admit that to someone who did, who took it for granted, who grew rich by doing it. 'Not to make money. Just to have a voice . . . writing must be great therapy.'

Verity shook her head, firmly, neatly. 'It's my *living*, Alma. In any case, it didn't save *me* from going to therapy.'

'*You* went to therapy?' Alma was shocked. How much did they really know about each other?

'Certainly.'

'You never said a word.'

'There's still something faintly shameful about it.' And yet, to Alma, she looked a little smug. Verity's life was going well, too well; she looked too beautiful, too sure she was wise, sure that her recipe would work for others.

'What was it like?' Alma said, grudgingly.

'Fascinating. I went in full of fury with Ian, but within a quarter of an hour I was sobbing about my parents. It's bloody interesting, honestly, Alma. All these old feelings come back . . . and they're every bit as strong as they were, as if they had never been left behind, as if they'd gone on happening, just hiding somewhere where you couldn't reach them—'

'But that's what I meant just now,' said Alma, touched against her will. 'When I was talking about wanting to go back. It's as if there was something . . . I don't know. A secret . . . something lost. A lifetime ago, in my childhood. And I sometimes feel that I have to know, one day before I die. But I'm afraid . . . and maybe it's already too late . . . and I'm angry. I feel someone stole something from me.'

'Well that's what you'd talk about, if you went.'

'In that case I'd better go on my own . . .'

'Paul is twenty-odd years of your life, you know.'

'I don't want to talk about this any more,' said Alma, suddenly utterly depressed, feeling the brandy turn black on her. She was a person, not half of a couple. She did exist, didn't she? Even her best friend didn't seem to think she did. All her life it had happened, these instant, paralysing surges of desolation, bringing with them the conviction that no one cared, no one understood or could possibly help her. 'I have to go home. I've been out too long.'

'Because of Zoe?'

'Yes.' But it was only partly true.

'Alma, you can't feel guilty every time you step outside the door.'

'I always leave the light on, now. And I have my phone machine on even when I'm home, in case I go out and forget to switch it on.'

'Poor darling . . . but none of it will make any difference. She'll come back when she's ready. It's out of your hands.'

51

'Don't say that. It makes me feel even more helpless . . .'

'I'm telling you the truth. Trying to . . . Why don't you stay with me? You've very welcome.'

'No. I really want to get back.'

They embraced each other, though Alma was angry, and Verity kissed her, tenderly, and Alma said, swallowing her anger, telling one part of the truth she felt, 'You're a good friend. My best friend.' And then wished she hadn't been so generous.

'I haven't upset you, have I?' asked Verity, looking into her friend's dark eyes.

'Well . . . it's just the way I am at the moment. Volatile. It's not your fault.' She patted Verity's shoulder, a half-hearted reassurance.

But Verity took it as a sign to press on. 'Remember to think about therapy. And . . . Paul does love you. We all do.'

Alma turned away, waving one hand in a gesture which could have meant anything, but actually said *leave me alone*. As she racketed across blank, orange-lit London in the back of a ramshackle minicab, with the alcohol draining, leaving her cold, she thought, if two people who are so fond of each other manage to leave each other feeling so bad, what hope is there for the rest of the world?

Yet later on, as she stretched in her bath relaxing into the warm palm of home, uncurling into the kindness of the water, she no longer felt angry with Verity. She'd been unfair, ridiculous. With those she knew best, Alma's pain leaked out. She expected too much, was unreasonably touchy . . . and even then, she didn't know what she wanted. But Verity was her best woman friend.

The sister my parents never gave me. A good mother, unlike my own.

She stepped from the bath and shivered convulsively, clutching at her towel to keep her warm. There was a line of night beneath the bathroom blind. The enormous world was outside the window, a grid of strangers, of emptiness. She pulled down the blind and felt a little safer. She didn't dry herself; she stared at the floor, in a brown study as the bathroom cooled.

She thought, we spend most of our lives groping after another version of our first family. Trying to find a less threatening father, trying to find a listening mother. Trying to find a less cruel space where the children we were could live again. Walls which would hear us and remain standing. Windows through which we could safely dream. No one to peck or pull at us; only to contain the sea within us. Only to help us not to drown.

And if we could find that place of light, the old wounds would be transfigured.

And I would survive. Entire, speaking. No longer broken, no longer torn. Not the dull list of what I have, but what I am. What I might have been. I was never empty; such grief, such love, muffled beneath the false floor of my being. And if at last that was understood (but why was she crying? half-naked, weeping, a woman of water in the bathroom mirror) – I should be forgiven by my own children.

– Yet she still didn't know what they had to forgive.

8

IT WAS ONLY EIGHT WEEKS after Zoe left that Alma applied for a proper job. She had no mortgage, but heavy bills. The house was large, and had to be heated. There were tiles to replace, wood-work to paint. She had to keep a hold; she had to make money.

At first, she thought she would take on more editing. She would work more hours in the pale green office she had converted from her old play-room. It was a large room, pretty, overlooking the back garden, the limes changing colour, the apple leaves falling . . .

There was a phone, which did not ring. By the end of the third day, she sat blankly staring, remembering the games they had played in that garden. The tree-house Paul had built for the children; Zoe aged ten, with a crown of red apples, waving, shouting, then crashing down, bringing half the fruit and the tree-house with her – but she was all right. The mercy of that. Now it didn't matter that she'd been all right.

Alma gazed at the clear blue autumnal sky, across which migratory birds briefly swept, the edge of the formation breaking, shivering . . .

Zoe would be cold, Zoe would be frightened, why did she have to go in July, with so few clothes, with winter coming?

Soon it would be time to stop feeding the fish. It seemed so hard, not to feed them in winter. My lovely daughter. I liked to feed her. She was a good eater. I liked to cook for her. Who's going to feed her? Who will protect her?

Alma sat by the glass, her pen barely moving. After two months she couldn't stand it any more. She answered a job ad in the local paper.

*　　*　　*

Portico and Sheen had opened the branch in Kemble Hill in the boom years of the 1980s. There had been a Portico's in Harlesden for a dozen years, but the Kemble Hill branch was a flower of its decade, a sign of faith in the bright new Britain. Alma, who lived three hundred metres away, must have walked past their window a thousand times with only the usual dilettante glance at the pictures of houses to see how the price of her own was doing. There had been the years of the adrenalin rush, when she could think how rich they would be if they sold, getting richer, richer, so rich it was embarrassing – and then the inevitable years of decline. Not wanting to look, no longer a pleasure. Looking only to mortify the flesh.

Behind the photos, you caught a brief glimpse of well-groomed desks and keen young faces. At first the office was always full; as the eighties ended, it was emptier; the keen young faces were outside the window, staring as if at a road accident, wondering when it would be time to start looting. Evidently, though, the firm was still ticking over, or why were they advertising for staff?

She tried several outfits before settling on a creamy beige skirt and jacket which definitely made her hair look blonde, not white, and made her dark eyes rather startling. She put on her only pair of high heels. A workman whistled as she walked down the road, the metal tips sounding like horses' hooves compared to her usual flat ballet shoes. It was quite a pleasant sound. So was the whistle. Yet the old Alma hunched her shoulders with shame, for being whistled at must be her fault; till the new Alma hissed, *Don't be ridiculous. It's not your fault. Are you a woman or a mouse?*

She considered her options, and whistled back. His torso was exemplary, his face was ugly. 'You dirty old woman,' he yelled, delighted. She'd evidently taken the wrong option, but she walked on with a spring in her step.

'You have a degree,' said James Portico doubtfully, making it sound like a mild form of smallpox from which her recovery was not assured. He had a deep brown voice, doggy brown eyes, and a confusing manner in which profound brown gravitas alternated with sharp bright flashes of greed. He was somewhere between forty and seventy.

'Thirty years ago,' she said reassuringly.

'What we require is – well, fairly basic,' he said, smiling and smoothing his waistcoat. A very good suit, she thought. Not that I'd know . . . Paul only had one. 'Clerical work, really. General backup. Jerry and I tend to deal with the clients, financial details, that sort of thing. You'd mostly be typing out particulars of houses, keeping our mailing list up to date, taking dictation, drafting letters . . .'

'I've had twenty years' experience in publishing,' she said. 'I've been using a word processor for ten of those. Spelling and punctuation are my specialities.'

'Well that would be nice,' he said with cautious enthusiasm. 'None of the secretaries ever could spell.'

'So really I'd be – a glorified secretary?'

'Er – uhn – no, not exactly. But yes, well.'

'That's fine,' she said. 'I don't want to think. I want to be very, very busy. I want to earn a wage, and be near my home, which is just down the road, in Arbutus Street—'

'Very good houses. Pricey but good. I don't suppose you're considering selling?' Two thirds joking; one third serious.

'If I do you'll be the first to know. If you give me the job, that is.' To her surprise, Alma found herself smiling, perkily, feeling a real small rush of high spirits. Another world; another life. 'I'm – good with people, if that helps –' (Gwen had forced her to be good with people, watching them carefully, accommodating) '– I think I'm tactful. And quite persuasive . . .'

'We generally go for – less experienced people . . .'

Alma welcomed his tact; he meant *younger*, of course.

'. . . which is why the pay is really quite modest.' He was interested now, mildly wooing her. 'But if circumstances in the business changed, and you liked it here, and we liked you, you might get on to selling, and then there'd be commission. It's quite substantial, on our larger houses. And there are incentives. For good results. That's why we're in this racket,' he said, suddenly looking twenty years younger, pivoting slightly on the back legs of his chair, as raffish a movement as his weight allowed, and Alma grinned back, knowing she had the job.

*   *   *

And after three weeks when Alma typed form letters and stuck photos on particulars of flats, Jerry Sheen went off to live in Lanzarote, though his name still dignified the sign outside; and Alma came into her own.

Or rather, into other people's. Into other people's houses. Empty houses from which life had gone. Alma brought other homeless souls to look at these abandoned bodies, these echoing shells, to see if they could live there.

Somewhere to live; to be more alive.

They brought their hopes to Portico and Sheen.

9

IT WAS SATURDAY. Alma was working at eleven. She had letters to write before she left home, and the garden needed a good clear-out. Things were running down towards winter.

The house seemed to be full of dozy, half-dead insects trying to get in from the cold. Once Paul would have seen to them, dispatching the wasps, sparing the spiders but putting them outside 'where you girls won't see them'; his job, the man's job.

– He always called Zoe and me his girls. And I loved it; I think that Zoe did, too . . .

Alma sat in her study, one eye on the clock, writing yet another short, polite letter with yet another small photo of Zoe, asking yet more strangers if they'd seen her daughter, sorry for troubling them, grateful for their help, though little help was ever forthcoming. By now she could do it on automatic pilot, only feeling the pain when she picked up the photo, the small pale mugshot, passport-sized, which Zoe had had taken for a school trip to Germany. A year ago, only a year ago . . . Now she had a hundred copies of that photo.

Sighing, Alma pushed it in the envelope, pale green, shiny, a picked-off leaf. The drawer was full of them; pointless riches. Outside the window, the trees were thinning, the lawn was choked with yellow-brown cast-offs.

Good job Paul's coming round to see to it tomorrow.

That warmth, quickly stifled, because Paul was coming round. She'd grown used to him; she depended on him.

– *Too much. It only encouraged him.*

Across the patio, outside her window, a last Daddy-long-legs staggered, fell, unable to fly, unable to crawl, doing painfully slow and elaborate gyrations as he tried to lift his long body over blades of grass, a crashed biplane with its tail hanging downwards, head rearing up, desperate to live. It seemed to be making for her French doors.

They die in winter, all of them, don't they? So why do they try to get into the warm?

It was painful, watching his disastrous odyssey. It was suddenly uncomfortable to be in the room. Somewhere a fly buzzed, abortive, trapped, as eager to escape as the Daddy-long-legs was to get in, a sound like something electric gone wrong that made the house feel malevolent.

So get out of the house, she told herself, crossly, licking the envelope, putting on her coat. Sitting here brooding just made her feel guilty. Guilty over Paul. Sorry for Paul. She had to think about herself, for a change. It was time to think about herself.

At Portico and Sheen she was an Alma she liked, crisp, confident, capable. Wasn't she? Surely she was.

It was true she agreed to do extra work when letters weren't finished by half-past five, since Ashley, the new secretary, who had taken over the 'general backup', had to catch a train to Harrow, where her mother waited.

It was true she did a lot of the evening appointments, since Mr Portico liked to get home, and Kevin Hough, the other 'negotiator' – for Alma was now a negotiator – had a demanding social life. 'Boys will be boys,' Mr Portico smiled. 'And frankly, my dear, you have a better touch with clients.'

It was true Alma hadn't quite sorted out with Mr Portico the question of payment for out-of-hours work, since she only got commission when the sale went through.

It was true she made coffee more often than the others . . .

Brooding on all this, she homed in on the coffee.

I'll talk to Ashley. Make a joke of it. Tell her I'm too old to do manual labour. Or Kevin. Maybe the boy should do it. At least sometimes, when he isn't busy.

It had to be easier with new people. It had to be easier when she was at work.

In her private life, it was hard.

59

Her private life had a cast of thousands from the fifty years she had been alive. Neighbours who knew she would always listen, calling to her as she walked down the street, holding her arm (and they were claws, talons), sure she would never break their grip although they must have sensed her haste, her panic . . . but only after they had told their tale would she manage to say, imploringly, 'I'm just rushing with this to the post, actually,' 'I'm dreadfully sorry but I have to go, I'm picking up Zoe after school,' 'I have a train to catch, forgive me.'

Forgive me, please, for having a self, something which cannot be entirely at your service.

There were plumbers who told her their life-story while she wished she had never offered them coffee. She would stand chained to the kitchen table, her face miming interest and sympathy while her mind shrilled *I'm busy, let me go*. There were workmen paid to fit cupboards or mend gutters who flirted in ways she didn't like but became – what? There was a phrase for it, she thought, telling herself that now at last she would change, she would be clear and ruthless, she would slap them down – she became fatally complicit with them. Fatally complicit, that was the phrase. Because in the end they were stealing her life; because in the end she might die of it.

It was as if she had to wait to see what they wanted, and then had to apologize for not supplying it, soften the blow, make some amends. But they knew she knew the thing they desired, and so she was stained, already half-possessed. They knew she felt they had rights over her.

And so they stayed longer, and were less pleasant. After they had gone she felt exhausted, drained. *Go fuck yourself*, the other voice said. *Go lie in front of an articulated lorry*. It even spoke aloud, occasionally; on rare occasions it broke into the open; but always too late, too far down the line. And most of the time she could hardly hear it.

Once her friend Sheilah recommended a builder who had worked till lunch-time, then come into Alma's study, sat down in her armchair, huge, brawny, because she had asked him to sit down, because it might be rude to keep him standing on the threshold – and proceeded to make suggestive remarks, till the study seemed tiny, and she a speck of dust, faceless, brainless, a raw squirming midget, baring her teeth and staring paralysed.

When he eventually went, she had telephoned her friend.

'Did he try to get fresh with you, Sheilah?'

'You must be joking,' Sheilah said. 'Do I let builders get fresh with me? Are you saying that bugger tried it on, Alma?'

'Not really,' said Alma, deeply ashamed.

'It's your fatal attraction,' Sheilah said.

– Fatally complicit. Fatal attraction.

Sheilah herself was another problem area. She was a television researcher who for years was on the brink of becoming a star. Alma had known her since they were both thirty. She was lively, sharp, and self-obsessed.

She would breeze in and light up the room, her neat blonde head on a greyhound neck, bright blue eyes, glowing skin, that gentle, perpetual sunbed tan that she knew one day might become less gentle – always bringing gifts, not quite the right ones, expensive clothes surplus to a show's requirements which didn't suit her and wouldn't suit Alma, though Alma always accepted them gratefully, boxes of chocolates as big as TV sets, cheap champagne removed from Hospitality.

Five hours of bubbling anecdote later, the house would be headachey with cigarette smoke, Alma's cheeks would be stiff from smiling, Alma would start to feel blank and used. It was all right if these visits were far enough apart; it was not all right if she came too often.

And yet Alma loved her, in a way, and was resigned, by now, to the glazed expression that clouded the blue of Sheilah's eyes if Alma talked about herself, or said the wrong things, about pain or failure.

– Now I'll have to make changes, Alma decided. We can't be friends if I can't be myself. My new self, whatever that is. She hadn't seen Sheilah since Zoe left, fearing the blow of her friend's inadequate responses.

One day she would ring. Alma dreaded it.

But I'll use my new skills, she told herself. This job must have taught me to be business-like. I'll say I'm too busy to see her at the moment. And I *am* very busy at weekends, since they nearly always ask me to work Saturdays . . .

(And I don't say no. Should I sometimes say no?)

But wasn't she a self she liked, at work? Wasn't she grateful to get out of the house?

The doorbell rang, making her jump. So loud, the doorbell when you were alone.

She hurried to the door, looking at her watch. A dark head behind the blur of the glass. The usual split second of hesitation, but you couldn't spend your life being frightened of shadows. Alma drew herself up and opened the door.

A thin dark girl stood on the doorstep. Zoe's age. Not much older. Alma looked again; far too thin. The near-skull of the anorexic, smiling too hard, too painfully. Older than Zoe. Wearing sandals, in November.

'Good morning,' she said. A childlike voice. With a soft Scots burr; why had she come so far? A large black bag sat at her feet, too heavy, surely, for those thin wrists. There was a gap between her sleeves and her gloves. Alma saw a shadow that she hoped was not a bruise.

She thrust a piece of paper at Alma. It was a crudely printed list of goods, her calling card, her reason for existing.

– Soap, three kinds. Boxes of soap.
– Bath salts. Bath oil.
– Dish–cloths. Tea–cloths.
– Sponges. Washing–up brushes.
– Gloves, Oven. Gloves, Rubber.

Alma looked at the girl's own gloves, holed wool.

She had all these things. They were what she had to offer. She was hauling them around with her fragile arms.

Not the dull list of what I have . . .

'Morning,' said Alma, struck with pity, staring at the list for inspiration. She did not have the time, but the girl stood before her. Her terrible smile, her awful need.

Now she was flashing identification at Alma, something vaguely fake-looking cased in plastic. It seemed kinder not to look too hard. And she mumbled something garbled about the unemployed.

'It's giving employment to the unemployed. It's very cheap. It's for a good cause—'

'*Which* unemployed?' Alma asked, irritated.

The girl stared; her eyes pleaded.

'Never mind,' said Alma. 'I'll buy something.'

There was nothing on the list that she possibly needed. The soap would be harsh; the shampoo would be chemical. Alma liked to cosset her hair. The bottles would sit in the bathroom unused.

'Bath oil,' she said with determination. 'I'll take a bottle of Bluebell Bath Oil.' – Her photo of Zoe in the bluebell woods. At least the smell would remind her of Zoe.

'I haven't actually got the Bluebell,' the girl said, in her sweet Scots voice. 'I've got the Lavender.'

'I *hate* lavender . . . I'll take the bath salts, never mind.'

'I havena got the bath salts, sorry.'

'But they're on your list. Why are they on the list?' Time was ticking on. This had gone far enough. The house was getting cold, with the door open.

'You see, I can't actually carry everything.'

'Of course,' Alma muttered, stricken, sorry. 'Look, what *have* you got? I'm sure there's *something* . . .'

(But why, she wondered, did she feel so responsible? Why was the girl more important than her? Why did she have to supply her needs?)

'The dish-cloths are useful,' the girl said quietly.

'I'll take two dish-cloths.'

'They come in packs.'

'How much is a pack?' But Alma didn't wait to hear. At least she wasn't poor. She would buy her freedom. 'Never mind. I'll take three packs.'

The girl looked amazed that this had become so easy. Her voice was suddenly business-like. 'There's four in a pack. That's seven pounds fifty.'

'*Seven pounds fifty?*' Alma asked. She went and fetched a ten-pound note from her bag. But she shouldn't be giving ten pounds over the doorstep. There was something wrong with her. She couldn't say No.

Still, she couldn't have a fight with this ghost of a girl.

'I've got some very nice sponges as well,' the girl said, taking the note between long white fingers, her prominent eyes avoiding

Alma's. 'They're good value. I'll just show you some.' She was bending already to the maw of her bag.

'*No*,' said Alma with sudden vehemence. 'I mean, no, I'm sorry. I've got to go to work.' Work, she thought. She was safe at work. She had a job. She was good at it.

Of course, these young people have no work.

The girl handed over the dish-cloths, chastened.

Twelve dish-cloths I didn't need, thought Alma. But she couldn't blame the girl. She didn't blame her.

'Thank you,' she said, taking them, trying to summon some warmth, some kindness. 'Jolly cold job you've got at the moment.'

The girl was fumbling about her person. (All her clothes were old. Her coat didn't fit. Skinny as she was, it strained at the buttons.) She was silent for a second, then spoke in a rush, staring straight at Alma, outfacing her, desperate.

'I haven't any change,' she blared, abruptly. It was like a recording; this was all pre-recorded. 'I'm very sorry. I've got no change.'

Alma stared at the coloured mosaic of her floor, too angry to speak or look at her. 'That's not very satisfactory,' she said. 'How can you sell things if you have no change?'

The thin frame shrivelled in the face of her anger. 'I haven't taken any money today.' The mark on her arm was yellow and purple.

'All right, take it,' Alma said. 'Go on. It's all right.'

And the note disappeared towards the girl's pocket: wavered; stalled; perhaps she was ashamed.

'*Please* take it.'

'Thanks,' said the girl. She didn't look up.

Both were relieved when the door closed between them. One had taken too much, one had given too much. From such skewed transactions, no joy could come.

But I had to, thought Alma. *I couldn't refuse her.*

She stood paralysed in the hall for a moment, but the time on her watch was five to eleven, she had to get out, she had to get to work, she had to act, to assert herself.

*   *   *

The light as she opened the door was bright. The air was fresh and definite.

Other people's lives seemed unimaginably different. Firm and opaque, not plastic, like Alma's.

The self was where they lived, these lucky people. Where they could rest, and feel comfortable.

For Alma, the self was never at home. It was something she used; an uncertain limit. The shield or membrane between her and the world. Her self was a membrane, porous, yielding . . . she needed a shield.

Give me a shield.

The sky said nothing. It was dazzling white. Glancing back into the hall, she was blind as a mole.

– My voice, my face might be all I would need if only I really believed they were mine. If I lived in my body a different way.

Was that what she'd lost? Was that what was stolen . . . ? The simple possession of her own body.

Too long ago ever to recover . . . ?

But Alma was determined to find it again.

Perhaps they were one, her face, her body . . .

She let herself out of the house with a sigh.

10

ALMA DROVE DOWN MORTON AVENUE, and stopped outside
number fifty-two. She had two appointments to show clients
round houses which were already empty, the first through a death.

– Though houses were never empty, she had realized, since
working at Portico and Sheen. The door chains and window locks
and double glazing and five-lever deadlocks and draught excluders
did little to stop life getting in.

Spiders spun, ants crawled, wasps slept, flies lay legs-upward
on window sills, the odd Red Admiral snoozed on a table-top,
London dust sifted in like rain, a soft grey stain along the window
frame. The halls became choked with violent-coloured adverts for
minicabs and time shares in Spain; a month or two meant a log-
jam of free papers, yellowing glossaries of missed opportunities.

I suppose people think, when they make their final exit, that
time stands still, behind the front door. But it can't be still. It
can't be stopped. We swim in it; we drown in it.

Thank God that Zoe was a good swimmer . . .

The thought came like a small benediction as Alma stared at
the blank face of the house. Whatever else happens, I don't think
she'll drown. That one thing I did do for her. She loved the water.
Loved the freedom . . . Maybe she never had enough freedom . . .

The name of the would-be buyer was Crowther. They were
Kevin's clients, and she'd never met them, but they'd been on the
books for long enough to survive two cullings of the mailing list.
Hard to please? Not serious? They had a flat, she remembered, in
a good part of Kilburn, that Portico and Sheen were selling. There
had been two offers, both slightly below the asking price, as was
normal, and Portico and Sheen had recommended acceptance, but

the Crowthers had said they would wait for something better.

'Sticky customer. Probably nuts,' Kevin had told her yesterday. Kevin acted as if most of the clients were nuts, so Alma didn't take much notice.

'Are there children?' she asked. 'Why do they want a house?'

'Dunno,' he said vaguely. 'But everyone does. Want houses. Not have children . . . I don't,' he said, with boyish charm, smiling his most beautiful, white-toothed smile. He had a monkeyish face, over-animated. He tried to be tough, but the warmth broke through. 'It's death having kids, at my age. I want to get on. Make something of myself.' He sat in the sun, basking in his plans. 'Have you?' he asked suddenly. 'It's different for women.'

'Yes,' said Alma, turning away, feeling sick, as usual, at the prospect of explaining. To someone who would never understand.

Ashley knew about Zoe. She was a kind woman. 'Cup of coffee, everyone?' she'd said swiftly, getting up from her desk. 'And will you get a shift on with that letter, Kevin, or I'll never get it into today's post.'

'I'll make the coffee,' said Alma. 'I need a break.'

And she did sometimes like to get away from her desk, which was a little too near the window for comfort. She sometimes felt people were staring at her, but of course they were looking at the photos in the window.

Now she sat in her car in the November sunlight, waiting for the Crowthers to show up. She checked, automatically, the tools of her trade. She had her electronic tape measure, her clipboard with instruction sheet, her camera – not that she'd be needing it. She had no photographs to take. It was an aspect of the job she rather enjoyed, priding herself on making the properties look more attractive than Kevin ever managed. A bit of greenery cunningly included, a carefully-chosen angle that would make the house look larger . . . It wasn't exactly lying, was it? It was simply putting the best face on things. It was the job. She liked the job . . . She had not brought the mobile phone. There was one in the office that she and Kevin shared, but she hadn't been into the office this morning. In any case, she never seemed to need it.

She hoped that the Crowthers would come on time, for her next appointment was twelve o'clock. Morton Avenue was not a bad street, 'this ever-popular residential street', it said in the particulars, as if most streets consisted of factories and bus depots. But it was quite a pleasant street, in truth, a mixture of short terraces and semi-detacheds, a little wider than average, with orderly gardens. The sort of street that said life was good, if you mowed your lawn and clipped your hedges, if you walked the dog and cleaned the car, if you combed your hair and caught the post . . . Alma patted at the springy mass of her hair. A street that promised nothing bad would happen.

Just like Arbutus Street, she thought, rather bitterly. And inside the neat boxes there could be mayhem, beatings, murders, quiet abuse . . . Things never made known, things that won't be remembered. Lost children. Lost people.

A dark shape moved round the corner of the house and she realized the Crowthers were already there, probably trying to get a view of the back garden. She got out of the car with a professional smile.

'Are you Mr Crowther?'

He was in his late twenties, tall, not fat, smartly dressed in a dull sort of way. Blouson jacket, tie, pressed trousers. The sort of trousers Paul would never have pressed. And the sort of man who might well buy a house. Good, she thought. Not a time-waster. Handsome from a distance, but prissy mouth. Computer programmer? Salesman? Burglar? – for it suddenly struck her, he might not be Mr Crowther. He could be anyone. How would I know?

'Are you from Portico and Sheen?' he asked. 'I thought Mr Hough was looking after me.'

– That was all right then. 'Good morning,' she smiled. 'I hope I haven't kept you waiting.'

'I have no particular objection to a woman,' he said, in a way that meant he most certainly did. *Prat*, she thought, and smiled, blankly. 'I've been here quarter of an hour already.'

'I'm sorry,' she said automatically, though she knew that she'd been exactly on time.

Dentist, she thought. *Taxman. Policeman.*

She dismissed the unpleasantness and thought about the house.

There was always a small thrill about going inside. Looking into people's private places. When the houses were still furnished, even more so; it was like soap opera, without the cast – the intimate secrets of complete strangers.

'I must say, the outside doesn't look much.' His mouth was mean; he was definitely aggressive. She started to feel less conciliatory.

'You can't tell much from the outside, usually.'

'I made it clear that I wanted four bedrooms, but for some reason he keeps sending me three . . .'

'It depends what price bracket you stipulated. They'll send whatever is in that price range. Four-bedroom might be that bit more than you can manage . . .' She hoped he would be stung by that tiny shaft. Buyers' pretensions were fairly predictable. He wanted her to think he was a four-bedroom man. They all liked to think they could have more than they could pay for.

The hall was cold, but the back of the house smelled pleasantly of dust and warmth. With no windows open, the back rooms were suntraps on a morning like this. A lucky morning. Her spirits stayed resolutely buoyant; always more sales when the sun was shining. 'There you are,' she said hopefully, opening doors, closing doors, playing the hostess, using her charm. 'Here is your front room . . . your second reception . . . large kitchen . . . quite pleasant, isn't it?'

'I'm sure the particulars said "kitchen-breakfast room".'

Alma glanced down at her clipboard. 'This *is* what we'd call a kitchen-breakfast room.'

'Just now you called it a kitchen.' He smiled a small smile of stupid triumph, and she suddenly thought, he's tall, isn't he. Tall and fit. And not terribly nice . . . and I haven't got the mobile phone. I'd feel better if I had the mobile phone.

'I'm sorry, sir,' she said, very formal, deferring to him and distancing him. 'Would you like to see upstairs? I'll wait for you down here,' for she didn't want to go upstairs in front of him, showing her undefended back. There was no reason for her to go with him, since all possessions had been removed from the house; no reason, indeed, for her to come at all, since he must have been offered the key to the house, but for some reason he'd asked to be escorted.

Because he's lonely, she told herself. I bet there's no wife; he smells of loneliness. Because he likes a bit of power over people. Next time, Kevin can do his own dirty work.

'I'm not sure I'll bother.'

Was he sneering, or leering? 'That's up to you sir.' She didn't meet his eyes, not wanting to see what insult was in them. 'Three double bedrooms, it says in the particulars.'

'*Double* bedrooms? Now you're talking . . . Why don't you come upstairs with me?'

This time the innuendo was unmistakable, and he was very close to her, grinning at her, so fear gripped her ribs and contracted her stomach and loosened her tongue, which had been swelling, knotting – 'I'm afraid I'm expected at another appointment. Perhaps you could come back another day,' and she turned on her heel and walked towards the door, hoping he would not see she was shaking, snatched open the door upon the sweet bright air.

'I haven't offended you, I hope? Career girl, are you? No sense of humour?'

'I have to lock up,' she said, still not looking at him, wishing she could slap him, scratch him, shoot him. '*If* you don't mind,' for he stood in the hallway, sullen, still excited, thwarted, glowering.

'Very unprofessional,' he said as he left, passing too close deliberately, knocking against her with his shoulder. 'You haven't shown me round. I shall make a complaint.' He was just a sulky boy, but his rage made her shiver.

You're all right now. Stay calm, thought Alma. Women passed in the street; a dog barked; a child cried. She was no longer in danger, if she ever had been. 'I suggest you speak to Mr Portico on Monday.' She walked towards the car, her own lovely car, with the shadow behind her, into the sunlight. She thought it was over, she opened her door, but he could not bear to be defeated.

'You're a tight-arsed bitch,' he yelled at her. 'I know your kind. I know what you need –'

She turned the key, wrenched her door open. Whatever he was saying collapsed in the sunlight.

'Can't take a joke,' he trailed off lamely.

She drove off fast, past the careful lawns, the well-fed roses, the castellated hedges, the neat blind windows which had seen nothing, which never saw anything, which gleamed in the sun.

She was half an hour early for her next appointment, which was with a young couple, her own clients, heavily pregnant, first-time buyers. She felt sick, but she couldn't let them down.

She parked, without thinking, by the red-brick bulk of the school where Zoe had gone when she was little, arriving by some homing instinct at the place where she'd stood so often in the past, waiting for the child to appear.

She switched off the engine. Her heart was beating. Yet nothing had happened, had it, really? He was just – a bit cheeky. He was a yob. All mouth and trousers, she told herself, but her hand on the steering-wheel had not stopped trembling.

First time for everything, she told herself, for hitherto nothing like this had happened; the clients had been boring, or stupid, or obstreperous, but none of them had ever been suggestive, none of them had tried it on with her.

Why today? she wondered, staring at the brick, the bloom of sun on the smoky red brick, the aberrant, determined straggle of green where a plant had found its feet on the crumbling mortar. The building was asleep, infinitely peaceful, waiting for Monday.

Waiting for its children. As I once waited.

– Was it my outfit? My makeup? My hair?

She was wearing a perfectly ordinary dress, knee-length, black, that she'd bought last week, with a wide cowl neck which she thought was flattering. The shop assistant had said it was flattering. 'Lovely with Madam's ash-blonde hair,' she had said, in a particularly mealy-mouthed way which told Alma that secretly she thought it was grey. All the same, it was true; the dress flattered her. And the skirt, unusually for Alma, was straight. Some would say tight. With a four-inch split. Alma peered in the tiny eye of the mirror. She looked upset. Her pupils were tiny, but her irises stared in their nets of mascara. Because she was pale, her lips were too red. I'm over-made-up, she told herself, feeling sick and ashamed at the revelation.

Then another voice, Alma's own angry voice, said *Christ,*

71

woman, have you gone crazy? A piss-artist tried to frighten you and you tell yourself it's all your fault?

Blood began to creep back into her cheeks. She got out of the car and stood in the sunlight. She had parked on the bridge, facing the school. Her feet felt quite steady as she walked to the wall and gazed over into the wide, deep railway cutting which basked in the sun of the late autumn day; all down the banks there were squares of allotment, patches of colour, patiently tended, a tilted scarecrow, a green-painted shed, a black cat sneaking through the cabbages, a white-haired man digging slowly, steadily. Thank God, she thought, I'm safe, nothing happened. Pink-tasselled asters shone against the green, and the windows of the shed flashed gold in the sunlight. A ripple of joy ran through her, spreading. The railway lines sheered away into the distance, a long sheaf of steel, crossing, diverging, dazzlingly bright as they sloped into the future. Glad to be alive. She was glad to be alive.

She turned back towards her car and the school loomed before her, a cavernous body of soft red brick, and she was suddenly pierced by its immense silence, its quiet desolation, its nakedness. There should have been voices, hundreds of voices. Thin high voices like a web of silver wire, an arch of bright voices soaring over the playground, laughing, screaming, complaining, explaining, too young to be anything but musical in all the wild sweetness of their different excitements.

She heard Zoe's voice. She heard Zoe call her. Then a child's feet came running behind her – but when she turned, gasping, it was the newsagent's girl, a plump child, glossy-haired and shy with strangers, her black plaits jumping like living things, frowning and shouting as she chased her mother, who hurried on ahead towards the station.

Watching them, Alma was pierced with envy. The mother was impatient, looking at her watch, unwilling to wait and take the child's hand. Taking her for granted, as I once did Zoe. Every day when I came to collect her I just took it for granted that she'd be there. I loved her, of course, but I should have worshipped her. I didn't quite see it was a miracle. Like the sun, and the asters, and the cat in the cabbages.

I was rejoicing, wasn't I? When she might be dead. I was thanking God for looking after me, for saving me from bloody

Mr Crowther. Kill me, God, and look after Zoe. If you exist, look after her.

She was leaning on the car, eyes clamped shut, when an unctuous voice spoke in her ear.

'Are you all right, Mrs Bennett? You look a little strange.'

It was the local vicar, who had confirmed Adam in the face of his parents' inertia, and tried to get Zoe done as well. But Zoe had quietly dug her heels in. *Maybe he was right, though, after all. Maybe God only protects his own.*

'I was praying, Mr Langham,' Alma said, and smiled, a strange, tight smile which left him confused, uncertain whether she was teasing him.

There was a pause, and then he decided she wasn't. 'Any time and space is a good place for prayer . . . Good day to you.' He touched his cap, and was attacked by a wasp, savage with winter, buzzing like a saw, and he stood there batting at it foolishly, spinning irresolute on the pavement. He had a most unfortunate Adam's apple, which lurched in his throat like a bobbing toad, sometimes under and sometimes over his collar.

Normally Alma would have been paralysed, but she was fresh from her victory over Crowther. 'Good day to you, Vicar. Must be off.'

She drove away to her next appointment.

11

WHAT IF NOTHING IS LOST, nor can ever be lost . . . ?

Alma glanced down from the window of Adam's old bedroom where she was trying to sort out his things and saw two male backs bent in the garden, Paul and Adam weeding together, so evidently father and son, though Paul was dark-haired and Adam was fair; the same broad shoulders, the same long arms, Paul's legs slightly shorter, proportionately, otherwise they'd both have been six-foot-sixers. They were joshing a little, pushing each other, laughing in the way they used to laugh. Adam had always been close to his father.

It wasn't often that they were together like this. Never now, she supposed, in this relaxed way, instead of in some café or some rented room. They were at home, for once. At home again. They looked perfectly natural; there as of right. I evicted them, she thought, ashamed. And now I tolerate their return when it's useful. Well they are being useful, I'm glad to say . . .

My men. I used to think of them like that. I was always proud to see them together. It's nice to have men. It separates you from those who never married. And the white-haired sisterhood of widows . . . I'm not ready for that, not yet.

And yet, individually, they both annoyed her. Too far away to speak, they allowed her to be tender, their vulnerable backs and necks exposed. Paul had his hand on Adam's shoulder.

I've done them harm. I didn't mean to.

They were clearing the Michaelmas daisies, which had ramped out of control this year, wonderfully prolific of mauve and crimson buds and then touched by mildew like dirty snow, their flowers the dull silver of disease. Spreading to the roses, the Anchusa, the cornflowers. Now it would all be ripped out and burnt. Men, she thought. How they love bonfires. Once we would have made it a party, a barbecue . . .

Why aren't I better at clearing and pruning? I'm never quite ruthless enough, am I. Men love their axes and their secateurs . . . I'm scared to cut right back to the ground. I can never believe the plants will grow back again.

It was just the same clearing inside the house. I want the space, I crave light and air . . . but the things. They hold me. The old things grip me. Unnaturally heavy with all that time. I don't really want them but I fear to be without them, in case they hold secrets, in case they're the key . . .

That ridiculous hat Aunt Eileen gave me because I once dressed up in it when she got up a play for the village children. I don't want that day to be thrown in the rubbish . . . It was sunny and windy, there was blackcurrant wine which the children were allowed to mix with water, the Closs twins were sick, I was practically the star, Aunt Eileen let us make up our own words and said we were good, she said I was marvellous . . . It rained. We sheltered under a tree. She brought out some tarts. There was a rainbow . . . Marmalade tarts, very slightly burnt, utterly delicious. Aunt Eileen's magic.

But the memory had faded, taken out too often, thinning, breaking, the ghost of itself.

The hat was once cream, with a scrolling feather as elegant as a poet's quill pen. Aunt Eileen had thought Alma might be a writer. 'You've got a way with words,' she used to tell her. 'But Mum always says the cat's got my tongue.' 'Does she?' asked Eileen, interested. 'That's what *our* mother used to say to us. It's just a saying. Don't take any notice . . .'

Now the hat looked like something the cat brought in, dis-coloured with mould, the felt indented, an upturned mushroom, too old to eat. The feather was mangy, greasily serrated.

And yet, I wore it, in glory, that day.

Alma hesitated, and put it back in the cupboard. A defeat, maybe, but she wasn't quite strong enough. She didn't have that many happy memories.

Other people's things should be easier to jettison.

With the children's things Alma had long ago had to learn to be tough, for children were like snakes, constantly shedding the skin of habits they had outgrown, skating boots, roller-skates, stamp albums, modelling kits. And clothes; a long straggle of multi-coloured oddments, slowly getting larger and more expensive, a dervish of rags whirling away into the past.

But everything had changed now the children had gone. Now their ordinary possessions had power. Zoe's possessions, at any rate. Nothing should be touched; not a thing should be changed. All must be left so that she could return and take up life where it was before, not a heartbeat lost, not a single breath missed, so the appalling wound would close up in an instant . . .

– I shall throw that boy's old things away, thought Alma, considering Adam's heaving back, slightly narrower at the waist than his father's, the healthy red of his cheek as he turned, looked up at the window, waved a hand, his shiny fair hair, his easy smile. Adam liked to act as if everything was simple. He was puzzled and hurt by her complications.

Why couldn't he clear his own mess away? His football kit. His dreadful posters of rock bands that he now despised. His teenage LPs, some of them sleeveless, old-fashioned as liquorice, warping in the sunshine. He had played those records so thunderously loud, he was always in the house, we could never escape him . . . The noise was an assault, a statement of intent, a shattering barrage from the occupying force. Not that he minded when we shouted at him; he never made much fuss about turning it down. It was our counter-attack, the expected move. No hard feelings. He never seemed to brood. Whereas Zoe never played music loud. She went out to dance, there were no confrontations . . . She quietly did whatever she wanted. Resisted us by doing without us.

Oh God, I wish she'd shouted more often, I wish she'd told us what was going on . . .

We did talk, though, didn't we? We were close? I kept telling the police, 'We're a close family, we've always been a very close family.' They had nodded, expressionless, taking few notes, which Alma supposed was because there was so little she could tell them which could possibly explain the thing which had happened. The terrifying, impossible thing . . . Which to the police was nothing, was ordinary, was probably explained by their failure as parents.

'Mum,' Adam called. His young man's voice, the voice she had known as it broke and deepened, now overlaid with a faint city veneer, the hint of a drawl in the upper-class manner but also something clipped, hip, pseudo-transatlantic. She supposed all young lawyers talked like that. She smiled down at him, all the same. Trying to grow up. It was charming, touching. And he was her son. She opened the window.

'Do we get some lunch, Mum? Dad wants to know.' She saw Paul wincing, shaking his head. So Adam was supposed to carry the can.

'Well I'm not cooking anything,' Alma yelled. She saw heads turning two gardens along where the Elsevier sisters had lived for years. They were bent over their pond's completely blank surface. Alma made her voice sweeter, kinder, more motherly. 'I'm sure there's something in the larder.' She didn't want the neighbours thinking she never fed them. That her kids ran away because they weren't looked after.

As soon as she'd said it, she was annoyed. She had wanted the men out of the house by lunch. She had planned to go to the Hayward Gallery which was showing a major Bonnard exhibition . . .

Paul's eager, over-eager voice broke in. 'I could just nip out and buy some soup and cheese – maybe some chops, some vegetables . . .'

Paul pretending to be helpful, though really he was planning the kind of hearty lunch that he longed to eat, planning to occupy her kitchen for hours, to make a family feast that proved life went on, that things were normal, things were fine . . . He's like Mother, she thought. Spends his whole life lying.

– But he wasn't like Gwen. He wasn't lying. He was trying to mend things. To rebuild life as it was before. He liked his food, his home, his wife.

But I don't want to be in a list of Paul's things. I don't want to be a sodding wife any more.

Alma forgot about the Elsevier sisters. 'And who the hell's going to cook all that?' she yelled, irate. 'Because I'm very busy.'

She felt she was busy, though the facts were against her – she'd been sitting brooding for an hour or more.

The men exchanged looks. 'I am.' 'I am.' Both of them could, then. Jolly good. She smiled, despite herself, and pondered how unreasonably grateful women are, when men occasionally do the things that they do all the time . . .

'That's all right then,' she said, and turned away.

I wish I didn't have to be so fierce, she thought. I wish it wasn't such a wrench to stand up to them. I wish I could just say it, without strain, without screaming. And even then, I didn't manage to say No. They'll be here in the house until it gets dark, and I'll miss the day, I'll miss my chance . . .

The men were planning menus in subdued voices as she closed the window and sank down on the bed. Poor Paul and Adam, all the same, she thought. Because I know them, I can let rip. Because they go on loving me, whatever I do . . . they go on loving me, they have to love me . . . *as I love Paul*, the thought concluded, before she had the presence of mind to deny it. *Love allows things. Love allows . . . love allows us to be ourselves.*

It arrived like a present slipped through the glass, light as water, immensely soothing, something she could sip and fall asleep, and she pulled off her shoes, lay on the covers, the sun-warmed chenille like a cat's soft coat. It caressed her cheek; she stretched, relaxed. To her amazement she was drifting, twitching, half-hearing the burr of the motor-mower, last mow of the year, then Adam laughing, doors and birds, a child, a child . . .

Love allows. It was liquid as music. Safe with her family, Alma dozed.

She slept and dreamed, as usual, of Zoe. She was following her daughter up a high mountainside which her rational self told her must be in Wales, since the mountains of her family were Welsh, but these were precipitous, patched with ice, tall clumps of willowherb where the snow had melted. Too dark and too bright, flickering sunshine, too bright to see clearly where the path should go, and after a while Zoe drew ahead of her, her white dress flowering and fading on the rocks, now melting, now freezing, which couldn't be good for her, too near the edge, beyond which the land plunged and ten miles away, in still golden light, the opposite range of mountains crawled, their snowfields untroubled, supporting the sky. Here it was falling, but Zoe wouldn't wait. 'Be careful,' Alma called, kept calling, had been calling for hours, but the sun and wind snatched it, and instead the words that echoed back from the rock face were 'Be a good girl, please be a good girl . . . if you love me, Alma, be a good girl . . . I love you dearly, child, be a good girl . . .' And to her horror Alma saw her mother ahead of her, blocking the path where Zoe must climb, not seeing her grandmother but waiting for Alma, and her mother's voice drowned Alma's cries, her own mother's voice stopped her speaking to her daughter, Gwen crouched on the path like a cairn of stones and as Zoe tripped and fell and Alma's lips opened, trying to tell her to use her wings and fly across to the other side, fly for the safety of the faraway mountains, somebody shouted, close at hand, 'Cat got your tongue? Cat got your tongue? *Alma! . . . Alma! . . .*'

'. . . Oh, you're asleep. I'm sorry, darling. I thought you were annoyed with me.' She opened her eyes on the familiar room, its familiar clutter, Paul's familiar face, loving, anxious, nervously jovial.

'I fell asleep,' she mumbled, blurred. 'Did somebody shout "Cat got your tongue?"?'

'Not me,' he said. 'I was calling your name. Sounds like your Ma. The soup is ready, by the way. With herbs from the garden.'

'I'm not very hungry.'

'Please,' he said. 'For Adam's sake. He never sees us together.'

His eyes were very blue, very direct, the eyes of a decent man asking for something. His face was twenty years older than when they first met. They had lived those twenty-odd years together. His hair had got very grey at the temples; was it since they split up? She'd never noticed before. The skin of his cheeks, looser, reddened. His mouth. Still full, not very happy. Dry from working in the wind. *If you love me*, those blue eyes said. *For Adam's sake* . . . she must love her son.

There was no anger to help her. 'OK,' she said.

12

AS SHE SAT AT HER DESK in the window of Portico and Sheen on Monday morning, Alma was sure she was being watched. A dark shape, beyond the glass. A large shape. A large shadow, for the sun that day was particularly bright, he was looking *between* the pictures, not at them, a man was definitely watching her . . . then he was gone. No, it was nothing.

Don't be ridiculous, she thought.

The phone rang constantly, as usual on Mondays. There were the follow-ups from weekend appointments; most people viewed at weekends, of course. Offers came in on Mondays. It was a day for new resolves, new hope. There were always enrolments on Monday, too. People felt up to moving, on Monday, up enough to phone the estate agent's, at least, though only half of the callers would fill in the forms. More of them, apparently, since Alma's arrival. Alma was always nice to people on the phone, whereas Kevin could be cheerfully impatient. 'Time-waster' was his favourite word. His time, he felt, was too expensive to be wasted. Or would be one day, when they paid him right.

Mr Portico, whose office (a cubicle, in fact, with a deep leather armchair where he'd been known to fall asleep) was just to the side of the others' shared space, had not looked in on them this morning, and his door was closed, unusually. It allowed Alma to indulge in reverie, whenever the buzzing phone allowed her, though she had innumerable phonecalls to make.

That was her job, really, phoning people up, following up leads, encouraging people, landing the clients who hadn't quite decided which estate agents to use. They had to keep the figures up; the figures, apparently, were shaky this year. Mr Portico monitored them every Friday; the number of houses on their books, the number of what Kevin called the 'appos', meaning the applicants, or appointments, people who were seriously looking to buy, the number of offers, the number of completions. They had to maintain something called *board presence*, too. Board presence was monitored monthly. Every 'For Sale' board was an advertisement, bearing, as it did, their phone number in orange. Their main local rivals were Garret & Garret, who had an office just down the street. Kevin was obsessed with Garret & Garret. Their boards were very slightly larger than Portico's, a lurid scarlet and royal blue. When too many Garret boards appeared in a street, Portico and Sheen would put canvassing letters through the door of every house on the row, pointing out (falsely) that they had several 'unencumbered buyers' looking for something in the area.

There were other darker features of the job that Alma tried not to know about. Sometimes Kevin and Mr Portico could be heard debating whether it was time to 'do a board smash'. This always made Kevin laugh a lot. It must have had something to do with Garrets'. And then there were the repossessions. Too much of their business was repossessions. Mr Portico, in his courtly way, preferred Kevin to handle the repossessions, and Alma was very glad of that. The people whose houses were being repossessed quite naturally resented the estate agents who were selling the roofs above their heads on behalf of the hated mortgage company. Occasionally Kevin got physically threatened. Perhaps this upset him more than he let on; he always told the story as if it was a joke. But in such cases he greatly enjoyed going back with the bailiff on the day of reckoning, watching the eviction, changing the locks. Alma didn't like to think about Kevin's enjoyment. She wanted to like him. She did like him, actually. She wanted to like the work, the job, the new chance it had given her.

She had what she suspected was a slightly childish dependence on Mr Portico's good opinion, so when he was watching she worked extra hard, but when he wasn't she sometimes compensated, partly to show fellow-feeling with the others, who slacked, on occasion, quite without guilt. If Kevin's Himalayan peaks of adrenalin briefly flattened, he would phone girlfriends, or girls he evidently wished were his girlfriends, though the responses Alma inferred between his jocular intimacies didn't seem encouraging, and soon he would be back on the job again, chasing, chasing, every inch the salesman. When Ashley flagged, she would phone home. Alma felt envious of Ashley sometimes, for her mother was apparently 'a great giggler'. Gwen had never giggled. Were they happy together, that mother and daughter? Happier, perhaps, than most married couples?

One week Ashley had been off sick and Alma phoned to see how she was. The voice that answered was like Ashley's, but older.

'Who was that I talked to?' she asked Ashley next day. 'She was really kind.'

'Oh . . .' said Ashley, sounding embarrassed. 'That was my mother. She lives with me.'

'Rather you than me,' said Alma, impressed.

'No,' said Ashley, very pink by now. 'I love her, see. It's . . . OK.'

'I couldn't live with my mother,' said Alma.

– What were their lives really like, Alma wondered, these others whose space she shared every day, whose breath she breathed, whose faces were becoming almost more familiar than her family's? They were nice to each other, good pals in the office, grateful for each other's basic good humour – but were Kevin and Ashley less unhappy than her?

They were both in their twenties. Things happened in your twenties.

– Or else they didn't, which was worse. Ashley sometimes mentioned a man called Nicky, but it didn't seem to be going anywhere. Perhaps nothing very much ever happened to Ashley . . . But that was arrogance, wasn't it. As if things that happened quietly at home with her mother didn't count like acts in the sexual drama.

I could do without the sexual drama myself, thought Alma. The last acts are exceptionally grim. At least these two are young. At least they're not worrying the bone of something. Paul and I have got down to the bone.

For yesterday had turned into a total disaster. The first mistake had been the bottle of wine. 'I bought it just before afternoon closing,' Paul had said, with slightly forced casualness, knowing that she might choose to object, but Alma liked her wine, these days. It blunted pain; it moved the world away, and when you woke up, things might have moved onwards.

Except that this bottle was an Amarone, heady, garnet-red, over fourteen per cent alcohol, and Adam drank beer, steadily, silently, disdainfully declining his share of the wine – 'Young people don't drink wine at lunch-time' – so that before the chops were on the table, Alma and Paul were on their second glasses, and volubly drunk, at first good-tempered as a surge of false love lit up their bodies, then jokily contentious, almost normal, then plain contentious as they got to the fruit, didn't feel like eating it, wanted to drink more.

'There's some Cointreau,' said Alma, 'but that's disgusting.'

'Haven't you got anything else?' asked Paul, incredulous, loftily disapproving. 'That would never have happened when I lived here.'

'Actually,' said Alma scornfully, 'it was you who cleared us out. All those empty bottles you shoved back in the cupboard. Well, there was some Southern Comfort, but I drank it with Verity.'

'I could just do with a Southern Comfort,' he said. 'So how was Verity? I've seen her too, you know.'

'So she tells me.'

'She's a very nice person.'

'You don't have to tell me, she's my friend.'

'I've always liked her. I think she likes me.'

'I'm very happy for both of you . . . Adam, dear, could you make us some coffee?' Alma knew what Paul was working up to.

Adam could feel the atmosphere was changing. 'Shouldn't we go back in the garden, Dad? Before the light goes?'

'Make us some coffee, like your mother says. I did the lunch, so you can do the coffee . . . Did Verity say anything about us?'

'Us?'

'Us. Our marriage. For God's sake, Alma. You and me. You know what I mean.'

'We talked about most things. I can't remember. Why are you being so nosey?' she asked. 'What time is it? I've got things to do. I want to go to the Bonnard exhibition.' But she already knew it was much too late.

Paul was picking the skin off an orange, throwing the pith on the table, as usual. He would never use his plate. He would never pick it up. 'Because of what Verity said to me. She thinks you and I ought to try again.'

'Ah.'

'She thinks we ought to go to therapy. You and me. It's called couple therapy,' he explained helpfully, prolix with drink.

'She said something about it. I told her she was wrong,' Alma said, lunging at the table to scrape up the pith and splitting her fingernails. 'Bugger.'

'You find out about the past. Amazing things. Verity had it, you know . . .'

'*You* go,' she said savagely. 'But I won't bother. I'm living in the present. I'm thinking of the future.'

The orange was dry, lustreless. He tried one segment, then spat it out with a grimace of distaste that made him look ugly. 'You've turned into a different person, Alma. I don't know who I'm talking to.'

'Black or white?' called Adam from the kitchen. 'Sorry, Mum and Dad, but I'm going to have to go. I hope I'm taking someone to a film, tonight.'

Alma got to her feet. 'Could you give me a lift?'

'You bitch,' said Paul. 'I'm talking to you. Don't try and avoid me. We have to talk.'

'You'd better talk to Verity,' said the new Alma, the angry Alma who hated him, who enclosed a weeping, shuddering Alma, an Alma who wanted to kiss him, hold him, curl in his lap, burrow into their past.

'Mrs Bennett,' said Mr Portico, in a tone that indicated he had called her name before, 'are you busy, or could I have a word?'

Recalling herself, Alma smiled automatically. 'Of course,' she said. 'Fire away.'

'You might prefer . . . perhaps in my office . . .'

She gazed at him, puzzled. He sounded peculiar. 'Here's fine by me,' she said. 'I mean, isn't it?'

The office went quiet, glad of the distraction.

'I've had the most curious call,' he said. 'From a man. A Mr Crowther. Kevin's client.'

'Oh yes,' said Alma, dismayed. 'I was going to mention it, Mr Portico.' It had actually slipped her memory, in the aftermath of Sunday's events.

'Wally,' said Kevin, succinctly. 'Bit touched.'

'*Is* he . . . ?' Mr Portico sounded relieved. 'You see, he just made some rather startling . . . allegations. And he's removed himself from our books.'

'What did he say?' said Alma, annoyed, feeling a warm tide of anger rising.

'Perhaps you could give me your version of events.'

She stared at Mr Portico levelly. She realized how shallow her affection for him was. 'I can tell you what happened, if that's what you mean. Not *my version*.'

'I didn't mean to suggest . . .'

'Mr Crowther was unpleasant, and then suggestive. Threatening, in fact. Sexually suggestive.'

'Wanker,' said Kevin sympathetically. 'Thought so.'

'He claims you were rude,' said Mr Portico. 'He claims you refused to show him round.'

Under three pairs of eyes, Alma felt her control slipping. Her mother's voice spoke in her ear. *Don't be rude, Alma. You upset Mr Crowther. Surely you could have been nice to our friends?* She was blushing, hotly. She wanted to cry, as she had cried whenever her mother accused her. No one would believe her. There was no point. She couldn't read the expression on Portico's face; he stood in the window, between her and the light.

'I wasn't rude,' she said. Her voice was fatally childish. 'I wasn't rude. I wish I had been.' Her breath wouldn't come; her heart thudded. Then she heard Crowther's voice, shouting, and anger returned, life returned. 'He called me a *tight-arsed bitch*, as it happens. That's pretty rude, isn't it? He's a big man, too. I was . . . frightened. He wanted me to go in the bedroom with him. I thought he might rape me . . .' And then asininely, because what she said had sounded melodramatic, 'Perhaps I imagined it, I don't know' – trying to bite back the words as soon as they were out.

Mr Portico was silent, and then turned towards her, the light revealing his sad, lined face. 'I'm really sorry, Mrs Bennett,' he said, and his voice was very slightly quavery, his voice held something like tenderness. Or could it be excitement? – I'm paranoid, she thought. 'My niece was assaulted at university. The things you ladies have to put up with.'

'Bastard,' said Kevin. 'Piss-artist. Cut his goolies off. Not you, Mr Portico. Of course.'

'Sounds a good idea, Kev,' said Ashley.

'I extend our apologies,' said Mr Portico. 'On behalf of . . .' He trickled off into ponderous silence. Did he mean on behalf of his firm, or his sex?

'Poor you,' said Ashley. 'Would you like a coffee, Alma?'

'Please,' said Alma, smiling at Kevin, smiling at Ashley's kind young face, her sandy eyebrows raised in sympathy, her pale blue, wide-open eyes. How comforting it was to be believed. At home she had never been believed. So she could never speak; never truly speak. Now she was reinventing herself. It was never too late. She would find her voice.

Here she could avoid the old mistakes.

With new people. In a new place . . .

– That irritating shadow in the window again.

13

THAT EVENING, unusually, she phoned Paul. The landlady's voice didn't sound very friendly, as if Paul had told her a thing or two, none of it favourable to his wife.

'Do you want me to call him?' she asked Alma, as if this was in doubt, as if it was an effort.

'Please,' said Alma, controlling resentment. 'Sorry to trouble you.' The woman sounded young, middling young, lower middle-class trying not to be. We're trained from birth, she thought, to make these farcical, insane distinctions. How should we explain them to visitors from Mars? – and yet, I'm absolutely sure I'm right.

'Alma.' He sounded reserved, but anxious. 'Is anything the matter? Is there any news?'

'Nothing about Zoe . . . No. Look, it's partly about yesterday. I mean, I'm sorry. It wasn't very nice of me. You did come round to help.' (Yet even as she said it, she was thinking *damn*, I'm sorry we quarrelled, but it wasn't my fault. If he hadn't insisted on that sodding lunch. If he hadn't bought that bottle of wine . . .)

'Perhaps we shouldn't drink.'

'Not with each other, at any rate . . . have you spoken to Adam?'

'Yes.' (Of course he would have done. He had always been a careful, responsible man.)

'Was he OK? I mean, did we upset him?'

'You'd never know, would you. He said "It's cool," in that funny voice he's learned from his friends. Then he asked if I thought we would get back together –'

Oh no, thought Alma. Please let's not have this conversation.

'– and I told him, frankly, I don't think it's likely.'

Which was the last thing Alma expected to hear. She felt oddly hurt, unpleasantly pre-empted. As if Paul were somehow letting her down. 'Is your landlady listening to what you're saying?'

'Sorry? Why? No, she's gone next door.'

'Oh. So anyway . . . Adam. You think he was OK.'

'Yes. I think he's in love, in fact.'

'He didn't tell me.'

'I expect he will. If you listen to him.'

The implication was unmistakable. 'Since when have you spent so much time with your son? Since when have you two been such close friends?'

'Let's not quarrel. You have a point. We've got much closer since you chucked me out. So I have to make an effort to see him. He's a nice boy. He's a lovely boy.'

'You don't have to tell me.'

'Ah,' he said, infuriatingly, the neutral 'Ah' that meant total disagreement. There was a silence, fraught with antagonism. Then he said, more friendly, 'Look, thank you for ringing, anyway. I did feel bad after yesterday. So . . .'

His tone was valedictory, but she hadn't said what she wanted to say, and she felt a little panic; was he busy, was he bored? Was there someone there? Might it be a woman? If it is, I'm glad, she told herself. But she wasn't glad. She needed to talk to him. 'Something happened at work,' she told him.

'Oh, work,' he said, without enthusiasm. She had started the job after he left home. In his mind, the two things were not unconnected.

'Are you interested?' she snapped, unfairly.

'I was watching television, that's all.'

'I didn't know you'd got a television.'

'Peeky has. She lets me watch it.'

'Who the fuck is Peeky?' she asked, rudely.

'For Christ's sake, Alma. It's my landlady. Her name is Priscilla. Everyone calls her Peeky . . . *we're talking on her telephone*.'

'Sorry. Can I tell you what happened, or not?'

'Carry on.'

'I don't know why I didn't tell you . . . There was a man I had to show a house on Saturday. He was horrible. He . . . tried it on. I was on my own with him. I got frightened.'

'Bastard! Alma, darling. Why didn't you tell me? He didn't

touch you, did he? Are you all right? Are you upset? Shall I come round? Why didn't you tell me?' His rush of concern was gratifying, the instant surge of protective love.

'I don't know, I thought I was over it, but then he rang up the office and complained, so I had to tell them, and I wanted to cry, I somehow thought they wouldn't believe me –' She was ready to cry on the telephone now.

'So that was why you were in a bad mood on Sunday,' Paul said.

Her desire to cry in his arms shrivelled. 'I wasn't in a bad mood on Sunday.'

'I think this job is dangerous. Do you remember what happened to that young girl, what was her name, Suzy something –?'

'Lamplugh. I'm not a young girl. I'll be OK.'

'They shouldn't send women on jobs on their own.'

'Great. In that case, they'll stop employing women.'

'But they send you off to meet some complete stranger—'

'Actually no. He'd been on the books for ages. Look, really it's just one of those things that happens. But you're . . . my friend, Paul.' She was crying now, undone by a sudden surge of affection, wishing he were here in the room with her. 'So I wanted to tell you.'

'Let me come round.'

There was a pause. The unfair thing was, she felt better already, because he had listened, cared, loved her. Because she had cried. It was ten o'clock. If he came, he would inevitably stay the night. They had slept together once since they separated. Mess, she thought, sleeplessness, complications.

'You're a sweetie,' she said, and it sounded patronizing, but she meant it from the bottom of her heart. 'I think we'd better not, at the moment.'

'Why not?' Now he would be difficult.

She couldn't think what to say. 'Why does your whatsit call herself Peeky?' she asked, at a tangent, curious.

'Alma. Answer me.'

'I just want to sleep, and forget about it, really.'

'Now *I* shan't sleep for worrying . . . never mind. You should have a word with your boss. There must be some safeguards. Something you can do.'

'There are. Someone always knows where we're going . . . But the truth is, it's just like the rest of life. Life is dangerous, isn't it? The fact is, there are maniacs out there. But he was just a wanker, as Kevin would say. I handled it quite well. I was almost . . . proud of myself.'

'Still need to tell your old mucker though, don't you?'

'I suppose I do.'

'I wish . . . I wish. I wish you needed me in other ways. Not just the faithful old dogsbody.'

'Yes.'

'I might not be here for ever, you know.'

He had never said anything like that before. It must be bravado; he so clearly adored her. She ignored it. Zoe. Talk about Zoe. 'I sent off some more enquiry letters. Nothing's come back, of course. Nothing helpful.'

'She will come back,' he said, but despairingly. 'I've always felt – she'll just turn up.'

'I wish I did. But thanks, Paul. You've been really kind. I feel better, honestly.'

'I'll go back to my film, then. I've missed half of it.'

'Sorry, sweetheart. Goodnight, Paul.'

Alma wondered if the endearment cut him. She said it because she was turning him down. A consolation prize he knew cost her nothing.

He sighed down the phone. 'Goodnight, Alma.' Then, just when the phone was nearly back on the wall, his voice shrieked, and was salvaged from limbo; '– and be careful, Alma, please be careful. Zoe will need you . . . All of us need you.'

'I know,' she said, 'but what about me? There's more to life than being needed.'

'I didn't mean that—'

'Goodbye,' she said.

14

MR PORTICO WAS NOT A FEMINIST. To his generation they were terrorists, homebreakers. He could not imagine that anyone he knew, anyone normal, could be a feminist. Mr Portico was unreconstructed. Alma was charmed and amused by him, though he would have enraged her if he'd been thirty years younger.

'Which afternoon will you be taking off?' he asked her, on her second day.

'How do you mean?' said Alma. 'I didn't ask for an afternoon off.'

'Our lady staff always take an afternoon off. Firm policy,' he said with a benevolent smile, pleased to be offering this largesse.

'Is it?' Alma asked blankly, gobsmacked. 'You mean, every week? What for?'

'Shopping, of course,' he beamed, vastly. 'How else are you going to get your shopping done?'

'I've never come across this before.'

'I'm glad you've come to work for an enlightened firm. It was my dear wife's idea, originally. In the first years of our marriage she worked in a bank. Before I could afford to keep her, that is. She had to shop on Saturdays. Madness, she said. And so when I started my own business, we gave all the married women an afternoon off.'

'Just the married ones?' Alma queried.

'They have to shop for the family, don't they?'

Alma wondered if she should explain to him that she was living alone, but decided not to bother. 'Thanks, Mr Portico,' she said. 'Thursdays would be nice, if that suits everyone.'

When she tidied her desk every Thursday lunch-time and gave her letters to Ashley to post, picked up her jacket, smiled goodbye, Mr Portico looked especially avuncular, as if he were imagining her afternoon, busily filling her shopping trolley, buying cake-mixes and frilly loo-roll covers.

'Bye, Mr Portico.'

'Goodbye, my dear.'

Ashley, on the other hand, looked quizzical. Ashley was single, and worked five full days. Ashley knew quite well that Alma lived alone, but when the two women had a beer together and talked about this foible of Portico's, she had been cheerful, not envious. 'Go for it, Alma,' she said. 'I would . . . I mean, he's barking, but go for it.'

Ashley often told people to 'Go for it.' She and Kevin both loved catchphrases. They were tools, techniques for handling life, for sounding as if you were on top of things, and they seemed to work; they were both unusually cheerful. – But then, they're not thirty yet, Alma thought. Less time for bad things to have happened to them.

Alma did not head for the supermarket. Alma went home, and took off her skirt, and pulled on jeans and a big red sweater that she only subliminally recognized as Paul's, red desert boots and big silver earrings. They glinted gaily against her pale curls. The springy shoes made her feel young and cheerful. From behind, she thought, I must look like a girl . . . not that I want to look like a girl.

OK, I wouldn't mind looking like a girl. But I really don't want to *think* like a girl, or suffer the way that teenagers do . . .

Locking the door. Zoe, Zoe.

She wasn't going shopping, she was off to the Hayward to see the exhibition she had missed on Sunday. All her adult life she had gone to galleries, at first tentatively, shyly, not knowing what to do, not knowing what was expected of her, feeling this was the pastime of elected others, richer people, more educated people, who had imbibed culture at their mother's breasts . . .

(I probably got morality instead. I was breast-fed; for nine months, she told me. I was curious when I was breast-feeding Adam, and I asked her, and she got that tight, closed look, but she said, as if I was attacking her, 'You got your breast-feeding. Nine months' worth of it,' as if she wanted me to pay for it. And it was difficult with Adam, but with Zoe I loved it, and I fed her for ten months, to outdo my mother. And because we were happy. Happy together . . .)

It was when Alma left home that she'd first tried a gallery. And found that the pictures expected nothing. They hung there, silent, they let her be, they suffered her to approach and drink. The other people looked at the pictures, not her. And so the self-consciousness drained away, and soon she entered galleries eagerly, freely.

Alma sat at the front of a Number 11 bus which butted its way through the weekday traffic. The November sunshine was brilliant again, making everything look filmically vivid. The bus's big windows swarmed with life. A black mother wound in African costume of patterned maroon cotton turned and laughed, one child in her arms, another at her feet, clinging to her hem as the woman roared with laughter, showing one gold tooth, talking to the driver as he stopped for a moment in the river of cars and shouted repartee; a fruit stall glowed and bulged with colour, oranges, lemons, mangoes, grapes, blushing red pawpaws, purplish figs, elongated yellow planets of melons, everything fatly curved with juice; three seagulls squawked and hovered nearby, skating down gullies in the fumes and noise; a white cat streaked across the zebra crossing, head down, yowling, disapproving of the city; a horde of orange people held up the flow, shaven heads bowed over their instruments, bobbing, turning, chanting at the crowd, smiling smiles that looked no less youthfully attractive because their bearers were probably brainwashed . . .

Certainly brainwashed, Alma thought.

Glorious colours, saffron, peach, golden yellow, sunset red, every possible interpretation of orange . . . Sun people. They were beautiful. So why did they suddenly look mindless, vacant, their movements synchronized by something sinister, their shaved heads showing the coarse shine of bare skin?

– Zoe would never do that. I don't believe it. We weren't really religious, nor anti-religious, we never let them think life had simple explanations . . . Shrouded in orange, bald and shining, gleaming with their frighteningly similar smiles, she could no longer see, as they receded in the distance, what gender they were, how tall, how old. Not Zoe, she thought, but they could have been anyone. Someone's daughters, someone's sons. Like the children who followed the Pied Piper of Hamelin. What crime, she thought, have we parents committed? What huge dishonesty? What tiny lies?

It was a minute or two before she opened her eyes, clenching her lids against the pain.

Outside the window life still leaped and blazed, no dimmer, no less because of her suffering. On the corner of the street a thin androgynous redhead was juggling, white-painted face, baggy trousers, holed tee-shirt, and the red and green balls went tumbling and dancing, bright against the buildings and the heads of the crowd, looping up, sweeping down but never quite falling, the thin arm swooping on the ball at the last, scooping it up again, skywards, skywards . . . and the juggler seemed to wink directly at Alma. Close up his face was much older than his body, but the whole ensemble was liquid, ageless, part of the dance, part of the juggling. If she could somehow be part of it too. Of the painless life the other side of the glass.

As a child, what she saw had been her secret talisman. Mother and Father didn't know where I was looking. When they were telling me off I would look outside the window and fix on the poplar in Mr Oswald's garden . . . Its heavy golden column, swaying in the light.

I tried to share the trick with Zoe. I tried to point out the beauty of things. Maybe it was counterproductive, as if I was saying I'd been there before her. But Zoe was definitely . . . artistic. The paintings she used to do at Junior School were inspired, brilliant. I encouraged her. I couldn't have been more encouraging, though I sometimes pressed her to do her best . . . But she stopped, for some reason, as a teenager. Still came to exhibitions with me, it was one of the things we loved doing together, I think she liked it, she never demurred . . .

I soon learned to keep quiet, though, when we looked at things together. A peculiar closed look came over her eyes, and her head and neck stiffened as if she were butting something. 'Right, Mum,' she'd say, '*I'm looking at it.*' And I would get offended, and move away. Until I realized that she was growing up, that I

94

needn't open doors for her any more. The ones my mother never opened for me.

The stairs up to the Hayward were a blind coil of roughened bone, like the inside of a shell abandoned by its inmate. The wind had gnawed its way in, and howled. The sun hadn't been here, today or ever. Once you were inside, you couldn't see out. Alma pulled her red jumper down under her jacket and ran upstairs two at a time. There were feet behind her she tried to ignore; *that bloody Crowther isn't going to spoil my day*.

As she emerged at the top into great gusts of freezing sunlight, the presence behind her tapped her on the arm. 'Homeless,' he said. He was young, fat, gormless, with quite decent clothes and a streaming nose. The end was reddened by cold or drink. 'Spare me twenty p for a cup of tea.'

'You made me jump,' she said, annoyed. 'Wait, I'll get you something –' He might really be homeless. And Zoe might be homeless, for God's sake. In any case, Alma always gave to beggars, though she didn't often look them in the eye. She took out fifty p and prodded it at him.

'Fanks,' he said. 'Very kind of you. You're a nice lady.'

It was quite a speech, not the usual muttered 'thank you', but excess didn't make her better disposed towards him. Too fat, she thought. More tactful to be thin, if you're begging . . . though she didn't want them to be skeletal.

'How do you know I'm nice?' she asked him, and hurried on in across the esplanade of concrete, into the gallery, out of the cold.

She'd first fallen in love with Bonnard in Paris. There was a big exhibition called *Les Intimistes*, which meant little to her as a nineteen-year-old, but the light, the textures were endlessly delicious; light chalky or pearly, luminous or blazing, surfaces saturated with light. Bonnard, Vuillard and Roussel.

She soon decided she liked Bonnard best. There was something childlike and archetypal about his figures that was infinitely moving. He had kept his child-self; it spoke to her, whereas

Vuillard's people had already grown up, with the neat small heads of respectable adults, living in a world of immaculate pattern.

She was suddenly happy. Three floors full of Bonnards.

The nudes in the bathroom were lovely, as always, but not the paintings she was looking for. The bedrooms were radiant, and made her wistful, would she ever again slip inside that glow, the world of two behind the glowing curtain? When life was a thing of plenty, of benison, instead of loss. The light of the flesh.

What Alma wanted was the garden scenes. She wanted the chequer-board of growing things, of human figures basking like flowers, of loaded tables and sun-soaked geraniums and still small clouds that would never rain. She found them finally, alive and warm, in a chilly corner of the upper gallery.

The present was there, made permanent. Live in the present. Could she live there? She sat and stared at one picnic scene until she could feel the heat of the day, until she knew she was inside that picture, inside that moment, part of it all, alive for a second in the eyes which had seen it, part of Bonnard, and *he has not died*, she thought, exultant, transfigured for a second, her skin prickling, *there is no death, since there is this painting, since I – since we –*

But the glory faded, the spasm retreated. The painting remained as lovely as ever, and she stared, puzzled, trying to recapture the thing she had been on the verge of thinking, something she was sure would have explained everything, released everything, made all whole . . . She sat there alone till two loud teenagers came and stood in front of her, touching each other.

'Fabulous, isn't it?'

'Absolutely great.'

'Wish we could buy it.'

'One day, I promise . . .'

'I love it. I love it.'

'Love *you*,' he said, and they glided onwards.

They were Zoe's age. Older. Not much older. Smarter, harder than Alma's daughter but how would I know? she thought, despairing, she might have changed, she must be changing . . . She might be in love. She might love a stranger.

Alma tried to reconstruct her train of thought. It was something to do with love, she thought. Loving the picture. Loving the painter.

Love somehow lets you into the picture. Allows you to enter. Love allows.

So if I look, I can move through time. I can leave my body, the prison of my body. Escape at last from the knot of my flesh.

My wounded body, she found herself thinking . . . (What a curious thought. Was her body wounded . . . ?)

She could slip inside those golden, childlike bodies. Walk through the gardens. Lie in the fields. Lie still and naked in the wonderful light. All would be explained, redeemed, forgiven. They would all be there (for the faces weren't specific; Bonnard's rune-like faces allowed any names); all Alma's loved ones. All that she loved.

All the lost children would be free and found. They would lie outside time. They would stay together. They would need no words. She would feed her daughter. Food would be given them. They would survive.

It was only half-past three when Alma emerged from the shelter of the gallery into the world. The wind attacked; ice in her face. She felt like a target for a knife-thrower, trying to shrink within the outline of her body, but she turned up her collar and jogged towards the bridge, glad of her springy, youthful shoes, glad of Paul's jumper underneath her jacket.

A grey figure sat at the top of the steps which took her up on to Hungerford Bridge. His face was grey; he was wrapped in grey plastic. He had no hat, and greasy hair which the wind was whipping across his mouth. In any case, he didn't try to speak. He didn't even look up. Perhaps his shame was too deep, or perhaps it was a tactic, how could she tell? But his terrible greyness, she could see that was real, the grey of being cold with no hope of relief.

He had a cardboard box, in which some coins lay, not many, most of them brown, a few small and silver. Beside it was a notice which protected him from speech. HOMELESS, it said. IN LONDON LOOKING FOR WORK. THANK YOU FOR YOUR

KINDNESS. The writing was spidery, careful, rather beautiful. His downcast face was thin, sensitive. His skin, in close-up, was roughened by a rash.

Alma fumbled in her bag, unsuccessfully. Only five and ten p coins came out. She didn't want to stay here for ever embarrassing him, blocking other people as they hurried by. At last she found a pound and dropped it in his box. It fell with a satisfying, heavy thud. His head bobbed briefly, a muffled 'Thank you.'

She turned to go and then stopped, irresolute.

He knows, the voice said, a tormenting little voice. *He must know Zoe. He knows where she is.*

– If you don't ask, you'll never find her. Don't be a coward. Go back. Ask him.

She knew it was mad, but she walked back and crouched beside him. To her horror, he shrank away, afraid. His eyes darted about like insects.

'Please,' she said. 'Sorry to bother you. I'm looking for some-one. I lost my daughter . . .'

When he found his voice it was surprisingly normal, reedy, educated, still frightened. 'Sorry, I haven't seen any little girls.'

'You don't understand. She's a teenager. She's run away . . . she might be living rough . . .' Alma was fumbling in the pocket of her jacket for a photo. It came into the light, too small, a poor likeness, of course he hasn't seen her, of course he won't know her . . .

She could see he wanted her to go away, but she held up the photo, silently insisting.

His eyes focused on it for a second, then he shook his head with a violent movement, and before her eyes his face was riven by a stream of blood which poured from his nose, a sudden flood of bright drops on the plastic, great splashes on the ground, on the coins in his box, a little splash on her desert boots.

'Oh dear,' she gasped, 'I'll get you some tissues –' She dug into her bag, into her jacket, her jeans, but there were no tissues; she cursed herself. After a minute or two of watching him bleed, asking impotently if he was all right as he dabbed himself with the useless plastic, she walked away, shaken and ashamed. She felt as if she had assaulted him.

She was still clutching the picture of Zoe, but the blank little face was disfigured with blood. It seemed unlucky to throw it in the river.

She walked on across the bridge in the bitter wind. You could see bright water beneath your feet, shining in the gap between the planks. Everywhere the wind cut through like a blade.

All across the bridge, at intervals, the grey figures suffered, the hunched figures, standing or sitting while the world walked past them, ignoring them as if they were statues. Made lifelike, though, by a trick of the light. Almost lifelike; half alive. Alma too walked past, averting her eyes. There were too many of them, too horribly many.

She closed her eyes, briefly, and saw the bright blood. These lost children, with their poor pinched faces, bent at child-level but mysteriously aged.

She stopped and gazed across the bridge's iron rail, trying to take in the thick curve of the river, the cold wide glitter of its golden water. The expanse of the Thames let in a swathe of stern light, a white sword cleaving through the complicated rooftops, the elaborate gulleys and domes of money. Offices, not houses. Museums. Galleries.

Nowhere in sight where people could live, where they could crawl in from the wind and rest.

She suddenly longed to be in her own home, to be safe inside, to be out of the glare. The sun sank lower, too large, too bright, a vast yellow ball of frozen brilliance that gave no warmth, offered no comfort.

Yet the winter light worked its familiar miracle. Even the iron bridge became beautiful, with its rust-red struts and its exhausted statues, and the beaten metal of the water below, crawling for ever but never moving, and the tiny blinded eyes of the towers, the grids of minuscule gilded windows . . .

Hard to believe that there wasn't a pattern, that the beauty of the scene didn't mean something, that the city, from this distance a child's world of palaces, wouldn't open up as the sun went down, as the grey men shivered back into life; that the shining porticos wouldn't yield, that the empty halls wouldn't take them in.

Alma closed her eyes again and saw her picture. Her golden Bonnard. Then the fountain of blood . . .

There was no meaning. Only energy. Only life pushing on, leaving the weak behind.

And pictures could only preserve a dream. Keep the light on the wall as the sun diminished.

15

'USE IT OR LOSE IT,' said Ashley cheerfully, looking with unabashed appraisal at Alma's middle as she sat at her desk. 'I mean, you're sitting here all day.' She picked up something in Alma's expression and backtracked hastily. 'I mean, you look fine, Alma. You look really great. From behind, people would think you were my age . . . *That's not what I meant –*'

For Kevin had burst out laughing, swinging back in his chair with his hands behind his head. 'Girls! Miaow! Fucking tactful, Ashley.'

Mr Portico's door was shut again; he had been known to chide Kevin for 'unparliamentary language', '– though I bet *those* sods swear like fucking troopers,' as Kevin would point out, once Portico was gone.

The conversation had begun with Ashley waving two complimentary tickets to a new Fitness Centre which was opening in Burnham Rise, one tube stop away. 'Come with me, Alma. It'll be a good laugh. They seem to have the lot – sauna, sunbeds, martial arts – that'd suit Kevin – T'ai Chi, dance, you name it, they've got it –'

'No thanks,' said Alma. 'Though I ought to do something. I used to run. I used to go swimming—'

'Use it or lose it, Alma . . .'

When the office was briefly silent again, except for the silky tic-a-tac-a-tic-a of the word processor, and the click of Kevin's retracting pen (for he could not keep still; he was never still; they were constantly reminding him not to kick his desk, not to tap his feet on the marble-look floor; the biro was the least of possible evils) – Alma found herself exploring her stomach muscles, pulling them in, straightening her spine, trying to feel if it was all still there. I don't think about it, just because I'm thin. But thin bodies ought to be looked after too. I think I'll start going to the pool again. Get a nice swimsuit. Maybe this evening.

Her head, she found, was rather bowed, and she hauled it upright, shook her shoulders down, and smiled a practice smile to her left where she could see her reflection in the big window. Its impressionist vagueness told her she was pretty, she was still quite pretty, still quite young.

The window was seven-eighths obscured by house advertisements in neat columns; it was Ashley's job to put them up, and Kevin liked to tease her that one or other was crooked, and then when she had climbed into the window, squinting, he'd say 'Just winding you up, Ashley'. Shadows of punters came and went on the busy pavement outside the window. Sometimes people would linger for hours, but most of them never came inside.

Sometimes they were only three feet from Alma's shoulder. She had to remind herself they were looking at the houses. There was a large shape on the pavement today, somebody just behind Alma's reflection. She suddenly focused on an eye looking through. It was a man, she realized, looking at her, he had caught her smile, he was smiling back. She looked away quickly, feeling exposed. She had a vague impression of strength and youth, and of someone who approved of her, someone who didn't think she looked better from behind.

From behind, people would think you were my age, indeed. She turned back to her work with a little sigh. I was your age once, Ashley, don't forget. And you'll be my age, and probably look it.

– And yet, she liked Ashley; Ashley meant no harm. And Kevin. Both of them definitely liked her. Their comradeship meant a lot to Alma, in her oddly denuded, solitary state. And usually they didn't make her feel old – though I'm *twice* their age! Is it possible?

Use it or lose it. Well, she's right.

'Was that T'ai Chi, or T'ai Kwondo, Ash?' Kevin was asking, as Ashley put her coat on, ready to catch her train to Harrow.

'What?' she asked blankly. 'D'you mean the Chinese lot? The ones who want a flat somewhere in Harlesden?'

'The fitness lark,' he explained, patiently. 'The one you've got tickets for. I can't imagine why Mr Portico employs you . . . Did you say T'ai Chi, or T'ai Kwondo? Because T'ai Kwondo is a martial art.'

'Told you,' said Ashley to Alma. 'Our Kev is interested in martial arts. Come on, Kev. Smash your desk in two.'

'Can you take this packet to the post, Miss Hughes,' said Mr Portico repressively, entering abruptly and silently, with one of his rare accusing stares. 'Mr Hough, you are working this evening, aren't you? There are two or three valuations to do. And a few little awkwardnesses to follow up. A client I suspect of doing a private . . .' Private sales were the estate agent's nightmare. The vendor and purchaser conspired together to cut the estate agent out of the deal. 'It's more than a suspicion, actually. The client has taken his house off the market, the applicant says he's not looking any more, and Alma only introduced them on Tuesday. I think a home visit would be very helpful.'

'Ah,' said Kevin. 'Leave it to me.' He whistled, briefly, to show confidence. 'Trust me . . . Uh, Mr Portico . . . I never had to crack one of these myself. Jerry Sheen was red hot on private sales. Any words of advice . . . ?'

'I understand,' said Mr Portico heavily, walking from the room with a self-satisfied smile, 'that you're very interested in martial arts. You could always tell them about your hobby.'

'Ha bloody ha,' said Kevin sourly once he was safely gone. 'I was going to go down the pub with Charles.'

'I think he gets fed up with us,' said Ashley, putting on her lipstick in her compact mirror, small pale face frowning, pouting. The bright red always lit up her face, echoed her red hair, made her bold and striking. 'It's not nice to be the one on your own . . .'

'You're a kind person, Ashley,' said Alma.

'– and I think he was joking about martial arts,' Ashley added, with a scarlet smile at Kevin.

I'm not so sure, Alma thought. I'm not quite sure how far he would go . . . and I'm not quite sure how far Kevin would go.

'Taking the piss, was he?' Kevin was outraged. Then he looked sheepish, and Alma was glad. 'Bit of a relief, actually. I've not actually *done* any martial arts. I've got the videos, though. I'm working on it . . . so where's this new Fitness Centre, Ashley?'

16

THANK GOD FOR MARKS AND SPENCER, which was open that day until eight. Once, Alma thought, I would never have dreamed of buying a swimsuit at Marks and Spencer. Of such small changes comes middle age. On the other hand, Marks had been getting more youthful, and Alma was surprised to discover that some lines seemed distinctly too racy for her, cut at the sides to above the hip-bone, plunging to a cleavage she no longer owned. She settled on something svelte and black, one-piece, of course, but with narrow straps and an elegant V, front and back.

– But it's boring, she thought as she got to the checkout. No one will look at me in this –

And she went back and changed it for the same model in brilliant pink, Schiaparelli pink. The colour of sunrises and seaside rock. Lipstick, she thought. Flamingos. Roses. This'll turn the grey blonde, if anything will.

She didn't go home; she went straight to the pool. The car park was crowded as it always had been in the days when she arrived in a rush with Zoe, anxious adrenalin tightening her stomach, scouring the rows of cars for a space . . . I'm glad I'm on foot, I'm glad I'm not late, I'm glad I only have myself to look after, I'm sad I only have myself to look after.

The front of the building looked oddly faded, the paint splitting, the glass dirty. It was always so sparkling. So vibrant. So new. How many years can it be since I came?

Zoe was twelve when she gave up lessons. Four years ago. Not so very long. But everything has changed. Everything. I thought things would always go on the same . . .

Don't think, Alma told herself, welcoming the bustle of divergent bodies inside the Centre, the familiar smells of perfume and sweat and chlorine wafting across from the pool. She was a little shy now, in the changing-room, not wanting the young women with their pared-clean outlines to see the small tucks and folds in hers, the places where flesh had yielded to bone, though they smiled at her amicably enough.

She felt better in her swimsuit; she felt good; she felt great. She walked tall and slim to the swimming pool, the adult part, of course, divided by a wall of glass from the children's pool, though the cries of the children bounced off the glass, faint but definite, bird-calls, laughter –

A few eyes followed as she walked to the deep end, feeling very bright pink and very exposed. Male eyes. Assessing, approving? She preferred them to look at her now, all the same, while she still had her wild cloud of curly pale hair falling over her shoulders like a veil. Once it was soaked and stuck to her skull she would feel really naked, skinny and bald.

I wish I didn't have to think what I looked like. All women have to think what they look like. I wish I were a man, and could stare myself, and not give two hoots about the paunch and the baldness. They never seem to mind, do they? They never seem embarrassed by their little defects. They slob along, looking pleased with themselves, not even bothering to pull it in, while we are never unaware of being watched . . . We even watch each other in the same spirit . . .

And now she was happy that she had her pink swimsuit. It was a shield; it was a spear.

Once she was swimming, the selfconsciousness left her, she became her body, she became the water, she released herself into the confrontation between her will and her lack of practice, refusing to swim badly, for she was a good swimmer, neat and stylish, she could turn like a fish . . . but when she tried to vary her twenty lengths of freestyle with two of butterfly, she felt exhausted and gave up halfway on the second length, flipping over on her back, letting her limbs go limp.

It's no disgrace, she told herself, as the breathing eased, as the stitch relaxed. I'm fifty. Nineteen lengths isn't bad. (Yet she used to do fifty without stopping, without hurting; was it really me, she wondered; was it really only four years ago? – Perhaps I was slowing down even then. I could do it, though. I'm not the same person.)

Use it or lose it, Ashley said. It's true; you turn your back for a minute, and when you turn round, things have changed for ever. She sculled herself gently to the end of the pool, enjoying the warm embrace of the water, the sense of safety, of babyhood.

– My mother never taught me to swim. Not that there were swimming pools everywhere then. I can't remember playing in the bath. I must have done. She must have played with me. Surely all mothers play with their daughters. But she never relaxed, or hardly ever. There was always something to clean or tidy, always some duty to perform. She thought life was hard, and she was right . . .

Aunt Eileen played with me. Eileen played. Eileen and I went swimming in the sea, and she held my hands and pulled me along until I was less afraid of the water, and she always wore that enormous costume, it actually had legs and peculiar bones, it made her laugh but she kept on wearing it . . . the sea was wild but we played in the rock pools. Paddled for hours. Floated bits of wood. The water got so warm in the rocks. The baby shrimps must have loved it there, little thin-shelled things, skittering about in their salty play-pool . . .

Alma forgot where she was, briefly, letting herself drift like a sun-warmed shrimp, abruptly found herself entangled with something large and hairy, and heaved out of the water, spluttering. He was a big hirsute black man with a shaved bullet head, and he laughed as he shook the water off him. 'Whoah,' he said. 'Drunken driver. I'm in my lane, and – wham!'

'I'm sorry,' she said. 'I'm frightfully sorry.'

'Fraightfully sorry,' he said, parodying but in high good humour. 'No problem. Any time you want to bump into me, that's fine.' And his glance slid over her, easy, appreciative, a man enjoying the look of a woman, before he slipped back into his stroke again. And she smiled hugely, enjoying his enjoyment.

She did two more lengths on her back, trying hard, just in case he or anyone else was looking, her arms very straight, her kicks steady. Coming out of the water, she enjoyed the slight tension in muscles unused to being flexed. The shower, when she got there, was gloriously hot. After a moment's hesitation, she decided to strip like the teenage girl who was washing to her left, though on the other side someone around Alma's age was scrubbing gingerly around the edge of her one-piece, peering at the others with wounded eyes. Alma slipped off her suit and let the boiling water flood over her shoulders, her breasts, her nipples, her tingling thighs, beating at her head like a summer rainstorm, turning her hair into heavy tails which swung across her as she shook herself, standing there long after all the chlorine was washed off. She smiled at the teenager; the teenager smiled back.

Coming out of the changing-room she looked at her watch. Seven forty-five; she was suddenly starving. At home there wasn't much, and she'd have to cook it. – *Stay here. Eat here. You like it here.* Without thinking, she went upstairs to the café and ordered a baked potato and soup.

And so she was here, in the familiar place. How they pulled her back, the familiar places. She had never left the house of her birth . . . She sat down where she'd sat so often with Zoe. Sat down, as always, at a table for four. Zoe loved the chips. She always had chips, chips and a sandwich and an orange juice. Only had the sandwich because I insisted, and made her eat it before the chips. Not that she finished it. I always did. Or else the children. If there were children.

Half looking up from her coffee, she saw them standing as usual by the vending machine, watching its contents like a television, then gazing around them with guarded hope. 'Baked potato,' a voice from the counter shouted. Walking across, she saw more of them, standing alone looking through the glass observation windows at the figures swimming down below, leaning together in the shelter of a pillar. She looked at them, let them see her looking. Not a smile, which might be threatening, but the friendly look, *I see you, I know you*, which had always brought them to her in the past.

Then she went and sat down and waited for them. The potato was too hot, she scalded her tongue, turned it into a thing of leather. She watched the lost children. She waited for them.

*　　*　　*

After half an hour she knew they wouldn't come. They wouldn't come to her because she was no longer a mother. Without her child she could not be a mother. She was invisible to them, just one more stranger.

They had got younger, she had got older. The ones she had known would have long ago gone to whatever adolescence they could hope for.

It must be nearly time for them all to go home. It was later than when she used to come with Zoe, and the mothers of young children had all disappeared, rushing away to their next appointment . . .

Nearly everyone left was here on their own. A few males with papers, the anxious middle-aged woman she remembered from the shower, who sat eating chips, distractedly, scratching at her blue-grey hair with a fork, an old man chuntering over some tea, a young white male who looked like a weight-lifter, thick neck swivelling to every passing female, a beautiful young woman in a skin-tight purple tracksuit who kept crossing and uncrossing her elegant legs, sipping an orange juice, biting her nails, a swimming instructor eating chocolate biscuits and flexing one arm again and again, worrying away at it, flexing, relaxing, circling his wrist, backward, forward. And me, she thought. I'm on my own, too.

She had read in the paper only last week that more and more people were living alone, reading it with dispassionate interest until she realized it was her they were talking about.

And my family. Now we're all alone. Paul and I. Adam, Zoe. Paul in Ealing, in a smelly bedsit owned by someone with a ridiculous name. Me rattling around in a four-bed house. Adam in an attic room in Bloomsbury. And Zoe . . .

If I only knew where she was. I wouldn't mind where, or what she was doing, or if she didn't want to see me, if only she'd let me know where she was . . . But she won't, will she. She doesn't trust me. It's my punishment. For everything I've ever done wrong. I must have interfered too much. I bossed her about, I know I did . . . for wanting her to be best at everything . . . I'm sorry, Zoe, I let you down, somehow I wasn't the mother you needed . . . if only I knew where I went wrong. But there were worse mothers. There are. I know it.

Alma stared at the solitary ghosts of the children. *Come to me, please*, she willed them, silently. *I'd love to talk to you. I need to talk to you. Somebody wants you. Somebody needs you. You used to come and sit with me and my daughter. Now she's lost too, and I need your company . . .*

But the children were not there for her needs. Too needy themselves, too blindly needy. In any case, they had begun to vanish, slipping away into the darkening streets, taking their chance in the dangerous city, like Zoe, she thought, like my beautiful daughter. I've come too late. They've forgotten me, as I forgot them, didn't think about them, didn't realize they had something to tell me, didn't want them to be part of my family . . . but they were, weren't they? And they've gone away . . .

It used to be as if they recognized me. Knew me. As if there was a password that was never spoken. As if there were some knowledge that would soon be shared, but Zoe stopped wanting to be with me, and I stopped coming here, and we lost contact, and I lost touch with that part of myself before I ever quite knew what was there. And yet I still feel they could tell me something . . . Alma frowned, impatient with her numb sense of grief, finished her coffee, pushed away her potato.

'Penny for them,' said the white weight-lifter, in a voice that was over-confident, hiding nervousness. 'Mind if I sit down beside you?'

'No . . . I'm just going, actually.'

'I been watching you. You got fings on your mind. Don't go rushing away, I'd like to talk to you.'

His sheer bulk, his friendliness, paralysed, stifled. She couldn't get up; she smiled, weakly.

'You're a nice-looking lady. I saw you in the pool.'

'Thank you.'

'But you're not 'appy. On your own, are you? Pretty woman like you shouldn't be on your own.'

Alma willed herself to mount some defence. It was a classic pick-up, he was crowding her, but it was hard to get cross when his tone was so friendly, and a tiny part of her was pleased to hear that he'd seen her in the pool and thought her attractive. She

109

caught herself stroking the wet coils of hair away from her face and stopped, annoyed. I don't have to be nice to him, do I? I don't have to talk to him. He just presumes that no woman wants to be alone . . . His smile was kind, but too intimate. His hand on the table was the paw of a bear, pale underneath its pelt of brown hair.

'Go on, give us a smile.'

This was getting easier. Alma couldn't bear being told to smile. It had happened quite often recently, when she hadn't had a lot to smile about. She could feel the anger beginning to gather. Anger, her friend. The other Alma.

'Won't cost you nothing.' He was leaning forward, smiling what he thought was a winning smile. One tooth was discoloured; he was over forty.

But younger than me. Thinks he's doing me a favour.

'You shouldn't tell people to smile like that. Women. We're always being told to smile –' She tried to smile, to keep her voice level, to be informative, not abusive. 'You don't know what other people have on their minds.'

'Don't get heavy,' he said, still smiling, his smile slightly fixed, unsure what was wrong. 'Relax. What's the matter?'

She cast wildly about for something sufficiently terrible to tell him that would not reveal her real pain. She had to save that suffering; it was all she had left. To tell this oaf would dirty it for ever. 'My mother has cancer. She's dying, actually. I can't sit here grinning like some stupid great ape –'

As soon as she'd said it, it seemed too violent. She'd whacked him with it, right between the eyes. There was only one possible model for the ape.

''Ere, 'old on . . .' he was taken aback, his smile shattered, flushing dully, 'are you calling me stupid?'

She was on her feet, gathering her things, already going. A few heads turned; his voice was loud. Perhaps he often failed to pick women up.

'I'm trying to tell you to leave me alone.'

'I was only tryin' to be kind, wasn' I?' He hissed the words, looking thwarted, venomous. 'Women's Lib, are you? Imagining things. I just felt sorry for you, that's all.' He stood up suddenly; his chair crashed over, and his flush deepened. He looked huge, like that, but pathetic, as well, perhaps registering too late what she had said about her mother, perhaps ashamed, now the whole café was watching him.

'Thanks,' she said neutrally, defusing it. 'Thank you. I appreciate it.' As she walked down the stairs she had a sense of him still there, his big arms loose, his face hang-dog, wondering why he'd gone wrong yet again.

Damn, she thought, I won't think about him, I wish I could just say he was a pig, pure and simple, which he probably is, instead of thinking that he's lonely, that I should have somehow . . . *catered* for him, that I had some duty to be kind to him. Men. Bloody men. They play on our niceness . . .

And the children, she thought. Up there on their own. With men like him, so obviously lonely. It doesn't bear thinking about, does it? So we don't think about them, and they go on suffering . . . Unless it's true that their innocence protects them. That incomprehension is a kind of wall.

That's what I need, incomprehension. Because men like him . . . predatory men. I can always smell them, their terrible hunger. The sorrow of always knowing what they want. To penetrate me, to be let in. And they sense it, they see it in my eyes. And then there's no barrier, because I know them, and those who know are expected to provide. I'm one of the available, the walking wounded. Especially if they're tender. Especially if they're warm . . .

As if she had been born to look after them.

As if it were . . . *one of the family.*

As if when they were there she stopped existing, as if she had lost her right to exist.

And I become nothing. I lose myself . . .

So where does it come from, that terrible openness? When did I lose my innocence?

Who did the thing that was done to me?

How long ago did I lose myself?

She was confused, not knowing where they came from, these dim questions that formed with such pain.

– It's just Gwen, she thought. Just Mother and Father. Always telling me to be a good girl, always telling me to think of others. It isn't a mystery. It's just my mother. And Father always shouting, scaring me . . . And so I was too good for years and years, the good daughter, the good wife . . .

I even taught Zoe to be a good daughter.

So did I do the same thing to her? Oh God, oh God. Did I just repeat things? Did she have to leave home because she'd lost herself?

. . . Because without a self, how would Zoe survive, how would Zoe deal with the predators?

No, it's not true. I'm not my mother.

I loved my daughter. Zoe isn't me.

On the bus, Alma found she was grinning, remembering what she had said to the weight-lifter. I told him Mother was dying . . . Freudian slip, wishful thinking. But the grin was quickly frozen by shame.

I shouldn't wish that on anyone. And the old, their lives are so hard to imagine . . . Harder than ours. Harder than mine. And they're alone, both of them, her and Aunt Eileen.

They're so far away. Getting smaller and older.

– *Maybe I should go and see them.*

That little rush of pleasure at the thought of pleasing them. They'd be so happy she was coming, she would be a good girl, a good daughter . . .

No, she thought. This time it's for me. I have to be able to talk to Mother. As an adult. Telling the truth. Asking her things . . .

But it didn't seem possible. Unimaginable. A vague sense of hopelessness crept up like mist.

Eileen, though. I can talk to her. She's always talked to me, hasn't she? And yet, she's elusive about my mother.

Of course she's her sister. Those old loyalties.

The house looked darker than usual that evening; she hadn't been home before going to the pool so the normal light didn't glow in the porch, mimicking life, repelling strangers, beckoning, perhaps, to a runaway child. Alma rushed inside and put too many lights on, turned up the heating, emptied the clammy wet things from her bag. The house came alive, reluctantly. It had been ice cold; she had only just saved it.

If I left it too long, I think it would die . . .

Before she took her coat off, Alma poured herself a sherry and telephoned her mother in Wales. Gwen shrieked with delight at the news of Alma's visit, was wildly vivacious for five minutes, then wound down towards her discontented mode when Eileen's name was mentioned.

The sisters still saw each other every week, like clockwork, though they lived fifty miles apart and Gwen didn't drive, so that Eileen had to drive there and back through all the Welsh weather in her terrible old van . . .

'It's embarrassing,' Gwen grumbled to Alma on the phone. 'You'd think she was a gipsy, to look at that van. She always parks it right outside the house, bold as brass, where everyone can see it.'

'She does come to see you, Mum,' said Alma. 'It's a long way, isn't it? She's fond of you.'

'She gets her dinner,' Gwen said, annoyed. 'The best dinner she gets all week. She was always a hopeless cook, was Eileen. But she's a big eater. I mean, meat's not cheap.'

'You like to see her, though,' said Alma.

'I don't mind it,' Gwen sniffed. 'She gets lonely, you see.'

Alma said nothing. It was Gwen who got lonely. She'd never made friends, unlike her sister, not the kind of friends who spent time with her. 'It's a bit of a tie though, every Sunday. She gets sat down and won't stir till six. And I do get tired, at my age. And then I have to go straight out to chapel. And she never comes with me. I have dropped hints. But your Aunty Eileen's too good for chapel.'

'Mum, I'm not religious, either –'

'Probably the fault of your aunt, is that.'

Alma wanted to say No, but the words didn't come. *So my one rebellion was someone else's fault . . .*

'I'll tell her not to come, with your being there.'

'*Mum!* I love Aunt Eileen. I want to see her. I'll go over to her though, that'd be best. Saturday lunch, maybe Saturday tea . . .'

'But I hardly ever see you, Alma.'

Alma took a deep breath and hardened her heart. 'She did a lot for me when I was little. And as you say, she must get lonely. She won't be there for ever. I'm going to see her.'

The pink swimsuit dripped high over the bath, swinging in the breeze, the drooping panicle of some huge orchid, lighting up the bathroom, cheering her up.

Not a bad day, Alma told herself. I stood up to the weight-lifter. I swam nineteen lengths. I'm a middle-aged woman who stood up to my mother . . . it had taken so much effort to make such a little stand, but the deep pink suit swung above like a trapezist, brilliant and bizarre; life could not be predicted; time could suddenly break into flower . . .

17

PAUL SAT IN HIS OFFICE at ten-past seven, with the darkened school stretching out below him, for the clubs were all over, the athletes had vanished, even the cleaners had smoked their last fag, put away their polishers, all gone home. But he was still here. God in his heaven. Brooding above it in his box of light . . .

Except he didn't feel remotely god-like. What was he? Dogsbody, social worker, policeman, accountant, hard man, soft man, beggar-man, thief. Zoe used to adore that game. She could never get the names in the right order. Her favourite was 'sailor'; sailing away, she always wanted to go round the world . . . And maybe she is now. But not as we imagined. We told her we'd help her, after her degree, never doubting that she would do a degree. Little plans, little dreams. The obtuseness of parents.

I should know. I waste my life on bloody parents. Today had been wrecked by two different sets of parents. They fuck up their kids and then they send them to us and complain that we can't put them right. They worry about them, but about the wrong things. They say 'He's got no confidence,' and then spend half an hour criticizing the kid to me in front of him, and don't make the connection. They give them their own tellies and let them sit up till three a.m. watching slasher movies and then complain that they're always tired, as if their schoolwork is exhausting them. They tell me 'She was a very bright baby' as if I've somehow put the lights out.

Most things seemed to be his fault, which was all very well, in theory, for he often said, to console his teachers, 'The buck stops here,' and 'I've got broad shoulders,' or, more factually, 'Look, they're paying me for this,' because at least he was less underpaid than the others. Paid quite enough for him; he had never been greedy. Though life was more expensive now he lived alone. For this temporary period of living alone, because he would not think of it otherwise.

But his shoulders weren't quite so broad as usual, now his own private life had broken down, now he was just another separated parent, like the ones who came to see him all the time to explain why Fiona was acting funny, or why Darryl had done badly in his exams. 'I understand,' he always said, 'I'm so glad you've come to see me. We understand.' Knowing Fiona and Darryl would get used to it, eventually. It was change that upset them, and the threat of change. Now he understood in a more heartfelt way, understood how unhappy the parents were themselves, how they were pleading with him to be kind to their kids, to make everything right, to forgive them for failing, though of course they never said anything like that. Be God. Be Daddy. But he couldn't be God, and at the moment he didn't feel up to being a convenient hate figure either, as expected.

I'm just like you, he wanted to say. Things have gone wrong for me as well. I've done worse than you. At least your kids are still here. I've messed up so badly that my daughter's gone missing. And then he would go into a kind of fugue state as the parents sat and battered on at him, a flood of words he no longer heard. So what, he wanted to say, you're right. Don't leave your kids here. Don't trust them to me. I'm no good. I've lost my own already.

He couldn't be bothered to explain or apologize. In any case, he thought, they mostly just want to talk. To talk at me until they've talked themselves out. And then they can flounce off triumphant and tell their neighbours what they said to me. 'I told the Head, I told him . . .' And perhaps they feel they've achieved something. At least they've complained about life to someone, at least they've registered their discontent . . .

And who do I complain to? How about me? I used to let off steam to Alma, every day, till she must have been sick of it, and mostly she listened. And sympathized. She was a good wife. She was . . . selfless, really. I was sure I was lucky. And lucky people think they'll always be lucky.

It was other people who got divorced, so I could be supportive to my deputy when his wife left him for her chiropodist, I could be supportive to all the staff who've had 'family problems' since I've been here . . .

Only now it's me. And I don't want to tell them. I don't want them to pity me.

– In any case, it's only temporary.

But I miss my wife. I miss the tenderness. I miss her body. I miss my home. I miss being able to talk about the kids . . .

Adam had seemed very quiet, recently. My tall boy. My awkward boy. Of course he's a man, I must remember that. So odd to see someone grown from a baby nine inches long to a gentle giant. Taller than me. Kinder than me. Too kind, perhaps. I've always thought so . . .

Alma got impatient when I worried about him. Alma always said that Adam was fine. At least we could talk, when we were still together. I wonder if Law is too pressurized for Adam . . . I didn't much like the look of his room . . . too small. Too lonely. Too far away . . . I guess I still don't accept that he has left home. He was my friend. We were mates, buddies –

The body Paul had cuddled, now bigger than him. He still embraced Adam, but rarely, awkwardly, their bones too heavy, shoulder to shoulder. He didn't want to embarrass his son.

They go away. They all go away. But how can you believe that, about your own children?

– And oh, I miss Zoe. My lovely daughter.

After Zoe, or someone very like her, was spotted at the St Sebastian Day Centre for the Homeless, he had started on a crazy, exhausting programme of searching for her on the streets. It was the last week of his holidays; some of the schools had already gone back. Zoe had not. She had not gone back. It was early September, but summer hung on, dirty and sullen where the traffic roared. Of course he'd seen her everywhere, her untidy curls, her coltish walk, her terrible defencelessness . . . how often he had hurried after someone, yelling her name . . . the wrong name. The baleful glare of some startled stranger.

The first time he looked for her in Lincoln's Inn Fields he'd been astonished by the island of green tented space in the middle of the frowning frontages of some of London's grandest buildings – the Royal College of Surgeons, the Inns of Court. Occasional barristers still strolled in fluting pairs around the perimeter path; under the trees, though, squeezed between the bushes, spread-eagled across the green heart of the space, homeless people sat or slept, surrounded by a straggled detritus of possessions. The makeshift benders or tents were the worst, made of layers of polythene and flattened boxes, bent too low over the bodies they protected, encasing them more like coffins than houses. The terrible humility of those poor shelters, abasing themselves at the feet of the lawyers. You couldn't see what bodies slept inside. For all Paul's desperate hunger to find Zoe, he couldn't bring himself to disturb the benders. They were too nearly alive, like dirty chrysalises from which living things might crawl, injured.

Instead he'd walked around, miserably, cutting his fingers on the edges of the photo of Zoe he clutched in his pocket, not managing, on that first visit, even to speak to any of these weather-beaten people, so different from him, a clean-shaven man in a good jacket. He'd wandered in a dream, on the paradisal green, with the birds singing of the end of summer, between the tanned strangers in their frozen postures, stunned into slow motion by tiredness or hunger.

By a blue octagonal shelter in the centre of the Fields a more lively group of men stood talking and laughing. There was another noise he could not make out; the thud of feet; a girl shrieking; perhaps a fight? . . . Something behind that central shelter. As he passed it he saw every window was broken.

Then the dream opened up; it had flowered in joy. For Zoe was suddenly there, where she should have been, ringed by other girls in white and navy, bright-cheeked, panting, laughing girls, two teams of schoolgirls absorbed in playing netball on the pitch in the middle of Lincoln's Inn Fields, and the little group of men were cheering them, raggedly . . . Zoe's curls jumped in wild profusion as her pink arm caught the ball, then paused, her whole young body tensed to shoot, and she sent the ball flying towards the net . . .

But she missed, and turned, in disappointment, and stared

straight through him, and *was not Zoe*, was another girl from another school, plainer, younger, more ordinary . . .

If only Zoe were still ordinary. Zoe was no longer one of the lucky ones; shining faces, shining hair, aiming the ball at the net in the sunshine. Zoe had changed sides, he knew it in that moment. Zoe had gone; she had moved outside.

At his own school, here in his familiar haunts, girls of her age were a perpetual torment. None of them knew, of course, how it cut him, the intonation of a flying voice floating Zoe-like down the corridor at break, a young back running in a school raincoat, one particular fifth-former who from behind had Zoe's dark curling mane of hair . . . 'Afternoon, Mr Bennett.' She was rather sweet, old-fashionedly polite, from a family of girls who all played the recorder and did poorly at exams. But she gave him a bad feeling by not being Zoe. 'Afternoon, Sarah,' he would smile, the actor.

Liar, actor, psychopath, therapist . . .

We always had plums when we went to Mum's. She bottled them, from the tree in the garden, and Zoe loved them, so on nearly every visit Mum made plum pie, sweet soft red fruit with a delicious edge of tartness, and Zoe would line up the plums on her plate and get quite upset if the rhyme went wrong and she ended up a thief or a beggar-man . . . quite soon she got ruthless and quietly stole our plum-stones to make the rhyme come out to her liking.

'Ooh Zoe,' Mum said, one day when Zoe was still quite young, four, five, I can't remember, 'you're going to marry a sailor, how exciting!'

'She's not,' said Alma. 'She's going to *be* a sailor.'

'Yes,' said Zoe. 'Be a sailor. Not get married. Be a sailor.'

– Will she never get married, because of us? Is that what happens to the children of parents who split up?

What a ridiculous thought. She might be dead, and I'm worrying in case she never gets married . . .

But I want my grandchildren, he thought. I wanted to enjoy them together with Alma.

Sex is so weird. It's so short-term, it makes you live totally in the present . . . but it's also the thing with the longest shadow. We go into the future through that strange short act. And it makes us crazy, all of us.

Like the parents who come in here frantic with anxiety because they think their kids are having sex. They all act as if they'd never had sex themselves, as if no teenager ever had sex before. As if I taught them how to do it at school. Whereas Nature bloody *intended* sex for teenagers. Three centuries ago all my girls would have been pregnant . . . but I can hardly point that out to the parents.

So I lie, instead of admitting that I know that half the older kids are having sex. Sexing each other, as they like to put it, though that always sounds like chickens, to me . . .

Alma was sure Zoe wasn't having sex. 'I *know* her,' she said, in that reproachful way, as if I didn't have a clue about Zoe. And it's true, all that was a mystery to me. Of course, a mother would be closer to her daughter . . . Alma was close, maybe too close, always prying and giving advice.

When Zoe ran off I was sure, at first, that a boy was at the bottom of it. It seemed so obvious that sex was the answer . . . I was wild with jealousy and worry. She could have been pregnant, or any damn thing . . . But Alma said it was out of the question. And I was relieved when she told me that. Of course I know sex is perfectly normal, but it's different when it's your own little daughter . . .

To think of another male touching her. The body I held, stroked, kissed . . . Now Alma tries to say that she did it all, but I know it's not true, I held her, I bathed her. I probably didn't do my share of the nappies, but Alma always got there first.

I remember so well how I longed to see her. Sitting on the tube, coming home from work, imagining Zoe waiting for me, she was two or three, and we had a nanny, Alma was working with an author in the office, some child-care guide, was it, for a tight deadline, so I had the luck of getting home first, and there she would be. Toddling down the hall. 'Dada, Dada.' Her enormous grin, those tiny teeth in an expanse of red gum, her little round face transfigured with pleasure. The way no adult face ever looks. Her whole body, dancing with pleasure. Her little legs running, a baby cowboy, sturdy, bandy, running to me. Her hands reaching up. Two plump pink hands, all palm, so open. Holding my hair, pulling my hair, pulling me close to have my kiss, which meant twenty kisses, fifty, a hundred. 'Daddy home.' And the sun came out. What man would not adore such a welcome? No wife ever gave it. No mistress, no friend. I sometimes think no one's ever loved me like Zoe, in that all-embracing, adoring way. All I had to do was be the right person, the expected, awaited, beloved Dada.

– And she thought I was so funny, too. I've always loved to make people laugh. I did it at school when I was little, I try and do it in the staffroom now, it's the only power I have, making people laugh. Once I could do it with Alma too; she looked so pretty, when she gave up and laughed, helplessly, weeping, coming over and kissing me, patting my shoulder. 'You do make me laugh.' She would sometimes say 'Make me laugh' at bedtime, when she lay there tense after a day of overwork. And in those days I could. And she'd start to relax, and she'd turn to me, and then we'd make love, don't think about that, it's too painful . . . She stopped laughing long before we stopped making love. And then everything stopped. And she pushed me out.

– But Zoe always found me funny. The corniest joke, the most obvious imitation, my Japanese accent, borrowed from the students I used to teach English when I was young . . . even when she was a teenager, and getting more sophisticated, so I began to be a little afraid of her, she loved her old Dad, she loved to laugh. And I adored it, making her laugh, my pink-cheeked girl, her wonderful laugh . . .

It makes me sick with rage when Alma says I never talked to Zoe enough. Because my way of talking was making her laugh. And she made me laugh. We just had fun. Perhaps it wasn't enough, but it wasn't . . . nothing. I loved her, I loved her more than my life, and Alma can never take that away.

It's because she's so afraid she was a bad mother. She has to make me feel I was a bad father. She questioned everything we ever did, till I was almost relieved when she told me to go, so I could get away, and hug my memories to myself.

I may be deluded, but I still feel . . . Zoe liked me. She loved us both, of course, I know. But . . . we got on, didn't we? We were . . . good company. Perhaps she'll miss me. And so she'll come back.

He heard footsteps echo in the corridor. They paused, then there was a tentative knock.

'Mr Bennett? . . . Ah, just checking.'

It was Bob Vernon, his caretaker, whose dogged affection Paul had earned by giving him three weeks' paid leave when Bob's small son had meningitis. He was a man of few words, not popular, but Paul and he had an oblique friendship, framed by the labyrinths of school, over which each man in his sphere presided. He was one of the few Paul had told what had happened.

'Bob,' said Paul, pleased to see him.

'You all right then?'

'. . . Managing.'

Bob looked distressed, pulled at his lip, which was always smoky-blue with beard, though he told Paul he shaved three times a day.

'No good news then?'

'Nothing yet.'

'How's Mrs Bennett?' He said her name with savage emphasis; he didn't approve. Probably, Paul thought, because her hair is untidy.

'Oh fine, fine. Perfectly well.' Paul heard himself conveying that he was hard done by, but he couldn't resist Bob's silent sympathy.

'Women,' the caretaker said darkly. 'They don't bloody know when they're well off.'

Paul said nothing, embarrassed to agree. He was a feminist. But he did agree. He did agree, with all his heart. *I was a good father. A good husband.*

'You should get off home,' Bob told him, gruffly. 'You'll wear yourself out, here till all hours.'

This was a major speech for Bob. Paul knew what it meant. He appreciated it.

'Thanks, Bob,' he said. 'I'm on my way.'

Bob loped away, thin, lugubrious, powerful. A good man to have on his side.

Paul closed his briefcase, switched off the light, walked downstairs, out of the heavy front door. Turned to double-lock, and saw the graffiti. 'Mr Bennett is SEXIN . . .' Interrupted, thank God. Would be removed tomorrow, by Bob.

Though who the hell do they think I'm sexing? he wondered. I should be so lucky. Who would want me? That's part of sex. Knowing you're wanted. Getting inside. Coming in from the cold. Being accepted . . . enfolded . . . *mothered* . . .

He caught himself back. What a strange thought. Why link sex with mothering?

I suppose my mother once loved my body . . . That primal tenderness, so long ago. Putting up with my weakness, my smelliness . . .

Now no one seemed to want to touch him. And it meant so much, being stroked and held. Being found . . . lovable. That someone should find him lovable. His ageing, horny, hairy body. His giant needs (and they grew, with loneliness.) No one might ever want him again. He was grateful, now, and half-amazed, that Alma ever loved him, and regularly . . . That they had made love such uncountable times. Sinking into the wet warmth of her body.

Whenever I wanted to, she let me.

– *But did she love me, or did she just pretend?*

The sharp wire of doubt, after two decades of doing it.

Did she sleep beside me all those thousands of nights? Were we really a couple? Were we . . . *complete?*

Now it was over, he ached with disbelief.

No wonder teenagers want sex too, they're at an age where they can feel so lonely, as if no one will ever like them or want them . . . And some of their parents don't really want them. Can't wait to get them out of the house.

– *But we want Zoe so very badly.*

He tried to think 'we', tried to be loyal.

But part of him thought Alma drove Zoe away. She was such a mixture; too gentle, too fierce. She had no idea how fierce she could be. Remnants of Welsh Methodism? Gwen's savage standards? Home didn't always feel comfortable.

If she knew I'd left home, Zoe might get in touch.

If she knew where I was, she'd come to me.

18

THE FIRST DAY THEY NOTICED the newcomers, it was a bright day which threatened rain; stormy sunlight between great black clouds. Kevin arrived in an immaculate cream raincoat. His credit card bills must be enormous. Ashley was flustered, ten minutes late, carrying a red and white furled umbrella.

Alma had been first to arrive as usual. She had boiled a kettle for their first cup of coffee.

'Did you see them?' she asked. She knew they must have seen them.

'Wot?' asked Kevin. 'Who?'

'I saw them,' said Ashley. 'What are they up to?'

Alma peered across at the other side of the road. 'Sitting down,' she said. 'On the pavement.'

'Oh *them*,' said Kevin. 'The wotsits. The dossers. They won't be there long. There's nothing for them here.'

'What will they do if it rains?' asked Alma.

The other two came and stood beside her. All of them gazed at the little group of figures almost directly opposite the office. Pale faces, dark bodies, clumped together between the phone boxes, which must have offered a little shelter.

'Go under the railway bridge,' suggested Ashley.

'Sod off out of it, I hope,' said Kevin.

'Must be awful being homeless,' said Ashley. 'You'd never guess he's got a kind heart, Alma.'

And Kevin and Ashley smiled shyly at each other, glad to stop thinking about the homeless. They went back to their desks. The day began, but little bursts of reminiscence kept breaking out; they had enjoyed their evening at the Fitness Centre.

'Ashley in a leotard. I tell you, it's enough to frighten the horses.'

Ashley giggled, smoking her biro like an imaginary black Sobranie.

'– To be honest, Alma, she looked pretty good. Whereas me, in my cut-away leopard print G-string –'

'You didn't, Kevin.' Ashley grinned at her. 'He didn't, Alma, he looked quite respectable. You wouldn't expect anything else, would you?' (For Kevin was a notably elegant dresser, perhaps a little on the stuffy side, not a bit like his vocabulary.)

'Well,' said Alma, tickled by the pair of them, 'I'm glad you two had such a good time. Good job I didn't take the ticket, Ashley . . . anyone want coffee, I'm just making some?'

But while Ashley was out of the office at lunch-time, Kevin came and perched on Alma's desk. He had a self-important air. 'I wouldn't want you to get the wrong idea,' he said. 'About Ashley and me. I mean, there's nothing in it.'

'What?' said Alma. 'Why should there be?'

'Nothing carnal,' he said, with parody salaciousness that made her smile, despite herself.

'You're ridiculous, Kevin,' she muttered. 'Ashley's got a boy-friend, anyway.'

'Now there you're wrong. You mean this Nicky guy, don't you? I asked her if he was coming with us, and she says they've had a barney. She thinks it's over.'

'I see,' said Alma, meaning nothing by it, but Kevin's little eyebrows shot up above his glasses.

'You don't,' he said. 'Now Ashley . . . she's a really nice person, like you once said. But I don't want to break her heart, do I? She's an older woman, isn't she?' He saw her reaction, blushed to his hair. 'You're different, Alma, you're married.'

For some reason it was easy to be honest with Kevin. Because he was so buoyant and so outrageous. 'Kevin,' Alma said. 'I want to tell you a few things. First of all Ashley's nearly the same age as you. I can't believe she's more than thirty. Secondly, she's taller. And I very much doubt that you could break her heart. She once told me she likes tall blonds. You're not exactly Stefan Edberg.'

'Swedish tennis-player, right . . . ? *Right.*' He looked stunned

for a moment, got up, walked around, his familiar twitchy movements more erratic than usual, hands spreading and clenching, not
looking at her – the duck-like bob of his gait looked irrepressible,
but suddenly he sat down, deflated. 'Uh – well yeah, Alma, OK.
That was quite a speech. I hear what you're saying. I mean, I didn't
mean to sound . . . I suppose I was a bit out of order there, Alma.'

'Don't give it another thought, Kevin. I don't suppose you will,
in any case.'

But he looked at her very earnestly, through the expensive
frames of his glasses. 'No really, Alma. I've got a lot of respect
for you. *Respect*,' he added. 'Now that's very important,' as if he
might gain it by talking about it. 'By the way,' he added, brighten-
ing, 'on another topic. I think you've got a fan. He's a bit of an
Edberg himself, actually. Course he might be for Ashley, but she
doesn't sit near the window.'

'What are you talking about now, Kevin?'

At that moment Ashley came back from lunch. Kevin looked
shifty, but Ashley didn't notice. 'He's there again,' she said,
grinning. 'Alma, don't be obvious, but look out of the window.
Kev and I think he's a fan of yours. He came in yesterday when
you were at lunch, and got some particulars off Kevin, and then
he asked where the other lady was.'

'You're imagining it,' said Alma, peering, but the sun was out,
and the dazzle was confusing.

'Well he's very nice-looking,' Ashley said.

'So d'you reckon he looks like Stefan Edberg, Ashley?' Kevin
asked with heavy innocence, and Alma suddenly thought, he's a
bit jealous. It's him who likes her, of course it is. It's the other
way around, he's turned it all around.

'Not totally *un*like,' Ashley observed, judiciously. 'Amazingly
perceptive of you, Kevin.' Then her head went down, and she
gave a kind of sneeze which Alma knew from Kevin's face was
an involuntary titter, as the door opened and Edberg came in.

Alma spoke firmly to protect the poor man from embarrassment. 'May I help you, sir? Good morning.'

He leaned across her desk and shook hands. The touch was
surprising, but rather pleasant. So many of the clients never even
said 'Hallo', and it ended up making you feel de-personalized, as
if you were a thing attached to a desk.

And he was unnervingly handsome, in a clean-cut forties matinée kind of way, except that his dress was entirely modern, a leather jacket, but soft and expensive-looking, navy not black, and a maroon silk shirt, no tie, so you could see the curve of his neck, she had always liked the curve of men's necks, yellow-blond hair, soft and thick, cut high at the back and floppy on the forehead . . . He was tall and slender, with cheekbones like cliffs. He reminded her of someone. Not Stefan Edberg. Someone . . . intensely, shockingly familiar. Must be some film star . . . *must be gay.*

But he didn't sound gay. Was not remotely camp . . . He smiled at Alma, friendly, direct. *All the same, he's much too good to be straight.*

'Good morning,' he said, in a light London voice. 'I'm interested in houses.'

'Three-bed? Four-bed?'

'I live alone,' he said, and Ashley sneezed again, and Kevin got up and walked over to the window where he straightened some photographs, coughing. 'Three-bed would do me. Up to a hundred and twenty.'

'We have quite a good choice, in that case, sir.' Alma tried to make herself sound more formal than usual, avoiding his eyes as she looked through the files. But she was registering something, or imagining something. He was looking at her, not the sheets she gave him.

'There are others, but I'll have to get them photocopied . . . Ashley, could you copy these? Let's take your details, sir.'

'I'm not sure I want to register yet . . . I don't want sheafs of stuff coming through the door.'

'We need your name, all the same, I'm afraid.' He was so very blond. Could he actually be Swedish? He had large white teeth; faintly greasy skin, but the bones were so good that you hardly noticed. His eyes, when she made herself meet them, were striking, a rather pale blue behind thick dark lashes, dramatically different from his corn-coloured cow-lick. Must know he's good-looking, Alma thought. Must know what effect he has on women . . . but who was it he reminded her of? She made an even greater effort to sound cool. 'Is your own property on the market?'

'Not yet.'

'We always advise people to put their property on the market.'

'First I want to get some idea of what's available.'

'Otherwise we're not usually in a position to put forward any offer you care to make.'

'I'll cross that bridge when I come to it.'

'Fine. Name . . . ?'

'Edwards. Simon Edwards.'

Ashley choked on her way out of the door with the sheets she was photocopying for Alma. Alma turned her desire to laugh into a smile.

'Excuse me if I seem to be staring,' Simon Edwards said to Alma as she wrote down his name. 'But you remind me of someone. I don't know who.'

'I'm sure we haven't met,' Alma said, and smiled properly, because she had not been imagining his gaze, because he was not, therefore, excessively interested, but merely a man who was reminded of someone just as he reminded *her* of someone, life was full of coincidences like that . . . and they smiled at each other, for a moment, quite warmly, and she thought, how nice to see a beautiful man, someone young and clean, with good teeth and bright hair, how nice to feel he likes looking at me, even if I only remind him of his mother . . .

She handed him his form. 'Could you fill in the rest? It's quite simple to put you on the mailing list.'

'Oh, you don't have to bother with that . . . I can pop in and pick stuff up. You see I often pass by, I'm a youth worker at the Burnham Rise Youth Project, just up the road.'

– Well dressed for a youth worker, Alma thought. 'I'll get you those other details,' she said, and left him sitting there while she walked out of the room to look for Ashley.

Ashley was sitting by the photocopier, wiping her eyes. 'Simon Edwards,' she hissed. 'It's too good to be true. It's him to the life, isn't it?'

'Not really my type,' said Alma, 'but he does remind me of someone . . . not Edberg.'

'What's your husband look like? Was he your type?'

'I can't describe him. I don't really know. Big. A bit scruffy. Brown hair. Pink skin.' She gestured vaguely, scrolling gestures that indicated 'a bit of a mess'. 'When you know someone that well, you don't really see them.'

'I bet you'd never not notice Edberg.'

'*You* show him round then,' Alma said, stooping to pick up the photocopies that Ashley had managed to scatter on the floor. 'He's not wearing a wedding ring.'

'So, you looked!' Ashley teased.

'Lay off, Ashley. I mean, I'm still married.'

'Doesn't stop some married women I know.'

Simon Edwards left with a polite thank you, clutching the details of some thirty houses. Glancing at his back as he went through the door, she thought there was something faintly absurd about him, slightly oversized, too deliberate, too handsome. Too Aryan, maybe. Too pure a dream. The puppet hero from a TV film.

Yet her thoughts crept back to him, every now and then, through the slow afternoon, as the sunshine died, as grey rain drifted over and pattered at the glass, as November closed down upon the little lighted office, and Ashley said, 'I'll turn the heating up. It's going to be real winter soon.'

Rain was bad news, at Portico and Sheen; there were always fewer customers when it rained, fewer people who thought it would be nice to look at houses, and fewer of those who looked would buy, because they all wanted sunshine included in the deal. Sun, and luck, and hope, she thought. Nobody seemed to have a surplus, at the moment.

The few people who came in seemed like refugees, thin and dispirited, without proper raingear, some of them blatantly sheltering from the weather, others what Kevin now called 'TWs' since Alma and Ashley had both started objecting to the regularity with which they heard the phrase 'time-wasters'.

But the use of the initials made Alma even more uneasy. Not that Kevin meant any harm by it, but Kevin never meant any harm by anything, not even when he rode shotgun with a bailiff doing a repossession. 'It's the job, isn't it?' – another of his phrases, the phrases that helped him sail through life. TW somehow reminded her of the War, or of other wars, or of massive disasters, huge disasters that had happened somewhere else, while they sat inside, bantering and laughing. It sounded like POW, that was it. Prisoners of war. Displaced people.

129

Which they are, some of the people who come and stare. Some who don't even get inside. Some who just hang around near the window. The look in their eyes is so desperate, sometimes. As if they're staring in at a lighted Christmas tree, and know they will never get any presents. And we sit here making jokes about sex and looking down our noses at the ones who 'aren't serious', which is what we say when they have no money, as if they come in here for a laugh, whereas really they do it out of terrible hunger, hoping, I suppose, for a freak or a miracle, or why would they ask 'Nothing under thirty thousand?' when they know there's nothing in the window under fifty, but a tiny part of them thinks God will look after them, God or Fate or whatever they believe in, maybe Mum up in heaven, I don't know – a tiny part of everyone who comes in here believes there is a house for them, if only they look far enough, a tiny warm space which is marked out for them, and the price will be right, and they will come home. And they look at us, and we say 'Nothing, sorry.' And they go away just a little more defeated. And we exchange looks, and think 'time-wasters'.

There were shadows outside the wet windows even now, as she checked their weekly copy for the local paper, breezily declaring Portico and Sheen to be 'Fast, Courteous, Efficient'. Even now, in the cold, in the twilight, they gathered round the lines of fluorescent-brightened photographs, the little red-roofed arks with their blur of garden made perfect by distance and the veil of rain, enlarged by Alma's camera-angles. Figures in anoraks with plastic rainhoods. People, she thought, who didn't seem to be able to afford an umbrella to shelter them, let alone a roof . . .

And behind the tourists, behind the time-wasters, behind the dreamers, across the street, she glimpsed them again, the new-comers. The ones who had been further off before. The ones who were migrating from the centre of the city, encroaching on the places where normal people lived. White faces, grey bodies parked on the pavement. Between the phone boxes, shining wet, under the plane trees, which dripped, dripped. Beneath the streetlights, which came on at four, so no one could ignore them, lit up like a stage set. And yet they were ignored by the people who passed, busily, hastily, people shopping or hurrying home, normal people who didn't lie on pavements, normal people who lived inside.

Not seeing the newcomers who sprawled at their feet; sleeping, some of them; singing; burping; shivering in the soaking rain. Drinking from small bottles wrapped in newspaper. Some of them young, even very young.

Lost people. Homeless people. Dossers, derelicts, down-and-outs, all the names, Alma thought, we give them to cover our confusion and embarrassment. Really we just want them to go away (and she did want them to go away) and they would go away, very soon, she was sure. They would get tired of this pitch, wouldn't they? Right opposite us is hardly tactful. Right opposite an estate agent.

They make us feel bad. They make us feel guilty.

– She thought gratefully of Simon Edwards' glowing smile, the easy health of his tall young body.

'Doing any viewings tonight, Alma?'

'No – but I have done, every night this week. I wonder when it's going to quieten down. Mr Portico says it gets very quiet, in the run-up to Christmas.'

'You'd think people would get more desperate, wouldn't you?' Ashley remarked, frowning at her fingernail which yesterday's aerobics had split to the quick. 'What's the saying? No room at the inn.'

'That's not a *saying*, Ashley,' Kevin put in. 'I mean, it's what the geezer said to Mary and Joseph.'

'I *said* it was a saying.' Ashley had turned pink. She was very sensitive about her education.

'It was *true*, wasn't it?' He pressed his advantage. 'No room at the inn. I mean, it was a fact.'

'Bible studies?' Mr Portico inquired, looming on the threshold with a sheaf of papers. 'Could you type these, do you think, Miss Hughes? If you can tear yourself away from Mr Hough's theology.'

The phone rang at five o'clock on the dot, and Alma answered it, and it was Simon Edwards. His voice on the phone was warm and young. She couldn't help feeling a little breathless; so different from most of the voices that phoned.

'I'm interested in two of the houses you gave me. Is there any hope of an appointment today?'

'Probably depends on the vendors, Mr Edwards. Tell me the properties, and I'll check.'

'Brierton Avenue and Oakeshott Road.'

'I think we've got the keys . . . shouldn't be a problem.' They were both near the office. Walking distance. She thought of Ashley. 'Could you hold the line?' She pressed the 'secrecy' button. 'Ashley. It's Edberg. Could you show him two houses?'

'It's not really my job . . .' She had stood in for Kevin or Alma on one or two appointments, but strictly speaking her job was just clerical.

'Who's going to object? But only if you want to.' Alma didn't want to, she wasn't sure why. 'No one has to know except you and me.'

'And the Schoolboy Wonder,' Ashley said. 'Kevin will poke his nose in. Won't you, Kevin?'

'So what. Look, he's hanging on. You'd share the commission, if there was a sale . . . want to, or not?'

'All right,' Ashley said. 'Tell him six o'clock.'

'We can meet you at six o'clock,' Alma told him. They agreed the details, then he made to ring off, saying 'See you later.'

'Not me, actually. It'll be a Miss Hughes.'

'Oh,' he said, 'oh, all right,' but it was perfectly clear that he was disappointed.

Alma couldn't help feeling gratified.

Kevin hummed a lot, over the next twenty minutes, and didn't seem to be concentrating.

'I could run you over,' he offered Ashley. 'It's on my way.'

'But it's stopped raining . . . and it's only a three-minute walk, Kevin.'

'Just thought you might be stiff from yesterday.'

Ashley ignored him. Alma observed him. He was still not getting on with his work.

'Don't think I'm getting neurotic or nothing,' he said in a minute, looking at Alma. 'But I'm thinking of that wanker, what was his name, the bastard who gave you a fright the other day. Crowther, that's it. I mean, have we got an address for this Edwards geezer? Are we sure he's kosher?'

132

'Of course he is. Someone that good-looking could have anyone they wanted. He doesn't have to come in here to meet girls.'

'Well you may have a point. All the same, give us his form.'

Alma fished it out and gave it him. He looked at it, frowning. 'He hasn't even given us a telephone number. No address, either.'

'Didn't he?' said Alma. 'I asked him to fill in his own details . . . but I know where he works. He couldn't be more local. The Burnham Rise Youth Project, just up the road.'

'He says he does,' said Kevin, grimly, and picked up the phone book. 'Right, let's try them.'

But the outcome of the call was boringly ordinary. They knew his name; he did work there. 'Just keeping the address book up to date,' said Kevin, ringing off swiftly, disappointed.

'Quite the little private eye,' said Ashley, but Alma could see she was impressed. 'Kind of you, Kevin.'

He didn't want them to think he was soft. 'Private dick,' he said. 'Hurr hurr.' He stared at his signet ring for a moment. 'The Youth Project's no kindergarten, from what I hear.'

'What do you mean?' Alma was curious.

'Nothing . . . just rumours. People pushing drugs. So what if he is. At least he'd have some cash.'

All the same, as Ashley left to walk to the house, having checked her makeup and brushed her thin head of soft red hair into a fluffy halo, she paused in the door. 'You did think he was all right though, Alma? Kevin going on about it's got me worried.'

'Of course he was. And gorgeous with it. Go on, enjoy yourself,' Alma told her. And then, 'Don't forget the mobile phone.'

Home could feel terribly quiet and empty after the cosy badinage of the office. Why were all offices obsessed with sex? – Because we're not allowed to have sex in the office.

How quickly they had become like family, Kevin and Ashley, now her family were gone. How important it seemed that the three of them got on. How tender Alma felt towards the young ones' flirtation.

– And yet it's all empty, really, she reflected. I don't know them. They don't know me. We can't help each other, in the middle of the night, when daughters disappear, and parents die, and life is too real to joke about . . . Would any of us care, if the others were in trouble?

It's an anaesthetic, I suppose, my job. Stops me thinking. Stops me feeling. Paul knows that. That's why he resents it. He hates me talking about Portico and Sheen.

And Kevin. Is he nice, or nasty? He's kind to us, but with the public . . . I don't think he thinks they're human, really. Or he wouldn't say the things he says. He thinks anyone on the repossession list has asked for it by not keeping up their payments . . . Well he doesn't think *at all*, really. Not where work's concerned. He just gets on and does it . . . 'It's the job, isn't it.' He says that so often . . .

He'd said it when she asked him once if selling repossessions ever worried him. 'The only thing that worries me is losing the sodding keys . . . It's the job, isn't it. Life's too short.'

And she had accepted it. Not pursued it. She didn't want to think about the dark side either, the misery outside the plate-glass window. She liked their bright little cocoon of an office, its buzzing phones, its busyness, the adrenalin high, the foreglow of money, not quite in their hands but just over the horizon.

Alma suddenly felt trivial, disloyal. I hardly thought about Zoe all day. Or Paul. I rarely do, in the office . . . or Adam, she appended, even more guiltily.

– I'll write to Paul's parents, she thought. I miss them. They were good to me. They're family. I don't know what to say, but I'll write to them. It shouldn't be hard. I did love them.

Especially his Mum. She was a bit like me.

Obscurely, it felt like doing something for Paul, and when she'd finished the stilted, affectionate letter Alma walked through the rain, which was falling again in straight icy sheets that seemed endless, unstoppable, part of her sorrow, the walls of her sorrow – walked to the post-box on the corner. By the time she got there she was half-drenched; it was the kind of rain that soaked straight through her coat, poured down her neck, squelched into her shoes – and she thought, briefly, of the newcomers, under their street-lamp, opposite the office. They would be so wet. They would be so cold. But it was too much for her; she couldn't solve it.

She posted the letter and felt brave, and virtuous, as if she was making things right with the past, as if she was pulling her life together, sending the mute little square of white across hundreds of miles to the Bennetts' cold house.

It's for you, Paul, she thought, as she slipped it inside.

19

IT WAS EDBERG, however, who tapped her on the shoulder in Kemble Hill High Street two days later, making her blush and pant for air. He was older, by daylight, but wonderfully handsome. Unreally handsome; people stared at him. His eyes were the scintillating blue of blue glass. His head was almost too big for his body . . . and yet, his body was very large. His eyebrows were heavy, dark, well-shaped . . . was it possible that he darkened them?

'You're getting blown away. Come under my umbrella. Come for a drink.'

'Oh . . . oh, hallo . . . thanks for asking, but . . . I've got to get back. It's the end of my lunch-break.' She felt herself blushing.

They stood stalled for a moment. He was staring at her.

'Is it Miss Bennett, or Mrs?'

'Mrs,' she stuttered. 'But I'm separated.'

– Why did I tell him?

Too late; she had told him.

This time his interest was unmistakable. His hair was thick and soft and yellow. Too yellow to be true. Touchable. There was nothing more exciting than someone else's interest . . .

And yet, she didn't really want to touch him. He was rather too big, too young, too alarming, too impossibly glamorous for her to touch – and in any case, she was too long out of practice. It was almost unthinkable. And yet – Alma wanted Edberg to want to touch her. And she did think about it. She thought a lot.

For a week she thought about him at work, at home, in bed, in the bath, in the supermarket, where tall blond heads turned out not to be Edberg.

Ashley had reported him to be polite. 'Not interested in me, I can tell. He asked if you were in the office every day. There's something about him, I dunno . . .' And she wouldn't be drawn; she really didn't know. 'Not really my scene, appointments. I'm not tough enough to be a negotiator . . .'

'Do you think I'm tough?' asked Alma, surprised. Yet she knew she could be tough with people, sometimes. The right people, she hoped, on the whole. Greedy vendors, welshing applicants. And her children, of course, when they didn't try. Occasionally. Hardly ever, surely . . . Alma was a gentle person, wasn't she?

'Well *Kevin's* tough . . .' said Ashley. Kevin looked pleased. He stroked his cuff-links. 'I know my limitations, Alma. And I like to get home. You understand.'

'Your mother,' said Alma.

Ashley reddened, nodded. 'You'd be better at dealing with someone like Edberg.'

So that was that. He was Alma's pigeon.

There were few things in life, she thought, one morning, remembering the man as she dragged herself awake, stretching luxuriously, surfacing into the sweetness of the thought, more enjoyable than knowing someone fancies you. When *you* fancy *them* as well. And there are no corollaries, no complications, no future events when things could go wrong, for she was sure there would be no future events. How could there be, with someone two decades younger? More, she told herself, to make it more impossible. *Quarter of a century younger.* There. This deliciously content-free sexual frisson.

And she wafted downstairs feeling distinctly cheerful, dressed, she realized, rather better than before, better than before she realized people noticed, making more of an effort, her eyebrows plucked – to find a letter on the tiles of the floor. So cold to the touch, her tiled floor, and the letter was flimsy, with an old person's handwriting. A square of tissue-paper skin on the stone.

With a shock, she recognized Rita Bennett's handwriting. Rita, replying to my letter. A little shock of guilt, worry, fear. What if she's cold to me. What if they haven't forgiven me. Naturally there's nothing to forgive . . . but guilty, guilty, she thought, I'm guilty. And lusting after Edberg. Rubbish, fantasy. I'm a worthless person. No good. Useless.

Reality returned, desolate and chilly.

They had always welcomed her, praised her, cherished her, worried about her when things went wrong. 'My lovely mother-in-law' was how Alma used to describe her, crowing to friends about her good luck. They had telephoned daily after Zoe's disappearance, offering to come, to help search, to do anything. Their love for her had never been conditional. She was Paul's wife; they adored their son.

– And then I threw him out, Alma thought. They couldn't believe it. They couldn't understand it. They coped by pretending I was ill with grief after losing Zoe, so that they could still love me.

The letter, when she brought herself to open it, was short, and sad, and apart from the emotional ending, rather wintry. It is winter, she thought, for all of us. We're all older. We're all sadder. Maybe my letter to them was bland. Maybe I hurt them by sounding bouncy. I just wanted to sound . . . as though things were the same.

'Darling Alma . . .' So she was still their darling. But the rest of the letter was not reassuring.

Paul's father had had a slight stroke. It was 'relatively mild' – *relative to what? relative to death?* Alma wondered – his speech was 'hardly affected', but the lines were gripped with loving worry, Rita thinking aloud about what she had to do, what he could no longer do for himself, what was going to happen – and then catching herself back. 'I'm sure everything will be all right in the end. John's always been as strong as an ox.' And Rita herself had had 'kidney trouble'. She didn't elaborate on this. 'We haven't been ourselves, with worry about John, and this kidney trouble.' Both of them, Rita said, thought constantly of Zoe. They hoped above everything to hear some news. 'John talks about you often, Alma. He's sure you and Paul will get back together. He knows how much you loved each other. We hope you're not too lonely, dear. You are in our prayers, as you always have been. Perhaps you will come and see us one day, but we understand how busy you are.' And then the magical conclusion, the line that Alma's mother could never have written, the line every daughter wants to read, that every child wants to hear from their parents' generation, from those who go before and look back and judge us. 'You are a good and lovely person.'

Reading that phrase, like a benediction, Alma found the tears running down her cheeks. Because they're old, Alma thought, they get down to essentials. They say the things they want to say in case they don't get another chance. They don't get distracted by the rush of things happening like middle-aged people do. My letter to them was just stupid gossip, trying to pretend that life goes on. And it does, it does. But people fall behind. The weak, the old, the ill, the lost ones. The abandoned ones. The forgotten people.

I abandoned Paul. I cast him off. I forgot his parents. I decided to survive. I rejected Adam. I wasn't interested in anything except my suffering. I hugged it to myself like an egg. As if something new could be born of it . . . what's the matter with me? I'm a horrible person . . .

What have I done to Paul? she asked herself, in agony. I spend my time fantasizing about that meaningless bloody male model of a man . . . while Paul's alone, in some horrible digs, worrying about his parents' illness.

At six o'clock that evening, the earliest time Paul could possibly be back in Ealing, she rang his landlady.

And he answered the phone. So far, so good. She didn't even have to get past Peeky.

'Paul, darling —'

'What on earth's the matter?' He was agitated by her unfamiliar warmth.

'Are you all right?'

'Why shouldn't I be?'

'I just had a letter from your parents.'

'Oh. How do they sound?'

'*Paul* – you didn't tell me they'd been ill.'

'You didn't ask.'

'But they were always so well,' she found herself saying, foolishly.

'Yes. People often are, though, till they get ill. And they're not so young any more.'

'What does she mean by "kidney trouble"?'

'I wish I knew. She hates talking about illness. Particularly about her own illness – it's as if there was something disreputable about it. And suddenly the house is full of illness. You know what bikers and walkers they were—'

'Have they stopped walking then?' Alma couldn't imagine the Bennetts not walking, striding along in their crêpe-soled shoes, their white hair bright against their red and blue anoraks, ignoring the rain, ignoring the stiffness which must have been creeping over their bodies.

'Well Dad can't manage any more. He can get to the end of their road, and that's it.'

'She said it was mild.'

'She says "relatively mild", that's the phrase she uses to everyone.'

'That's right—'

'It is relatively mild, compared to some strokes. He can talk, thank God. But he's lost co-ordination, and a lot of movement. Still, he can talk. Why don't you go and see him, Alma? Before he has another. Which sometimes happens. He's fond of you. I mean, if you're worried about them, go.'

It was unpleasantly as if he were calling her bluff, yet her feelings for them were perfectly genuine. Someone was shouting to Paul in the background, and he called something back that Alma couldn't hear.

'Is anything the matter?' she asked him, unhappily. She wanted them to be close, but this call wasn't working.

'My supper's ready,' he said casually, but Alma imagined a hint of bravado.

'What do you mean, your supper's ready?'

'I get tired, Alma. I come home knackered. You must remember what I'm like after school. Peeky noticed. She offered to cook. I pay her a bit more, and she cooks every evening.'

'Very cosy.'

'Well, it is less bleak.' He was gentle, factual.

Alma felt ashamed of her sarcasm, and panicked by the rush of jealousy that flooded through her, miserable, icy. 'Well you'd better go, if your supper's ready.'

'No, look, it's OK. She'll understand . . . It's kind of you to worry about my parents.'

As if they were no longer her family. As if it were merely 'kind'

140

of her. 'Maybe . . . we could go and see them together.' Alma couldn't quite face the idea of going on her own. What if they rebuked her? What if they cried? – *What if they died while she was there?*

'I think that would give the wrong impression,' he said.

'What do you mean? We're still married, aren't we?'

'Come on, Alma. You've given up on us.'

'How do you know?' said Alma, petulant.

'You have, haven't you?'

There was a silence. She couldn't find words for her confusion of feelings.

'Be honest, Alma. You want a divorce.'

'Stop telling me what I want, will you?'

'– Don't you, then?' His voice was definitely hopeful. Warming up at last. She was shivering.

'No,' Alma said, in a small, tired voice. 'I don't know what I want. I think I want to see you.'

'I've got to have my dinner—'

'I don't mean *now* . . . look, couldn't we go and see your parents together? I'd feel so awful if – well, you know. Not that it'll happen, but if one of them died, and I'd never gone to see them since Zoe ran off.'

'You really mind about them, don't you?'

'Don't sound so surprised!'

'It's just that sometimes you seem so far away. And I start to imagine you have no feelings. Maybe it's easier to see you like that.'

'Paul . . . I do still, you know, love you. Just because I don't want to live with you . . . just at the moment . . . it doesn't mean . . .'

'You do love me?'

'Yes.'

'You *do*?'

'*Yes.*'

'*Alma.*' There was a long pause, then. 'Alma. Listen. I've got to go. You know how I feel about steak and kidney pudding –' He sounded quite different, definite, invigorated, filled with new energy because she'd been tender. Or was it just Peeky and her bloody pudding? '– so I'll do you a deal. You can think about it.

141

I'll come with you to see Mum and Dad if you will agree to come to couples therapy. Just give it a try. If we hate it, we'll chuck it.'

She was taken by surprise by a surge of relief; *he wants us to try; he still loves me.*

'OK,' she said, 'it's a deal. I'm glad. We'll work out the dates when we've both got diaries . . . just one thing. I'm going to Wales. See Mum, and Eileen. A long weekend. Soon.'

'Are they all right?'

'Yes . . . it's me. It was my idea. I wanted to. I'm going to try and talk to Mum. Properly. I'm determined to. I'm still angry with her. I have to try . . .'

'It's never worked before, has it . . . aren't you banging your head against a brick wall?'

'*Don't* say that.'

'Sorry . . . OK, maybe it will, this time. While there's life there's hope . . . it makes no difference to the couples therapy. There's a huge waiting list. Certainly not before Christmas. I'll ring tomorrow. Goodbye, darling . . . Bye. Take care.'

She put the phone down and sat smiling at it, stupidly. Her cheeks felt warm. Even her hands felt warm. She poured herself a drink and enjoyed every mouthful, the amber glow spreading upwards, outwards.

– And yet, the house itself felt chilly; in a moment she felt cold; she pulled on a jumper.

Alma drew the curtains, and noticed that the sycamore outside their bay window had lost more of its leaves. It made the room brighter, by daylight, but harsher. The year was turning. Time was passing.

– I hope they can fit us in before Christmas. I hope we can go and see Paul's parents.

Because although this phonecall had ended so warmly, she'd noticed they took longer to warm up each time, as if each time they started from somewhere colder, somewhere more precarious and remote. As if the gaps between the calls were getting longer and longer, which perhaps they were, she thought, surprised; she'd been busy, and preoccupied with Edberg, and Paul was definitely calling her less.

Once he was calling me almost every night. Every night, in summer. So different, then; she had sat there wearily, holding the phone away from her ear because the urgency of his feelings made her sweat, naked on the bed in the heavy heat.

The world's got colder, hasn't it. Paul's got colder. We're forgetting each other. Maybe one day I'll leave it too long.

– That fear, as if someone or something were dying.

She could read about time and entropy without believing a word of it, as long as the sun shone or artificial lights blazed, as long as the world buzzed outside the window, as long as she sat on a rattling tube where dozens of people contained their energies, waiting to burst out at the correct stop; or in a summer garden, with lawns being mowed and the neighbours rowing *sotto voce* nearby . . . It was impossible to believe that things just ran down, when you saw how everything was pulsing and shifting, breeding under stones, diversifying, multiplying . . . transforming always into something new. Nothing stays the same. Everything goes onward . . .

But it wasn't like that in the middle of the night. When the world lay still, in its little death. When everything slept but frogs and cats, and Alma, reading in her empty house. When you knew the frost was deep outside, when you knew that the bodies which stretched in the streets wouldn't all start moving again in the morning. When you knew your daughter might be one of them. When you couldn't look after her any more, feed her, clothe her, keep her warm. When you could no longer keep her alive.

When you could no longer make new life; when your body was too old to make new babies. When everything shrank and closed upon you. When you were alone, with time slipping away. Letting go of things, forgetting what mattered . . .

It's Adam, she thought, as she fell asleep, *I'm forgetting Adam* . . .

She forgot, and slept.

20

ALMA NEEDED TO TALK TO SOMEONE. She was being pulled in such different directions, towards Paul and away from Paul, into a future where other men desired her and back into the past, where the parents huddled, growing more remote, more needy, older . . .

And perhaps she needed to tell someone, also, that a man as handsome as Edberg had made a pass at her. A man so handsome, and so young. Perhaps she wanted to talk about lust, for she was troubled by lust, as well as loneliness. And pleased by lust as much as troubled. Probably the sodding menopause. She needed to talk to Verity.

'I'd love to, Alma, but I've got to finish the fair draft of this by the end of the month, and Ian's kids are coming this weekend.'

'I'd love to see you,' Alma said, pleaded, a little ashamed of herself for doing it.

'Boot's on the other foot now, isn't it?' Verity said, after a little pause.

'What do you mean?'

'Well – just that before, you were the one with all the commitments, and I was the one who needed to talk.'

'Was I?' said Alma. 'I suppose I was . . . I'm sorry, Verity, was I always too busy?'

'Don't sound so stricken,' Verity said. 'In any case, you had a right to be busy . . . Look, if you need to come over, you'd better come over. But you know how I get, with a book to finish. Tunnel vision. I'm sorry but it's true . . . the book comes first, or it would never get written . . . Anyway, Alma, is there any news?'

There was a pause, then Alma said, 'No, not really. Look, I'm

144

all right. Sorry to bother you . . . Good luck with it. The finishing straight. Come round for a meal when it's over.'

Alma made herself sound composed and cheerful, but the effort left her flattened. Damn, she thought, why couldn't I say I do need to see you, I really do . . .

Why can't *I* have needs? Even with my friends?

Why am I this grinning, miming creature?

– And underneath, such emptiness. The stolen truth, the thing that would not speak, the self that could not find its voice. *I'm quite all right. Sorry to bother you.* Under the ice, sinking deeper and deeper.

It seemed like insult to injury when Sheilah Fenwick rang her at work.

'Alma, I've got to talk to you. Just have to see you. When are you free?'

Alma's heart plummeted. Another long session of listening, of watching Sheilah's blonde head bob and shake, watching her terrible animation, watching her fingers, crusted with rings, scattering ash as the stories flowed . . .

'I'm a little bit busy this week,' she pleaded, but she knew she didn't sound firm enough. The pleading note implied that Sheilah had rights.

'No, it's got to be this week. Got to be.'

'Well what if it can't be?' Alma tried.

'Can you speak up, darling, I can't hear you . . .'

But Alma couldn't. To give in was simpler. She stared at the little patches of light reflected in Kevin's designer glasses, wishing she had his rubbery chutzpah, doing what he wanted, always bouncing back again. She said nothing. Other phones rang, in the void, and Kevin switched into frenetic activity. Alma treasured her own silence. Maybe Sheilah would think she had died.

Since no invitation was instantly forthcoming, Sheilah was forced to make one of her own. 'Look, there's that new wine bar at the bottom of your high street. I'll take you there. It'll be on expenses. Which night are you free . . . ?'

'Well like I said, I'm not sure . . .'

'What are you doing on Friday? Nothing? Thought not. Great – I'll see you at seven.'

'Eight,' said Alma, bargaining weakly.

'Eight,' Sheilah agreed. 'Byeee!'

Of course she was late, as always, so Alma had to sit there, cursing her, sipping a glass of acid red wine she did not like but didn't want to waste, wishing she'd remembered to bring a paper. Imagining people were looking at her, thinking 'She's a bit old to have come for a pick-up.' Noticing that people were not picking her up. Feeling the self-protective slump of her shoulders, rounding inwards to protect her breasts; feeling herself shrinking into her chair, though it was narrow, smart, uncomfortable. Meant for younger bodies, which wouldn't sit still. Alma sat still, and stared at her wine.

This is entropy. I'm it.

There was a little ripple of heads turning, and Alma knew that Sheilah was there, the usual explosion of long thin limbs and expensive leather and blonde-feathered hair, strawberry-ish, currently, and cleverly cut to show tiny, aristocratic ears . . .

– Though why I think that I can't imagine, since I know her family were poorer than mine; we've all been brainwashed; too late to change us.

She was very striking. Alma felt a surge of pride to be the friend of someone so glamorous. Some of it must rub off, she thought, kissing Sheilah warmly, enjoying her perfume. Warm and floral, yet dry not sweet. Something very expensive, surely . . .

– And then again, why do I think it must be expensive? Flowers aren't expensive. They smell sweet.

'Where do you get your hair cut?' she asked Sheilah. 'I keep on meaning to cut all mine off. Now Paul's not there to tell me not to. And yours always looks fantastic.'

'You're joking,' said Sheilah. 'You've got beautiful hair.'

'Mine? Grey and untidy?'

'Grey? It's not. It's fantastic hair, I've always been jealous. All those curls, and I bet you never touch it. It takes me hours to get mine like this. And costs me hundreds of pounds a year. And I worry about it all the time. I bet you never give yours a thought.'

This was a revelation to Alma. 'Do you really think so? Do you really like it?'

Sheilah reached her thin hand across the table and stroked a thick strand, curled it round her finger. 'I'd swop my car for hair like yours.' She was proud of her car, a bright blue Aston Martin which would keep her in debt for the next ten years.

Alma started to feel more cheerful, and the goodwill led her to wave for the wine list. 'I'm buying the wine.'

'I said, it's my treat.'

'You buy the food, I'll do the wine.' And she chose a bottle which was slightly more expensive than either of them would be able to detect, though it was certainly Sheilah's turn to treat her – they so often ate at Alma's house. Damn, she thought, as she fished in her handbag, apologizing to the waiter as she did so. 'I'll pay for that now . . . my purse is stuck, sorry.'

'Very well, young lady.'

The two women exchanged glances, mocking, long-suffering. Another one. The world was full of them. And yet, the complicity drew them together. Two women friends, two old friends. Two women who were no longer young ladies.

'I'm too old to finish this disgusting glass of red just because I've paid for it, aren't I?' said Alma. 'There must be something I've learned from being fifty.'

'*Shhh*,' said Sheilah. 'Don't tell everyone.'

'I'm not ashamed of being fifty. Are you?'

To her surprise, she saw that Sheilah was annoyed. 'I'm forty-eight,' she hissed at Alma. 'I don't want to advertise the fact. You never know who's here.'

Alma couldn't take her seriously. 'It's just that we used to be the same age . . .'

'Look, you could pass for early forties any old day. It's defeatist to get old. Let's not talk about it.' But Alma was staring at her goggle-eyed, and Sheilah was forced to explain, *pianissimo*. 'Alma! In television, fifty is *death*. If you're female, that is. It's beyond the pale.'

'Right,' said Alma. 'We've got that straight. I think you're loony, but I've got the message.' It was refreshing, disagreeing with Sheilah. Normally it was too much physical effort to check her in her onward flood. She does look good, Alma thought.

Greyhound bone structure, faultless makeup, and the enormous film-star smile, which she does all the time, through nervousness, but until you spot that it looks terrific. And yet, there was something glazed about the eyes, as if a great effort were going on, thousands of miles beneath the skin, as if epic battles were going on, and someone was being defeated.

'Alma,' said Sheilah, glittering wildly at the waiter who was bringing the good bottle of Sancerre, 'when he's poured the wine I have to talk to you. Something really important.'

'You said so, on the phone.' And so, it begins. At least I have the wine to look forward to, Alma thought. And she is fun to watch. And the music is another consolation; quietly haunting, silver-blue, the smoky sound of a sax playing jazz. It evoked youth and spoke of its passing – though Sheilah wouldn't see it that way. The waiter leered at Sheilah as he poured, and she flirted back on automatic pilot.

'Two things,' Sheilah announced, raising her glass. 'Well, loads of things. So much has happened since I saw you last. The first thing is about you. Why are you looking so surprised?'

'No,' Alma lied. 'I just feel hungry.'

'It's about Zoe. Don't jump like that. No news, just something that might interest you. You remember George. I was crazy about him all last year. Independent director, very successful, well he was successful till the money dried up . . .'

'The married one?' Alma asked. 'The one you went to Brussels with? What on earth has this got to do with Zoe?'

'Well not directly. Wait. He's been making a film about home-less people. Seems to talk about nothing else. He's done all this reading, most of it depressing. Point is, I told him about Zoe. Her going off, and how upset you were, and the woman who saw her in that homeless place –'

'– *thinks* she saw her. It isn't certain.'

'OK, but let me finish. I told him how there'd never seemed to be anything wrong, and there wasn't even a row, was there? – and I mean, you and Paul adored her. Doted on her. You were a wonderful mother.'

'Thank you, Sheilah, you're kind,' said Alma. 'It really helps, your saying that. I spend my time wondering what I did wrong.'

'In any case, listen to what George says. He says nearly all of these homeless people have got terrible things in their past.'

'I know that. That's what scares me – thinking of her with these damaged people. If she is on the streets, and I pray she isn't.' Yet the image had settled, against Alma's will; Zoe, bedraggled, with her sleeping-bag; Zoe, tiny in the nets of the night. Zoe hungry. Zoe thirsty.

'Wait on, Alma, that's not the point. Oh – avocado and mozzarella salad, with garlic bread on the side, please. And some water. No, fizzy. What are you having, Alma? You haven't decided? Shall we make that two of the same? Great, thank you. – George says, nearly all of those kids have been abused in some way. Or rejected. They don't go home because they can't go home. They're not on the streets for trivial reasons.'

Alma took a long drink of wine, and listened, filtering her pain through the sweet flights of jazz, letting the alcohol trickle through her, a silver stream, a silver river.

'He says that she's bound to come back. Bound to. There's no good reason for her to stay away. I mean, life on the streets is hell, Alma. If that's where she is, she'll be home by Christmas.'

'It's true there was no frightful trauma . . . as far as I know . . . but you never know everything . . .' Hope rose through Alma, all the same. Dizzy hope. *She'll come back before Christmas.* 'He wasn't just saying that to be kind?'

'Why should he? He doesn't know you from Adam. By the way, how *is* Adam?'

'Oh, he's all right . . .' Distractedly. 'Does George really believe most of those kids are abused? I've read the same thing, but is it possible? There are supposed to be over three thousand children sleeping on the streets of London. Can there be that many abusers?'

'Well sometimes it must be booze, or illness, the parents can't cope, the usual shit . . . But some of them have been beaten or assaulted.' Her tone was impatient; too much pain, for Sheilah. She rarely allowed herself to register pain. She had had things hard; she wanted to be happy. 'I mean, Zoe was *spoiled*. She had everything.'

Alma thought, she's envious. Of course she is. Sheilah's own parents were divorced, and her mother had no money, bringing up four children on her wages as a school dinner-lady. Sheilah's adult life might look luxurious, but nothing could fill the emptiness of the past.

'We tried to make her happy.' That sounded coercive. Alma tried again. 'We tried to let her be happy.'

'Maybe you gave her too much, Alma. Maybe she had it too easy.'

The conversation was taking a turn for the worse. It was leading in the direction of 'treat 'em tough'. Alma had heard Sheilah go this way before. 'I don't believe you can give them too much,' she said. 'I feel it must be our fault, not hers. I blame myself. I blame Paul. I only blame her . . . for not explaining. But then I realize she couldn't explain. If she could have explained, she wouldn't have gone. And it must be my fault that she couldn't explain. I don't know about you, but I could never explain any-thing to *my* mother. Still can't. She never listens. She won't talk straight.'

'Of course she can't,' Sheilah said, scornful. 'Of course you can't expect to talk to your mother. Everything's changed from when they were young. You just have to get on with it. I did. These kids today expect the earth.'

There was a long silence while Alma thought. 'No,' she said. 'I don't think that's it. I think we expected too much from her. And it was mostly me.'

Sheilah was almost angry. 'But it's good when people expect something of you. My Mum expected nothing of me –' (in her agitation, her diction slipped back to something like her mother's must have been) '– except to be a dinner-lady, like she was. And look at me. I amaze my mother . . . But if I'd had something behind me. Someone who believed in me. I mean, I might have been really successful. It's as if . . . you can get to a certain stage, just under your own steam, and then . . . you somehow fall back, if there's nothing behind you. You don't quite believe things are within your grasp.'

'Yes . . . but what if you're not ambitious? What if you want to lead a quiet life? Like Zoe might have done, I realize now. And your parents are constantly telling you you're brilliant. Always expecting you to be best.'

'I can't imagine it,' said Sheilah, simply. 'But I wish you'd been my mother, Alma. You're a rock to me. I appreciate it.'

'Oh Sheilah,' said Alma, genuinely touched, clinking her glass, smiling, smiling. This real affection between them; how could she have forgotten it? 'You're being a rock to *me*, tonight. I'll tell Paul everything you said.' I'm a beast, she thought. I forget her sweet side.

Two hours later she was flagging severely, the bottle was empty, and Sheilah was in tears. Alma's empathy was exhausted. Alma was exhausted.

Of the two things Sheilah had wanted to tell her, the second, unsurprisingly, was all about her. Alma settled to this in good heart, but soon her heart felt old, dehydrated.

The unexpected: Sheilah was pregnant. Nine weeks pregnant, at forty-eight, which was her true age according to her birth certificate, she emphasized to Alma. It was an accident, completely unplanned. Her periods were irregular, and she had assumed she wasn't fertile any more.

'I don't know whether to congratulate you,' said Alma, trying to take this in.

'Well I'm very old, which I know has not escaped you . . .' Alma demurred. 'For this lark, I mean.'

'And is George the father?'

'I'm almost certain.'

'– You're not certain.'

'Well . . .' Briefly Sheilah sparkled, looked wicked again, nearer thirty than fifty. 'I had a little fling with a cameraman. He was absolutely gorgeous. All of twenty-six. He was really pushy with me, which is sexy . . .'

'I know,' said Alma, thinking of Edberg, thinking God, we old lags are so vulnerable. But it wasn't attractive, the thought of Sheilah briefly spreadeagled in the shadow of a camera.

'I had no idea I was pregnant. I mean, I thought it was just another big gap between periods. And then my breasts felt funny. And it rang a dim bell. And then I tumbled . . .'

'But you've never been pregnant before, have you?'

'Yes,' said Sheilah, unhappily. 'I was twenty-one. I never told Mum. She would have insisted on us keeping the baby, because it was family, I know she would, she would have wanted to bring her up herself, and I knew that then there would be no escape, for me or the kid, from that terrible poverty . . . You can't understand it if you've never known it. Don't judge me, Alma, I know you love kids. But at least I did have her. I refused an abortion. I got her adopted, and I howled and howled . . . I suppose my mother was right, in a way.'

'Yes,' said Alma, thinking. 'In a way. Once you've lost a child, you know there's nothing worse . . . but you know I've always been weird about abortion. Of course you were right not to have the abortion. I'm a good feminist, but I hate the thought of it . . . goes against nature. Something like that. I remember trying to explain it to Zoe. Many times . . . she said I was illogical.'

Sheilah looked impatient. 'It's not the *principle*, Alma. It's the reality, when people make *actual decisions* . . . anyway, I had her, and I lost her. And since then it's been too painful to contemplate. I could never think about having another. She'd be twenty-seven. I always cry on her birthday. It's a bit like Zoe, I don't know where she is . . . she's out there, somewhere, wandering around. Maybe with kids of her own. Somewhere on this earth.'

'You never told me any of that!'

'I thought you would disapprove of me.'

'What kind of a prig would I be?'

'Well, with you such a perfect mother and all . . . we childless women all feel guilty. It's fucking ridiculous, but we do. As if we're hard, or not proper women. I've always dreaded being asked the question, "Have you got kids?", and I have to say "No", and people look at you as if you're Lucrezia Borgia, whoever she was, I've never known . . .'

'A poisoner.'

'There you are, it's bollocks . . . I knew she was something pretty bad. In any case, it's all going to change . . .' And again she looked thirty; maybe nearer twenty; there was a glimpse of a rounder, sleeker Sheilah, secretly contented, cat with the cream. *My God*, thought Alma, *perhaps she will have it.*

'What does your doctor say about this baby?' she hazarded, tentative, unwilling to offend.

'Not a lot. They don't have time, do they? They can't give you antibiotics for it.'

'So . . . I mean, are you going to . . . go through with it? If the tests are all right? What does George say about it?'

'I haven't told him. I don't know what to say. I'm completely floored. That's why I had to see you.'

'Well what do you feel? I wouldn't even be asking . . . but it's your age, Sheilah, it's . . . scary, isn't it? You want it, don't you?'

'Desperately. Enormously.'

'And you're not afraid?'

'Absolutely terrified.'

'Well,' said Alma. 'If the tests were OK . . . I haven't got used to this yet, but, well . . . I think it would be lovely. A baby of yours would be a lovely baby.' And she felt a rush of warm emotion, a river of life, the upsurge of sweet unreasoning hope that came so rarely as she grew older.

'George is handsome,' Sheilah mused. 'It might look like him.'

'It might look like the cameraman!'

Sheilah hooted with laughter. 'Thank God I can laugh . . . I lie in bed at night thinking I'm going to go crazy, thinking "It's growing, and I can't stop it," and then thinking "It's growing, it's amazing, it's wonderful . . ." But Alma. I'd be seventy when the child was twenty-one.'

'I think it's my health I would worry about.'

'It *is* my health that I'm worrying about, mostly. What if I die in labour. What if I miscarry in some horrible way . . . all the risks are higher for someone my age . . . I mean, I've always been funny about illness because my mother always seemed to be ill. I can't bear to be with ill people, I stuff myself with vitamins, I only like fit men . . . and now I might be doing something really dangerous to myself. I *am* doing it. It's happening.'

'It's possible . . . you might lose it, in any case.'

'Of course I might. It's early days. And at my age, the chances of miscarrying are high. The doctor said that. She said "Don't get too excited." I said "I'm not, I'm in two minds." She said "Are you considering a termination?" And the way she said it just got to me, as if it wasn't a baby she was talking about, so I said "You must be joking," and she looked offended and a bit frightened and said "It's my duty to remind you of the options." She was all of twenty-five. I ask you . . . what do they know? What can a twenty-five-year-old know? . . . Now *you* tell me. What do I do?'

Only an inch or two left in the bottle. Alma thought, if she's pregnant, she shouldn't be drinking, but there's no point in making people feel guilty. At least she isn't smoking, which is fairly amazing.

Sheilah said, 'I have to have just one cigarette.'

'If it were me,' Alma said, 'which it couldn't be, because I'm o–l–d–e–r than you, say it in a whisper, I know I'd think it was a miracle and go ahead with it. Because I've lost Zoe, I'd see it as some sort of mad compensation.'

'Well *I* lost a daughter,' Sheilah said, and her terrible smile cracked, and her eyes became brilliant with tears inside their clenching wreaths of bright wrinkles. 'I lost a daughter, didn't I?' Her thin frame buckled, she covered her face and sat for a moment, snorting with grief, muttering, 'Oh God. Oh no. It's the booze.'

Alma stroked the hand that still lay on the table, crumbling its unlit cigarette. 'To be practical,' she said. 'What will you do about the father? How are things with George? Weren't you going off him?'

'Yes,' sniffed Sheilah, but back under control, her eyes a little red, her eye-line smudged. 'But he's a good father. Which is why he hasn't left his wife. Although the kids will both have left home next year and his wife is knocking off his best friend . . .'

'Don't you ever feel the world of telly is depressing?'

'I'll tell you this; it's better than Huddersfield. I've chosen my lifestyle, Alma.' Her face tightened again after grief's brief slackness.

'Well if he's a good father, like you say, and the baby's all right, it will need him. So tell him. And forget about the cameraman. Completely. What George says might help you make up your mind.'

'Yes,' Sheilah said. 'I know. It helps to have you say what I've more or less decided . . .' She paused, put the cigarette down in the ashtray, an unpleasant worm which had been trodden on and split, exuding brown matter from its broken back, and took out another, waved it, put it down. Picked up the bottle, poured out the last glass, too abstracted to offer it to Alma. 'But there is another complication . . .'

This was when Alma began to feel tired, dead tired, weary of life's long campaigns of attrition. Her body was tired. She was tired of the wine bar, tired of the strangers, tired of Sheilah, tired of the smoke, tired of the jazz, and the spiteful little spotlights peering at their faces. Her eyes were tired. Her head felt huge, as if the bones all massed together in her forehead, pressing her down, telling her to sleep. The day was too long; life was too long. It's age, she thought. I'm really getting older. But she had to concentrate. Sheilah needed her.

'This could be nothing, or it could affect everything. I haven't told a living soul. It's just that two weeks ago George had a letter from a woman he slept with eight years ago.'

Alma knew, in a sickening flash, what was coming. Had been coming to someone she knew for ages. Had been expected, and was finally here. The hammer-head hitting, hitting in her forehead.

'She's been diagnosed HIV positive. She thinks she was infected before she slept with him. Thinks so, but isn't sure.'

'God. Oh, Sheilah.' Their eyes locked, frightened. 'And you were sleeping with him unprotected . . . but wouldn't George be ill by now, if he was infected eight years ago?'

'I can tell you, I've rung every bloody HIV helpline. They all give slightly different information, and most of them said the chances were slight . . . but you see, there are people who don't get symptoms. Ten years or more after being infected. And if I were infected . . .' She trailed off, desolate.

'Is it that the baby might be infected?'

'There's a chance . . . but also, it makes pregnancy dangerous. I won't believe it . . . I daren't get a test . . . but in the middle of the night, I think about it . . .'

They stared at each other. There was nothing to say. The lights had gone up; it was half-past eleven, and the wine bar must be closing. Sheilah looked much older in the yellow light, her lipstick gone, her mouth unhappy, the snow-smooth surface of her makeup melted. And so must I, thought Alma. She could feel every muscle and tendon sagging. She reached for her coat, meditating dully.

Life pulls and stretches us. It wears us down. We get used to that, we endure, we harden, we batten down the hatches to protect our habits. But Sheilah's being asked to start growing again. Sheilah *wants* to start growing again. To transform herself. To split herself open. To put a new life before her own . . . and she might have blighted it before it's begun.

Suddenly Sheilah's face looked like a skull, a rictus of teeth with anxious eye-holes, Alma saw her thinner and thinner, then dying . . .

'We ought to go home,' Alma said, and smiled, a huge effort of warmth and goodwill, reaching up for the daylight from deep underground. 'I really think everything will be all right. Talk to George. See what happens. Maybe if the baby wants to be born, it will be.'

They stood outside in the cold road, waiting for Sheilah's taxi. In profile, by streetlight, she was a greyhound again, her marvellous posture, her small poised head . . . Alma tried again. She wanted to talk sense. She felt too tired; words were just coming from her mouth, useless words which didn't help anyone.

'All over London. All over Britain. People must be getting letters like George. And going through what you're going through. And statistically, I suppose ninety per cent of them must be OK.'

'Yes love,' Sheilah said, hugging herself, opening and shutting the clasp of her handbag. 'Statistically, how many forty-eight-year-olds get pregnant?'

'Well,' said Alma. 'Yes.'

'You think of funny things,' said Sheilah. 'I keep thinking about my cameraman. He was awfully sweet, after we did it. Only twenty-six, and he looked like a boy. Freckly nose. They have waists, at that age. He's got red hair. Auburn. He said he'd only ever slept with three girls. He was amazingly affectionate. And sort of . . . grateful. I thought at the time he was just doing it for a laugh, but I couldn't have been more wrong. And I think, how rotten if I gave it to him. I mean I've had my fun, and George has had half London, but this kid doesn't deserve to die. No one should die till they've had a life . . . And I can't explain why I won't see him again.'

'Not much of a laugh, sex these days.' The thought of Edberg went bad on Alma, joyless and sinister. And utterly trivial. She no longer wanted to talk about him. Alma wanted Paul. His arms around her.

The friendly yellow eye of a taxi approached. We all want to be safe. We all want to be looked after, borne through the night in a nice warm car . . . Sheilah hadn't had a lot of looking after.

They kissed, awkwardly, crashing cheekbones, Alma anxious not to seem to be avoiding Sheilah's lips, and yet repressing a vague unworthy fear.

'Well done,' she said. 'You didn't smoke once.' She wanted to give Sheilah a parting gift.

'Thanks, Alma. For everything. Glad you noticed. Keep trying, that's my motto. Got to do our best.'

Alma hurried home alone through the icy wind. December was coming. The real black cold.

But George had said Zoe would be home by Christmas . . .

Thank you, Sheilah. Bless you, George.

21

ALMA WAS STRANGELY CHEERFUL in the office next day. When she passed by the row of – what should she call them? dossers, tramps, down-and-outs? – none of the words was particularly pleasant . . . when she passed by the row of stained human beings who seemed to have set up permanently across the road from Portico and Sheen, she looked at them with distant pity; they were nothing to do with her. Of course Zoe wasn't going to die in a gutter with reddened skin and filthy hair. Of course not; Zoe was . . . normal. Normal childhood, normal family, nothing dreadful in the woodshed there.

My shining daughter. My healthy girl. It would be all right. Logic said it would. Logic, and George. Nothing was final. They would all look back at this and smile. Alma was sorry for Sheilah, terribly sorry . . . and then there was the shameful other side of pity, the creeping joy that it wasn't her, that someone else had been chosen to suffer, that the black shadow had passed over her . . .

'You look nice today. Meeting someone special?' Kevin asked her when she gave him his coffee. She noticed she had made coffee again at the moment when Kevin took it from her hand; the big signet ring he must have bought himself, his large square hand, hers white, ageing. I'm glad I made it, she told herself. I did it because I'm feeling better. Hope allows us to be generous (or was she a slave? She didn't really care. She liked Kevin, and he liked her.) Was she meeting someone special? She might be. Yes. Paul had said he would bring some wallflowers round.

'Probably my husband.'

'Well you would be, wouldn't you?' She had never told him they were separated. 'Your husband is a very lucky bloke.'

There was something old-fashioned about his flirtatiousness, his friendliness to both of them, his optimism, just under the skin of his barrow-boy cool, his flamboyant cheek, his preposterous language. She suspected he was vulnerable, as well. He was gauche, with Ashley; almost painfully clumsy.

'So will your wife be,' she responded in kind. 'I bet you'll be a lovely father, Kevin.'

Kevin retreated into monkey-shrieks of laughter to conceal his blushing pleasure at the tribute. 'Wot me a father?' he choked. 'Not unless it splits, hur hur hur. Sorry to be vulgar, Ashley. Though I'm sure you don't know what I mean. Hur hur . . . Hur.' Then he looked horribly depressed. Ashley gave him a withering glance. They had had some row that Alma couldn't figure, but nothing could dent her good humour today.

She was humming as she walked down the street after work, enjoying the red–gold late afternoon sun which had flickered back to life after a day of storms; enjoying the peaceful sense of people going home, having earned their money, earned their rest, looking forward to their papers on buses and tubes, to turning the key in their own front doors. Home, she thought. I have a home to go to. And maybe by Christmas they'll all be back. (Dimly she saw some kind of struggle break out among the dark figures who sat on the pavement, who sat at the feet of the normal people, but then someone laughed and the fight subsided.) We'll all be back, maybe. Back together.

Someone tapped her on the shoulder and her humming died. 'Alma . . . is it you?'

The face was utterly familiar, florid, tired, over-expressive, the furrowed brow, the exposed pink gums. But where . . . ?

A rush of grief, of dread. It was Thelma Hutton. 'Thelma,' she said, trying to conceal the jolt of pain.

'But you're looking well, Alma!' There was surprise in Thelma's voice, and Alma imagined a hint of reproach, as if she should not have been humming, or walking down the street with bright lipstick on.

'I'm not too bad . . . how's . . . oh dear, I've forgotten her name. How's everything, at St Christopher's?'

Thelma Hutton and Alma had both been on the committee

159

of the Parent Teachers' Association at Zoe's school. Thelma's daughter was in the same year as Zoe, though Zoe was in the 'fast track' stream, Lower 6A, known as 'The Hothouse' by everyone. What *was* the child's name, Alma wondered.

'Emily's fine. Very scratchy at the moment. They've got their mock A-levels. It's fairly ghastly. And she's playing Cordelia in the school play . . . Zoe loved theatre, didn't she?'

'Yes . . .' But Alma could hardly speak. The rush of longing was almost overwhelming, to be part of it again, not to be shut out, tea and sweet biscuits at parents' meetings, the smell of bleached cleanness in the staffroom where they met just after the cleaners had gone home, the crumbled grey lions which guarded the school gates, turned by time into soft-nosed lap-dogs, and on the rare occasions when she was free and Zoe allowed her mother to pick her up, the crunch of gravel as the girls came running, the first ones just before the final bell, headlong, coltish figures shouting and laughing as they escaped into the light . . . And sometimes she was happy to see me. Not always, but sometimes she was radiant. The gossip of the waiting mothers, crossing, meshing, complaining, boasting. The familiar glow from the teachers' praise, for they had always praised Zoe, always, ever since she was a little mite at infants' school, before her hair began to darken, before her limbs began to lengthen, when she was still rosy and curly and round, but she learned to read before anyone else – I didn't push her, did I? I *encouraged* her – 'Of course she's very forward . . .' 'Of course she's very bright . . .' 'Mrs Bennett, you must be very proud of Zoe.'

'Are they doing their mock A-levels already . . . ? Gosh.' Alma couldn't keep the wistfulness out of her voice. Zoe was missing it. Zoe wasn't there. The others pressed on, frowning and giggling, pulling at their hair, copying from the whiteboard. The others ran on, leaving Zoe behind. Zoe would have loved to have played Cordelia . . .

'Be thankful you're out of it!' said Thelma heartily, then realized, with a little gasp, what she had said. 'I'm sorry, I just mean that Emily's impossible . . . Dear, have you had any news of Zoe? All our thoughts have been with you. I mean, any mother can understand . . .'

You can't, Alma thought, *because you haven't been through it.*

'Thank you,' she said. 'No actual news, except that we know she's alive and well. Or she was in June.'

'Oh yes, someone told me, that special phone line . . . such a good idea.'

Alma had lost count of the number of times she had had to agree it was a good idea. Everyone preferred to be glad for her; everyone wanted to look on the bright side. Because, of course, it was easier. Because the dark side is unbearably dark. They think about it, all of them do. But they daren't mention it, as if I don't know. They smile, and pretend, and then go away and shudder. Damn them. Half of them want her to be dead.

'But we think she'll be home by Christmas,' she said, slightly too loudly; insisting. Saying it might make it come true.

'Oh,' said Thelma. 'Well . . . that's good.'

Clearly thinks I'm deluded, thought Alma. Mind touched by grief. 'There are studies,' she explained doggedly. 'By experts. When children leave home for not very serious reasons' (am I trivializing what Zoe felt?) 'they nearly always come back quite quickly. And winter's coming.'

Thelma looked at the pavement. *She's sorry for me.* 'Nights closing in,' she mumbled. 'I put the heating on last week.' The weather was something they could all agree about. 'How's Adam?' she added, on an inspiration, glad there was still a child to ask after.

'He's training to be a barrister.'

'Still living at home?'

'They don't, do they?' Alma answered defensively, feeling 'No' would have implied that all her children had rejected her.

'He must miss his sister.'

But she hadn't really thought about that before. Perhaps he did miss Zoe as much as they did. He had always seemed very fond of his sister, though Zoe got impatient with his earnestness, and he was sometimes jealous of her brilliance. And other times he was proud of her.

'All of us were so proud of her!' burst up from Alma's chest, out of her mouth, and the tears pushed up and overflowed, a steady haemorrhage of painful fluid.

Thelma looked stricken. Thelma panicked. Thelma preferred no raw emotion. 'Of course you were. Of course you were. I mean, my Emily was always a bit of a plodder . . .' *

But Emily was still there.

The unspoken ending hung between them in the cruel, the reddened golden air, which touched everything with becalmed beauty, the lie that it would all stay there for ever, the windows of buses, their scarlet flanks, the white ruff of hair of the old man on his bike, the heavy shoulders of the women with their shopping, their patient faces, heaving uphill, the plumes of breath from all the home-going people, walking alone but weaving together, the thin shawl of leaves on the London planes, trembling against the cool city sky which arched over them all, wild rose through indigo, and Zoe wasn't there, Zoe wasn't there.

Even an empty house is a comfort, thought Alma, pushing inside the door and out of the wind into a warm darkness which snapped into light at a touch of her hand.

Put them all on; the porch light, the hall light, the light on the stairs, let there be light. Closing the door behind her, leaving the rest of the world outside.

Thank God I have somewhere to live. Even a house with too much history, it doesn't matter, at least it's a home. Somewhere to kick my shoes off. Somewhere to plug in a kettle and brew an enormous pot of tea. The house smelled of lemon geraniums, and this morning's grapefruit, and (faintly) paint, where Alma had painted the dining-room white; like the smells of a body, diverse, familiar. Some things, at least, were still all right.

She'll be home by Christmas. Home by Christmas.

The phone rang. It was Paul, in a hurry. A crisis at school; an emergency meeting. They were cutting his school budget by twenty thousand pounds. Other local schools had been hit even worse. His voice blurred on; she didn't want to hear it. She knew what he was about to tell her – he wouldn't be bringing the wallflowers round.

'I didn't ask for them anyway. They're not my favourite flowers, wallflowers.'

'I know you didn't. It was just an idea—'

'Not a very good one. You'd better get on.'

'Yes . . .' he agreed, and she put the phone down.

But Zoe would be home by Christmas . . .

She made herself repeat it as she sipped her hot tea, *home by Christmas, home by Christmas*. The mantra seemed to have lost some of its power. Christmas was only six weeks away.

Can I really believe that she'll be home in six weeks? – that I only have six weeks left to suffer? I thought I would suffer for the rest of my life.

– If Zoe does come home, what will she find? Me on my own. Paul in Ealing. She'll be devastated. She . . . adored her father. (It annoyed Alma, that Paul could be loved so unquestioningly, with so few demands; it was *I* who took all the trouble over her; *I* who worried about what happened; *I* who put Zoe before my work. Sometimes at least. When did Paul do that? He just strolled in late, and Zoe loved him. I had to do all the difficult things, from being with her when she had her first filling to taking splinters out of her feet. He always thought everything would be all right, he thought children grow up all right by magic. He bought her sweets secretly, when I forbade them . . . The times he looked after her when she was little, it *occasionally* happened, I can't deny it, I mean I did *sometimes* have to go out, I'd come back and find them tucked up in bed, watching the television in the bedroom, and she would have chocolate round her mouth, and they'd look so contented, and I'd feel so angry . . . 'You're turning her into a couch potato. Why can't you read to her, or let her paint?' 'She's happy like this. *Right* . . . Your mother says we have to turn off the television.' And then Zoe would cry, and scream at me.)

All the old bitternesses flooded back.

She'll blame me for us splitting up. She'll take Paul's side. She'll start to hate me . . .

I don't care. Just let her come home.

Alma wandered into her study. The light was winking on the answering machine. It would be Zoe this time. Seeing Thelma was an omen . . .

But it was her mother's voice, with that edge of complaint. 'This is Mother, talking to that awful machine. Will you be bringing Adam when you come? It would be nice to see at least one of my grandchildren. I haven't seen him since his last birthday. Oh, and Alma . . .'

The voice wailed on, in fits and starts, greedily swallowing the tape on the machine, so no one else could telephone, so she could have no friends, no life of her own, I hate my mother, I hate my husband, I hate my daughter for leaving me . . . Alma sat crushed with depression as the voice dirged on.

I'm sure she likes the thing, actually. She complains, but I think she *loves* my machine. It can't interrupt her. It can't answer back. The monologue will go on for ever. Can never be changed. Cannot be stopped.

– And she really wants to see Adam, not me. But if Adam goes – even if he would – I shall never be able to talk to her . . .

She'd stopped listening long before her mother stopped talking, and switched it off, roughly, when the emptiness crackled, the glorious, neutral, absence of voice.

Absently, she noticed that the light on the answering machine still flashed. Was there another message after her mother's? She endured the maternal litany again, gritting her teeth in irritation, wondering if Zoe felt the same way about her.

Then a man's voice spoke. A London voice. An attractive voice, not entirely familiar. 'I do hope I have the correct Mrs Bennett. If not forgive me. It's Simon Edwards. The other day, you were too busy for a drink, but I hope I can tempt you this weekend. My telephone number is . . .'

Alma's heart pounded. Alma's heart leaped. She re-wound, swiftly. Alma pressed PLAY. Alma's heart played while her mother talked; hope made the monologue bearable. She bore with her mother, then heard him again.

It wasn't that she meant to ring him back. Not now, at any rate. Maybe never. It wasn't that she meant to *do* anything about it. It was more than enough that he had phoned. She would hug that fact to herself for weeks. That he was keen enough to look up her number.

. . . *A young male hunk wants a drink with me!*

She found herself whooping with crazy high spirits, 'Woo-hoo, Alma, whoopee, whoopee,' and polka-ing down the hall to the stairs, but before she went up them she had to go back, press the SAVE button and hear it yet again, her mother's long wail and then Simon's voice, a little bit husky, hesitant, polite, and what else could she hear?

'Testosterone,' she sang to herself as she bounced upstairs, 'what have you got, you got—'

The doorbell rang. She froze on the spot, guilty, nervous. How loud was she singing? Who could it be? The police? A neighbour in pursuit of her ladder? The Misses Elsevier would disapprove . . . She would have to pretend it was the radio.

Then her heart lurched, her treacherous heart, a great soft movement like foundations shifting, the earth cracking, hot joy flooding up, and she ran downstairs, biting her lips because she suddenly knew it was Zoe, Zoe, so Thelma *had* been a harbinger, and her bare feet leaped down the hall's cold mosaic –

But two steps away, she could see quite clearly that the figure outlined by the bright porch light against the patterned glass was too large for Zoe.

It was a tall man, with yellow hair, she imagined a cow-lick of yellow hair, and she realized she was afraid of him.

22

'YOU LOOK AS THOUGH you've seen a ghost! Mum! What is the matter?' His voice, in moments of emotion, still squealed a little, like the boy he had been.

'*Adam*. Adam. Oh Adam. I'm sorry, I think I'm going crazy with missing your sister. Through the glass for a moment I thought . . . You looked like someone else.'

'You're disappointed.' The boy, the boy; he stood in the doorway, his shoulders drooping. She tried to feel tenderness instead of irritation.

'Don't be silly, Adam. Come in. Take your coat off. I've just made tea, or do you want a beer?' She was aware she didn't want him to have a beer. Foolish of me; they all drink too much.

'Beer, please. I'll go and get it.'

'Fine.' Why does he always offer to do things? It's normal for mothers to look after their sons. '. . . How are you managing in that little room?'

'It is quite little. I miss home sometimes. I love my room here . . . I mean, the room that used to be mine.'

'Well it still is. You sound as though we chucked you out.'

'No, I didn't mean that. It's just that everything's different . . . it's not exactly home now, is it?'

'You're always welcome to come and stay.' But she said it flatly; it didn't sound right. She patted his arm, in the acrylic jumper he must have bought out of his grant. It felt hard and clumsy, the colour harsh.

'Can I really?' he said, a boy transformed, his big teeth, Zoe's teeth, gleaming for a moment, shining between his generous red lips, a little loose, a little soft, they reminded her of someone – not Paul's lips, not my lips, lips she did not entirely like . . . *stop this*, she told herself sternly. Why am I so horribly critical?

But why can't he see I don't want him to stay?

'I'd love to come and stay for a weekend. I could do my washing. And I'd do the garden.'

'Maybe you could come when I go to Wales . . . I'm going to Wales to see Gran and Aunt Eileen.'

He sat down, obviously crestfallen. Alma could have bitten her tongue.

'Oh . . . Yes. I mean, thanks . . . but well. It's just, I thought I might come when you were actually here. Then I could see you.'

'I'm sorry, darling. Of course you must. I'm not thinking straight at the moment.'

Half of his beer had already gone. At least he drinks it from a glass, she thought. He had a little beige moustache of froth, drying on his upper lip's blond stubble. He was tall and good-looking and affectionate and kind. Why couldn't she think of that instead? And a trainee barrister. She ought to be proud.

'I hope you know I'm proud of you.'

'Thanks, Mum.' Once again, that radiant smile, that look of delight, so bright, so naked. Then he looked at her very gravely, blushed, opened his mouth, swallowed, closed it, opened it again and stared at the floor, his whole body expressing a desire to speak, his hands making aborted thrusting gestures which set his beer swaying to the lip of the glass. He didn't quite spill it. He didn't speak.

'Do you want to say something?'

'Yes.'

'You aren't frightened of your mother, are you?' She heard herself, harsh, not encouraging. To her shame, she knew he was frightened of her. Not physically, of course; she would never hit a child, she prided herself on never having hit him, but it didn't take actual blows, did it. *Please let him speak.* She willed him to do it.

'– You needn't worry about Zoe so much.' It came in a rush, almost unintelligible, shooting out violently, running aground. She stared at him amazed.

'Is that *it*, Adam?' Again she heard herself; ironic, dismissive. Angry, too. How can he tell me not to worry? 'What on earth do you mean? Of course I'm worried. I'm mad with worry. I try to keep cheerful, but I worry all the time . . . if *you* were missing we'd be mad with worry.' That guilt again, for it wasn't quite true; boys were different; they always would be; men were different, weren't they? Bigger, tougher, less sensitive. Adam plodded on; he had never been a worry.

'I'm just trying to tell you, she'll be all right. *I know she will.* I don't want you to worry.' He had coloured deeply, but he was insistent, nodding his head with every syllable, staring deep into Alma's eyes, as if he bore a message from the gods.

'Don't be maddening, Adam. I know you're trying to be kind, but it's like telling a drowning man not to drown . . .' She remembered what Sheilah had said about Adam. 'And *you* must be worried. *You* must be upset.'

'Of course I have been. But . . . not now. I think she's all right. She'll be all right. You should stop worrying, honestly Mum.'

'Look, have you got religion, or something, Adam? It doesn't help me, groundless optimism.'

'Right. Sorry.' He stared at the floor. Why is he so easily deflated? It makes me feel uncomfortably powerful. 'May I get myself another can of beer?'

'Well leave some for me, won't you. Let's go for a walk round the garden. We'll just about be able to see . . .'

'I'd cut the lawn, but I think it's too . . .' Some flicker of annoyance on her face struck him, and he changed tack, his blue eyes pleading: 'I'll cut the lawn for you. You'd like that.'

'I would *hate* you to go cutting my lawn in the *dark*. I can't imagine anything more ridiculous.'

'Sorry.'

'Stop saying sorry!'

'Oh sorry . . . sorry!' His big pink hand shot over his mouth. His legs were crossed twice, knotted with dismay.

Why am I doing this to my son? What's the matter with me? What's the matter with us all? When we all lived in caves, did we quarrel like this? I suppose I'd be dead, at my age, and Adam would be a patriarch, and maybe things were better that way, maybe the generations weren't meant to grow old together . . . Maybe we should be like animals, who have no relations with their grownup children, but leave them as soon as they can fend for themselves . . .

Why does Adam mind so much about me? Why do I mind so

much about my own mother? She's eighty-two, I'm a woman of fifty, if we can't live our own lives by now, then when?

– But there's unfinished business. Business from the past. Such big parts of us are still tiny babies. Hungry babies, waiting to be fed.

'I've got a cottage pie. I could put it in the oven. And there's broccoli, I think – plenty for two. You always liked broccoli, didn't you? Unlike Zoe, who hated all vegetables—'

'But *I* got the spots.'

'Well you haven't now . . .'

'– And she was the one who ate the sweets but I was the one who got the fillings!'

Suddenly they were friends again, the tension eased, they could smile at each other. He came and loomed while she did things for supper, and she welcomed that shape, the benign male shape, his familiar voice with the cadences of Paul's, his laugh with the ghost of a lost voice breaking. The past, the past. It's round our heads, it hovers behind us, but we can't quite catch it . . .

On the kitchen door were the nicks with the knife that marked the children's passage from babyhood, Zoe's cut always below her brother's, the gaps increasing as they both got older. They wouldn't stand straight, they wouldn't stand still. Nothing stands still. It was incredible that this hulking man was once three feet tall. The marks floated, soared like rings of smoke . . . Then they'd got too old. There was an end to the series.

But the marks remained. She had never repainted it.

'Here, Adam. Come here.' She waved a long sharp knife.

'*What?*' he said. Was there a flicker of fear?

'I'm not going to cut your manhood off. I want to preserve you for ever on my door.'

He was childishly pleased; he stood straight; he stood still. The last mark was four inches above the others. She cut into the wood with a feeling of pleasure. Fun to be a vandal. Fun to have a knife.

'Mum,' he said, two inches away, her enormous son who had grown from her body, with his homely smell of clean hair and beer, but a man, he's a man, with a man's pores and a man's jaw-line and big pink knuckles – 'Will you write my name against the line?'

She removed the knife; it flashed past his face; *please may no one ever hurt my children. Their unmarked skin, their unbroken bones.*

'How old are you, young man?' But she was smiling.

'Mother, do you mind putting down that knife?'

'Sorry.' The light was so bright on the blade. 'Do you really want me to write your name?'

'If you don't mind . . .'

'Right.'

She wrote his name in baby print, extra legible so the children could read it, before she remembered that there were no children, he was reading Law, the children had gone.

They ate supper together in the dining-room from which she had bleached out family history, enjoying the sense of dispelling shadows as she painted over the bars of grey where the chair-backs had pushed time and again, the greasy patches where the same heads rubbed the same places year after year, all of them moving to the same rhythm, till suddenly the circle broke and they all staggered outwards into the light.

'You've made this look . . . different. Nice, though.'

'Better than it was,' Alma agreed.

There was a pause. 'Do you miss us at all?'

Those impossible questions that come with the answers clamped to their backs. She resented it, but said, 'Yes, of course.'

'Me, as well as Zoe? All of us?'

'What do you think? Of course! I mean what is this? Do you want to hear that I'm sobbing every night?'

His face betrayed panic, as it did so easily. 'No . . . I'm just trying to imagine what your life is like. Don't get angry. You've never been alone before, have you? Don't you think it's hard, being alone?'

It must be the beer. He was unusually intense. She wished he would get on with his cottage pie. 'Yes and no. But I fail to see . . .' And then she did see, and swallowed hard. 'Oh Adam. Are *you* all right on your own? I mean you've never been on your own before. You're OK, aren't you?' *Please*, she thought, *just say you're OK.*

'I'm fine. It's fine.' His tone said the opposite. And then he was eating his pie very diligently, pink cheeks busily bulged with food.

'Adam, darling. Are you sure you're all right?'

Damn, she thought. So I'm sucked back in. Trying to deal with my impossible family. Looking after them, when *I'm* not all right.

– *How nice it would be to go and listen to my phonecall* – the unworthy flash of a desire for pleasure, a longing for freedom, for selfishness.

'I wish you would come and see my room,' Adam burst out, incongruously, suddenly sounding all of twelve years old.

'Well *of course* I shall come and see your room . . . But you said it was a perfectly ordinary bedsitter. I didn't *dream* you would want me to see your room. I mean, I haven't been to see *your father's* room . . .' She knew she sounded shrill, protesting too much.

'That's different.'

'Why?'

'Well, it's not really his place. It's more part of whatshername's, Priscilla's, place.'

'Is it? You've been there . . . ?' A little bad feeling that Alma didn't analyse. 'In any case. Of course I'll come. What's it like?'

'Fine. Not brilliant. A bit . . . bleak.'

'I thought you said there were views over the city?'

'Well – rooftop views. You don't see people. Chimneys, gutters. That kind of thing. Pigeons, seagulls, on good days . . . I think it's a bit damp, actually.'

Visions of pneumonia, bronchitis, TB. A black wave of worry swept over Alma; she tried to fight it off by shouting at him, exploding, pushing away her plate – 'Why the *hell* did you take a room that was *damp*? How stupid can you *get*? You've always been chesty—'

'Mum, it's not my *health*. You've got it all wrong. I just sometimes feel . . . a bit lonely.'

'Is it damp or not? Eat up that pie.'

'It doesn't matter about the damp. I wish I hadn't mentioned it.'

'Your father will be furious.'

Adam ignored the familiar lie. 'Mum. Let's not talk about this any more.'

'If your room is damp, Dad will help you move. I'll ring him tonight and ask him to.'

'I don't want you to. I don't want a fuss.' He was cornered now, baffled, annoyed. He finished his beer defiantly.

'You're making the fuss. You said it was damp.' Alma knew she was being horrible, running tight rings around the big sad bull, sticking *banderillas* in his neck and back as he swung his head helplessly from side to side.

'The collar of my shirt's too tight,' he said. 'It shrunk when I dried it at the laundrette.'

'You could borrow one of Dad's . . .'

But Dad's shirts had gone. In his cupboard, only a patient row of hangers. Dad had gone. Zoe had gone. They looked at each other soberly, the big blond youth and his white-haired mother. A mute understanding. *Not many of us left. And it's getting late. We'll be nice to each other.*

Alma began talking at random, warmly, telling Adam about life at Portico and Sheen, making it as entertaining as she could, trying to talk about things without edges, things that couldn't turn in their hands and cut them. The tension eased, but Adam wasn't listening. He was looking round the room; looking for something.

'– Adam, are you all right? What is it?'

'Mum . . . there's something I came to ask you today. As well as just wanting to see you, I mean.'

'Well go on then. Ask. You can always *ask*.'

'It's embarrassing.'

'Surely I told you the facts of life –?'

'Ha ha ha.' But he blushed, slightly, and turned his face away from her quizzical glance; she remembered Paul had thought he had a girlfriend . . . Amazing that our *children* should have sex lives of their own.

'I'm short of money. I'm sorry to ask. I just thought, with the new job, you could maybe lend me some . . .' He couldn't sit still as he asked her. Every part of him seemed to be jerking, twitching, shamblingly at odds with the part next door, needing to escape her but nailed to the chair.

But Alma relaxed. Alma was grateful. That he should ask for something so simple, so contained. 'Darling, you've never asked for money before. Don't look so wretched. Of course I can give you some.'

172

'*Lend*, Mum, honestly . . .'

'Lend's no good. How much do you want? A hundred? Two hundred? Is it rent, or the gas bill, or an overdraft . . . ? Not that it matters. Just tell me what you need.'

He looked blank for a second – was he stunned by her agreeing? – then snapped into life, as if on automatic pilot, as if the impact of his words escaped him. 'Five hundred. But if you could manage it, a thousand.'

'*Five hundred* . . . Adam, are you in trouble?'

He had a queer stunned look, as if he didn't believe what he was saying either. 'Not really. Well, a bit. I just . . . need it.'

There was a pause, in which the central heating shunted. The house was shocked too; the house creaked awake. Something important seemed to be happening. *I must rise to the occasion*, Alma thought. He's come to me and not to Paul. He's *asking* for something, not suffering in silence. I have got the money. I've got it in the bank. Two thousand-odd left of Uncle Bernard's money . . . I was keeping it for an emergency, but this probably *is* an emergency.

'If you need it, that's fine . . . five hundred, to start with.'

'Mum, that's . . . terrific.' He blushed violently red, which made her realize how pale he had been, how the blood had swept back in a flood of relief.

'You can't . . . can you tell me what it's for, darling?' At once she wished she hadn't asked; it seemed to detract from the grandeur of her gesture.

'Actually . . . actually I can't. I wish I could. But it's something important.'

Alma was a very curious person, but she forced herself to stand up and smile. 'Adam, I'm really glad to do something for you. I know we sometimes seem to think too much about Zoe . . . but it's just, you know, that she isn't here. The prodigal daughter, or something. I . . . want to be a good mother to you. I'll go and get my cheque-book. I assume you'll take a cheque.'

She was joking, half-coquettish, trying to lighten the mood of embarrassment between them, but to her astonishment he shook his head.

'I really need cash. If you can possibly get it. Or it will disappear into my overdraft.'

'But I've never had five hundred pounds cash in my life . . . oh well, I suppose I shan't have to have it for long. When do you mean to collect it?'

'Tomorrow.'

There was something here that Alma hadn't fathomed, something which accounted for the sudden lurches into absolute decisiveness that Adam was making.

'Well . . . OK, I mean fine, but are you sure you're all right? You're not being hounded by criminals or something? You haven't started gambling, have you?' Alma hardly knew what gambling was. It was something men did, and lost all their money, but where would Adam have learned to do that?

'*Mu-um.*'

'Sorry, darling. OK. After work.'

They cleared the table, peaceably. Something was achieved. Something was settled. But Alma's mind still twitched at her tongue.

One last question escaped unchecked. '. . . And . . . you're not going to spend it on drink, are you?'

'*MU – UM!*'

'I'm sorry, really. But it is a lot of money.' Damn. Above all, she mustn't sound mean. 'Not too much . . . just . . . a lot.' And she smiled at him, and he smiled back, with sheepish knowledge; it was a lot of money.

After he left, she telephoned Paul. He was sleepy, but friendly; Peeky had to fetch him, which was a good sign. If he was sleepy and friendly, she was glad he was alone. She had not made up her mind to tell him about Adam. After all, the money was her decision. But Paul broached the subject of Adam unprompted.

'I'm a bit worried about Adam.'

'*You are?*'

'Alma, why are you over-reacting?'

'Oh, I just saw him and he seemed . . . a bit strange.'

'I think it's the girlfriend. The new girlfriend. Or the girl Adam wants to be his girlfriend.'

'She isn't a girl, if she's over eighteen.'

'Yeah yeah, I know that, but . . . never mind. Let's take it as read for once. Life's too short.' He stopped, annoyed, and she had to coax him.

'Please tell me about this girlfriend. He hasn't mentioned her to me . . .'

'Well boys can't talk about sex with their mothers . . . I think they'd had a row, that's all, when I talked to him on the phone last night. It's no big deal, he just seemed a bit lonely. He's a nice boy, Alma—'

'*Of course* he is.'

And there the subject died, until the middle of the night, when Alma suddenly woke up thrumming with anxious adrenalin, and sat bolt upright. A voice pecked in her brain.

It's the girlfriend, yes. Of course it is. They're pregnant. They must have got themselves pregnant. It's Paul's fault; I bet he's never really explained to Adam about contraception . . .

She caught herself back. Adam was twenty-one. It's *my* fault. I never talked to him about having children, I never explained how precious they are . . .

The girl must want an abortion. She doesn't love Adam. Or she does love him, but she doesn't want the baby. She's a student herself, she can't handle it . . .

But Alma was sure that Adam would want it. He'd always loved children, hadn't he? He was so tender with Zoe when she was a baby . . .

But he's weak. The voice pecked on, relentless. He can't stand up to this bloody girl. He's frightened of me, he's frightened of her.

He *isn't* weak, oh God, I'm mad . . .

She was going crazy. She lay down again, forced her body to relax. She would think of white; of clouds, of snow . . .

But it was her grandchild. Her first grandchild, and they would use her money to get rid of it. The child would be lost, would never be born – because of her money –

She could not lie still. The pain cut deep beneath her ribs.

I'll beg them not to. I'll give up work. I'll stay at home and look after it. There will be a child in the house again. My vanished babies will be back home.

She lay and wept, in the chilly night. The useless water soaked into her pillow. Suddenly impatient, she hauled out some tissues, blew like a whale, batted at her face. She was fifty years old. She must have learned *something*. She tried to think calmly. It would soon be getting light. She was a grownup. She had to work tomorrow.

It happens to all of us, she thought. We all lose them. We all lose our babies. They have to grow up and go away . . . They need us less, of course they do, they start to forget us, they forget. That time when their world centred on us. When they needed us so absolutely . . .

And then I didn't always want to be there. I sometimes longed to get away . . . it was hard to admit it, but she knew it was true.

Now *I* need *them*. I'm the hungry one. I miss my babies. Their weightless bodies, curled into mine like little blind puppies. So precious, in memory, those newborn bodies, no longer clinging, no longer exhausting.

That's what she would do. Look after their baby. She would mother their baby, and have another chance.

I'll be a better mother to my grandchildren.

– But first, she had to face her own mother.

23

ALMA TOLD A LIE TO HER BOSS.

'Mr Portico, my mother's not well. Could I possibly take Friday and Monday off so I can go to her for a long weekend?'

Alma told a lie in the bank, because she felt guilty drawing out so much money, because she felt the worn-looking cashier was regarding her as a flighty spendthrift. 'I've got to pay the builder today . . . terrible what they charge, isn't it?' A decent house-holder protecting her property, making sure everything was watertight. But the woman's jaded expression didn't change. She counted the money and shoved it at Alma, who looked over her shoulder instinctively. Would anyone notice she had all that money?

There seemed to be more customers than usual in the office that afternoon. More potential thieves, as it seemed to Alma. She had stashed her handbag with its immorally fat packet of notes in the drawer of her desk, but she could sense its presence, it glowed in the dark, winking a signal to all London's light-fingered. She swivelled instinctively when anyone passed near.

– And yet, she thought, it's not really so much money. Lawyers earn that much money in a morning. I hate lawyers. All the same . . . I'm glad my son will be a lawyer one day. I'm glad he won't be an estate agent. The perpetual shrilling of one of the five phone lines, or the electronic music of one of us dialling . . .

There were days at Portico and Sheen when nothing seemed to materialize, when all they did was update their files or canvass people who weren't interested or chase after offers which were fading away. There were days of ferocious stress and excitement, when Kevin started to yell into the phone, impatient with buyers raising fatuous objections, pressuring the cautious, hassling the weak, riding his revolving chair like a jockey, hunched over the receiver, willing them on, but once they were over the finishing line he was a pussy-cat again, all pleasure, all charm.

Kevin was working towards his bonus for exceeding this half-year's quota of fees. On the previous six months he had done this easily, but this half-year had been more up-and-down, and more down than up, recently. In any case, in Kevin's opinion Mr Portico's incentives weren't high enough. He had heard they were higher, at Garrets' down the road . . . No wonder they were hungry, at Garrets'.

But it wasn't just the money that motivated him. Kevin genuinely felt that he knew best. He could see all the pieces on the board, Mr X who would move if Mr Y could sell, Miss Z who could buy if Mr A would insure a slightly risky property, Mr A who would only believe this was urgent if Kevin tracked him down on his mobile phone . . . chains of people depended on him. Chains of people whom he could make happy, if he could move the pieces to promising new places. Chains of people full of glorious potential, and he could be God, if they would only let him, and he hung there, sweating, on the stressful days, bombarding his clients with high voltage will-power.

There were only rarely afternoons like this one, when promises of money fell into their laps like fruit; when it seemed they could not put a foot wrong. Offers came in on three properties which they had started to think of as no-hopers. Two contracts were exchanged without the usual last-minute labyrinth of delay. A surveyor failed to pick up the damp which would almost certainly have stopped the sale. An insurance company which was being difficult came up with an acceptable quote on a house. Two clients agreed to lower their prices to a level where their flats might actually be sold, and an excellent conversion of four two-bed flats was offered to them in preference to Garrets', though Garrets' was just across the road from the flats.

'Like someone's birthday today, innit?' Kevin addressed them with a beatific smile after the news came through on the second exchange, way back in his chair, hands behind his head.

The phone rang again. They looked at each other. It was quarter past five; they all wanted to go home.

'One of the offers fallen through,' said Alma. Kevin's hands stayed on his head. Ashley rummaged busily in her handbag. Alma sighed, and answered the phone.

It was the Gurneys, the young married couple who'd been looking for a flat ever more frantically as Greta became more pregnant; frantic for a home yet unreasonably choosy. They were Alma's clients. She wanted to help them, but she sighed as she recognized his worried voice.

'Hallo, Mr Gurney. How can I help you?'

'We'd like to have another look at the flat you showed us a month ago. You remember, Durham Road.' Everyone thought they were her only clients; everyone expected her to remember. 'The sellers had already moved somewhere else . . . well, we saw in your update that the price had gone down.'

'You'd like another look?' Alma's voice lifted. The Gurneys never looked at anything again. The Gurneys had always been disappointed.

'Well we would.' He seemed doubtful, as if she would refuse him.

'That's fine,' she said. 'I'm delighted you liked it.'

'Well we're not sure yet,' he said hastily, defensively. 'We want to see it today, if possible.'

'Today's a bit difficult.' She was meeting Adam. Kevin should be going to the Fitness Centre with Ashley.

At once his worry returned full force. 'I'm afraid it's got to be today,' he said. 'You see I'm anxious about Greta. She's seven months gone. I mean what if we don't get in somewhere before it arrives?'

'Yes,' said Alma. 'I'll speak to my colleagues.'

She rang off, and appealed to the better nature of her colleagues. But Alma's colleagues knew all about the Gurneys. 'Timewasters,' said Kevin. 'And I've worked my arse off today, Alma.' 'I'm sorry for them,' said Ashley. 'But I'm just starting to get somewhere with my Jazz Dance. I mean, if I'm late they'll think I have no commitment. And in any case, it's not really my job . . . you *are* having two days off, next week.'

'I'll do it,' said Alma. Reproaches always worked.

She rang her son, and arranged for him to come after six-thirty. She rang the Gurneys. She checked her bag. It was in the desk drawer, she knew it was, but the money might have seeped away through the cracks . . . Nothing felt safe, in her life, just now.

The old chestnut had a little truth in it. Women alone did feel vulnerable. There was no one there to absorb the shocks, to calm her down, to pick her up.

And men alone, I suppose, she mused. Paul always liked to be looked after.

But not all men. Some men are hunters.

She drove to meet the Gurneys, who were cold, as usual. Ever since June they seemed to have been shivering, waiting reproachfully outside bleak buildings, while the bulge under Greta's cheap jacket grew bigger. She was pale and large, with beautiful eyes, exquisite grey eyes in the face of a fish. He was narrow and fussy with a neat black moustache that tended to quiver when he looked at kitchens. He took too much interest in them, of the wrong kind; 'Greta wouldn't want to cook on *that*,' 'Greta wouldn't want to look out on *that* when she's doing her washing-up.' Greta was passive when he said these things, even faintly proud, as if it were a sign of his love for her.

'Cold, isn't it?' he demanded.

'Well, it is nearly December,' Alma parried.

'No hope of us having a roof over our heads by Christmas. Come on, Greta, let's get moving.' Greta found moving quite difficult now.

Alma had never doubted the Gurneys' honesty, but now she had the five hundred pounds in her bag she found herself watching them narrowly when Greta squeezed past her for the hundredth time to check that the bathroom step wasn't dangerous.

The Gurneys, perhaps as a result of the pregnancy, saw the world as a cruel and predatory place, poised to reach up and grab at their ankles. Carpets were 'probably artificial', humming with static electricity, handles of doors were at children's eye-level, windows waited to suck babies from cots.

'– Of course, no house is perfectly safe,' said Alma. They nodded, but reproachfully, as if she was unkind to confirm their worst suspicions. But they were patently softening towards this flat. When Ted began to call the second bedroom 'the nursery', Alma knew the sale was almost made.

'The garden is a feature,' she said. 'A lot of two-bed flats at this price have no garden. Or a shared garden. You wouldn't want to share.'

'We wouldn't,' said Ted, very definitely, allowing himself a tight-lipped smile, pleased to be the sort of man who wouldn't share things.

They stood in the kitchen and looked out on the garden. It was a small square of unmown lawn, with a gnarled, nearly leafless tree in the middle.

'But I find the garden slightly disappointing,' said Ted, his moustache twitching self-righteously. The subtext was always: *we deserved better.* 'Not a lot of character.' They said that often. Character costs more money than you've got, Alma thought grimly.

She looked at her watch. It was ten to six. She needed to escape; she needed the clincher. She was tired of deferring to the Gurneys' whims. *I exist too. They're stifling me.* She peered through the dirty glass at the tree. Probably apple. Probably diseased.

Then Alma told a lie to Greta Gurney.

'Does your husband realize that's an apple tree? Almost certainly a James Grieve, I think. It's one of the nicest apples. Very English. Old-fashioned. A bit special . . . Imagine your child in the apple tree, biting into a beautiful juicy apple . . .' Have I laid it on too thick, she wondered? But she had enjoyed it. And it was her job.

'I wouldn't want him to *climb*,' said Greta. But the picture had clearly worked its trick. 'Come back, Ted. Did you notice the James Grieve apple tree? We wouldn't need to spray it. We'd have lovely healthy fruit . . .'

But not for long, thought Alma, if you never spray it. She smiled at the Gurneys, entirely reassuring. And then she told a lie to both the Gurneys, because she wanted them to make up their minds and go home.

'Think about it,' she said. 'There's no hurry at all. Though there is one other person very interested.'

Alma ran the Gurneys back to his parents'. They were quiet in the car, but she could sense tremendous agitation in the seat beside her, where Ted was sitting, naturally, though he was only half the size of his wife.

'Greta,' he said as Alma drew up outside a grim block of council flats, 'I am going to speak our mind.'

'Go ahead, dear,' Greta said.

'We think it's us,' Ted said. 'We think it might be us.'

'Does that mean you want to buy it?' Alma asked. She wished they would get out of her car. It was his self-importance that annoyed her, though it had its touching side as well. They thought they were the first pregnant couple in the world; they thought their baby would be the first baby.

'We wish to make an offer,' Ted affirmed. 'Accept no other offers,' he added, nervously.

'It's not up to me, of course,' Alma said. 'It's up to the vendor, but—'

'Does that mean we might not get it?' Greta wailed. 'I mean, we've decided. That wouldn't be right.'

'If your offer's OK, I'm sure you'll get it . . . now I'm sorry, but I have to go and meet my son.'

'How old?' Greta asked. It was the first time she had ever shown the slightest interest in Alma.

'Twenty-one,' Alma said.

They stood on the pavement under the streetlight and stared at her, trying to read their future. Alma realized that to them she had power; she had a home, a job, a car. She had done some of the things they dreamed of doing. She was fully grown-up; she had a grown-up son. They wanted to know if they would ever have anything.

Alma told a lie that she hoped would come true.

'I'm sure you'll be lucky,' she smiled at them, wanting to help them, wanting to like them.

Greta suddenly smiled back, no longer fish-like, smiling over the top of her enormous belly, smiling like the sun coming over a hill, and in a second Ted had joined her, his hand on her shoulder, a small real smile which untidied his moustache, dissolved his frown, made him look quite human.

24

ALMA HAD PUT THE CAR in the garage and locked it, before she remembered that she needed toothpaste. She couldn't be bothered to get it out again. The late-night chemist was on Kemble Hill. She looked at her watch; it was twenty-past six. Adam was always late. She would walk and get it. She took her bag, remembering too late the heavy parcel of notes inside it. Close to her body. She hugged it, concealed it.

I wish life wasn't about buying toothpaste, she thought, as she trotted in her ballet-shoes beneath the frosty haloes of the streetlamps. Where one was broken, she could see stars, just the faint pricking of the brightest stars, all the rest concealed by the busy glare of London. I wish we could see the stars at night. I wish I had time to think about things. I wish I really felt I knew what I was doing, over halfway through my life, at the beginning of winter. Running down the road on my own in the darkness.

I wish I knew what would happen to my children. I wish I could remember what happened to me. I wish we could know about the future, and the past.

More of the streetlights were broken, down here. One flickered on and off, irresolute. She passed lightly through the rare pools of brightness. It was very fragile, really, the city, and the body, and the dark was huge, and everywhere.

The present is just running for a toothbrush, she thought, or answering the phone, or being desperate for a drink, or trying not to be late for the future. The immediate contact, or missed contact; the smile from Greta Gurney at the last moment, or the wrong number, or the dropped glass. Trying to sweep up, to keep abreast; trying to placate, trying to explain. Trying to be nice though she feared she wasn't. Always reacting, never acting, and then the light was gone and it was too late to change things. Gone into the past, into the night behind us.

And the future was blinder than the past. The future was the gap that opened at your feet; you could only try not to sprawl headlong. On the morning Zoe went, I had no idea, I was half-asleep, I hadn't even pulled the curtains, I thought her note was just a bit of rubbish . . . then the light fell on it suddenly, it came into the present, it *was* the present, it was everything, it had that senseless, absolute power, cancelling the past, destroying the future . . .

She turned the corner on to Kemble Hill High Street, where the orange city light flattened everything. She bought her toothpaste, consulting her watch; she had seven minutes to get back home. She checked the presence of the envelope of money as she slipped the purse back into her bag. It looked like a letter, it looked ordinary, but it made her handbag feel electric, and she came back on to the street feeling raw, aware that the night was full of other people, some of them friendly, some of them not.

Strange to pass the window at Portico and Sheen, just another passer-by glancing at the photographs, glimpsing her speeding reflection in the glass, a slight, angled figure with pale, blowing hair, smaller than she thought, going faster than she thought.

'Heyah!' came an incoherent groan. 'Heyah the fuggy rallah ye doon!' It was the homeless people just across the way, faithful to their pitch, theatrical by night, lit up in weird poses by the brilliant streetlight, far louder now that the traffic was less, no longer upstaged by the passing shoppers. 'Go ya din see the bleedy fuggy heah, man?' Then, more distinctly, half on his feet, but swaying, the man in possession of the bottle said, 'Come 'ere. Why don' you? Say 'allo. Come 'ere.'

'Hallo,' said Alma, thin and prim, in a hurry. They must be so cold; her breath rose in a cloud. Strange that they choose to sit opposite our office. Perhaps they don't know where they are any more. I wonder if they have any idea of time . . . There aren't any boundaries for them, are there? Every day the same. More or less. Waking and sleeping. Everything blurred. A kind of endless present, I suppose, since they don't have a future to plan for – do they? – and what kind of past can have brought them here?

But perhaps they dreamed endlessly of the future. The only

place not closed to them. Being poets, or postmen, or sheep-farmers . . .

Alma was cheered for a second; then not.

She knew that their dreams would be locked in the past. Terrifying dreams where they were always the victim, always frightened, always too small, and no one would stop and listen to them.

She hurried away on the other side.

She was vaguely aware of someone behind her as she crested the hill and headed down towards her turning. She thought for a moment that someone called her name, but then she realized that it must have been the drunk with the bottle, and she walked on swiftly, clutching her bag.

Turned left into the darkness of Caversham Road which would lead her back home in time for Adam. The darkness seemed darker, the streetlights rarer. She'd complain to the council, she'd get something done, she wouldn't start worrying about the feet, she was much too old to be scared of the dark . . .

She began to run, which was noisy, and stopped her hearing what she feared to hear. The panting of her breath and the slapping of her handbag combined with the thud of her feet on the stone, and her chest began to hurt, and her heart began to hammer, but she couldn't slow down, she had to keep going . . . And now she was sure there was someone behind her, someone running, someone shouting . . .

She struggled to wriggle her key free of her pocket as she ran on more raggedly, the energy leaving her, and now the feet were closer behind and she realized – as the house grew nearer, as she saw her garage, her laburnum tree, the beautiful, deserted curve of the bay – that she wouldn't have time to get in through the door, that as soon as she slowed the man would be upon her. *Paul*, she thought, if only you were at home, back from school, tired but waiting for me, if the lights were on, if they were all still there, if I could slip into the past and hide . . . But there was only this present, this paralysing fear, and she almost fell, and then he was beside her.

He touched her on the shoulder and she turned, frozen, no

sound coming, just gulps of raw breath, he was black against the streetlight, black and big, a ruff of light like a lion's mane, if I give him my bag perhaps he won't kill me . . .

And then he moved so he stood in the light. His face was huge, dazzlingly white, utterly familiar; the light was blinding: she couldn't take in what was happening. His yellow hair; a slash of yellow hair. The light pinned her, shocked, belittled.

'Simon,' he said. 'I didn't frighten you, did I? I've been calling to you from way back on the hill. Simon Edwards . . . I recognized you.'

She bent double in the effort to get her breath back, wanting to be sick, the blood pounding in her ears, and the anger, red anger, the anger was with her, releasing her from fear and politeness.

'You fool! How dare you! How dare . . . you should *never* follow a woman like that. Are you crazy, running after someone in the dark?'

'Oh dear. You were frightened, weren't you. I'm sorry.' But his voice was curiously calm, with a silky, almost teasing quality. 'I'm truly sorry. But I telephoned you. Did you get the message? You didn't phone back.'

'I hope you are sorry! I'm soaked in sweat.'

'Are you?' Again, that note of teasing intimacy. 'Won't you let me make amends? A drink, a meal?'

It sounded like *let me make love to you*, and against her will, something in Alma stirred. But she was still angry. Her voice was cold. 'I'm in a hurry. My son is coming round. I have grownup children. He's twenty-one.' Her rational side pushed him away, telling him what ramparts of family protected her.

'Saturday then.'

'No . . . I'm going to my mother's in Wales.' *You don't have to explain. Just say no. You have a right to say no.*

'You're very lucky . . . my mother's dead.'

'Well it's not all joy, going to my mother's.' Her voice was more normal now, her body had unknotted. He was just a young man whose mother had died. He no longer sounded over-confident. His head was down, his body language was submissive. And yet she had felt such terrible fear . . .

'I've got to go. Sorry I can't ask you in, but my son will arrive at any moment.'

186

'Of course. So we have a date for the following Saturday? Thank you for forgiving me for frightening you.' His voice was polite and deferential, but surely she hadn't agreed to a date. Still, it felt too churlish to disagree. She wanted this over; she wanted to get in. And he did seem sorry. She had over-reacted.

I'll meet him once, and that'll be an end to it.

'Well . . . perhaps. A lunch-time drink.'

'You're not free in the evening? I could take you to dinner . . .'

'Sorry, it'll have to be lunch. I'll ring and confirm.' She still couldn't make her voice quite steady. Damn, she thought. Damn, damn. She had managed to leave herself a little get-out. *But why the hell had she said sorry to him?*

'I'll see you to your door. Mustn't have you being frightened.' He was laughing, a little, he half took her arm. At the door he bowed, slightly; the light on his hair.

'Bye,' she said nicely, but a little voice inside said *Bastard*, it was you that frightened me, it's a little bit late to play all protective. And a third voice said, *But so tall, so blond*.

'Bye,' he said. 'You're a lovely lady.'

And she grinned, she was grinning, as she shut the door, the meaningless rictus of the lovely lady, if they tell you you're lovely you have to look lovely, a grin of deference, a grin without pleasure.

25

ADAM CAME LATE, scruffy, ordinary, wonderfully familiar, her darling son, blinking at the light, smiling at his mother.

'I'm so glad to see you. Have a beer, darling.' She wanted to give him whatever he wanted, beer, money, motherly love; he was her son; he wasn't a stranger. 'I've got the money. I'm itching to get rid of it. And you go carefully, on the way back. Get a cab, for God's sake. There are maniacs on the underground.'

'There are maniacs everywhere, Mother dear.'

She'd decided to say nothing about her fright. 'Yes.' And our children go out into this world. We can't keep them with us. We can't protect them. 'Are you hungry, dear? Can I get you something?'

'I wouldn't mind some crisps. Or some peanuts.'

'Trouble is, I don't buy them, now no one else lives here. It was you and Dad who liked nuts and crisps . . . There are apples. Bread . . . I suppose I could cook . . .' But even Alma could hear her lack of enthusiasm; she still felt weak from running down the road. She wanted someone else to cook for her, she wanted someone else to look after her.

'Thing is, Mum, I'm meeting someone later.'

'Fine . . . but promise me you'll go home first and leave the money. You can't take five hundred pounds on a pub crawl.'

'Mum! I don't go on *pub crawls*.'

'All right, Adam, sorry. Here it is. Count it. No I will, just to make sure it's all there.'

Today he looked happier than yesterday. I suppose it's the money. Well, that's good. The notes felt attractive, crisp and slick, the solid opacity of the whole packet, clicking together as she counted them.

'Mum. I want to ask you something else.'

'Not another five hundred pounds, I hope.'

'No . . . it was something you said about going to Gran's, next weekend, and I could come and stay, if I wanted to . . . well can I?'

'I thought you said you'd rather come when I was actually here.'

'I know. The thing is. There's this other person. Could *they* come and stay?'

A whole constellation spun before Alma.

Of course, the girlfriend. The mysterious girlfriend. Her early morning terrors returned. They do want an abortion, after all. Maybe she's booked in for next weekend. Maybe she wants to come here to recover. In this very house . . . *No.*

'It's a girl, isn't it?'

'Yes.' He went red.

'Shouldn't I meet her, before she comes to stay?'

'There isn't much time before next weekend.'

'Do you really like her?'

'Yes.'

There was a pause. If I don't ask him, I'm being a coward, I'm letting him think that no one cares . . . 'Adam. Will you tell me what the money is for?'

'It's *difficult*, Mum –'

Then it *was* an abortion.

'I don't care. I'm worried. You'll have to tell me. I can't hand out money for God knows what.' The gloves were off. She played the mother card, suddenly decisive, peremptory, the card that Gwen had always played with her.

Adam told a lie to his mother.

'I owe it to someone. I have to pay them.'

Alma looked at her son and suspected he was lying. 'Adam dear . . . you haven't got this girlfriend pregnant?'

'Mu–um . . . *Mum*. What do you take me for?'

'Well I mean. I presume . . . you *are* twenty-one . . .'

'*Mother*. I know how not to get people pregnant. Dad talked to me about it when I was *fifteen*.'

Alma's spirits bobbed up. Now he was clearly telling the truth. His agonized scorn, his embarrassment. 'I'm sorry, Adam, I've embarrassed you.'

'You haven't.' Talking about it only dyed his cheeks darker.

'Mothers always embarrass their children, don't they . . .' Relief made her light-headed, over-talkative. 'I just began to worry, in the middle of the night. You know, I would *love* to have a grandchild . . . not yet, perhaps, but when you're qualified.' She smiled at him, but his smile was stiff. Come on, she willed him, cheer up, it's all right. They're so bloody touchy, these adolescents . . . 'I'm going to drink a little of your beer.' She had taken his can and emptied it before she remembered how Paul used to hate it when she said, 'I'll just have some of yours.' Yet they were her men. Couldn't they share things with her? Wouldn't he share her good mood? They always thwarted her . . . She went and fetched him another can.

He sat caressing the money with his free hand.

'Here's to Great-Uncle Bernard, Adam. It's his money, actually. Here's to families. Here's to . . . *our family*' (she could scarcely get it out) 'and here's to the family you'll have one day. And Zoe. Let's pray that Zoe will.' Alma had always longed to see Zoe's children. They had talked about them, two girls and a boy.

'Zoe,' said Adam, leaning across, slopping her beer as he clinked his can against her glass, my clumsy son – 'here's to Zoe. She'll be all right. And Uncle Bernard. And . . . you, Mum. You've been really kind. I am grateful.'

It was very nice to be called 'kind' by someone, not to be thought a terrible wife, not the sort of mother who would lose her daughter.

'Look,' said Alma on impulse. 'You can bring her here. I'll give you a key. Enjoy yourselves. Use the washing-machine. Don't bugger it up, will you? Do a bit of gardening, if you have time . . . You won't, of course. Be happy, Adam.'

She stood in the doorway and watched him go. She wished his tread was more confident; she wished his back were entirely straight. She wished she had done better with Adam.

Perhaps this girl will mother him.

The baton would be passed to someone else. Lack would be carried on into the future, always hoping to be made good. Her awkward child might find a new mother. Someone to contain that terrible hunger . . . To quench his thirst. He was always thirsty.

Nonsense, she thought. I'm a very good mother. I've always

loved him. He knows he's loved . . . in any case, I gave him the money. And the key to the house. What more could he ask?

Adam's all right. Adam is *fine*.

26

PAUL SHIVERED AS HE STOOD on the pavement outside his school on Saturday morning. The day was wild, an electric blue across which cold clouds chased each other. The light was merciless upon his hands; he had forgotten his gloves; those hands looked old. Veined pink crêpe. He stared at them. It didn't matter. There was no one to notice. Storms were promised later, but not yet, he prayed.

The coach was there, with its bored driver. Paul was there, with three placards which the wind kept blowing across his feet. The parents weren't there. His mood was grim. He had been up till two a.m., in Peeky's freezing garage, painting slogans in black gloss paint. The brush had been too thick. The letters were crude. The cardboard was nailed to pieces of wood which would probably break before the march left the park. He had done his best. He always did his best. How many heads came on marches like these? Heads liked to sail above the storm. But Paul was here. He was always here. That was Alma's complaint, that he was always here . . . Never at home; always here.

– Well someone has to care about these kids, he told himself, turning up the collar of his coat. Because their parents bloody don't. Some did, of course, vocally, passionately. Not always helpfully; the father who regularly bashed his own kids would come in roaring with outrage because young James had to do detention for rudeness. The mother who only sent sweets for packed lunch and whose child had no gloves in winter weather would come in and scream in the office because no one had rung home to say the child had cut her knee in the playground. He sometimes thought it was themselves they hated; it was as if they became furious with the school when it showed a faint echo of their own behaviour.

But the parents who came today would be stalwarts. If anyone comes, he thought anxiously, scanning the grey distance for friendly faces. Today was a day of protest against the massive cuts to the education budget. The parents of all Brent schools had arranged a march and rally in the centre of Wembley. The schools were losing millions; they already had insufficient books, a bare minimum of staff, leaky buildings, no money for swimming lessons, no money, no money. These cuts would bear right into the bone. He would no longer be deciding whether to buy new maths books or get the boys' toilets repaired; now he would know that he could do neither. Let bloody Brent council come and run this school, he thought, if they're going to take away more of our money. Let them come and see how easy things are. Let them come and deal with Julian Dean. Or Darryl Smith. Or Wendy Hope, if they take away the money for Special Needs. They have needs, these children. They are bundles of needs. They are so very hungry, and so very angry. These men in their offices have no idea. They have never seen children come into a room and start throwing chairs to get attention. They have never seen children white with rage, helpless, hopeless, scared of themselves, afraid that no one can contain their anger. They don't know how destructive one child like that can be in a classroom of thirty children. Because he needs someone just for himself. He cannot share. He doesn't know how to. He has never felt there was enough to share. And if we can't give these kids some of what they need. If they go on into the world with their ravenous hunger, their frightening capacity for breaking things up. It will be too late to make things right. If we fail them now, they will go out and be killers, because they have learned we have nothing else to offer.

His hands were white with cold. He had a paper, but his fingers were too clumsy to open it. The case on the front page was sickening. Two teenagers were on remand accused of murdering a three-year-old girl. They had taken her to some waste land, tortured her, battered her with bricks, tied her up, poured petrol over her, set her alight. People had heard her screams for over an hour, but no one had come to help her. The boys were twelve and thirteen. They had a history of truancy and petty crime. A neighbour of one of them was quoted as saying, 'He was a naughty boy, but no one ever thought he'd do something like this. I blame the schools. And I blame the parents. His mother is a slag.'

The newspapers had all been vocally appalled. It seemed to be news to most journalists that children of this age were capable of killing. If they saw some of our children, they wouldn't be surprised, he thought. Any teacher could tell you that some of the kids in their classrooms are angry to the point of murder. Their thwarted energy. Their desperate boredom.

And just as this happens, they cut money to schools. They give us less help instead of more. They think it's easy to take money away from children. Candy from babies, they think it is. They think these kids will be kids for ever. They shove them away into dark damp buildings without enough books or computers or care. If they're off the streets, they think it's OK. Not that they can keep them off the streets if there's nothing in schools that's worth turning up for . . .

But these kids will grow up. These kids will come back. They'll burst out of the darkness and into the light. They'll come looking for the adults who neglected them. They'll come looking for someone to make good what they've lost. They'll know they've been cheated. They'll want their revenge. When these politicians are old and weak, the kids they've short-changed will be big and tough. The only power they have will be the power of their bodies, but they'll use that strength to make us take notice. They'll do to the weak what was done to them when they were helpless, when they were weak. They'll find the old. It won't be hard. They'll find their own children; even easier. They will make them pay for every penny they lost. They will hand it on, what was done to them.

'– Mr Bennett! Mr Bennett? Are you all right?'

Paul was astonished to find David and Helen O'Flanagan two feet away from him, shouting eagerly. They had brought their younger son, a freckled, clumsy, likeable boy. The O'Flanagans were good parents. At meetings they found it hard to stop speaking, but they were always ready to help with things, digging the school garden, collecting money, storing smelly rags for jumble sales.

'I'm sorry, I was thinking about these cuts . . .'

'Disgusting, isn't it. We have to do something.'

They were straggling up in twos and threes, wrapped up like tents against the freezing wind, most of them past the first flush of youth, draped in every possible variety of anorak. Decent people; unglamorous. None of them had wanted to come today. All of them had other things to do, the shopping, the washing, the cleaning, the garden. But they had turned out because they loved their kids. And they would appreciate his being there. He was a popular head. He was available. He drew strength from his quiet popularity. Most of them gave him a smile as they turned up. There were ten of them; then there were fifteen. Black and white, talking, laughing. They were united by the cold, by adversity, by the quixotic nature of what they were doing, making a protest to the deaf, shouting at the wind, defying the waves.

SAVE OUR SCHOOLS
STOP PUNISHING OUR CHILDREN
KIDS NEED SCHOOLS
SAVE OUR TEACHERS

As still more arrived, the group became noisier, starting to have the air of a party, as they stooped to read each other's placards and made jocular suggestions for slogans to chant. They left ten minutes late, with over forty people: four-fifths of the coach, not bad, he thought; nearly all the names we took have actually turned up. He felt safe, with his parents, buoyed up by their mood, by his sense of belonging, of being needed.

It's different for me, he thought, as the old bus bumped and rocketed through Kemble Hill, through Burnham Rise, on towards Wembley, where dozens of other coaches should be. These families have given up their pleasant weekends to come and do something they feel they ought to. Whereas I'm almost grateful to be here. I'm with friends here. It feels like . . . family. I've always had that feeling about my school. It's another way of being . . . a father. You'd think it was more difficult than being a real father, but it isn't. Distance makes you safe. I'm fond of these kids, but not painfully. I don't need them as much as they need me. They don't ask me for love; just help, and fairness.

And time, of course. I've always given them that. Alma would say I stole the time from my other family. My real family. My painful family. The family that's broken up around my feet. And without them, my weekends have been pretty lonely.

Pip Kelsey loomed over him, half fell with a shriek as the bus turned a corner, sat down suddenly beside him, with a gasped 'Do you mind?'

She was wind-blown, flushed; *pretty*, he registered. But also annoying. He knew she liked him. She taught piano, and had three daughters, about whom she worried incessantly. They were lovely girls despite her worries, and they treated their mother with amused tolerance, sometimes strained past all reasonable limits when she arrived at school in the middle of the morning, frantic because someone had forgotten their vest. Her face had a slightly avid look. Over-sympathetic; over-interested. She's found out what's happened to me, he thought. Oh God. I thought I could escape all that.

'How *are* you, Mr Bennett.'

He had told her a hundred times or more that she could call him Paul, but she managed to make the 'Mr Bennett' more intimate, an ageing schoolgirl with a crush on the teacher. It was difficult when mothers did that. Head teachers were like doctors; attractive through power. It wasn't personal, so it wasn't flattering.

'*Paul* . . . I'm fine. Good turnout today.'

'But how are you really? You're being so brave . . . I know about what's happened, you can talk to me. One of my friends is a friend of Mrs Bennett.'

That bitch Alma's been talking about me.

'We have every hope that Zoe will be back by Christmas. Adam is fine. Doing well at his Law.' He adopted the tone of a public address, bluff and cheery, staring straight ahead, but he felt under-mined, he felt exposed, he felt that everyone was looking at him, pitying him, thinking him a failure. I didn't want this. I can be strong, at school.

'Your poor daughter . . . in this terrible cold.'

What she said was so simple, so undeniable. He felt the tears pricking at the back of his eyes. He saw that she wasn't just feasting on disaster. He lowered his voice, and looked straight at her.

'I know,' he said. 'But I can't bear to think about it. I mostly get by by not thinking about it. Do you understand, it's hard to talk.'

She was flattered by the confidence. She briefly clasped his hand. Her hand was dry, and very hot. 'Of course,' she hissed. 'I shan't say a word. I just want to say . . . I think you're wonderful. Why are these teenagers so ungrateful? My daughters are the same. I can never do enough. The more I do, the less they like it.'

She was someone he would never be able to talk to. He didn't try. He coughed, explosively. 'Sometimes they need to be left alone . . . everyone needs to be left alone.'

She took the hint and lurched away just as the coach ground to a halt. But the scent she left behind was sweet, slightly peppery. *I need a woman. God, I do.*

They drew up in a crooked caravan of coaches, from which other scruffy bodies spilled, trying not to lose their scarves or their placards. The forty-odd parents from his school were absorbed into a milling crowd of hundreds; maybe thousands, he thought, staring. They fanned like ants across the park's wet grass, and began to struggle their way into a line, single-celled creatures building an organism, headless, tail-less, full of awkward life.

From such weird biology hope might come. From people making themselves part of one another. Paul stood slightly to one side so he could watch it happen, the amicable disputes, the jockeying, the shouted praise for each other's banners, the friendly contempt with which people treated the left-wing splinter groups trying to plant dozens of pre-printed placards through the crowd: REVOLUTIONARY COMMUNIST PARTY SAYS STOP THE CUTS. Hands took the placards gratefully, then tore off everything but STOP THE CUTS. The soi-disant communists seemed not a whit dismayed, as if this always happened to their placards. They're part of it too, Paul thought. We all are.

And they shambled like a monstrous caterpillar, hundreds of hands held up like hairs, bearing white leaves with their heartfelt words, out of the park, on to the streets. The clouds were darker now, but there was still blue sky. Paul was with them, Paul was within them, borne along in the thick of the crowd. There was something about them; something shining. They were doing something. They were here to be counted. They were embarrassed, they were selfconscious, but they were also conscious that they were being brave. Most of them were people who had never marched, most of them had never demonstrated in their lives. It was hard for them to march where the cars should go, to take up space in the middle of the street, to be stared at by everyone who shuffled down the pavement, to be glared at by most of the people in cars who had been hoping to get on with their Saturday shopping. It was strange for them to be flanked by police, however friendly the police might seem, flanked by police like powerful people from whom the high street must be protected. And so perhaps they did have power. Was it possible that they had power? The caterpillar began to chant. Ragged bursts of singing began to break out. 'What do we want?' 'No Cuts.' 'When do we want it?' 'Now.'

Children had come on the march with their parents. Their enjoyment was simpler; they smiled, they laughed, they darted about between their parents, their placards dipped and soared and swayed. These children were a magnet to children on the pavement. They pulled the sleeves of their shopping mothers. They pointed to placards; STOP PUNISHING OUR CHILDREN. DON'T THROW BRENT KIDS IN THE BIN. As the full length of the march began to unfold on to the high street, as the caterpillar stretched to its full extent, life on the pavement drew to a halt. People stared, uneasy, frowning at the slogans, trying to make out what was going on. They were reading, some of them moving their lips, muttering, turning to talk to each other. There was a weird pale light, as if this was a show, the last grave tableau before some disaster. Unearthly light; it made them all solemn.

SAVE OUR SCHOOLS, the caterpillar chanted, swaying, growing, full of life. s–o–s, they called, they shouted. SAVE OUR SCHOOLS. SAVE OUR SCHOOLS, IT'S NOT TOO LATE. SAVE OUR SCHOOLS. Now most of the people on the pavement had stopped moving, they stood and stared, they stood straight-faced, puzzled, shy, like people at a funeral, people who hadn't known till then that anyone was dying, people who were watching a tragedy enacted in slow motion.

'This is England, isn't it?' Paul heard a man say. 'We always had free schools in England. They can't be going to cut the schools.' But his face was sober; he knew they could. Now the rows on the pavement were part of what was happening. Thousands of people breathed together.

Then someone in a car which couldn't get through right down at the front of the procession, someone in a hurry to get somewhere, someone in a rage in a small box of metal, started blasting on his horn, blasting, blasting. He wound down his window; he began to swear. The horn blast stopped while he shouted obscenities. The swearing rose above the sound of the chanting, but then the chanting rose again, s−o−s, SAVE OUR SCHOOLS, then the horn blasted, then all the cars in the blocked queue behind who couldn't even see what the delay was about began to blast their horns as well, brutally, mindlessly, a corporate frenzy.

And then something else. Something hissing and rustling. A change in the air, a change in the light, a great darkness, a great dying, a drenching, drowning, blue unfurling of pent-up tonnes of November rain, a wave of grief, a silencing deluge, stopping the hooting, stopping the chanting, muffling it all in a tide of black water, and the column broke, the pavements shuddered, people began to turn and run, the caterpillar sprawled and blurred and the placards drooped into oblivion.

For a moment I thought we were going to fly, thought Paul, who held ranks, with most of his parents, the rain running icily down his neck and flapping wet trousers against his legs; for a moment then, we were going to take off. It was possible. There had been a moment . . .

But now the remainder of the body of the march stumbled on towards the gardens where the rally would be, wet and silent, under English skies, the narrow skies of more modest hopes, the narrow skies of disappointment. And he stuck it out; most of them did; they stood beneath bare dripping trees and listened to what passed for oratory from the official speakers under their umbrellas; the microphone howled sporadically, but the words that remained suggested not much was lost: '. . . and so, brothers and sisters, I made representations to various Tory members of parliament . . .'

The children were all bored. The children were gone. You could see a few figures, black as liquorice in the distance, playing on the swings in the soaking playground, the playground there was no money to maintain, the playground nobody thought was important.

Rain made Paul's eyelashes stick together, rain blurred everything near and far. His gaze kept creeping back to the playground, seeing his daughter, as he always did, that figure, surely, with the mass of dark hair, on the edge of things, her face invisible.

They were what mattered. The distant children, vanishing, now, through the veils of rain.

27

THE NIGHT BEFORE she went to Wales, Alma dreamed about her mother and father. The house, although it looked as it did today, was really the house where she lived as a child, and she was expected to sleep in her study, although there was no bed in there. She came out crying in her pajama top, realizing too late she had forgotten her trousers. 'I can't sleep here. There isn't a bed.' 'You're just being difficult,' her mother said. 'You've got exams next week, and you've got to study.' 'I could find us another house,' said Alma. 'There are plenty of houses at Portico and Sheen . . . there would be enough room for another baby.'

But she knew she had said the impermissible thing, and her mother's mouth closed down like a trap. 'Then you'll have to sleep with Mr Edberg,' Gwen said. 'I'm sure there's plenty of room in there. Do you know how to get babies? Dirty girl,' and the terror began to rise in Alma, the terror of what was behind the door, and it drove her upwards, trying to wake as her mother pushed her back into the room and she realized, on a wave of relief, that it was Simon Edwards, it wasn't − . . . *who?*

Travelling to Wales was like being reborn, a long cool birth in a kind country, as the slow train slipped down its wet green groove through low woods and damp fields into the round Welsh hills. Alma had decided to be kind to herself; it was surely time to be kind to herself. She had never liked long drives alone, and so she had decided to travel by train. She could sit and be still while the world moved past her. It was misty, close, everything intimate, the telegraph wires against thick creamy clouds like matted fleeces, the birds huddling. There were no far vistas. The air was cold, but she pushed the wings of the window apart, breathing deeply, cold but clean.

Alma had some letters to write on the train, but put the pad away after a cursory start. She didn't want to miss this journey . . .

It must be time to live the present more fully. She sometimes felt that life had slipped by while she did all the other things she had to do.

When the children were babies I was always working, and yet I longed to get back to them; I would sit in my office, impaled by images of them in the arms of the nanny at home. Then when Zoe had croup or the nanny got sick and I was forced to stay at home, I fretted all day to get to work. Wherever I was, I was always somewhere else . . . and I vowed, 'One day I'll be less busy,' and one day I was, but they weren't babies any more. It was the same when Paul and I were first married. We told each other, 'Soon we'll have more time together,' because we were in love, and that was all we wanted. And a few years later we did have more time, but the honeymoon was over, we were used to each other . . . and maybe we missed the thrill of it all by putting things off into the future.

It was a trick, the future; a distraction. The only reality was here and now . . . but enjoying the present was so hard to do.

Alma sat and stared at the grey plastic table-top, lost in thought, till the coffee-trolley came. It would soon be midday. She bought a packet of sandwiches. Limp and clammy. She pushed them away . . . Then she realized half the journey had gone by, and she hadn't been watching, she hadn't been noticing.

I always think *duty first*. I was taught from babyhood, *duty first*. Do the hard things first. Save the best till last. Never put the TV on until you've washed up. Never go to bed without cleaning your teeth. Never go for a walk until the house is tidy . . . but sometimes it got dark, while you tidied the house, sometimes it began to rain . . . sometimes if you saved the best till last you found you had lost it along the way . . .

It was Mother who always said 'Duty first.' The house was always immaculate. The bills were paid the day they arrived, but the fun was put off; time for that later. So there wasn't much fun.

There wasn't much laughter. And now finally Gwen was left on her own, with two husbands dead and the mortgage paid off and everything shipshape and a nice little pension.

Duty was done, but she was old. And her only daughter didn't really want to see her . . . The long weekend that Alma first envisaged had shrunk to two days; as much as she could bear . . .

I want to see her, but not on her terms. It was the first time Alma had seen Gwen on her own, without Adam or Zoe, for twenty-odd years . . .

And a little ripple of nervousness tautened Alma's stomach, shivered her neck. She stretched in her seat, she straightened her back. She lifted her legs in front of her, flexed her ankles, her long slim calves.

My body, she thought. Fifty years old. Not so bad for fifty years old. It grew from her. I grew in my mother . . . What do parents feel as their children age? The bodies which were babies, growing older . . .

Did they love my body? Were they tender to it? Before I could speak, or run, or remember. When I was defenceless, did they defend me? The big ones, the old ones. Looking down on me.

There was suddenly a shadow between her and the light. A ticket collector? She looked up; it was nothing.

She did use to cuddle me, my mother, not passionately, like Aunt Eileen did, but holding me close, holding me still, kissing my forehead, stroking my hair . . . Never for long, though. There was work to be done. And everything was in moderation. But I know she loved me, and thought me pretty, especially when I was being good. So what does she feel as I begin to grow old? My face getting thinner. My hair greying. Are they sad that it happens to us as well?

But she still hugs me. She still kisses me.

For Alma these embraces were complex. Her mother had shrunk to bones and wire. She would clamp herself on like a limpet, for seconds that seemed like hours. Alma had to be the rock, because her mother was the limpet. Alma was supposed to be stronger than her. Gwen's conversation was a dirge of complaints, with the implication that Alma should deal with them, Alma should somehow redeem it all.

– But part of me still needs a mother. I don't want to be a mother to her.

There were three stops to go when she shook herself again, out of the past, into the arms of the present, the welcoming day outside the glass.

The green, the grey, the clouded country glided by, round then hollow, reassuringly the same, still unspoiled, limpidly maternal, the sheep nestled on their solid little hillsides, the small stone farms in the curve of the valleys, the road winding like beaded ribbon around the gentle limbs of land. Not many beads; not many cars. Were there any people left in Wales?

– *I'm your child. Take me back.*

'You're looking thin,' said Gwen. 'Oh dear, you're so thin!' But her voice was a screech of friendship and pleasure, and she squeezed Alma to her like the baby she had been. 'I haven't slept a wink. I've been so excited . . . I got Helen to drive me to Cardigan yesterday, spent all day shopping, I was that exhausted, I thought I'd sleep but I didn't sleep a wink . . .'

'You shouldn't have worn yourself out shopping. I don't eat much. And Helen's getting on . . .'

'You're not on a diet?' Gwen's voice was shrill. 'Don't say you're on a diet when I've done all my cooking.'

'I haven't dieted for thirty-odd years.'

'– What do you mean, *Helen's getting on*? We're all getting on around here you know. I'm eighty-two, but I don't complain.'

This was plainly untrue, but Alma let it pass. 'Are we getting the bus?'

'Taxi, isn't it. I mean, this is a special occasion, Alma.'

A dirty black car waited outside.

'Afternoon.' The driver's face was dour.

'Alma, say hallo! It's Mr Jones! Don't say you've forgotten Mr Jones! They go away and they forget us altogether . . .'

Gwen's hair was freshly permed, a crinkly helmet, a habit that Alma had never understood since her mother's hair was naturally curly, like hers, but when she had asked her about it one day her mother stared at her amazed and said, 'I couldn't have it all wild, Alma. I have to be tidy. I like to feel tidy.' Her face was tiny, a mask of tough bones with a small neat mouth painted much too pink, the blueish pink of a girl's first lipstick. She had false teeth, perfectly white and regular; though only three teeth had had anything wrong with them, Gwen considered false teeth an improvement. They had changed her face, for old photographs showed her with natural teeth as large as Alma's, her lips more fleshy and protuberant, a different face, freer, more animal. She had dragged the spirit from her face by force.

'Do you think I look well?' she asked her daughter as they drove through the village at a funereal pace. 'Have you noticed my new scarf? I bought it yesterday. In your honour. I've been so excited.' There was a pleading quality to what she said: *love me; praise me; don't disappoint me.*

I'll try not to disappoint you, thought Alma, mute in the palm of her mother's needs.

Refusing all offers of assistance, Gwen brought a vast pot of tea to the table. 'I know you never bother with a pot, but you'll have to humour an old woman.'

'I do make tea in a pot, Mother. Of course I do, when the family's there . . .'

'You always stained our mugs. You liked to use those bags, in a mug.'

'But that's ages ago, when I was a student.'

It wasn't ages ago, to her mother.

'This reminds me of just after Father died. You and me were on our own, like this. You came to look after your mother. You've always been a good girl, Alma.'

'I remember. Adam was very young. I decided it was better to leave him with Paul . . .' And it was hard, so very hard. I wanted to be at home, not here. I didn't want to deal with my mother's grief, and I couldn't deal with Father's death. His incoherent anger in that final week, after his stroke, and I should have felt sorry for him, but I didn't, it was just like all the other anger, really, he had been in a fury so much of his life, and Mother had always tiptoed round him, and always made *me* tiptoe round him. And then I failed him at the last. Adam got ill, I travelled back to London, and Father died when I was still on the train . . . I came back to help Gwen deal with the body. To order the sherry for the funeral. Which caused a huge row, since Mother is teetotal.

'I don't think I was much use to you. Well, maybe with the practical things. Sorting old letters. Throwing away his clothes.'

'We didn't throw away his clothes.' Gwen's eyes flashed, indignant. 'I never would have thrown away Father's clothes.'

'Sorry . . . what did we do with them? We gave some to the Chapel, didn't we? And some of them went to Aunt Eileen to sell . . . by the way, what's arranged about Eileen? I thought that tomorrow would be a good day.'

'But you said you were coming by train,' said Gwen, in what seemed a complete *non sequitur*.

'What?'

'Well, I thought, Alma's coming by train. So she'll never be able to go and see Eileen.'

'*Mother*. You said you would tell her. You haven't fixed it, have you?'

'Don't look at me like that, child. I can see you're going to be cross with me.' Gwen mimed anxiety, defencelessness.

She's about as defenceless as a mamba, thought Alma, and yet she couldn't break the spell. 'I'm sorry, Mother. I'm not cross with you. It's just that I do really want to see Eileen.'

'Maybe she could come over here after all. I did tell her not to bother, this Sunday. Said I was busy, so as not to hurt her feelings, before you start telling me off for nothing . . . I'll ring her now and say Sunday lunch as normal.'

– And as normal, nothing will ever get said, it will all be social, trivial, safe.

'*I'll* ring her, Mother. I'll go to Tresaith. There's a perfectly good bus—'

'There *was* a bus. They stopped it last year.'

'I'll ask Mr Jones. I've got plenty of money.'

'I suppose it's an outing. I could show her my scarf—'

'Mother, I'm thinking of going alone.'

'Well everyone will think it's odd.'

'What?'

'You going to Tresaith on your own like that, when they know you're only here for two days. Don't want to spend time with your own mother.'

'They won't think any such thing.'

'Why don't you want me to see my own sister?'

Alma felt herself drowning, unable to resist the clutch of her mother, steely, wily, illogical. Ignobly, Alma passed the buck. 'I'll ring her, and see if she asks us both. After all, she isn't very well off, you're always saying she's poor, Mother.'

Gwen pursed her lips and took up the tea things, washed up noisily, outflanked.

'May I ring her now, Mother? Sorry, shall I help you?'

'It's already done, if you haven't noticed. We ring when it's cheap rate, round here. This isn't London. It's the middle of the day.'

'I want to give her *warning*, Mother. I promise to give you the cost of the call.'

'Money,' said Gwen, unfairly. 'You young ones think everything is solved by money.'

'I won't ring her if you don't want me to. You don't want me to ring her, do you?' I can be unfair if you can, thought Alma.

'Well of course I'm not saying that . . . You've only just arrived, and you're snapping at me.'

Alma rang Eileen. Her rich, cracked voice, pickled in the elements, humorous, loving. Buoyed up by the first moments of hearing Alma, lifted by the happiness of knowing they would meet. Everything was so much simpler with Eileen. She said what she meant. No complaints, no guilt.

But Alma noticed that the buoyancy waned. As they decided on details, Eileen grew tired. She was a little hoarse, a little flat. Perhaps she had a cold. But she sounded older. At seventy-nine, youth couldn't last . . .

But Gwen had never sounded young.

'Toodle-oo,' said Eileen; she was young again. 'Give my love to Gwen. Toodle-oo, Flower.'

'What's happening, then?' asked Gwen, suspicious.

'She sends her love. She sounds a bit tired.'

'You won't go tiring her out then, will you. At least you've had a chat. See her next time—'

'We're meeting tomorrow in Tresaith, at midday. Mother, she

207

wants to see me. I shan't stay long enough to tire her. It's work that tires her, I expect. Still on the road, at seventy-nine—'

'Funny kind of work. Always was.' Gwen sniffed. She hadn't worked since she married Jack. She hadn't taught for fifty-five years.

'She enjoys it though. It's fun.'

'Funny kind of fun, in winter. Driving round these roads in that heap of scrap iron. *Figure* of fun, more like.'

'Lots of people couldn't manage without her. You used to tell people that, when they asked.'

'Sticking their noses in everywhere . . . People were always nosey about Eileen. She's family, isn't she? I had to stand up for her. It's different now though. Nobody needs her. People have cars. They can shop in Cardigan, or Aberystwyth, when they go there . . . It's only the old dears depend on Eileen.' This change seemed to give her satisfaction. Maybe Eileen could be lazy and respectable at last.

'Well – she'll see them out then. That's a good thing.'

'Huh,' said Gwen. 'In any case, you'll be back for tea, won't you? Dafydd and Helen are coming for tea. They're dying to see you, honestly. A bit disappointed that the family's not with you, but they'd still like to see you, Alma.'

'I don't know. I want to have some time with Eileen . . .'

'They've been such good friends to me,' said Gwen. 'I should have been so lonely without them, with you so far away, and hardly ever visiting . . .'

'But Eileen's *family*,' Alma said gently. 'You always said that family was what mattered.'

Gwen turned to her with a mouth like someone swallowing a wasp. 'Well maybe I was wrong,' she said. 'I mean, you've all gone off and left me, haven't you? I don't know if blood's thicker than water any more.'

'Mum,' said Alma, feeling the onset of panic, it was all going wrong, there was going to be a scene. 'It was you and Father who decided to leave London. And Father *died*. He didn't leave you. And I have my own family in London. Otherwise I would come more often.'

'Well you're all alone now,' said Gwen, pugnacious. 'And you wouldn't let your mother come and comfort you. We could have been company for each other, but No . . . Still, that's the modern way. Nothing's like it was.'

'Mother, let's go and sit in the garden,' Alma said. 'Now the mist has lifted it looks quite sunny. I *have* come to see you. We've got lots of time. Father would have wanted me to see Eileen. He was fond of her, wasn't he?'

'D'you think I'm not?' Gwen's little eyes flashed, bright wet slate in their cupboards of bone. 'She's my sister. I know all about her. Don't you go telling me about Eileen.'

'You're upset,' said Alma. 'I'll make some more tea. I'm sorry, Mother. I seem to be putting my foot in it.'

She took her mother's hand, tiny, cold, not much life left in it. But then it squeezed back, clutched her hard, and her little mother was attached to her chest, hugging her forcefully, reaching up to kiss her, and Alma tried to respond but too late, so her lips pressed on hair, wiry, resistant, while her chin was left wet from her mother's offering.

'There,' said her mother. 'There's a good girl. Tea would be lovely. You're a good daughter.'

28

SO ALMA WAS A GOOD DAUGHTER AGAIN.

They shopped in the village in the afternoon. Alma was paraded in the village stores, in the post office, and the paper shop, which Gwen was filled with indignation to be told was closing after Christmas.

'But the children buy their toys in here!' There was a stand of cheap toys, all priced under three pounds, cheerful plastic things in transparent bags.

'Well there aren't many children left, Mrs Thomas. And the parents haven't got any money, have they?'

'How am I going to get my paper?'

'They'll probably send some from Pontyglas to the village stores, but there'll be no delivery.'

'Everything's getting worse.' She was reproachful, as if they could have kept going if they wanted, as if she expected them to try harder.

'We know, Mrs Thomas, we know. We've lost a lot of money on this business.'

'Oh well,' she said, surprised. 'I suppose you have, then.'

As they smiled their way down the village street, she confided in Alma, 'They're newcomers, see. They haven't got what it takes, have they? You have to be tough to survive up here.'

'Mum, it's all over the country, the recession. No one's got any money to spend.'

'They all expect to be millionaires,' Gwen hissed. 'Father made do with an honest living. Maybe he'd hoped for more, but when he didn't get it . . . Father was a stayer, not a fly-by-night.'

'Well even the banks are making people redundant now. It's not a safe job like it was in his day.'

'I know that. Your mother does know some things. The bank

in Pontyglas is closing. Do they think we can keep our money under our beds? I mean what do they take us for, in London?' It was as if she had never lived in London, now the source of everything bad and modern. It was as if she had never left Wales. 'Soon there'll be nothing left, up here. We used to have a bakery, and a dairy, and a wool-shop by the chapel, believe it or not. They came from miles around to that wool-shop. Owen's Mam used to send me wool to London, and I knitted the most beautiful things, little cardies for you, just like shop-made, no one could have told the difference, Alma . . .'

Alma clearly remembered those cardigans, identical except for their slow increase in size, pink with tiny patterns on the cuffs and edging, cream pearl buttons, small and close together, what seemed like hundreds of tiny pearl buttons, and as a child she would fasten them with infinite patience only to find, when she got to the top, she was a button out, and would have to start again.

One day she had asked her mother for a jumper. 'A jumper would be very quick to put on.' 'Boys have jumpers, girls have cardigans.' 'I want to be a boy then.' Alma burst into tears. 'Crying for nothing,' her mother said. 'I'm going to knit you a new one soon. You can choose the colour of the pattern on the edges.' 'I don't want patterns. I want a plain jumper.' 'You're a difficult child. You're just ungrateful.'

I never did that to Zoe, thought Alma. She was always allowed to choose her own clothes. Her mother's voice continued in the background, and Alma switched on again, with an effort.

'. . . We'd *starve* up here if they had their way. No food, no toys, no newspapers . . .'.

Gwen wasn't remotely political. 'They' meant the enemy, the townies, the Londoners, the young and lucky ones, the faceless Others. Rich and careless. Hasty and nasty. Sometimes they seemed to be connected to Alma, and Alma had a duty to speak to them.

'I know what you mean,' Alma soothed. 'Everything's changed since Father was small. I suppose he must have got more upset than you, because this place was his childhood, wasn't it. And he was a Welsh speaker –'

'– They're not the only ones who love this country. I was born in Cardigan, so what's the difference? Your Grandma was dead against our learning Welsh. She thought the future was about speaking English. She was ambitious for us, you see . . . I think I disappointed her. I was supposed to be the bright one.'

'Was Grandma ambitious?' This was news to Alma. You forgot your parents also had parents, that the chain of duty swung on for ever.

'Well maybe I shouldn't say ambitious. She wanted the best for us, let's say. I would have gone to college if there'd been more money . . . if she had had a boy, it might have been different, but she had two girls, so she put her hopes on me.'

'What did she want you to be?'

'A teacher. Well, I was a teacher, uncertificated, you know I was, but not for long . . . because I met Daddy, and followed him to London, which Grandma shouldn't have complained about, since she was so keen on everything English . . . but she wasn't happy that I gave up work. Daddy didn't want his wife to work. And I thought we would get pregnant straight away . . .'

The sun angled down the narrow grey street, the deep little gully where their lives were lived, and illuminated Gwen's slate-blue eyes, making her look almost pretty for an instant, softer, now, as she looked into the past, to a time when everything wasn't already decided.

'But . . . I wasn't born till you were thirty-one.' It hadn't occurred to Alma before. They must have had difficulties getting pregnant.

'Never was a child more welcome,' said Gwen, and the phrase was the phrase she always used, and Alma realized that the opening was gone, there were to be no more questions, the lid was back on.

But I won't give up. I shall ask questions.

'Were you really happy with Daddy?' she asked. 'You were in London, weren't you. Before the war. And you were in your twenties, without any kids . . . did you have fun? I hope you had fun.'

'Of course we were happy. What a silly question.' Gwen was indignant.

'What was he like?'

'I'm tired,' said Gwen. 'What's got into you? Nice. Very nice. Of course he was. He was . . . a nice man.' And she added, crossly, as if that proved it, 'He was *your father*. Of course he was nice . . . all the other girls were jealous of me.'

'I know he was my father. Let me carry that bag. That's why I'm asking. I'm just interested . . . I know he was handsome, and blond, and kind. I half-remember him cuddling me, and he wasn't cross like Father, was he . . . ?'

'Father did his best. He had a hard life. He was *very* intelligent, he came from Wales expecting to make something of himself . . . but he wasn't smarmy enough for the City. He wasn't posh enough. He was always passed over . . . My knee is bad, *bach*. Must you walk so fast? It isn't good for me, with my heart.'

They had left the main street, turned up the hill again out of the village, past a thicket of holm-oaks, and Alma enjoyed their blue-black sheen out of which a bird suddenly burst, then another, two wood-pigeons batting up into the sunlight.

Slowly up the hill, me and my mother, her and her mother, struggling on upwards . . .

'Lovely to walk, to be in the country.'

'Not so lovely with legs like mine. I don't know what I'll do when I can't get to the village.'

Gwen had never driven; it was men who drove. She'll ask to come and live with us, Alma thought, and then corrected herself; she'll ask to live with *me*.

'It's rotten luck, two husbands dying,' she said, and took her mother's arm, tried to fold its sharpness under her own. Neither of us have much flesh on us, do we? Wouldn't take long to turn us back to bone.

'People think they can help, but they can't,' snapped Gwen, shaking her off. 'That's my arthritic arm . . . you seemed happy enough to get rid of *your* husband, Alma.'

'I *wasn't* glad. I was very unhappy. Maybe we'll get back together one day.' That shaft had hurt; tears stung her eyes; how can someone so ridiculous have such power to hurt me?

'I knew you would only make yourself unhappy. Marriage is for ever, our generation thought.'

'How long were you married to Daddy? If he died in 1945 . . .'

'Nearly ten years. Though it was different, in the war . . . I was married to Owen for twenty-three. We stuck at things. We made a go of them.'

'Mother, I've been married to Paul for twenty-five years. Which is a quarter of a century.'

'And then you just go and throw it away . . . You young ones, you don't value the past.'

But the past is what fascinates me, thought Alma. The past is the place I am trying to find. It's always just over the next hill, just out of sight, or not quite in focus, hints and glimpses, never the whole, and you won't help me, you won't hear me, you don't want the truth, you just want things tidy . . . You just want things to be comfortable.

'– I'm sorry, Alma. It was wrong of me to say that. It's because of my knee. It makes me short-tempered. Pain does, you know. I hope it never happens to you.'

Gwen was trying to be kind; yet her closing remark somehow sounded as though she meant the opposite.

In through the gate, the creaking gate, the gate that would creak and hang for ever, she will live for ever and tell me nothing, she will shuffle onwards, blind and deaf, clutching the past to her chest like that handbag. And it's my past too. It's my past too!

The evening slipped by uneventfully. Alma had primed herself to try again, to be gentler, more tactful, but more persistent. But there were television programmes that Gwen wanted to watch, and guilt-inducing reasons why she had to see them: 'They're company, you know, when you're on your own . . . It's like seeing friends. I thank God for the telly. I think I'd go crazy without the telly –'

This latter was said with a skittish little laugh which told you that *she* could never go crazy.

Alma tried to respond in kind. 'I know. I tend to watch telly really late at night. Old films and things. Black and white films.'

But her mother was already on her way to the set. She had never used a remote control. 'I like cheerful things. Situation comedies. Laughter's better than moping, Alma.'

And perhaps there was some truth in what she said; there was a kind of comfort in sitting there together in the womb of the overheated living-room, united by the flickering light of the screen and the gusts of laughter from the studio audience, and no one ever died, in these comedies, no one ever minded, no one remembered, no one ever screamed or ran away.

Every now and then Gwen looked up at Alma, checking that she was enjoying herself, and Alma smiled obediently.

'There you are,' said Gwen. 'I knew you'd enjoy it. I bet you never watch *that* in London.'

'No,' said Alma. 'I certainly don't.'

Gwen stared at her hard, but decided she meant nothing.

29

GOING TO AUNT EILEEN'S was a glorious escape, though Alma had only been home half a day. Sunday morning felt like a party, one of those days November stores like gifts and then suddenly, flamboyantly unfolds, so blue, so gold, clear as washed glass, the twigs cut black against the glittering sunlight, the leaves more striking now half of them had gone, each presence sharpened by the absences, a thousand twists of lemon spinning on the wind. Such a clean wind, a playful wind, and three white ponies chased across a field, prancing and charging like two-year-olds, and Alma felt young, in Mr Jones' taxi, though he drove across country at his usual staid pace, and met all her efforts at conversation, made to secure her mother's approval, with dark little grunts like chewed wads of tobacco.

– And now the familiar swoop down to Tresaith, looking down on the weeds on the roofs of the cottages, peering to the left as they swept round the bend, hungry for the first glimpse of sea –

That first bright glimpse, then the bay opened up, dazzling white then dazzling blue. Alma had always loved the sea, though she only knew it from holidays, had always felt at home by the sea. But it's because of Eileen, she thought. I always felt at home with her. Always half-wished that she was my mother. Sometimes I almost believed she was . . . It was such a comfort when Gwen disapproved and Father raged and everything was awful, and it always seemed to be all my fault, Mother made me feel it was all my fault. 'You've annoyed your father again, Alma.' Now I can see it was just a game, something to do with him and her. They were using me, but I couldn't see it. They were *abusing* me, in fact.

The thought came forcefully, an angry jolt to her body in the car, but she swallowed, relaxed, reminded herself that she was going to be happy. Eileen never manipulated me.

Eileen played real games, childish games, football and leapfrog and sandcastles and climbing. Aunty Eileen . . . she'll be waiting for me.

Alma's heart rose up on a crest of pleasure, this was how going home should be, she leaned forward in her seat, she clutched the box of chocolates in its rustling paper, she peered into sun – but just at that moment a dark shape loomed in front of the car, they braked suddenly, Mr Jones yelled, Alma jerked forwards, the chocolates fell, and they shuddered to a halt, tilted sideways, nose down, half off the road, engine roaring.

The dark shape was batting at the windscreen and shouting, and Alma suddenly realized it was Eileen. 'Crazy bloody woman,' said Mr Jones, and she did look wild, with her coat unbuttoned and her long grey hair whirled out in great sea-serpent loops by the wind. 'Alma! Alma! I came to meet you!', and Alma was up and out of the car and Eileen crushed her to her icy cheek, she must have been standing out here for hours, but her lips were warm and slightly roughened, as always, and her green eyes shone, and she laughed with pleasure, hugging Alma, patting her, stroking her hair. The two women stood there smiling at each other, interrupting each other in happy broken sentences, not listening because their faces said it all, until Mr Jones gave a great blare on his horn, leaned out of the window and shouted, 'Ten pounds! And you'd better shift, or else there'll be an accident!'

'Are you starving?' Eileen asked when they got into the cottage. Out of the wind it felt like summer, the sun making golden squares on the floor, gold and rose on the faded red carpet which had been here ever since Alma remembered and its red and purple flowers, once large and dramatic, had softened now, turned hazy and dreamy, the pinks and mauves of early evening, but time's getting on, time's slipping away, for when Alma looked properly around the room she saw the paint was cracking, the window-panes were furred across with a mist of yellow dust, the catch was mended with Elastoplast . . . 'Because I haven't cooked. I thought we'd go out. Have a picnic. If you won't freeze. Have you come in your city clothes, my child? I'll get you a jumper. You can fit my boots.'

And in five minutes Alma was kitted out, in football socks which mysteriously appeared as if Aunt Eileen was always playing football, black rubber boots of vintage design, a purple scarf which had misshapen in the wash and a huge blue sweater with yellow ducks.

'You look like a teenager in that lot,' said Eileen.

'But I'm grey,' said Alma.

'You look blonde to me.'

'You haven't changed in twenty years.' Alma said it before she'd really thought about it, saying it because she wished it was true, but as they came through the door into the full blaze of sunlight she saw that Eileen was a little more stooped, and thinner, surely, but 'Come on,' said Eileen, 'race you to the beach,' and she skipped down the path like a three-year-old, making Alma pant to catch up with her.

'I'll carry the bag,' she offered, all the same.

'Good . . . It sometimes catches me in my left shoulder, but otherwise I'm better than ever, I'll make use of you, since you're here.'

She limped very slightly as they walked down the road.

'Is your boot hurting?' Alma asked.

'No . . . funny thing is, I'm better dancing than walking. That's the way with age. It's best to be dancing. Gives you no time to notice the aches.'

'Mother isn't dancing.'

'Your mother never did.' It sounded final, but after a pause as they stepped down gingerly on to the shingle Eileen added, 'But it's not her fault. It's how we were brought up. It was the first world war, and our Mam, your Grandma, was very religious, and superstitious, and thought it was unlucky to have too much fun, with people dying . . . She was strict with your mother. Gwen was the clever one. They gave up on me altogether, Flower.'

'Did Mum get all the attention? Were you jealous?'

Alma's mother would never have answered that question, would have found it shocking, but Eileen didn't flinch. 'Sometimes I must have got fed up. I wish they'd seen more good in me . . . but I think it was the other way round, mostly. Maybe Gwen was jealous that I had more freedom.'

She always had seemed free; didn't care; wasn't shockable. Gwen always said 'Eileen doesn't trouble tuppence,' but she said it damningly, shaking her head. As a child Alma never understood why it was bad not to trouble tuppence. It sounded very good not to worry about tuppence, which wasn't that much, it would only buy four bubble-gums or a sherbet dab; if you lost it, you hadn't lost much. Then she saw it went with another one of her mother's sayings, muttered as Gwen hovered for hours at the market comparing the prices of the vegetables, 'Look after the pennies, girl, and the pounds will look after themselves.'

Eileen can't be rich, thought Alma. Gwen has a decent pension from both her husbands; Eileen has never married. Never bought property, either. That was another one of Gwen's complaints. The cottage was on a peppercorn rent, but one day the aged man who owned it would die. 'Sufficient unto the day, that's her. She's never thought about the future.'

But her present is so much more fun than Gwen's.

Eileen stooped, in two stages, but without too much effort, to pick up a flat stone and skim it at the water, straightening again, her hands on her knees, smiling into sun to follow its trajectory against the white breakers, up over the blue and down again, crinkling her eyes and licking her lips, there were the big teeth that ran in the family, yellow as a horse but she's still got them and they've kept her face humorous and young . . . Eileen laughed as her pebble hit the first time, jumped, jumped, jumped – went down. 'Not bad for an old 'un,' she said, turning, so youthful, suddenly, that Alma kissed her. Salt on her lips. This sweet late sun. She won't last for ever; every time is a blessing. She enjoys everything, that's why she's wonderful.

She lives in the present. She fills it up. She stops to enjoy it, even if she's late, and she always is late, for every appointment, my mother's still shocked when Eileen's late for lunch even though she's been late every week for the last dozen years – or early, like she was just now, for me, madly early, because she's excited.

'Excited' was a bad word in Gwen's vocabulary – 'Don't get all excited,' 'She's over-excited.' Excitement was dangerous, disruptive, irrational. Maybe sexual even. Alma thought about that. But all children like to be excited. All children think that excitement is fun. When you were with Eileen, life was exciting.

'Where shall we have our picnic?' she said. The first beach was wide and open, creamy sand beyond the long band of shingle, the beach where holiday-makers came in summer, where tents would appear, where the kiosk was open from May till September. The tourist beach, where the children ran races. Rocks cut it off to left and right.

'We don't want to stick on this beach, do we?' Aunt Eileen asked disdainfully. 'Let's go over the rocks to the waterfall beach.'

'Will you manage?' asked Alma.

'Will I manage indeed. I manage to get there nearly every week, without any nieces fussing over me.'

And yet it was difficult for Alma to watch her, surging up over the large flat rocks, a leaning cone of blueish purple topped by her whipping strands of silver, without imagining her toppling, falling, as if everything precious had to be lost . . . Which it will be one day, but live in the present, enjoy the present, Eileen does.

'Come *on*,' Eileen called, turning, precariously poised on the skyline. 'What are you waiting for? There's no one down there.'

'Coming, Aunty.' Alma leaped up behind her, enjoying the feel of the rocks through the rubber of her boots, enjoying her muscles, enjoying being young. Relatively young . . . not yet old.

It was as Eileen said. There was no one down there, just a steep little beach which would grow at low tide, shining sand from which the black rocks jutted, in the centre of the cliffs a long narrow waterfall, plaiting, unplaiting, plaiting again, dropping its net against the green cliff-face, narrower, thought Alma, than it was last year, just a trickle in places, but jumping in others, pattering on to the sand below and then spreading out in a silver tree across the beach and down to the waves. The far end of the beach was a deep V-shape where the sand cut far up into the rocks, completely protected from the sea-breezes.

'We picnicked up there before, didn't we?' asked Alma.

'Lots of times. So let's stay by the sea, instead.'

Gwen was consoled by repetition; Eileen always wanted to do something different.

'Shouldn't we find somewhere more sheltered?'

'I like it here,' Eileen announced, pitching camp on a flat-topped cairn of rocks. 'I like the wind. I like wet sand. I'm going to take my boots off, if you'll give me a hand. It takes me ages on my own.'

Her feet were all of seventy-nine years old, gnarled and humped and veined like wood, hazel-nut brown, with segments of nails that looked like encrusted lobster shell.

'Your feet are like sculptures,' Alma grinned, holding one briefly in her hand. 'I wouldn't like to have to fight with one of those.'

'They just growed,' said Eileen. 'It's life did that. I'm fond of my feet. They've done a lot for me. I can't feel the pebbles, but I hate tight shoes . . . I've had these boots for fifteen years.' She gasped, briefly, as her toes felt the water, and then she was off towards the first tiny wave.

'I'd better join you,' said Alma. 'I can't be outdone by an eighty-year-old.'

'Seventy-nine,' shouted Eileen over her shoulder. 'I'll have a party for my eightieth. Something to shock my sister.'

They began to walk through the shallow waves together, making small splashes in the sloping lace, and the cold of the water felt fresh and alive, the sand underneath it smooth and firm.

'I've got tomatoes and cucumber and ham sandwiches and beer and peanuts and oranges,' said Eileen.

'I'm glad there's some beer,' Alma said. 'It's still dry as a desert at Mum's. Do you remember the row when I ordered sherry for Owen's funeral? But *he* drank sherry. It was reasonable. I wonder what she thinks would happen if she had a drink. I suppose all the dangerous things might leak out . . .'

'Let's sit down and open the beer,' said Eileen. She paddled a bit further, though. '. . . What dangerous things?'

'You know Mother,' said Alma. 'She doesn't like to talk about feelings. Or the past. In case it stirs things up. Stirs her up maybe. But I'd love to ask her about Daddy – my real father – I mean I hardly remember him – and about Owen – and about my childhood.'

'She doesn't say a lot,' Eileen agreed, opening a bottle reflectively, watching the little sigh of froth. 'What do you really want to know?'

Alma sat and thought. The problem was, she didn't *know* what she didn't know . . . all she had was a sense of loss.

'I sometimes feel . . . as though something's missing,' she began, slowly. 'I can't quite explain. Part of myself. I sometimes feel paralysed with people. As if they exist and I don't. As if . . . I have no will of my own, as if it's been stolen . . . I don't know. Sounds crazy.'

'I'm listening. Help yourself to food. I'm sorry you missed my tomatoes this year. Baby ones. They were delicious . . . these great monsters must come from Europe. Go on, eat. But don't stop talking.'

'I wonder if it was Owen's fault. He was always angry. Well, not always . . . I felt like an ant when they were rowing.'

'He was a funny little man, really,' said Eileen. 'No sense, all feeling, Owen.'

'Anger?' said Alma. 'It's not a feeling, is it? It's a way of bullying people, isn't it?'

'Well you're angry now,' said Eileen. 'Is that a feeling?'

'When I'm angry, it's a relief,' said Alma, slowly, thinking about it, the sensation in her chest of something expanding, getting stronger, getting bigger. 'I feel more . . . honest, sometimes, when I'm angry.'

'I daresay he did too . . . I'm not sure my sister is always very honest.'

'Did you like Owen, then? I assumed you wouldn't have . . .'

'Not a bad man. But not *my* cup of tea.'

'He frightened me,' said Alma. 'They crushed me, the pair of them. I had to be good. I didn't have to argue. Then when I came here you let me run wild. Thank God you did. You listened to me . . .'

'Still do. How old are you, dear?'

'I'm fifty.'

'You still seem a child to me . . . I suppose you still seem like a daughter.' She reached out her hand and patted her niece's; Alma found tears springing to her eyes.

'I wish I had been your daughter . . .'

'Well we can adopt each other, can't we. No one else is going to adopt you, at your age.'

It was a joke, but true, and real, something never to be

forgotten, impossible for anyone to take away that pact between them with the wind and sun.

'I don't like to bring it up,' said Eileen, 'but I've thought of nothing else, since I first saw you – . . . How are you coping? Is there any news?'

She didn't have to say Zoe's name. It had hung in the air between them all along. Its giant zero scored the skies.

Zoe on the beach. Both the kids loved Tresaith, loved the long scramble down the rocks to Penryth. Loved all these beaches.

– Loved this beach.

Her little body ran across this beach. She had climbed the rocky ramparts to the waterfall beach first when she was only two, and Adam was seven. Alma had taken her nappy off. Chubby and bandy; adorable. Chortling and shrieking with pleasure as she climbed . . .

Zoe at eleven in bleached denims, with her golden tail of hair bobbing, swinging, her trousers rolled up to different levels, her sturdy gold-pink chest and shoulders, she had danced in the waves and stained her jeans with salt . . .

'Not a word. Nothing. If only . . . I think about her all the time. Wondering what I did wrong.'

There was silence. Just the seethe and sigh of the waves, and then the seagulls' sharp complaints. Alma glanced across at Eileen and saw that she was crying, the contours of her face almost unchanged; she could have been smiling, gaze fixed on the sea, seamed and cracked, the kind face of the watcher, but the tears fell down like a waterfall, a bright veil over a face of rock.

'Don't cry, Aunty Eileen . . . Do if you want to. I cry at night. I soak the pillow. I wake up at two and it's cold and damp.'

'I'm *annoyed* with the child,' Eileen said. 'Once we knew she was alive, I was furious . . . Everyone needs to get away some-times, but it's cruel not to let you know where she is. Gwen talks about her non-stop, you know.'

'She's hardly mentioned her to me.'

'She doesn't want to upset you, Alma.'

'It's not talking that upsets me.'

'You think silly things,' said Eileen. 'I think, she could have come to me. I would have given her a place. I wouldn't have got at her.'

So she does it too, Alma thought, chewing. Like Mother. Who really believes that if only *she* had talked to Zoe . . . but in Eileen's case, it isn't ridiculous. Zoe loved her. She loved coming here.

And then something else struck her, unpleasantly. 'Do you think I got at her then?'

The painful question. Waiting for the answer. It didn't come; Eileen was swigging beer, the brown bottle tipped up against the sky, the sun winking through it, her head tipped back, tautening her throat, how can she look so young . . . ?

'You were . . . a good mother. And so proud of her. But you can't help being your mother's daughter.'

'Are you saying that I bullied her? But I *wasn't* like Mother. I'm *not* like Mother . . . At least we made her feel like somebody. *I* never felt like somebody.'

'I didn't mean to hurt you,' Eileen said. 'You were a good mother. Let it rest.'

'I didn't mean to snap . . . I prefer the truth. No one tells the truth, in our family.' Alma was tense, not looking at her, hunched forward on the rock, pressing its sharp edges into her calves. 'I wish I knew all you know, Eileen –'

Just at that moment an electric drone like a distant helicopter began, grew louder, an electric lawnmower, louder, a motor-bike, they stared at each other, and 'Oh no, not one of those bloody things,' Eileen spluttered, peering round to the right, full into sun, and there suddenly plunged across the silver-blue sea a vast black missile, roaring, whining, a weapon, surely, churning and fuming, and then Alma screwed up her eyes and managed to make out a wet-suited figure riding the fury, careering in triumph across the bay, and it was a man on a water motor-bike, bucking and leaping with the power of the machine.

'Bloody great penises, aren't they?' said Eileen, gritting her teeth and watching indignant as it crossed the stretch of sea in front of them and carried on down the coast to the south.

Alma burst out laughing. She was used to Eileen, but her frankness was always a wonderful relief. 'I've never heard Mother swear,' she said. 'And I've never heard her say the word penis. Amazing, isn't it. Not even a *damn*. Not even when she broke things, or locked herself out.'

'You don't take after her in that respect, Flower.'

It was fading, now, a grumble, a rumble, passing away to upset other people.

'You think I was too proud of Zoe, don't you?' asked Alma. 'You think I pushed her too much. You're right.'

'I don't want to judge you,' said Eileen. 'She was a clever girl. Still is, I know . . . And you always wanted the best for her. But was she ambitious, do you think? Part of her just wanted to have babies.'

'I don't believe that!' Alma was outraged. 'She wasn't much more than a baby herself. Of course she wanted to go to university. What life would she have if she didn't do that . . . ?' But the indignation faded, slowly. Maybe Eileen saw sides of Zoe that she never saw. 'Is that what she said when she talked to you? What was she like with you? When she came on her own?'

All the parts of Zoe's life that she had never seen. What Alma had missed when she was at work, when other people picked Zoe up from school, when she went to friends, as she grew older, and I was glad of the empty house, glad that I could get on with things . . . and all the time Zoe was growing away. Until in the end she could not be found.

'She was lovely, of course. Goes without saying . . .' Eileen considered the question, sucking voluptuously on one of the monster tomatoes she had scorned. 'Well really she just wanted to do nothing. That's what she'd say, in so many words. She came to the beach, and swam, or sun-bathed. Sometimes she seemed to sleep all day. Last time she came, I think she was in love.'

'Of course she wasn't,' Alma said.

'Probably a crush,' said Eileen, but Alma wasn't listening any more. 'You know how crushes can be at that age.'

'I wasn't very good at letting her do nothing,' said Alma. 'I've always been afraid of wasting time. I liked her to get on with things. I always want people to get on with things . . . I'm getting itchy feet even now.'

'Now you do sound like my sister,' said Eileen. 'Gwen believes in getting on with things . . . Aren't you eating that sandwich? I'm sure you're too thin.'

'She was a year ahead at school. The head talked to me before she put her up. And she was in the fast stream, of course . . . I wanted her to do what she was capable of. I didn't want her to be bored . . .' Alma knew that this was not the whole truth. She swallowed her sandwich in a hard lump that stuck uncomfortably in her throat.

'Gwen always used to talk about you being stretched,' Eileen said. 'And you were young for your year, like Zoe. You took your eleven-plus a year early. It used to drive me mad, she said it so often, "She's a bright child, they need to be stretched." One day I told her, "She'll turn into spaghetti if you keep on stretching her all the time."'

'I never thought of that,' said Alma. 'People do talk about their children being stretched. They say it all the time. But it's so violent, isn't it . . . ?' Pulling their little bodies out of shape. Long and white and floppy like forced winter plants . . . 'Maybe Zoe felt stretched. But she should have told us . . . she could have told us, couldn't she? Paul and I weren't frightening parents. He didn't lose his temper like Owen always did.'

'Have an orange,' Eileen said. 'They're good.' They were a bit chewy but the flavour was fresh, the life was still in it, tart and bright.

'Why are you so different from Mum?' Alma asked. 'Why is it so easy to talk to you?'

'I can't sit too long or I'll stiffen up . . . finish your orange and we'll walk some more. Maybe we could go on over the rocks to Penryth . . .' Eileen stood up, effortfully, shook off the crumbs, started to pack. Was the conversation over? But Eileen was thinking. 'You can talk to me because I'm not your mother. Maybe all children make their mothers feel guilty.'

'Mother doesn't feel guilty. She thinks she's perfect.'

'She doesn't usually show her feelings. We're chalk and cheese, we always were . . . just like your two, Alma. Adam and Zoe aren't a bit alike.'

'No.'

'Haven't heard from Adam for a while . . .'

'He's fine. We think he's got a girlfriend,' said Alma.

'Good for him. I hope she's kind. Funny, I always thought he was the fragile one. I thought it would be Adam that'd give you trouble.'

'Oh, *Adam's* no trouble,' said Alma, dismissive.

And then she thought about the five hundred pounds; about

the day when he'd sounded so lonely. How he'd wanted her to go and visit his room.

'– Well, he usually keeps cheerful, anyway. And I think he likes his course,' she finished.

'He'll be rich one day, if he's a barrister,' said Eileen.

'That'll be fun,' Alma said, automatically.

If anything can ever be fun again.

Life must go on, we must go on . . . but we can't go on and leave Zoe behind. There were four of us. We were a family.

The four of us. A family of four . . .

Eileen was leading the way across the bridgehead of rocks that divided the waterfall beach from the next. Starting on the long trek down to Penryth. Out of the sun, the wind felt chill.

'I'll see how I get on,' she called over her shoulder. 'I'd like to get to Penryth beach again.' But each step was a hauling operation; winch up her foot, drag up her body.

'It's a good half-hour over the rocks,' said Alma. Eileen gasped as her knee caught against a spur of stone.

'Don't distract me,' she snapped, unlike herself. 'Don't fret. I want to get on with this.'

Alma realized her aunt wouldn't get to the top. They wouldn't even get to the next little bay. But she held her peace; she waited, shivering, clutching the bag with its empty bottles. And she was proved wrong. Slow but steady, Eileen got to the top, rested, went on, slowly and carefully over and down. Then she was back on level sand.

'Eileen . . . remember we'd have to walk back as well. There are hardly any buses from Penryth, are there?'

Eileen waved her hand dismissively, not even looking back over her shoulder. The sand was easy, but there wasn't much of it, and after this beach the rocks began in earnest, a solid belt of rock for a quarter of a mile. Eileen was so full of fight. She had an epic quality, pushing at the wind, pushing at the sun, bulky where she had once been slim, but strong; seventy-nine years strong. Stooping to check where each foot was going, and thank God she does, Alma thought, because if she slips and breaks a bone, how long will it take to get people to help her?

– That terrible imagined sound of a bone breaking, like a rifle-shot.

Please may she stop, Alma prayed. I love her for trying, but she's too old.

'Do you want to go on ahead?' asked Eileen, pausing a little way up the first slope of the big stretch of rocks they had to cover. 'I didn't realize I'd got so slow.'

And Alma heard again the deep bone-tiredness that she had noticed first on the phone, and Eileen's face wasn't right, not the right colour, and the corners of her mouth were working.

'No point in going on without you,' she said.

'Leave me alone,' Eileen breathed. 'Get on with you.'

It was too windy to argue. Alma went.

'Damn,' she heard behind her. 'Damn and blast. Damn you, damn you. Damn you to buggery.' Eileen was swearing in the wind. Alma clambered on, but tentatively.

Like giant cobblestones, every one different, rocks covered the beach from top to bottom. The distance to Penryth looked deceptively short, but not a yard of it was easy going.

– She'll have to decide. I can't tell her. She's been on this planet longer than me.

'Alma,' Eileen shouted. Alma turned round. Now she would give up: thank God for that. Eileen was perched upon a granite pillar, looking like a sea-witch with her wreath of grey hair, until you looked down and saw her huge black boots. 'Bring us that bag. We forgot to eat the peanuts.'

Alma pulled out the peanuts. Eileen looked a bit better. They ate them, neither of them saying anything.

Then 'Tide's coming in,' they said, virtually together, looked at each other, laughed out loud.

'Two minds . . .' said Alma.

'It is though, isn't it? Funny, I thought it was going out. I really thought we had a chance to get there.'

'Let's go home and have some tea.'

'You lead the way. I'll take my time.'

They stopped to catch their breath on the waterfall beach.

'When did you last go along to Penryth?' Alma asked Eileen,

loving her, stroking a strand of grey hair from her mouth.

'Last summer,' said Eileen. 'Took me half a day. I love those rocks. All my life, I've loved them . . . but I'm glad we got beyond the waterfall beach.'

'Look, *I* would have stopped at the *tourist* beach,' said Alma. 'It's thanks to you that we got this far.'

'Well you have to keep going,' Eileen said. 'Life shrinks, you see. Not for you. Not yet. But you get to realize – you've stopped doing certain things, going certain places. It just creeps up on you. And then if you don't make an effort, you know you'll never do them again . . . well, maybe I'll never get to Penryth again. But I bloody well tried. It was a bloody good try.' She looked cheerful again, her colour back to normal.

'Are you sure you're OK?'

'Never better,' said Eileen.

'I think you're terrific,' Alma told her.

'Mutual admiration club,' said her aunt.

All the same, Alma heard her laboured breath as they set off again over the last set of rocks that divided them from the tourist beach, the children's beach with its wide flat sand. And she heard her sigh, a different sound; a sigh of acknowledgement that this was a struggle.

'Nearly back,' said Alma over her shoulder.

This beach was lovely in a different way, less protected than its rocky neighbours but radiantly open, its easy slopes one sheet of light, footprintless, a swathe of white silk along the flank of the sea.

Eileen made it back, of course. Alma was waiting. They stood together, shoulder to shoulder, looking at the light, companionable, quiet.

'So empty, isn't it?' Alma said. 'Off season, of course.'

'It's not just the time of year,' Eileen said. 'Twenty years ago there would have been children even in December. Day like this, they'd all have been out. I sometimes wonder where all the kids went –'

Alma saw them emerging, gingerly at first, a head, then an arm, from behind the boats. One or two getting up from the shingle bank. Three holding hands as they stepped from the sea, children wondering whether to return, could they come back to

229

the place where they were happy, not sure if they were welcome, quiet, listening –

She looked again. The beach was empty.

'Well where did they go?'

'The towns, mostly. Bigger places. There isn't any work here out of season, so the young parents move to the cities . . . they go to England, some of them. They go to London. Like Owen. And your father. A few are still here. They need more playmates. Do you remember how many children used to play in my garden?'

'Cities aren't good places for children. Here there's so much space – city kids would go wild on this beach.'

'Your two did . . .' They didn't look at each other, walking up the beach, coming to the shingle, each of them knowing what the other was thinking.

'Mysterious, how childhood goes,' Alma said slowly, picking her way. The small stones were painful through her rubber soles. 'They seem so solid, children. So . . . complete. As if they could never change, or vanish. But they grow so quickly. They just sprint away. It seems they get to five, and then they're teenagers, and you can't believe they were ever little . . . And yet, I think about them all the time. As babies. As little children. I half-believe that they're still there, somewhere. But we can't reach them. We can't *touch* them. I dream about Zoe, and she's still small . . .'

The sun was too bright; she closed her eyes for a second. As she opened them again, she saw a flash of bare legs, small bare legs, sun-blanked faces, the children running shrieking over the pebbles, running for the sea, the lost pale bodies, wintry from being locked away.

'When I first brought you here, Alma, you were very small. Give me a hand, child, up on to the tarmac.'

Alma took the roughened hand, steadied her, supported her. Eileen wasn't light; she was a weight to lift. Once I was light, and she lifted me . . . I must be here too. My ghostly child. The child I was, and can never find.

'I wish I knew more about what I was like . . .'

'You were a darling,' Eileen said, hearing her emotion, trying to deflect it, trying to get home. 'Come on. We need a cup of tea.'

'Well all Mum ever says is that I was a good girl,' wailed Alma, indignant. 'And that can't be true, because what I most remember is being told I was selfish. Day in day out. And thoughtless . . . Now it seems she's forgotten all that. She pretends she's forgotten. I don't believe she has.'

'You're wrong,' said Eileen, with sudden vehemence. 'People get old, and they do forget. Sometimes they have to forget, to get by. They get too old to do the work of remembering.'

The speech left her struggling for breath. Though the tarmac road up to the cottage was smooth, the slope still told on them, after climbing the rocks.

Alma was aware that she had sounded sour. It was a lovely day. She wanted to be happy; she didn't want to make Eileen unhappy. 'I'm not trying to say that everything was bad. I know we were happy when Daddy was alive. Weren't we? Gwen always says he adored me.'

But her memories of Daddy were too remote. She wasn't much more than four when he died. She remembered his blondness. His tenderness. So big and handsome, with yellow hair. A cow-lick, was it, of yellow hair? But the photograph on Gwen's mantelpiece was black-and-white, neat, and meant nothing to Alma. Blond on the beach, in her memory. Them on the sand, the endless sand . . . And the terrible climax, his death without warning, Gwen's mad dry screams, as if the world were ending.

'. . . I think he gave me a ride on a horse. On the beach, I think. I wish I remembered. Or else there was a game . . . Muffin the Mule? And he smelled nice. Funny. I remember that. A sort of stinging smell, but exciting . . .'

'Probably alcohol,' Eileen said. 'Come to think of it, though, he did wear scent.'

Her voice was not encouraging. 'I'll make the tea. You're tired,' said Alma. *Tell me*, she thought. *Tell me something.*

'Yes,' said Eileen. 'But I'm all right. To tell the truth . . . I didn't like Jack. He was . . . a ladies' man. I don't want . . . to disabuse you, Alma –' The long word stuck in her mouth for a second, rolled awkwardly, choking, off her tongue. 'But I don't think it was all Happy Families.'

'Mum says how awful it was when he died—'

'Of course it was awful, that woman shooting him, and you not much more than a baby. And we never really found out what happened. All the same . . . I know he was your father, Alma. But I think Gwen was better off with Owen.'

Her voice, her face, spoke finality. She had said a lot; she would say no more. She was asking Alma, telling her. No more questions. I've done my best. I'm tired now. I am her sister.

And Alma gave way, as always. Eileen was a person. Her feelings mattered. She needed a rest. Alma left her in the kitchen.

– But am I a person?
Do I have feelings?

The bathroom had cobwebs behind the loo. The sun streamed in and made its report. The bathroom said, *old age*. This house belongs to an old person. Someone who can't quite see well enough to notice the small encrustations of dirt. The basin and bath were stained. There was a film of grey around the edge of the taps. Alma took the tooth-mug and watered the plants, which looked neglected, baked dry by the sun. They were surviving, but only just. She's too tired, thought Alma. She can't keep up. She still drives out in the van every weekday. The roads are awful. And winter's coming. But she has to keep going, or she'd feel she'd been defeated . . . it's as if she's giving up on the little things instead. Ceding unimportant bits of territory. The house has never mattered to her really, except as a place where people can come.

And people did come, as they sat drinking tea in the crowded, raggety, colourful front room with its bowl of withered oranges and its dancing dust and the piles of half-finished garments on chairs. There was not much time before Alma had to go, and half of her resented the two large cheerful girls who came knocking at the door, and were still planted four-square on the sofa when Alma's taxi came. They were sisters, eager, red-cheeked, over-weight, but enviable in their intimacy, their easy laughter, touching hands. In summer they worked in Skippers' Bar, but in winter they did alterations for Eileen, for her eyes were no longer up to fine stitching. When Alma left the older girl was arranging to leave her baby with Eileen one evening next week so she could go out with Ivor, and Eileen was saying she could leave him all night.

'Goodbye, darling. Take care of yourself.'

'I still do my share of taking care of other people . . . Thank God,' Eileen added. 'Otherwise I'd be lonely.'

'I hope I didn't tire you out with talking.'

'No . . . but remember. She is my sister.' It sounded like a reproach, but she smiled. 'And . . . Zoe will just turn up, you know. She has to. I pray for that every night, and you know I'm not one for praying.'

'If she does, I'll tell you first, after Paul.'

'Paul *and Adam* . . .' Eileen's green eyes sharpened. 'He's a lovely boy. And he loved his sister . . . Flower, you'd better tell your mother before me. Or she'd never forgive me. She's the grandmother.'

'You're kind, Aunt Eileen,' Alma called through the window of the car. Mr Jones was visibly tired of their goodbyes.

'We grew up together,' Eileen replied.

True, Alma thought. I grew up alone.

As the taxi toiled up the hill, something came back to her. Could Zoe really have been in love?

But No, she thought. Not without telling me.

She told me things. We're a close family.

30

ALMA GOT HOME just as Dafydd and Helen were leaving. Gwen was vocal in her disappointment.

'Here she is at last . . . look at the state of her . . . you look as though you've been out in the fields. She can look very smart when she wants to. She can. Now don't go rushing off . . . I'll make a fresh pot . . . Are you sure you have to go? Well then. Well then. Say goodbye, Alma. Give Dafydd a kiss . . .'

Nothing's changed, thought Alma. I'm still her little girl. But when the door had shut behind the Wyn-Ellises, they were on their own. She could try to be herself. She must try to be herself. To break the pattern. She had two hours left. She took a deep breath; her heart was beating. It was now or never. Plunge straight in.

'I've been talking about the past with Eileen,' she said. It was a challenge, although her tone was polite. Gwen knew what it was. She pursed her lips.

'Talks a lot of nonsense, Eileen does.'

'I asked her about Daddy.'

'It's none of her business!'

'I just *asked* her about him.'

'What does she know? She knows *nothing*.' Gwen was furious; they had been talking for two minutes, and she was already in a rage, flushed, shaking, her eyes too bright.

'She did *know* him . . . and it is my business. He was my father. She didn't say much.'

'You have no right to rake over the past!'

'What's the matter, Mother? I just want you to talk about him, don't you see? You always said Daddy was wonderful –' Alma was talking too fast, clumsy, placating. But it was too late to placate her mother.

'And so he was. But people have to make trouble . . . People make things dirty. It's their dirty minds.' Gwen had two spots of bright red in her cheeks.

'Mother, *I don't know what you're talking about*.' It was as if her mother had gone mad. Was this all just jealousy, because she'd spent the day with Eileen?

'If my sister thinks she can go making trouble . . .'

'She wasn't making trouble. For the last time. I *asked* her about him. You've got it all wrong. What *is* the matter?'

Gwen stared at her for what seemed like minutes before her little body began to relax, and the hectic colour in her cheeks began to fade. But she had looked . . . had she looked guilty?

'Oh . . . nothing. There was just some talk. People always gossip. And Jack was very handsome. Blond. Like a film-star. People always stared, when we walked out together . . .' Ordinary vanity began to creep back, the familiar, complacent story-telling tone. 'He said I was the best-looking girl in the village. And he would have been successful, if he had lived. I know he would. He was a real charmer . . .'

'Eileen said something about that.' *A ladies' man* . . . but I'd never tell my mother.

Gwen's voice sharpened at once. 'Did she now? I knew it. She was jealous, see. She couldn't get a husband . . . It was *nothing at all*. Nothing to worry about. Just that some people said, when Jack was killed, that he must have known the woman who did it. As if there had been something between them. Just because she had a child, people took her part . . . That was all it was, Alma, honestly.'

Yet it sounded as though she meant the opposite. Gwen often seemed to talk in opposites. The tight little yesses holding back the vast noes.

'You never told me that before. I'd like to know about him. I *have a right*. He's my father. Why won't you tell me?' Alma's voice was rising, against her will; she had never before told her mother she had rights; she had never before managed to remember them, in the paralysing presence of her mother's will.

'But why are you upsetting yourself?' Now Alma was angry, Gwen tried to sound calm. 'You've got enough on your plate. Your aunt's upset you.'

235

'Mother, it isn't Eileen.'

'What then?'

'It's . . . I don't want to have a fight. I don't want to make you angry. But it's . . . *you*, Mother.' (At last she got it out; after a lifetime of trying, she got it out.) 'It's you who upsets me. I want us to talk.' Her voice was skating up again, she couldn't control it. 'I want to know more about my childhood . . . I want to know *something* about my childhood. I want to be able to ask you things. *I want the truth! The truth! Do you hear me?*'

– She was actually shouting. She was blazing hot; her heart was thumping, thumping, thumping. She was enormous. She could burst this house. She could kill her parents with the force of her passion.

But Gwen looked shrivelled, muted, frozen. 'You're shouting at me,' she wailed. 'I think you've gone crazy. You're shouting at me!' She tried to stand up, but her knee gave way, and she crumpled, in slow motion, and crouched on the floor, thin arms round her knees, helpless, tiny, a white-faced infant, a wrinkled child, crushed to the floor by Alma's anger.

This was what Alma had done to her mother.

Gwen clutched at herself, a ball of frail bones, unimaginably small, her face animal, contorted, braying out terrible bursts of harsh tears which drew from Alma a horrified pity. This wasn't her mother, this suffering thing, this twisted, writhing living creature.

Alma managed to get her back upright. 'Mother, Mother . . .' Trying to soothe her, but the dry, corncrake sobs racked on. 'I didn't mean . . . you mustn't, Mother . . .' One strand of white lacquered hair had come loose and stuck up in the air, trembling, mad. Alma stroked it down. She held Gwen's head. She comforted her, as if she was a child. She gave what she had never been given; she gave more than she had to give.

Gwen was back in her chair. The sobs were ebbing. Alma began to breathe again. *But she'd disintegrate*, Alma thought. *She'd break into pieces before my eyes.* Whatever the truth is, it would tear her in two. I can't do that. I can't. She's my mother. I have to comfort her. I have to protect her.

And the tears were hushed with a fresh pot of tea, with

apologies, with sympathy, with urgent assurances of love; with a drawing of veils, with a long retreat.

And there was the comfort of familiarity, as she calmed Gwen down and cheered her up. To fight with her mother was indescribably frightening. To defy the tyrant. To upset the known order. It was sweet to bring back the status quo. Both had been frightened. Both of them were grateful.

'You're a good girl, Alma,' Gwen said at last, for the hundredth, the thousandth, the five thousandth time since Alma had stopped being a girl. 'That was a lovely cup of tea. Funny how different it tastes when someone else makes it for you. Probably it's just having company.'

– It was gone, Alma realized; she had blanked it all out. The whole incident was as if it had never been. 'I should come here more often,' she said automatically. 'Sorry we haven't had much time together . . .' Her coat was on; they were waiting for the taxi. 'Thank you for letting me go and see Eileen.'

– *Letting me*, she thought silently. *Just you bloody try and stop me.*

'She is my sister,' Gwen said soberly. Her little white hand clutched at Alma's sleeve, an unshelled crab, twitching, clinging.

That parting phrase rang in Alma's ears as the slow train rocked her back towards London. The sisters had known each other for nearly eighty years; for fifty of those they'd lived near each other, seen each other at least once a week. The weft of Gwen's life was disapproving of Eileen, defining herself by their differences. And Eileen faithfully drives over to see her, brings her free tights and underwear, never criticizes her. Gwen takes her for granted, like a piece of granite you never knew your home was built on.

– They were like two halves of the same person. (Or mirror-images? Good and bad . . . Alma's ideal mother, and the one she had.) There were pacts that no one could understand. Siblings went back further than husbands and wives . . .

As an only child, Alma could never know that.

That's why I'm so dependent on them for my past. There's no brother or sister I can ask. And every time I see them, they're a little bit older. Gwen has gone a little bit further off. And they'll

237

slip away, and I'll never know. I don't even know what I'm looking for . . .

Except that I need to be angry with someone. Not Paul, or Adam, or Kevin at work, or any of the people I get angry with. There was so much anger, just now, with Gwen. It felt . . . enormous. And we were both trapped. I was sorry for her. We were both so frightened . . . (I wonder if Mother has always been frightened?)

What demon had suddenly burst out of its box?

Looking back on it all, it seemed unreal; too shocking to have happened; too raw; too huge.

Did I really say those things to her? – That jolt of fear in her ribs. Did Mother crouch on the floor and howl?

Alma felt ashamed. *Why can't I just love her?*

Her heart began to beat, agitated, guilty.

But the land outside the window was calm and kind, not many lights as the dark came down, the familiar blue-grey spines of the hills, sinking into sleep like friendly animals, furred with trees, the clouds on their back. Don't make a fuss, they seemed to say, only human beings make a fuss, why can't you fit in, like everything else?

– Maybe Zoe was with the travellers. The bands of new hippies who roamed the country in dirty caravans, living rough. Maybe she was somewhere in the disappearing landscape, beyond the glass, the trees, the roads, one of those fireflies dancing in the distance, crammed in the back of some ramshackle truck. Happy, maybe. Having fun.

Just for a second she could see her so clearly that she cried out, softly, and an elderly man across the gangway raised his wild eyebrows over pebble spectacles.

'Toothache,' she lied.

'Dear me,' he quavered.

Stupid that it's painful to think of her happy, her laughing round cheeks in the back of the van, lit up for a second as they pass a garage, smiling and laughing with someone I don't know, scruffy and merry, bouncing through the darkness . . . Not that I want her to be sad, or lonely. But to think of her completely happy without us . . .

But they learn to do without us. That's what life's about. I've learned to do without Gwen so completely that I cannot stand to be in the same room . . . yet in a way I still need her. I always shall. I need her because she contains my past. Whatever I lost. My lost childhood. One day Zoe will need me too. Maybe Zoe will need me too . . .

Alma leaned her head back and closed her eyes. Going back into the smoke of the dirty city. Opened them again; the hinterlands of London. The dull net of lights that were secret lives.

Going where the children have gone before me. The swimming-pool children. All the lost children. They shouldn't be dumped at swimming pools . . . They deserve to have sea. They deserve to have sky . . .

She closed her eyes again, weary. Tresaith beach danced in the darkness before her, a dazzling window of white-tipped water. The empty sands, glittering, yearning.

Zoe, darling. Come back to me.

31

ADAM LAY ON HIS BACK on the earth in the darkness, feet down the hill, head propped on his rucksack. He was wrapped in a scarf that Great-Aunt Eileen had knitted and the overcoat which was his last present from his parents. The cold felt bracing, clear and sane. Not a lot else felt sane at the moment. The grass was wet; there would soon be a frost, but if he lay on his back he could see the sky, and if he turned his head a little to the left he could still keep an eye on the brightly-lit summit of Primrose Hill, where they were due to meet. The seat was still empty. No one around.

He wanted to see the sky, not London, which was spread like an illuminated map across the horizon at the foot of the hill, a grid of lights as far as the eye could see. He wanted to get away from London.

London meant panic, and stress, and failure, and trying to buy things he couldn't afford, and struggling to get to lectures on time, and then to take notes as fast as people spoke, and sitting through the early hours of the morning trying to write his essay for tomorrow, in the horrid strip of light in his room, the dry mean glare of the fluorescent light. He wanted to get away from the light. He would like to lie here and fall asleep, get darker and darker, colder and colder . . .

Nobody loved him. No one ever would.

London was the place of humiliation. London was the place where the beloved made you think she liked you and fancied you, pretended she wanted to stay with you, coaxed you into planning a dirty weekend – made me ask *my mother*, my mother, damn her, so now Mum's going to be curious – and then let you down, laughed at you, was amazed that you ever thought she meant it. 'Oh no,' she'd smiled, 'I couldn't possibly. Who on earth wants to spend a weekend in Kemble Hill? I mean if it was *Paris*, Adam . . .'

'I can't afford Paris,' Adam said.

Yet he couldn't believe she was really unkind. He hadn't given up on her yet. If he loved her enough, he would make her love him. It couldn't fail. He couldn't bear to fail.

The sky over London was never really dark, not like the wonderful skies in Wales, velvet black, free, enormous skies, carelessly draped in veils of stars, and he would stare upwards through Gwen's binoculars, which she said she kept for bird-watching, but he and Zoe thought she used for spying on the village . . .

I wish I could go to Grandma's. At least Grandma loves me. And Aunt Eileen. He wanted, fiercely, to hide in the darkness, to go somewhere else where no one could see him, no one from the house, or his year, or his class. But this sky wasn't a hiding-place. This sky was faintly orange, electric, the stars almost invisible. This was a wakeful, urban sky. Still, the grass was dark. The grass was kind. Cold and dark, and the rustling trees; if he closed his eyes, he could be anywhere.

They wouldn't care if I died, he thought; they couldn't care if I lived or died. *She* would, though. I know she would. He felt calmer now, and watched the clouds blow up, light orange clouds skimming up from the north, a thin fast skin flicking over the moon, so its pitted semi-circle quivered, alive.

– And I've got a spot. No wonder no one wants me. I'm only twenty-one. Life seems so long. How does Grandma keep going to eighty, with Mum not loving her, and us so far away . . . why don't Mum and Dad miss each other? Why doesn't anyone love anyone else?

Why doesn't anyone love me?

Tears of self-pity, which he knew were self-pity but decided to let fall all the same, welled up in his eyes, turning the sky to watercolour, making the faint stars bigger, splashier. *Dad loves me, though. Dad's good to me.*

He heard a shriek of laughter from the top of the hill and sat up, eagerly, but it was a couple, a pair of lovers larking about. One of them had a bottle in his hand. They stood on the bench; they were giggling, fighting. I hate them, he thought. I hope they break up. Stupid, noisy exhibitionists. The girl looks ugly and the boy looks stupid.

– But they made him feel colder, all the same.

241

He decided to get up, and buttoned his coat, jogged on the spot to warm himself up. Then he decided to go back up to the seat and nearly forgot his precious rucksack. Idiot, he thought. I'm just an idiot.

He wished she would come. He felt selfconscious now, lurking on his own with the couple there, as if all lone males were maniacs, which was what some women seemed to think . . . it's not fair, he thought, and the tears welled again. I'd never do a woman any harm. I just want to love someone, and be loved, I've got a lot to offer, but no one wants it . . . I bet that bloody couple think I'm a nutter.

'Good evening,' he said, to reassure them, but his polite voice sent them into peals of laughter before a 'Good evening, Squire,' came back from the leather-clad male, heavily satirical. Then he belched.

Die, thought Adam.

He sat on the bench, hands clenched in his pockets. Women forgot that men could get frightened. Mum and Dad always taught me that fighting was wrong, and I would do anything to avoid violence, but what am I to do if someone attacks me? Young men get attacked more than young women, the statistics say, but nobody believes them, everyone thinks only women are at risk.

He looked at his watch. Ten past. *Come on*. He did love her; he was longing to hear her warm, impatient voice call 'Adam!' – But perhaps something had happened. Perhaps she wouldn't come.

The couple wandered off, kicking at lamp-posts. Fifty yards away, someone smashed the bottle. I'm glad they didn't smash it on me. I'm glad they didn't decide to kick me. But he was angry with himself for being frightened.

– Two hands came round his neck from behind, a strong pair of hands clutched him, held him, and he shouted, convulsed with shock and fear, shouting so loud that he could hear nothing, but as he began to fight to his feet he heard her voice – 'Adam, it's me! Adam, you old silly! I didn't mean to frighten you.'

'Zoe,' he bellowed. 'For God's sake, woman!' Then '. . . Zoe, darling. Thank God you're here.'

They stood in the lamplight, hugging, grinning. 'All the same, I nearly died of shock.'

'I always used to do that to you. When you were buried in a book, and I was jealous.'

'How are you . . . ? I've got the money.'

'Mum or Dad?'

'Mum.'

'Well done. You didn't tell them . . .'

'I wish you'd let me. They're *suffering*, Zoe. If they ever find out, I know they'll hate me.'

'Nonsense. It's my fault. I made you promise.

'But if you're going to go back some day, why put it off? You could cut short the agony.'

'*Not ready yet*. Don't nag. You're my brother, not my mother.'

'I know . . . but I'm sorry for her.'

'Well how about being sorry for me?'

And Adam thought, though he said nothing, well how about being sorry for me, just for a change; just for a change, think about me. Somehow Zoe was always the focus of things . . .

But that was unfair. She was younger than him, and in a worse mess, and on her own.

'Shall we go and get something to eat?' he said. 'There's a pub down there. Are you hungry?'

In the brightly-lit pub, he saw her clearly.

Her weight had ballooned since leaving home. She used to be slim and sporty-looking. Now she was large, though she'd dressed to hide it, in straining jeans and a borrowed man's shirt. She used to be thin; she used to be smart.

'I know you're thinking how fat I am.'

'Course I'm not. It's just nice to see you.'

'Adam, you're sweet. But I'm fat as a pig. Mum would hate it, wouldn't she . . . ?'

'Course she wouldn't . . .' He felt sorry for her. 'I think they're more worried that you're starving yourself . . . they'd be relieved that you're not too thin.'

But Adam knew that Zoe was right. It mattered to Alma how people looked. He always made an effort when he went home, washed his hair, found a clean jumper. Yet his sister was still pretty enough to turn heads, with her flushed round cheeks and dark-fringed eyes, surprisingly green, greener than he remembered, and her tousled head of golden-brown hair, shaggy as a lion and as roughly groomed.

'She'd take one look at me and go through the roof.'

'She's miserable. She misses you.'

Adam felt thin and flat, as so often with Zoe, faced by her irrepressible high spirits.

'Is she all right? Is Dad all right? – Poor old Dad, chucked out on his neck.'

'I think his landlady's keen on him.'

Adam saw his sister give a shiver of displeasure, and wished he had not made the remark.

'I do want to see him,' she said, sadly. 'I loved my Dad. He was all right.'

'I still don't really get it,' Adam said. 'I mean, there are lots of *worse* parents. Mum can be a pain, but she's not that bad. And you two always seemed so close. I mean, you never even *rowed*.'

'That was part of the problem,' Zoe said. 'Are we going to have something to eat, or what? I may be fat, but I'm still hungry . . . I always worried about hurting her.'

'Don't you miss sport?' Adam asked cautiously, looking at her arm as she pulled off her coat, well-shaped, muscular, not yet fat, all the fat seemed to be on her face and neck and the middle of her body, under layers of clothes. 'You loved swimming. And hockey. And gym, didn't you. You were in all the teams. I wasn't.'

'I don't miss it,' she said vehemently. 'I'll have a beef pie with baked beans and chips, and a whisky with a lager chaser.'

'*What?*' said Adam. 'Since when have you been drinking whiskies with chasers?'

'I'll pay,' she said angrily. 'Give me my money. I can drink what I want. I'm not a child.'

She ripped open the envelope and paid for them both. She seemed to settle down when she started eating; or was it once the lager was slipping down her throat? She had a different presence from before; she was larger, louder, more aggressive. The change didn't make her more lovable, but he sensed a fragility underneath.

'I do miss swimming,' she suddenly said. 'Just lying on the water, creaming along. I'm too dirty to swim. And I wouldn't fit my swimsuit. I don't fit any of my old clothes.'

Something struck Adam with the force of a blow, staring at his sister, red-cheeked, plumped-out.

'Zoe . . . don't get mad. But you're not pregnant, are you?'

Tears began to trickle, like a tap turning on. She stared at the wall, and the flow increased. 'Not now,' she whispered, could say no more. 'Not now. I'm not . . .'

Adam sat in silence, patting at her arm, his stomach turning.

'. . . You *were* pregnant?'

'I wish I was still pregnant! I wish I was! I wouldn't care about anything . . . I wish I was fat because I was pregnant. But I'm not, am I? They took it away.'

'You left home because you were pregnant . . . my God. I've been so thick.'

'Maybe I would have left home anyway . . . She worried too much. She minded too much. It would have broken her heart –' She was calmer now, but the tears still fell, a slow release of the pressure within.

'I don't agree . . . she would have been all right. Mum loves babies. She's soft about them. She's talked to me about grand-children.'

'Now you are being thick,' Zoe shouted. 'Don't make it worse for me. I know! I know she loves babies, I know she hates abor-tions! I wanted an abortion! I couldn't face telling her! The awful thing is . . . maybe she's right. I feel unhappy, all the time. I feel empty. I feel . . . bad. I feel like a *bad person*. I never felt like that before.'

'I feel like that quite often . . . but you're not a bad person. You did what was best. How could you go to college, with a baby?'

'I don't want to go to college. I don't want anything. I don't even want to live, at the moment.'

Yet he could see her cheering up, as she said those things, those angry things he could never say. Those things he felt, and quickly stifled.

'Don't say that,' he said. 'It's unlucky.'

'I don't suppose I really mean it.'

I do though, Adam thought, but he smiled. 'It will all be better once you have your new place. It must have been horrible for you.'

'You can't imagine. You're a bloke.'

'I'm not a bloke, I'm your brother, damn it. I get fed up of being seen as a bloke. Men do have feelings. I care about you . . .'

'Sorry. I know. But you meet some bastards.'

'You are going to tell me your address, aren't you? It is OK, isn't it? The place where you're going.'

'It's two stops from the job. Of course I'll tell you. You can come and help me carry out some of the junk.'

'What junk? They have no right to leave junk in it. Not if you're paying out eighty pounds a week. Not if they're asking you for four weeks' deposit.'

'– It's supposed to be furnished. That's the junk.'

'– Actually, Zoe, *my* furniture's junk. You just put up with it, in furnished rooms.'

'I'd just like to make it nice. I want life to be . . . less awful again. I want to . . . make a go of things. You know, lose weight. Get my act together. Get on with something. Do well at my job. Don't look like that, don't be such a snob, it is a job, there were hundreds of applicants! I did well at the interview. I used my brains. I had a bath at a hostel. I made myself look nice.'

'I know, all right, don't be so touchy . . .'

'Mr Bighead Barrister, ashamed of his sister.'

'If I were ashamed, I wouldn't be here, and you wouldn't have your five hundred pounds.'

They ate for a while in silence. Zoe's drink disappeared with remarkable speed; she tossed back the lager, and looked at him expectantly.

'I'm not going to get you another whisky. You can have a lager, but that's your lot.'

'You're depressed about something,' she pronounced. 'You're depressed about me. Well don't be.'

'I could be thinking about myself for once.'

'No, it's me. Me working in Woolworth's.'

'Well since you mention it, it is a bit odd . . . I mean you were always the brilliant one. You were going to Oxford, they thought you'd get a scholarship . . .'

'They never asked me, they told me. Or . . . they asked me in a way which was telling me.'

'They would *faint* to know what you're doing. I think Mum imagines you on the streets, or shivering on Hungerford Bridge, collecting shekels from art-lovers . . . She goes looking for you, you know. They both do. Or else she thinks you're hitching round the world with a backpack.'

'That's typical Mum. Even when I run away, she wants to make a triumph out of it. She wants to think I'm romantic and brave. She'd love to tell everyone I'd been around the world. Well I bloody haven't, I've been in a squat, a dirty, disgusting squat behind Praed Street, and now I'm getting out, and I'm getting a job, and if she doesn't like it she can bloody lump it!'

'You never talked to *her* like that . . .'

'It isn't easy, standing up to Mum.'

Adam thought about that. Of course it was true. But Mum only wanted the best for them. Especially for Zoe. Her tremendous pride . . . 'It's not so bad, her being proud of you.'

'That proves you don't understand a thing about me.'

She's sure she's the most important person in the world, Adam realized, with a little sigh of weariness. I wish I could feel that just occasionally. She's sixteen years old, and misunderstood, and enjoying it, and it makes me hate her. *Mum and Dad love her, and she doesn't care.*

'I've got to go soon,' he said, coldly.

'I want another drink.' Her large sulky mouth. She was better-looking than he'd ever be; even fat, even scruffy, she was better-looking. She made him feel too blond, too transparent.

'You're sixteen. You're under age. Buy it yourself. But I think I'll shop you.'

'Big brother,' she said darkly, but then her mood changed as her fingers touched the packet of money. 'Oh well. Never mind. You brought me the dough. Will you walk me to the tube?'

'I ought to see you right back to the squat . . . will it be safe there, with that lot?'

'They're all my *friends*. Just because it's a squat . . .'

'Zoe, they're homeless – be reasonable . . .'

'Well that's another thing you don't understand. You look at people like them – people like *me* – you think homeless people are different. Because they look dirty, or a few of them are drunk – and everyone notices the ones who are drunk—'

'Don't get excited, I didn't mean—'

'They're *not* different.' She was standing up, over-animated, large, indignant, looking round for the way out as she over-rode him, shouted him down. 'Most of them are intelligent people. They're *normal* people, like you and me. They're not frightening. You just think they are. Well a few of them are mad, but mostly – it's just that something *happened* to them. Something very bad. Or too many small things. And they fell through the net . . . They're *not* different . . .' she repeated, lamely, her impetus going as she neared the door and a faint cool draught began to eat at the edge of her well-being. '*You* could be homeless. *I've* been home-less.' She looked over her shoulder at her glum-faced brother; whatever she saw irritated her. 'You've got so straight, now you're a lawyer.'

'Good job one of us is straight.'

They pushed their way into the chilly street. Ghostly siblings fought and jostled. As the true cold hit her, she turned and con-ceded, 'In any case, I shan't tell anyone I've got the money.' But her tone was grudging; she avoided his eyes.

Her walk was still powerful, athletic, bouncy inside her mound of clothes. She's still very young, he reminded himself. Very young, and yet she was expecting a baby . . . she couldn't be ready to be a mother. It was shocking to think of her as a mother. But moving too. She half-wanted the baby . . . I would have been an uncle. I'd have liked that. For a moment he was swept with tenderness.

– But she'd done something practical. She *coped*. She always coped. At someone else's expense. She gets her way. She always did. And she isn't grateful. She calls me *straight* . . .

They walked in silence towards the tube, into the orange flares of streetlight then out again, into the present then back into the past, both of them locked in their own trains of thought.

'Actually you're pretty straight as well,' Adam said to her, as they turned the corner and saw the red and white disc of the underground sign.

'How can you say that?' she expostulated, tugging at the ticket in her overstuffed pocket. 'I've seen more things than you ever will. I've lived on the streets. I've done things—'

'*Don't tell me.*'

'I found I could do without you all.' Her cheeks were blazing in the light from the station, her voice was rising, she looked almost ugly, her mouth was scornful, desperate. *What things had she done?* Was this really Zoe?

He wanted to shake her. *She was his sister.* 'Oh don't go thinking you're such a rebel. You've got yourself a room, and you want it nice. You've got yourself a job, and you're proud of it. I think you're still trying to be a good girl.'

The touchpaper lit in one flaring motion. 'Fuck off,' she screamed at him. 'Fuck off interfering. I don't need you. I don't need the family. You're so fucking smug. You think you know everything –'

And then the tears gushed, and she turned away, and he just caught a glimpse of her wet, contorted face before her feet went thundering into the station, and he skidded after her – 'Zoe!' – before a fresh wave of anger brought him to a halt; how dare she say that she didn't need him, when he'd just brought her five hundred pounds? How dare she say that she didn't need the family? He stood there irresolute, shaking with rage.

And she never asked about me, not once. And I let Mum think that the money was for me! He moaned with frustration, crumpling his rucksack. He was left with nothing; always empty-handed.

After a minute or two the anger drained away. She *was* just a child. He felt miserable. He'd offended her, and he loved his sister, and he hadn't even got her new address . . . He thought about abortions; blood and suction. She must be grieving. He hadn't been kind . . . And he'd lost his girlfriend, or never really had her. He didn't know anything. He was a fool.

He went after Zoe, he plunged down into the nightmare tunnels, but the platforms were empty. She was gone as if she had never been, lost in the maze under the orange-lit city, the labyrinth of winds and hidden knives and sudden blind endings, of mess and loss.

Later as he made his own way back, hundreds of feet below the thundering traffic, below the drains, below the rats, he thought he saw her everywhere, huddling with others in the corners of tunnels, their faces a peculiar livid grey colour, passing cigarettes from one to another, companionable but strangely glum, the lost children in their terrible numbers, growing up, growing older, still waiting for something, and he knew that they would never go home, and they waved as if he were one of them.

32

'THIS IS SO NICE,' said Paul to Peeky, suffused with simple gratitude. 'I can't tell you what it means to me.'

He saw her broad, shallow face flush instantly, from chin to hairline, and wished he had put it another way, but it did mean a lot, a tremendous amount, to come into Peeky's warm kitchen this Friday, hollow with hunger, his neck and shoulders strung tight with the tension from crazed kids and crazier parents, to find her kneeling in front of the oven, her pretty neck under a bell of blonde hair, the smell of beef casserole filling the room, steaming up the windows behind the check curtains, her strong bare arms, her happy smile as she turned and noticed it was him, and this was all for *him*, how could it possibly be, the warmth, the food, her kneeling, her smiling? 'It smells fantastic,' he hurried to say, not wanting to embarrass her.

'Taste it first,' she said, pert, cheerful. 'I like it too, cooking for someone. Long time since I had someone at home. Three years, must be, since Barry left.'

'Barry? . . . oh yes, of course, your boy.'

'My boy,' she said, with tremendous pride. 'Off to university. First in the family. I miss him though. Don't see him much.'

'You must be proud of him,' said Paul, absently, watching her pile the food on his plate.

'And you of yours,' she said. 'Your boy.' She knew about Zoe, though they hadn't really talked about it.

'I was proud of Zoe too . . . this is delicious. She was beautiful. She *is*.' He thought about it, his mouth full, his body responding, glowing, to the warmth. Where he was cold, now he was warm. Where he was hungry, now he was nourished. Where he was despairing, he was consoled. This was wonderful. She was wonderful. When was the last time he had felt happy?

'Shall we open some wine?' Peeky said timidly. 'I have *got* some. I keep some in.' The more she tried to make it sound as though she always had wine, the clearer it became that she'd bought it for him. He opened it flamboyantly, king of the kitchen, poured two large glasses, took a deep drink.

'I sometimes wonder about this pride business. I think we over-did it, with Zoe. Because she seemed to be good at everything. One of those children who are good at everything . . .'

'Was she? Lucky you,' said Peeky. She looked at him hard, with big round eyes. She wore a black cotton top that clung to her body. Her breasts, he noticed, were firm and young.

'But it didn't *matter*,' Paul persevered. 'The times I remember aren't when she won things, or got picked for things, or won prizes. I remember when we had fun. When she was little, and needed me.'

'Bless her heart,' said Peeky. 'You *do* love them, when they're babies, don't you?'

They ate in contented silence. Peeky re-filled his plate; he re-filled her glass. He took off his jacket. He saw her look at him approvingly. He drank some more. He thought about Zoe.

I used to love it when she came into our bed. Pajama jacket, never wore the trousers. Snuggled between us, always in the middle. Stroked my beard, complained it was bristly. Later I shaved it off, and she cried . . . her little round legs, her dimpled knees. Her feet would be cold, and she'd plant them on my thighs . . . She'd stroke Alma's hair, and if she didn't wake up the strokes would get rougher and turn into pulls . . . She would kiss us and bite us. Love-bites. She laughed at my cock. At Daddy's willy. She liked to look at it. Her wonderful innocence, children's innocence . . . how can parents abuse their children, when the children give us so much power? . . . Just by loving us, trusting us. And they are sexual, without knowing it. We can see that. We have to protect them.

Bathing Zoe. In the bath with Zoe. After her mother taught her to swim, she found she could float in our big bath, with just one hand, or an elbow, on the bottom, her head right back, her hair floating out, just a tiny pale circle of face above the water, and once I came in and thought she had drowned, her eyes were closed, a little Ophelia . . .

But her favourite thing was bathing with us. Having one of us in there with her, alongside her till she got too big, then facing each other from opposite ends, and she'd push her little knees between mine, my big ones mountainous compared to hers, enfolding her, protecting her, I thought I would always be able to protect her . . .

'Have you got toothache?' Peeky asked, concerned.

'No, I was thinking about my daughter.'

'Oh dear,' she said, all sympathy. 'You poor man. It's awful. And then your wife goes and lets you down . . .'

He didn't demur. Her sympathy was balm. She made him some coffee. She poured him some brandy. Time became fluid. The light was too bright. But magically, someone had turned it down.

They were sitting on the sofa, quite close together. She was telling him how her husband had cheated her. 'And then people get a good man, like you – a kind man, with a decent job, because Stan couldn't keep a job for five minutes – and they don't appreciate you! It's crazy.'

He was on his second brandy. Life was sweet. All kinds of pain had crept away into the shadows. This was the present. This was good. She looked remarkably pretty with her hair untidied, strands of blonde hair over her wide forehead. He looked at her knees. She wasn't wearing stockings. She looked at him looking at her knees.

'Aren't you cold?' he asked. 'It is December.'

'Are you?' she asked. 'You only have to say . . . I'm warm-blooded. Don't feel the cold.'

'I've never felt warmer in my life,' he said, but his voice sounded odd, as if his tongue didn't fit, and he tried it again, he wanted her to know. 'This is marvellous,' he said. 'Feel really happy. Doesn' happen often. Think I'm a bit pissed –'

The telephone rang. They jumped, guiltily, realizing how close together they were sitting.

'I bet it's your *wife*,' Peeky said, not bothering to conceal her annoyance. She answered it; held it out to Paul. 'Your *son*,' she giggled, covering the mouthpiece. 'They do pick their moment, don't they.'

And Paul realized, unequivocally, that she expected him to

make love to her, and he felt a hot rush of lust and excitement . . . plus a tiny cold shiver of anxiety.

'Dad,' said Adam, 'I need to talk to you.'

'Actually,' said Paul, 'I'm a bit busy just now.'

'I'm not feeling very good,' said Adam.

'What's the matter?' Paul asked, trying not to sound irritated, trying to sound interested and kind; but *he* felt good, for once in his life, so couldn't Adam feel good, couldn't he make an effort?

'It's complicated,' said Adam. 'I couldn't come round and see you, could I? Even stay the night?' There was a pause. 'I suppose I couldn't . . .'

'I've got a friend here,' Paul lied, clumsily. 'Of course you can, if it's urgent. But can it wait? Couldn't we have lunch, say, on Saturday?'

'Yes,' said Adam. He sounded hopeless. 'I'm sorry, Dad. I just feel depressed.'

'Everyone gets depressed,' said Paul, disloyal, watching Peeky bending over the table, her sturdy shoulders, her indented waist, the twin curves where her back dipped inwards to her spine. 'Everyone sometimes feels depressed, at your age. Look, see you Saturday – the Dog and Duck. We could go for a walk, after lunch.'

'Yes,' said Adam.

'Are you *sure* you're all right? Because if you're not . . .'

'Yes,' said Adam.

Paul put the phone down, and began to feel bad. A headache started to eat his pleasure, but Peeky felt fine, Peeky felt affectionate. This time she sat down touching him, and Paul realized he was going to kiss her, it was the only possible conclusion –

The phone rang again. 'Damn,' said Peeky.

And it was his mother, but she was someone else, smaller, more frightened, trying to be calm.

'Your father has had another stroke.'

'Is he all right? Are you all right?'

'His speech is very bad, this time. They say it might get better. He can still make it to the bathroom, but it isn't easy.'

'I'll have to ring Alma. We're coming,' he said.

'I'm not sure he'd want you to see him like this . . . it would only upset you. Maybe in a few days time . . .'

253

The conversation worried on. His stomach had dropped, hung in his pelvis, full of dread, deadly, metallic.

In the background, Peeky was cleaning the table, banging the saucepans on the draining-board. He realized the light had gone up again; he felt himself shrinking in its acid blast; the warmth of the food contracted, retreated, he became a small unhappy man, but he didn't want to, he wasn't ready yet, he wanted a little while to be happy . . .

'Shouldn't I come? I ought to come.' But he knew she would not tell him to come.

'You can't do much.' She sounded undecided. He knew that if he wanted he could bear her down, he knew she probably wanted him to over-ride her, tell her that nothing would stop him coming.

But he didn't really want to go. He wanted to stay here. He wanted life. She had never liked to bother her children; it was so easy to let her persuade him.

'Anyway, Anne'll be here this weekend.' She sounded happy that his sister was coming.

'Wonderful,' he said, but he knew he sounded empty. 'Great . . . so maybe we could do the *next* weekend.' Now that he was in trouble, he needed that *we*. 'Or before, of course, if anything happens. I'm having lunch with Adam this Saturday –' Trying to make his time sound full, virtuously full of family activity. But why am I doing this? I love my Dad. Yet he didn't know if he would love the changeling, the body with its terrifying transformations.

'Bless you,' his mother said, tired, loving. 'I'll ring again –'

'Take care,' Paul said. 'Take care of yourself.'

That limpest of formulas. He put the phone down. *He* should be taking care of *them*. As he stood there brooding, the radio came on, loudly playing a discordant love-song.

Peeky was washing up. 'Do you mind?' she asked him, briskly. 'I like a bit of music when I wash up. Are you all right? You look a bit funny.'

'My father's not well.'

'Oh dear,' she said, scrubbing at the casserole dish, but she didn't sound as sympathetic as before. 'Nothing serious, I hope.'

'Another stroke.'

'Oh dear.' She switched the radio off, but she went on with

her work. 'I heard you say you were going to ring your wife. Do you mind doing it now, while I do the washing-up? – Because I want to ring my son, later.'

'I've annoyed you,' he said, humble, miserable, but also wanting to ring Alma, to talk to someone who understood. He was almost sober. He'd make himself sober.

'No,' she said. She stopped washing up, and looked at him. 'It's just a reminder, that's all. Your wife still means a lot to you.'

And it was true, but as she turned, her breasts were so beautiful, she had been offering them, only half an hour ago . . .

'Well, yerrss . . .' he burbled, temporizing. *But you're nice too. You would be nice.* Not quite sober. Not wholly contracted.

But the phone rang again.

'It's for you,' she said, but she managed a grin that said the game was up. 'Not our evening, is it?'

'Who is it?' he hissed.

'Business, I think –'

'Is that Paul Bennett?'

'Yes.'

'We tried to phone you in the daytime.'

'Yes.'

'This is the North-West London Counselling Centre.'

'What?'

There was a pause, then the woman spoke more slowly and distinctly, clearly annoyed. 'You telephoned us. You registered for marital counselling . . .'

'*Oh* . . . Yes . . . I'm sorry . . . Yes.'

Sorry I did it. Sorry you've rung. He felt intensely guilty, caught out like this with Peeky. Would they know Another Woman had answered the phone?

'We have a cancellation for a six-week session. It's every Friday lunch-time at one o'clock. Forty-five minutes. If you want it –'

'I'll have to ask my w . . . I'll have to ask.'

That night he lay alone, as usual, in his creaky bed in Peeky's third bedroom, and his limbs were restless from the excess of alcohol, but he felt quite cheerful, as he tossed and turned. When he spoke to Alma, she was kind. Alma had been concerned about him. Alma had been eager to visit his father. Alma had agreed to start counselling on Friday.

255

Things would get better. Things might work out. They didn't all have to fly apart for ever. Thank heavens he hadn't slept with Peeky (though it would have been nice . . . what would it have been like?). Somehow the family would come back together. All for the best, thought Paul, and slept.

33

PAUL ARRIVED ALONE at the smart black door of the forbiddingly expensive address he had been given. He felt selfconscious ringing the bell, though the brass door-plate gave away nothing. *People would see him. People would know.* They would think he was a failure, or a narcissist. He wished he wore a notice saying 'BUSY HEADTEACHER. HERE BECAUSE OF FAMILY TRAGEDY.'

Inside, the building wasn't smart at all.

Still, I'm sure that Alma could still sell it for a million. It's four storeys. It could hold eight flats . . . I hate her working at Portico and Sheen. They're riff-raff, estate agents. Dishonest bastards. And yet she likes it. Really enjoys it. I hope she doesn't talk about it today.

The receptionist took his name and told him, 'Mrs Bennett hasn't got here yet.'

Into the little waiting-room, which was exactly like a dentist's waiting-room, or any of the rooms all over the West where people wait for unpleasant things to happen to them, listening to the clock, swishing magazines, glancing uneasily at each other, protecting their pain with walls of glass.

There were three people there already, one man, two women, all looking furtive, to Paul, with brief intervals of trying to look sanguine, *I'm OK, you're OK, we all know why each other is here and that's OK, as well* . . . Then they relapsed into furtiveness. Paul wanted to laugh, to break the silence, and was grinning when Alma came in like a whirlwind.

She's lovely, he thought, as the other man looked at her, noticing as he always did her wonderful wind-blown billows of tallow, her fabulous hair. She has mythic hair. Electra, was it? Medusa, maybe . . .

'What a *rush*,' she said, accusingly. 'Train didn't come. I got a cab, in the end . . . how on earth did you manage to get time off?'

'I am the head,' he said. 'I had nothing timetabled around this lunch-break. Of course I'll get back to find a pile of paperwork . . . maybe we could share a cab back.'

They sat smiling and talking about not very much, looking at each other, enjoying looking, for they couldn't take it for granted any more. The other victims seemed to be regarding them accusingly, as if they shouldn't have been talking to each other.

The receptionist came to the door. 'Mr and Mrs West,' she said. A man and a woman who had appeared unconnected got up without smiling and walked out together.

'I thought they were waiting for other people,' Alma whispered, and she touched Paul's arm. Paul thought Good, we're not as bad as them . . .

But maybe the Wests were still living together.

'Mr and Mrs Bennett.'

Up the stairs, four storeys of stairs, to the very top.

'Thirty people could be housed in here,' Paul muttered to Alma. She said nothing. On the third landing they crossed with a couple coming down, who passed within inches of them, not meeting their eyes; the woman was weeping, sniffing up loudly, failing dreadfully, snot on her chin, her hands stuffed with tissues, her face wet and boneless, temporarily re-made as a baby's.

Just before they went into the room and met their counsellor, Alma hissed into Paul's ear, 'I'm not bloody well going to do that.'

But the first thing they saw was a box of tissues, sitting on the table in front of the counsellor.

Alma was glad it was a woman, at least. She was younger than Alma, but not too young. Mid-forties, say. She wore a wedding ring. Both of them had feared they would get someone stupid, someone who would talk down to them; someone who lectured, someone who judged; someone who took sides, but not with them. 'But I'm sure they've been taught not to be judgemental,' Alma had said to Paul on the phone. 'I'm worried they'll do the opposite,' he said. 'Say nothing at all. Leave it all to us . . . and look where *that's* got us, already.'

Jeanette wasn't stupid. She was very quick. She had bright blue eyes which darted about, sharpening, softening, questioning. Alma thought, I like the look of her. And perhaps she'll like me. She was cheerful, too, which surprised them, after meeting the weeping couple; they'd expected someone with a grave demeanour, someone reacting to a traffic accident. Alma looked at Paul, and Paul at Alma. Both of them began to relax.

They began with a few of the facts. 'So you're living apart. When did that begin?' They told her about their daughter. She didn't ask much about Zoe; 'We'll talk about that later,' she said.

'But it's the reason we broke up,' Paul exclaimed, annoyed. 'We would never have parted if she hadn't left home.'

Jeanette said nothing, but she looked at him, and what he said no longer sounded truthful. 'We wouldn't, would we?' He turned to Alma.

'I don't know. Not just at that moment, maybe,' she said.

Jeanette had a distractingly pretty blouse, creamy lace, which made Alma think of Eileen, her strong brown feet in the lacy waves, the footprints sucking and filling with water, drawing in the sand to round them over.

Surprisingly soon, they came to the past. Jeanette had asked them about themselves, but both of them began to talk about their families. Paul was loyally affectionate about his. Alma listened in silence, and then began to dig.

'But your mother did everything in the house.'

'That was normal, at the time.'

'But she did get tired.'

'She loves my father.'

'Yes, I know she does, but we've talked about it, she's unfulfilled – she wishes she had travelled, she wishes she had gone on nursing –'

'She's nursing my father.'

'Don't be ridiculous, that's not the same . . . And your father never talks about his feelings. Your mother is *full* of feelings.'

'Well she's never said those things to me.'

'She did to *me*.'

They stared at each other, silently deadlocked. It felt improper to argue like this in front of Jeanette.

'We shouldn't be quarrelling about my parents,' said Paul,

trying very hard to sound reasonable. He so patently wanted the therapist to like him, and Alma shot him a dirty look, but the situation suddenly struck her as funny.

'No,' she said. 'Let's quarrel about ourselves, instead.'

'Right,' he said. He managed a grin. He went on talking, a little more cautious.

'Did your parents argue much?' the counsellor asked.

'Never. Hardly ever. Dad couldn't abide it . . . he was a very calm man. He liked things calm.'

'And you?' Jeanette asked.

'Yes. Me too.'

'Well I don't *enjoy* arguing,' Alma said. 'But if you keep everything quiet . . . if you suppress everything you feel that isn't happy . . . you explode, in the end. Or just wither. Don't you?'

Jeanette said nothing, but she was nodding at Alma. Then it was Alma's turn to talk.

'My father died when I was four. My mother's still alive,' she began. 'I can't talk to her. She won't listen.' She found anger rising, taking her aback. 'I have never, never been listened to. But recently . . . I began to try . . .' She had to stop to get her breath. 'It's not Paul's fault. I don't think so. I mean . . .' She turned to Paul, tried to touch his arm, but he was sitting too far away. 'You took me for granted, didn't you. I *meant* to say – you took me as you found me. And when I started to get angry – maybe five years ago? – I think it was me who minded. I felt so guilty . . . it made me guilty to be so angry. Sod it! Why should I always feel guilty? . . . You must get bored with women's guilt.' She smiled at Jeanette, tried to be urbane, tried to conspire with the professional, tried to rise above her predicament and above the tide of feeling that surged up through her; but her heart pounded, her throat felt tight, and Jeanette did not return her smile.

'Do you really feel boring?' she asked, simply. Alma swallowed, and pressed on.

'I wasn't allowed to have feelings. I think my mother was frightened of feelings. My stepfather was boiling over with anger, and we spent our lives trying to keep him calm. I was a naughty child, they always told me I was naughty, of course I was an only child . . .' Alma's voice was doing something peculiar, choking, contorting, letting her down.

'I *wasn't* naughty! I *wasn't* selfish! How could I be selfish with a mother like that? Why shouldn't I be selfish, for once in my life? I want to be selfish! I want to have a self!'

She realized, with shame, that she was crying. Oh, *not* the box of tissues. Damn the box of tissues. But Jeanette was handing her the box of tissues.

'I didn't want to cry,' she sniffed, dabbed. 'I didn't want to be like everyone else.'

'Everyone cries sometimes,' said Jeanette. 'It's not so bad to be like other people,' but she said it kindly, not patronizingly, and Alma screwed up the tissue and went on.

'I sometimes feel . . . I sometimes *felt* . . . I don't think I feel it so much any more . . . I try not to . . . I try to be myself . . .'

'*Say* it,' said Paul. 'Say what you mean.'

'I'm *trying* to,' said Alma, angry, despairing. Paul himself was not the most articulate of men. She tried to find the little core of pure pain where the truth must be hidden. 'I used to feel I hadn't got a face,' she burst out. 'I know that sounds mad, but I did. I used to be surprised that people could see me. And any photograph of myself looked good, because there I was, I looked like a person . . . I felt I didn't exist. Not really. I just reacted to other people. I couldn't say no. I could never say no. I wasn't allowed to. It was wrong . . . I had to give them whatever they wanted . . .'

'Who?' asked Jeanette, who was listening intently, bent forward in her chair.

'*Him*,' she was weeping. 'My parents . . . Father . . . I don't *know*. I don't *know* who started it . . . I had *no right* to say no to them . . . But I did have a right. I must have had a right! I did exist! I did have a self . . . but somehow I lost it. It was taken away. I don't know how. I don't know what happened.'

'"Father" was your stepfather, was he?'

'Yes . . . he was fond of me, but terribly possessive. They both imagined things, when I was growing up. I was very innocent, until I left home. But he always accused me of having boyfriends. He stopped me wearing lipstick and eye makeup. Wouldn't even let me get my hair done . . . . It was insulting, really. I was insulted . . . Once I came in from a dance twenty minutes late. I was sixteen years old. I had been *dancing*. He was waiting at the bottom of the stairs . . . He completely lost his temper, he chased me upstairs, he shook me so I fell backwards on the bed and then he hit me, when I couldn't resist him . . .' Alma's words spilled out in a torrent of rage, it was as real as yesterday and just as painful.

'It was an *abuse!*' she shouted, her angry voice, her real voice, the voice that would fight for her and maybe save her, 'I was *innocent! It was an abuse!*'

She stopped and wept, and the room was silent. Paul was looking at her, struck with pain, and Jeanette was concentrated, waiting.

Her words echoed. Alma heard them. She read their meaning in Jeanette's face.

'Why did you say that?' Jeanette asked. 'I wonder why you chose the word *abuse*?'

'Because it's true . . . not literally. I don't think so. He wasn't like that.'

'You wouldn't necessarily remember . . . most people don't remember.'

There was a pause. Alma saw a white wall, a blankness. A blind expanse behind the tears. The physical blankness of snow, or hot sand. In this painful blankness, a word vibrated. The word was hard. It stung. It hurt. Remember. What was she being asked to remember? 'I'm sorry. I've lost the thread of this.' As she spoke, the wall of white light contracted, shrank to a glimmer, a chink in the distance, and suddenly she felt she wanted it back; it had been bright, not dark; there was something behind it. She wept for it. She groped for the question.

'Let's go back a bit,' said Jeanette. 'When you say that you feel you haven't got a face . . . that is quite common among victims of abuse.'

'Let me be clear . . . you mean sexual abuse?'

'Do *you* think you might have been sexually abused?'

Alma tried to get a grip on herself, tried to put herself on the side of reality, tried to be strong, and humorous, and not a victim, not a case study, though the tears ran on, against her will, weeping from some far distant place, weeping for terror of the hot white sand. 'Everyone's been abused these days, haven't they? It's fashionable, isn't it, sexual abuse?'

'You were angry, and very upset, just now,' said Jeanette, riding the rejection, riding the sarcasm. 'You said you were innocent . . . *it was an abuse.*'

262

'I don't think I was abused,' said Alma. 'I don't *want* to think I was abused, of course. But . . . Father was not that kind of man. Owen was angry, but not furtive, not a lecher . . . I don't think. I mean, he had principles . . . it would have been against his principles. But there are other kinds of abuse, aren't there. It wasn't right, the way they treated me . . .'

'If they were still alive, it might help you to say so.'

'Only my mother, and I can't talk to her . . . I went and tried, just the other week. She remembers both her husbands as perfect.'

'Some people find it helps to write a letter.'

'I can't do that,' Alma said. 'She's old and frail. It wouldn't be right. She's supposed to have a heart condition. When I see her she seems so little and sad . . . yet sometimes I could physically murder my mother.'

Paul said, 'You never used to get so angry. I mean when we were first married, you never did. You began to get angry a few years ago . . . and then recently you seem to be exploding all the time. Mostly at me.'

'I'm sorry,' Alma said, automatically.

'No, I don't mind, I love you,' he said. Then he thought about it, and sat back in his chair. 'Actually it is pretty unpleasant.'

Which made Alma smile; he could still make her smile. And yet the tears had not stopped flowing.

'Can you think of anything that triggered the anger?' Jeanette asked. The session was drawing to a close; Alma noticed her looking at the clock on the wall, and a sense of panic constricted her chest, there wouldn't be time, it would never be spoken, it would slip away, that glimmer of freedom, that chink of light into a long-lost room, the light which fell on the child who was waiting, who had waited always for help to come.

'It was when Zoe went that I got angry all the time. When I lost my girl. My beautiful daughter. I felt I had lost a part of myself . . . I felt . . . there was a gaping hole in me.'

'It was the second time that you lost yourself,' Jeanette said, gently. 'We'll have to finish. We'll talk about this again next week.'

They got up to go, but there was something else. Jeanette's face said that they weren't quite done.

'We've forgotten to pay,' said Alma, guilty, her normal self again, a normal worry. *Why couldn't Paul have remembered it?*

'Thirty pounds,' said Jeanette. 'A cheque would be fine.'

They lingered in the street outside, not entirely friendly, but bonded by pain, the intensity of what they had just lived. Alma felt dizzy, not quite real.

'Shall we go and have a coffee?' Paul said.

'No,' she said curtly. But she didn't walk away. 'You're an old fraud,' she said. 'You tried to play Mr Nice Guy, didn't you? Just to get that woman on your side.' Her voice was accusing, miserable. Yet she didn't want to quarrel with him; it wasn't him that she meant at all; she hated someone, but it wasn't her husband.

'Didn't you like Jeanette?' asked Paul, surprised.

'Yes . . . but I don't think I believe her. That I was *abused*. It's too glib, isn't it?' She suddenly began to cry, and he took her hand, turned her towards him, away from the street, away from the faces of the passers-by, into his body, protecting her.

'Why don't you say what you think?' she gasped.

'Well maybe . . . I don't know . . . they must know their stuff. I don't *know*, Alma, for God's sake. I never thought of this before. I mean, you always seemed fairly normal to me—'

'*Are you saying I'm not normal? Yes! You bastard!* You *want* to think it's true, because then everything can be *my* fault, can't it?'

She wrenched her hand away from him, and marched down the road, half-sobbing with fury.

He ran after her. Her slender back. He took her by the shoulders, turned her round.

'*Alma*,' he said. 'I'm sorry. I'm stupid. I didn't mean it to sound like that . . . of course you're normal, if anyone is.'

'They're not,' she shouted. 'No one's normal. I'm not either. And *you*,' she added, suddenly half-laughing in the middle of her tears, for he was going on his knees, on the dirty pavement, 'you're a maniac. Kneeling in the dogshit. Get up, you fool. What are you doing?'

He was doing something he had done before, in the least likely places, to break the tension. His face shone with purpose, his eyes were tender, and yet he was laughing at them both. 'Forgive me,' he yelled, flamboyant, theatrical. 'I love you. I adore you. Marry me, please –' And then he was no longer laughing. 'Forgive me, or I shall kiss your feet.'

'Get up, you idiot.' But she was grinning. Her anger ebbed; her tears dried. She stroked his hair, perfunctorily.

When they were both upright, they found their energy had gone. The hour with Jeanette had left them utterly drained.

They went for a quick coffee in a nearby café. It was very noisy. The coffee was instant. They felt shy with each other in the dead light.

Long strips of fluorescent. Paul looked old. And so must I, Alma reflected. They sat round-shouldered on two hard bar-stools, facing the mirror which ran along the wall.

Here we are, she thought. Staring at ourselves. We look small and old and very separate. We do not like what we've found out. We'll never be a couple again.

Paul drank, without talking, looked at his watch.

'I'll have to get to school,' he mumbled, apologetic.

'You always did.' She tasted grit; sediment at the bottom of the cup. The old resentments, undiminished.

'Are you still upset?' he asked her, gently. 'I hated to see you so upset.'

'Yes,' she said slowly. 'I feel all stirred up . . . but it's absurd. It's just *not Owen*. He was frightening . . . but he wasn't like that. And yet, Jeanette pricked up her ears at once . . . she seemed so certain, didn't she? Yet I told her nothing, really, did I – how could I? It had never crossed my mind . . .' Tiny black feet crossed the blazing white sand. Someone small left behind and forgotten. Alma blinked in the harsh flat light.

'Perhaps you should forget all about it,' said Paul. A great gloom hovered just above him, then settled, a heavy bird clutching his shoulders. Weighing him down. He could not lift it. He was just a man; a normal bloke: he had a job to do, didn't he? A hard job. He was briefly, unfairly pierced with annoyance. Surely therapy should make you feel better, not worse? 'What good does it do, raking over the past?'

'That's what Mother said,' she told him, startled. 'Almost word for word. Last time I went home. I asked her – I *tried* to ask – about Jack. She went bananas. She sobbed and howled. I just wanted to know about my father.'

Paul was silent, uneasy, pulling at his cuff. He had remembered something; something troubling. He didn't want to get into this. He wanted things to be . . . safe – and yes, *normal*. Normal life. With his normal wife. But the truth . . . it mattered. If you loved someone. He stared at the floor. He did not speak.

(His shirt wasn't ironed, Alma noticed. No one was looking after him. She would have advised him against that tie. He needed a haircut. He had lost too much weight.)

'Well I did wonder . . .' He got up, stiffly, and produced a last effort to help his wife, a last try before he threw in the towel, '. . . when whatsername, the therapist, said what she said – this is probably nonsense, but it did occur to me . . . could she have been thinking of the wrong person? If anything did happen . . . what if it was Jack?'

34

THE ATMOSPHERE IN PORTICO and Sheen was gloomy. They had all been upset by an incident a week ago when a couple whose flat had been repossessed had come into the office, looking for Kevin. The man was half-mad, on the edge of violence; the wife was silent, utterly depressed, lugging a sleeping two-year-old, heavy and inert as a sack of bruised apples. Kevin, fortunately, was out of the office. Alma and Ashley had to calm the man down. Quite soon, the woman had begun to cry. 'It's not really my field,' Alma had said, trying to repress her guilt and fear. 'Mr Hough always deals with the repossessions.' The man had ranted at them for twenty minutes, while the phones rang, while punters strolled in, while the child slept a drugged sleep, while the woman wept quietly, constantly, and Alma was sickened by her own bland voice, answering the phone as if all was well.

– In any case, things were far from well. The housing market was dropping all the time; each drop in price meant a drop in commission, and the lower prices weren't landing the punters. Half the photos in the windows had PRICE REDUCTION stickers. Only Kevin managed to retain his bounce.

Alma got back late from the counselling session. It was no simple matter, re-entering the office. For some reason the Kemble Hill homeless had moved their pitch, a few days ago. Perhaps it was the seasonal movement of the sun, which meant that their old place opposite was out of the sunlight most of the day, whereas Portico and Sheen's windowful of photos still gleamed and shone as if business was booming. In any case, one night they had shifted. Perhaps they had crossed the road in the dark, trying not to get confused in the headlights, dragging their piles of bags and blankets, changing their minds, going back again, laughing, shepherded across by the sober ones, grandly waving the traffic on.

Two mornings ago, they were already installed, arranged along the pavement as if for a photograph, the oldest in the centre, with his matted grey beard, sitting upright with his bottle of cider, the rest around him like a retinue, some swathed in old blankets and dirty newspapers, looking from a distance like tribesmen in cloaks, holding a ragged council meeting. They were hunkered down outside Portico and Sheen, and there were more of them than there had been before. They stretched to left and right as well, thirty yards of bodies along the high street, and some of the faces were shockingly young, many of those unfamiliar faces were young, though they had the same grey and patient look, they were part of the same unlovely family, surely, the same sour tribe of the dispossessed.

But close up, what she saw was more disconcerting. Some of these people didn't look like dossers. A few of the men wore suits; not much more crumpled than Paul's old suit. They looked normal, didn't they? They looked like her. But younger. Stronger and younger than her. So what were they doing on the streets?

Without realizing it, she was staring too hard.

'What's the matter with you?' a man's voice asked. He was big, unshaven, perhaps around thirty, though his teeth weren't good. His jaw was strong. He was quite smartly dressed – shirt, jumper, old leather jacket. *But his eyes.* She had to meet his eyes. His eyes were living, large, brown. That shock when an object looks back at you. So these were people. Yes, of course.

'I wondered . . .' she said. 'I was surprised . . .' She felt stupid. '. . . There are so many of you,' she ended, simply.

'Don't you like to see us on your high street?' he asked. He grinned at her, enjoying her embarrassment. The others were listening, admiring him.

'No,' she said. '– I mean, yes. I'm sorry, I've got to get to work.' She fiddled with her handbag. Should she give them some money? But he hadn't asked her for any money. – *And besides, his voice was middle-class.*

'Well you're lucky, aren't you? Having a job.'

'Ask her if she's got a degree,' said a woman with straggly grey hair sitting near the big man. 'He's got a degree, him,' she said, gesturing at him admiringly with her elbow.

'I'm sure,' said Alma, sidling past.

'Well have you or not?' the woman yelled.

'Actually yes,' said Alma. It didn't seem enough. 'But I've forgotten it all,' she added. *Damn*. Why should she feel that she had to placate them? Some of the younger ones were jeering. But what was her crime? – She lived inside.

'She's OK,' the big one pronounced. 'She's got to get to work. Don't let them upset you,' he counselled Alma, with ironic charm.

'Thanks,' said Alma. And then 'Good luck.'

– She knew it was feeble, but was it – *patronizing*?

More scattered catcalls. She was nearly past them.

But not before she had noticed there were children, though she didn't allow herself to think the word *children*. Some of them were, but would not be for long. A small grey hand almost touched her coat, and she jerked to one side as she plunged through the door.

She did not want to think about them. She was very late, and over-excited. 'Over-excited' meant bad, she remembered. Gwen probably did think excitement was sexual, she probably did think sex was bad . . . Maybe Owen was frustrated. Jeanette could be right. Gwen wouldn't have his child. Maybe Jack was frustrated . . .

The office was hot. She must forget about all of it, the therapy, the homeless, the whole wounded world. No hope of that, but she made a great effort.

Her in-tray contained the monthly update, which couldn't go out until she had entered the new PRICE REDUCTIONS, fortissimo, and 'Withdrawn from Sales', pianissimo. People were taking their houses off the market, sick of keeping the place tidy for nothing, but it was a worrying trend. Mr Portico had been in a bad mood all week.

'Your boyfriend came in,' said Kevin, jolly. Alma assumed he was teasing Ashley. The badinage between them had acquired more of an edge in recent weeks, she had noticed; was Kevin laying siege behind this screen of teasing? He often pretended he thought Ashley was thick, which was not a tactic destined to succeed; in reality, Alma suspected that he thought her utterly adorable. But Ashley was phoning Nicky again, so the situation was far from simple.

'Are you away with the fairies, or what?'

Kevin was talking to *her*, Alma realized. 'Who?' she said. 'What are you talking about?'

'Don't act innocent,' said Kevin, and she blushed as she remembered Edberg. *Edwards*, I must use his proper name or I'll go and call him Edberg to his face.

'Oh,' she said. 'Mr Edwards. Does he want to see something?'

'Wants to see you, I'd say. Said he'd pop back some time next week.'

Alma had left a message on his phone machine, cancelling the Saturday lunch-time drink. She had thought that would be an end to it. But he was persisting. What did she feel? A flush of excitement. A little rush of panic. It was *flattering* . . . but he wasn't for her.

Kevin was looking at her with interest. It seemed amazing to him, who wasn't yet thirty, that anyone could fancy a woman over forty.

'I wish he wanted to see a house,' she said. 'We could do with *someone* looking at *something*.'

They felt like frauds, with so few results, though they kept on phoning, bright-voiced, persuasive.

'Mr Portico looks awful,' said Ashley. 'He was doing the books, yesterday.'

'There's always sod-all going on before Christmas,' said Kevin, airily, as if he had been in this business for years, as if he'd sailed through a dozen Christmasses.

'Well I feel depressed,' said Ashley, 'I feel as though something bad's going to happen.'

'Where's Mr Portico?' Alma asked, frowning at her update, cancelling, altering, enjoying the neatness of the figures on the screen, enjoying a space that she could control, where she could travel swiftly without hurting herself.

'He's gone to lunch with the accountant. Said he wouldn't be back till four.'

'That lot upset him,' Kevin said, gesturing uncomfortably out of the window. 'Poor bloody sods. They could go somewhere else. It ain't exactly an advert, is it?' The heads of the homeless could be glimpsed like a frieze, all along the bottom of the window.

'I'm sorry for them,' said Ashley, clicking her nails across her keyboard, thinking. 'But it looks awful. There should be a law against it, honestly.'

'Our lord and master said he was going to get the coppers,' Kevin said. 'They should move them along.'

'Where to?' Alma asked. No one said anything.

Then 'Bleeding heart,' Kevin accused her. 'Women. You're a sentimental lot.'

'I saw you give one a quid yesterday,' Ashley said.

'That's different,' Kevin said.

'Could everyone be quiet so I can finish this update?' Alma asked. 'Whatever good it may do.'

There was silence for a moment, then the phone rang. 'Damn,' she said. But she'd answered it too often; they left it to her.

'Mum,' said Adam. 'I'm glad to get you.'

'Adam,' she said. 'Are you OK? . . . I'm a tiny bit pressed, at the moment.'

'Oh,' he said. 'I wanted to talk.'

'No news of Zoe?' She always asked that, although by now she knew the answer, knew there would never be any news.

'I keep telling you not to worry about her.' He sounded strange, but she didn't have time to wonder.

'I just saw Dad,' she said, excited, pleased, before she remembered that it was a secret, the counselling was meant to be their secret.

'I'm seeing him tomorrow for lunch,' he said.

'Oh good.' That's a relief. So I don't have to worry about you.

'– but I wondered if I could come and see you this evening.'

'Oh,' she said. 'I wish you could . . . But I'm having supper with Sheilah and Verity. They're coming to the house . . . well you *could* come too . . .' (doubtfully) 'but wouldn't you be horribly bored? Poor Verity. Her father's died.'

'I couldn't come and stay the night, could I?'

'– You could. Of course. You *could* . . . But why don't you come tomorrow, or some time when I could talk to you? You could bring your washing, darling . . . but I *don't* really want piles of washing in the kitchen when I've got people coming in for a meal. I like the place to be decent.'

'Yes.'

But she had heard herself sounding exactly like her mother. The negative voice of her mother in her. *Keep the place decent*, Gwen always said, whenever she went out for a minute. As if she daren't leave Alma alone, as if Alma was bursting with indecency.

'Adam? You're very quiet.'

'Yes.'

'If there's something wrong, just *say* –' Impatient.

'No – I think I'd better go.'

'Well I do have something urgent to get done . . .'

'Bye, Mum . . .' A long pause; he hadn't finished. And then he had. 'Bye, Mum.'

She put the phone down.

'Right,' said Kevin. 'Ashley and I are going for a walk.' He was bright again; there was something afoot.

'Are we?' asked Ashley. 'Says who?'

'We can't just sit here *moping*,' he said. 'Alma's got her update to do, Mr Portico's out getting smashed . . . It's up to us to do something, Ashley.'

'Oh yes?' said Ashley, but her eyes brightened.

'Christmas decorations,' Kevin said, bringing out the words like an armful of tinsel. 'Cheer the old bugger up. And us. Spray-on snow. Balloons. Holly. Garrets' are all tarted up already . . .'

'Why not?' said Ashley, reaching for her handbag. 'I love Christmas. Big kid, me.'

'Well maybe we should have a crib,' said Alma. 'A stable scene. Put it in the window. *I'm telling you, Kevin, I'm not touching that window, with all the homeless watching me.*'

'I'd have thought a stable scene would be quite nice,' Ashley said, touching up her lipstick. 'No need to be sarcastic. Are you being sarcastic? You can buy them complete. My sister's got one in the front room by the telly. It's lovely.'

'She's not being sarcastic. Alma's not that type,' said Kevin, opening the door for Ashley. 'Why are you so touchy, all of a sudden? Bye bye, Alma. Hold the fort.'

Unfortunately, Kevin's belief that Alma was just being helpful prevailed. Unfortunately they followed her suggestion. Unfortunately Mr Portico got back late.

So that the office was a glittering thicket of tinsel, every bit of glass softly swathed in fake snow, the stable scene dead centre in the window, standing proud beneath the lines of photos with their festive red PRICE REDUCTION stickers, Mary and Joseph, a white-faced baby, a menagerie of beasts who looked ready for slaughter and some marvellous angels with wings of real feathers which served as a great attraction to the homeless, who bobbed about in front of the glass, pushing each other to get a better view – everything was beautifully ready for Christmas when Mr Portico banged in through the door, his eyes very red, his face very white, bringing the cold and dark in with him, and said, 'What the hell have you been playing at? Well you'd better all sit up and listen. The figures for the last three months were a disaster. I'm going to have to close this branch down at Christmas.'

He slammed next door to take his coat off.

Only Kevin recovered enough to speak. 'No room at the fucking inn,' he croaked.

35

VERITY WAS PALE, and her hair was unwashed, and her eyes lay in pools of blue-grey wax. Alma held her in her arms for a moment after their first embrace at the door. 'You should have told me what was going on . . . You poor darling. I'm just so sorry.'

'I rang last weekend. You must have been away . . . It wasn't something I could put on the answering machine.'

'I could have come and helped.'

'You've got enough problems. I mean, it was you who wanted to talk to me, and I was too busy with my bloody novel, I had the time-scale all worked out, the exact number of pages to do every day . . . Then the hospital rang and gave me the news. So I haven't touched the novel for the last three weeks, and so bloody what? It doesn't matter, in the end.'

'So your father never told you he was ill again . . . he didn't like to worry you, did he? I think the fittest ones make most fuss – my Mother will live for ever, and complain daily.'

Verity's father had gone home to die, and Verity had been with him 'to the end', she told Alma, as she sat on the carpet, grateful to talk, spilling it out, her colour coming back and her animation, crying a little, sipping her wine. 'I've just come back for clothes for the funeral.'

Alma was awed and fascinated. Verity had been where we all must go. Verity knew about something she did not, for Daddy had died far out of sight when she was only four years old, and Owen, after his week of muffled fury, had died when she was on the train back to London. She'd seen his combed and polished corpse, but she had never been through a dying.

'At least you did it right. Being with him. You were a good

daughter. What more could you do . . . I liked your father. He was *interesting* . . . He talked to me like an intelligent person. I shall miss him too, you know.'

'Well he really liked you, Alma. You made a great impression the very first time you came to Sunday lunch because you were reading *The Time Machine* . . .'

Verity's father was a literary critic, but he'd never praised his daughter's novels. 'I wish that Dad had liked what I do . . . He read them, I think, but he wouldn't say much. Just cryptic things which got under my skin like "You ought to decide who you're writing for" and "William Cooper does everything by suggestion", which made me feel I had gone to a party without putting my knickers on . . . He couldn't understand why I never got married. I think I was a real disappointment to him.'

'But you weren't,' said Alma, helplessly, and then remembered some evidence. 'Your books were always in his dining-room, lined up where everyone could see them, all together, dead centre in the shelves. I think he was very proud of you. But he was a *critic*, remember. He couldn't write novels. All critics are jealous of novelists.'

'There's my loyal ex-editor,' said Verity, chinking glasses, smiling at Alma, her first real smile. 'Thank heavens for friendship. And Ian's been marvellous. He came down and helped me for the last three days, which were grim, I can tell you . . . death isn't easy.'

'I'm sure,' said Alma. 'It frightens me.'

'Bricks fall on our head, don't they – there's a clear sky, then clunk, the brick. Never the brick that you were expecting.'

Alma looked at her watch. 'By the way – I'm sorry, Verity, I'd much rather have had you on your own, but Sheilah left a message a few days ago. Really miserable. Desperate to see me before she goes away—'

'She's always away. What a glamorous life.'

'Filming in Antigua, but I bet it's not glamorous. They work her like a donkey, and she's got no prospects . . . Anyway I left a message in return saying she could come to supper. Later than you, so we could talk. She's got a lot of problems just now . . . What is it with us? We've all got problems!'

'It's life, that's why. Just being alive. And middle-aged, so there's been time for things to happen . . . How late is she coming? I'm a bit hungry.'

'I'll get some nuts. Have some more wine . . .'

When Alma came back, Verity was watching the news. Buildings were burning in Sarajevo. Masonry fell from an orange sky. The cameramen were dodging bullets. Panicking children ran at the lens as if they could escape into their living-room. No aid planes had got through that day. After the break, it was Somalia.

Alma switched off after the first few shots, before the lingering close-ups of limping skeletons, the terrible grill-chested, spider-limbed children with their over-sized eyes, unblinking, unsmiling, the bones pushing through beneath the shine-thin skin.

'I can't bear this. Do you mind?'

They talked desultorily, waiting for Sheilah, but Sheilah didn't come.

'Was he – nice – at the end?' Alma asked. 'I know you had your differences . . .'

'You're on your own, at the very end. I was there, but he had gone away, really . . . he thought he was with his mother, you know. He'd gone back in time. He was a child . . . Very mysterious, that last pass. When the pain got very bad, he was on morphine.'

'So was the end easy?'

'No. It's hard work, dying, even on morphine. They fight to die. You can't do much . . . And he wasn't ready to die, you see. There were lots of things he hadn't done. Write his memoirs. Go to Argentina. He had a holiday planned for next year . . . He did put things off into the future. Then he must have seen that the future wouldn't come. And it's so hard to let go of things. Especially the things you never had. I watched him lying there, staring at the wall. Seeing the things he would never see.'

'Hard to come into this world, hard to go out.'

'I wouldn't know about birth, of course . . . that was his sorrow, really, that I didn't have children. I think it was grand-children he wanted from me. His way into the future . . . something like that.'

'He'll have to put up with your books instead.'

'Which he disapproved of.'

276

'Maybe that's the point. You can't control how you go into the future.' Alma thought, without Zoe I've lost my future.

'All his life he wanted to be in control . . . he hated not being in control of his body. Hated being bedridden that last week. Hated my looking after him. Hated it worse when we threatened him with nurses . . .'

'I remember him so erect. It seems cruel that he had to end like that.' Alma remembered him tall and straight, immaculately dressed, with a bush of white hair, never without a tie.

'The strangest thing was seeing him unshaven. He didn't want us to do it for him, and he couldn't manage, that last week . . . seeing the white bristles coming through his chin. It was like nature coming back, escaping his grip. Like the oak-saplings poking up all over the lawn because he couldn't keep up with the mowing last summer . . . And the cancer returning. He'd fought a good fight . . . I'm so *tired*, Alma. I'm *bone-tired*.'

How thin the skin was, Alma thought, that keeps us from chaos, that keeps us in control. If we thought about it more, perhaps we couldn't go on. Maybe that's why we need so many secrets. Maybe that's why the old won't talk to us . . . And why therapy is dangerous. Bringing us nearer to the void. When we have to survive. We have to go on. Until the time comes when we can't do it any more. Until time closes over us.

Sheilah came at ten, looking beautiful and haggard. She and Verity kissed, exclaiming at each other, a show of warmth which hid mutual reserve since both of them would rather have been here alone.

Alma went to the kitchen. Thank God for the skin of politeness, she thought. They were chatting away in the other room. She basted the chicken, put it back, topped and tailed the French beans, threw them in water. Tonight she didn't mind the cooking; pleasant to do something gentle, manual.

In five minutes Sheilah came through the kitchen at speed, en route for the garden, clutching something. 'Got to have a fag,' she called back to Verity. Then 'I lost it, didn't I,' she hissed at Alma. 'I started to bleed last Saturday. I did ring you—'

'I was in Wales,' said Alma, looking at Sheilah, torn with

sorrow, not noticing the chicken-fat that dribbled on the floor. 'Oh Sheilah. I am sorry.'

'There wasn't any heartbeat on Monday. Had a D & C on Tuesday. In, out. Like a fucking factory. Didn't even keep me in for the night.'

Alma was boiling hot from the open oven. Sheilah had lit up by the open door. Dirty thing, smoking in the kitchen. 'Excuse me, Sheilah, got to get near the sink . . .'

'I was just going in the garden. George is gutted. You'll never believe it, Alma, but *he's left his wife.*'

'Great,' said Alma. 'But the rest is awful . . . I'm sorry, Sheilah, can we talk in a minute?' She felt exhausted. Too many needs. *Why did I decide to have the two of them together?*

At dinner Verity explained to Sheilah, 'My father just died. I'm not exactly on form.'

'I just lost a child,' said Sheilah, angry. 'However much I try, I can't seem to lose my mother. I bet you liked your father, Verity . . . it's always the wrong bloody ones who die.' She had been drinking too fast; she sounded wild. Alma tried to mediate.

'Of course Verity liked him. He was a lovely man,' – slightly reproachfully, to Sheilah.

'I don't know if I liked him,' Verity said. 'I don't know if it matters, in the end. I think when it came to it I just felt pity. A huge pity, as if he was anyone . . . I can't explain. It was almost anonymous.'

'I felt sorry for my little scrap of a thing. I know it was only about an inch long . . . but I kept on thinking, it didn't have a chance. I've made a mess of my life, but at least I've had a chance.'

'Aren't you just a tiny bit relieved?' Alma asked. She and Sheilah knew things that Verity didn't. She couldn't mention it by name, but Sheilah had no such inhibitions.

'Oh yeah, I was so worried when I talked to you. Well, I decided to take the test – thought I might be HIV, Verity. Decided to be responsible. It took three weeks for the result to come back. It came back negative the day after I lost it.' The room was silent, stunned by her frankness, awed by the chasm they had just danced over, the pit of darkness, the place beyond. 'I want you to know something. Both of you. Even if the test had been positive, I would have gone ahead with it. Taken the risk. I would have *died* if I could have had a live baby.'

There was a pause. The quiet house absorbed her passion. 'I understand,' said Verity. 'I know how you feel. I felt the same way. I'm really sorry you lost your baby.' She touched Sheilah's arm across the table, her long slender arm in its black stretch lycra, the colour of mourning, clinging to life.

Alma felt excluded by the two of them. Childlessness gave them a terrible bond. They began to talk obsessively about adoption, about fostering, about foreign babies. How both of them longed to pick the children off the television screen, their longing to make them live again, the tottering skeletons who stretched out their arms, the abandoned children of Ethiopia, Somalia, Romania, Sarajevo, the Sudan . . .

Alma went and defrosted some sorbet. Everyone but her had voted for coffee. That meant they would stay in her front room for ever, and she was working tomorrow morning, no matter if they were closing at Christmas . . . The sorbet yielded mean slivers of rock. In the dining-room the voices continued.

All over London, all over Europe, Alma thought, all over America and Japan, wherever people are rich and infertile, the women are having these conversations. And all over the developing, the withering, world, where people are fertile and horribly poor, the children huddle and steal and starve, grow up without parents or food or love.

But the two things can never match. They seem to match, but they don't, they can't. The torture is that they *seem* to match.

In any case, Alma had been upstaged. She felt fainter by the minute and less vital in the face of the noise and energy of Sheilah's and Verity's feelings. The glimmer of light which had seemed so powerful that day in therapy began to seem abstract, tentative, nothing. Depression began to close down like a lid as she cleared the table and they talked on.

– She wasn't important. She didn't exist. She would never get rid of them, never, never.

'I've lost my job,' she abruptly announced, and was gratified to see them both turn towards her.

'Alma, you *haven't*!'

'Why didn't you *say*?'

'But you really enjoyed it! That's terrible!'

'When my novel's gone in, I can lend you some money –'

'They can't just sack you with no compensation. George is a shop steward. I'll ask him.'

It was comforting to feel their combined affection, their indignation on her behalf. Her depression began to drain away. She wasn't alone. She did exist. She had known both these women for over two decades.

'Would anyone like a Rémy Martin?' Both of them would; all three of them did.

'My God,' she said, smiling, expanding, 'we've all known each other since we were *girls* . . . We were in our twenties. Can you believe it?'

'I knew *nothing*,' said Sheilah. 'I was happier, though. I'm afraid growing old will be horrible . . . and it wasn't very nice being a child, either. I'd like the last bit of my twenties back. I looked . . . OK. Well, I looked pretty great, a photographer once stopped me in the street . . . I was with Peter, and he was sweet, and I thought I'd be famous, I really did. I was infinitely hopeful. Ridiculously hopeful . . . They treat you like candy, when you're young and pretty.'

'I'm happier now,' said Verity. 'I hated being plump, and unpublished . . . These are better days, for me. But there are losses . . . I'd like my parents to be young again. I'd like Dad to be what he was before. I hated seeing him so reduced. It's cruel, old age. It takcs everything away.'

'Cheers, girls,' said Alma. 'It's our turn next!' They were all half-laughing at their own solemnity.

'Alma,' Sheilah asked. 'What was your best time?'

'Not childhood,' she said. 'Though parts of it were lovely . . . In Wales, with my Aunt Eileen. You know the one . . . I suppose I think now, I mean now she's gone, when Zoe was young. When she was a child . . . when she was a child, and in my arms. I can't believe now that that was ever true, that she was there all the time and I took her for granted . . .'

'She'll come back, like I said,' Sheilah told her.

'I'll drink to that,' Verity added. They were pleasantly drunk. The three of them chinked glasses. They were women of the world. They had lived in the world. They were glad to have survived some of what life offered. They would never be innocent again, though Sheilah wished she could still be young . . . but just at that moment, they were proud to have come through, proud to have ridden the years together.

'To friendship,' Alma said. 'Let's never lose it.'

She lay in bed that night and was grateful for the bright nets of alcohol that lifted her up, although she knew she would feel rough in the morning, although she knew that her mouth would be dry, that she'd come downstairs with a splitting headache. The alcohol made the present enough, it held her in its golden hand, where past and future were comprehended, where nothing mattered, nothing was lost, where everything could be known and forgiven, where she herself could be whole at last.

Three was the cruellest time to wake up. No hope of morning. No glimmer of light, though a huge lorry dragged itself down the road. The whole house seemed to be turning, tipping, and the headache already rumbled at her temples. It was very cold. The glass of the window shivered, and her teeth held the faint vibrato of an ache.

Why was I so stupid? Why drink so much? The older I get, the less I can take . . .

The night was black, and full of horror. My God, she thought, no one is safe. My Zoe could be anywhere, freezing to death. Paul's father. And his mother. My mother looked older and frailer than before, and she had that pain in her chest when we hurried . . . Eileen was defeated by the rocks. Sheilah could have had HIV, or she could have died in pregnancy . . .

We're all being swept on into the future. And it's colder and emptier than before because so many of us won't get there . . .

And the counsellor. Jeanette. She was mad, Alma thought. She was a sadist, who liked breaking people down. She must tell everyone that they were abused. It was all made up, it wasn't the key, the crying was self-indulgent and empty . . .

Whatever was lost will be lost for ever.

36

SHE WOKE AT EIGHT, and things weren't quite so bad. The perpetual comfort of sun through the curtains, the glory of the blowing light, a day when the greyness had lifted again. Light, she thought. The look of things. Paul's father is losing his sight . . . thank God for mine. Thank God for it. Just as in childhood, it was Alma's comfort.

She lay and stretched against the warm sheet. Life crept back. Thought crept back. The new thoughts. The new feelings. Horizontal, life was bearable; horizontal, in the yellow-cream light.

By daylight, Jeanette no longer seemed mad. The thing she had suggested lay in the sun. A locked box, a sealed room, but a thing they had named. No longer nameless. Something which said, *you must deal with me*.

It was I who named it. I said 'abuse' . . . but I didn't mean it literally . . . not physically abused . . . not sexually abused . . . I *couldn't* have meant it literally.

Abuse . . . abuse . . . it meant so many things. To insult. To injure. To use . . . to misuse. As so many parents misuse their children.

As if kids were here to fulfil our needs. I've misused my children, Alma thought. I've wanted so many things for Zoe that really I wanted for myself. I wanted her to succeed too much. I wanted her to have a proper career . . . I wanted her to be musical . . . all the things that I never did.

– But my parents were worse. They were surely worse? I tried to give Zoe some sense of herself. Whereas Gwen and Owen just chipped away at me. Trying to make a statue they liked. Sending me away or stifling me. Constraining me. Bearing me down. Pressing me between narrow walls. Making me yield. I was always yielding. Yield, yield, till there's nothing left . . .

And Jack. My own Dad . . . my own blond Daddy. So impossibly big, impossibly handsome. Blond as a god to the child I was
. . . What did he do? Was he like the others? Did he press me
down? Did he smother me?

She strained to remember, but nothing came. Only the beach,
the blinding beach. There were no figures, only Jack and herself.
The child she had been waved from the whiteness, but her face
was a blank; the white heat erased it, and the distance blew her
words away. Was she waving and laughing, or waving for help?

'You adored him, Alma. You'd do anything for him.' Her
mother's voice, repeating, repeating, sighing like the sightless air
through the curtains, dying away, leaving nothing.

What did I do for him? What did he do to me?

The past, the past. The long-locked past. The mysterious room
which led off from the others. I'll ask my mother, I'll make her
tell me . . .

But she will know nothing, or remember nothing.

And maybe there's nothing to remember.

The child still waved, forlorn, darkening, and Alma willed a
message to her; I haven't forgotten you; I shall be back. I'll come
and find you, some day, somehow. If I could defend you . . . if
I could protect you . . .

She pushed back the sheet, stepped into the sunlight.

Alma ate her breakfast standing in her study, looking out at the
last scraps of autumn colour. The orange Japanese lanterns by the
frog pool, the berries reddening on the cotoneaster, the last yellow
hands of sycamore leaves waving spread-fingered on the blue and
white sky.

Zoe loved the garden. Just like me. We used to pick up the
leaves together, and that was a job that nobody liked, she was a
good girl, she was almost too good . . . I boasted of her to my
friends. 'Zoe's no trouble. She's a marvellous girl.'

Suddenly the sky was scattered with darkness, she looked up
startled and saw the starlings, great wheeling constellations of
starlings forming and re-forming on the breast of the wind,
moving as quickly as black blown leaves, but alive, organic, part
of a pattern, coming from nowhere and going again, briefly filling

283

the sky with music, faint but multiple, shrill, electric, a sound like the distant calling of children, thousands of children calling together. The sky was alive, and then they were gone.

And then Alma was completely sure that Zoe was still there in the garden, under the yew tree, just out of sight, where she used to take her tea in summer, Zoe would rush in with her gym kit swinging, kiss her mother full on the lips, rush upstairs and strip to her undies and then come down again smeared with sun-cream, grab the paper and her plate of sandwiches . . . 'Go in the shade,' Alma always said. 'If you must be half-naked go in the shade. You kids won't believe the sun's dangerous.' Later she would look across from her desk and see her from the study window; most of her body was behind the tree, but every so often Alma would glimpse her burnished head, her careless hand, the paper waving as she changed positions, or the languorous waves of one long arm, pale against the blue-green yew leaves, 'Mum, Mum, can I have some more tea?'

– Alma heard her calling. It hung on the air, with the flash of flesh, the brief ripple of newsprint . . . Somehow, it must all still be happening. And Sheilah is still pregnant, as she longs to be. And Verity's father is still shouting at the gardener, running like an athlete across the smooth lawns . . . and Paul and I still love each other.

We do still love each other, somehow. We do.

The epiphany faded, the shivers of joy which ran like mercury over her body calmed again as the sun went in, she saw from her watch it was time to go – but she did love Paul. They had been through so much. She wanted him back. She wanted him home. Together they could face the past. And the future . . . ?

She set off for work feeling almost cheerful, though she knew from a faint sense of distance between her body and her active brain that she was hungover, and would be all day; it was work placing one foot in front of the other. She wished she could stay and think in the garden, but she had to go and earn her money.

Things began to get worse for Alma quite quickly.

The frisky wind and sprinting clouds had woken up the home-less early, making them uncharacteristically active. A group of men were milling around the door of the office. The tall one who had talked to her wasn't there. One of them was busking with a two-stringed guitar, singing above its tuneless twanging in a plangent, remorseless nasal voice. Two others were collecting, one with a small cardboard box. The one with the box was plainly very drunk. She tried to ignore them; it was *where she worked*; giving to them was encouraging them, and she could see Mr Portico's dark bulk inside the window . . .

'Harrum yuh gonna give a tenpee even yafuggi bitch?' said the man with the box, lurching across her. He smelled of cider, petrol, urine and fried food. She would have had to push him physically, to pass. She wished she could, she hated being bullied, but his will was stronger. She opened her handbag, found two small coins, dropped them in the box. The crowd yielded. Two children stared. They stared straight at her. She was rich, she was mean. Perhaps they weren't children, they looked too serious, she hoped they weren't children, they were shaking, they were dirty – she turned away from them, and slipped inside.

'I don't know where they all come from,' said Mr Portico. 'I don't know why the police can't deal with them.'

'I'm sorry. I was forced to give them something.'

'Yes, quite. Don't worry yourself. I did too.'

Neither Kevin nor Ashley was in that morning. Mr Portico came and sat at Ashley's desk, checking records on the main computer. They worked in silence for a bit, companionable in misfortune.

There had been something of a row between him and Kevin once the news of the closure had had time to sink in. Kevin had stopped Mr Portico on his lowering, remote way out of the office and delivered a broadside on behalf of the staff: management should hang on at least until summer in case there was an upturn. 'We are all agreed,' Kevin had said, pink-faced, and Ashley and Alma had nodded, sheepishly. 'Can't pay two rents,' Mr Portico had answered. 'Can't pay the wages. Thinking of remortgaging the house already . . . We were going under, Mr Hough. I regret . . . I regret . . . I am sorry, everyone . . .' And his voice had stalled, uncomfortably. And so the protest had fizzled out.

But ever since Mr Portico had seemed different. Melancholy, guilty, wanting to be liked, though Kevin had resisted for twenty-four hours before his essential good nature prevailed.

285

The new Mr Portico was easier to like. 'Shall I make a cup of coffee?' he asked Alma now.

She managed not to say *No, let me*, and drank it with enjoyment. 'Thanks, Mr Portico, this is nice. It tastes much better when someone else makes it.' *I'm my mother's daughter . . . she says that . . . I* ought to ring her, see how she is. I'll do it before I go out on my appointment –

(But she knew as she thought it, that she probably wouldn't; she had to leave by a quarter to eleven; there were always reasons why things didn't get done, why busy children failed their parents, so the parents sat waiting, with time on their hands, waiting for the voices of the vanished children – *as I wait for Zoe, when I'm not busy –*)

'Better get busy,' she smiled at her boss, draining her coffee-cup and pushing it away.

The atmosphere that Saturday morning was macabre, with the Christmas decorations twisting and shining in the permanent draught that came under the door, the hanging garlands blaring HAPPY CHRISTMAS AND A HAPPY NEW YEAR FROM ALL OF US, and Mr Portico walking round the office sighing heavily and staring at his feet. No new customers were likely to come in, with the scrum of homeless people outside the door. Alma and her boss were on their own, and they knew the show was closing down at Christmas.

'I'll finish this update in any case, if the business is transferring to your other branch.'

'This was never the right venue for an office . . . And I never felt quite sure that all the staff were behind me—'

'Oh, I'm sure they were,' Alma said, shocked. 'All of us really enjoyed working here. We'll miss it. Truly.'

'Mr Hough, I'm thinking of,' he said, weightily. 'His *attitude* is odd.'

'Oh, but Kevin has always admired you!' she lied. 'You're a kind of role model for him. I think he's the career estate agent, if anyone is. So naturally our closing down was a blow . . . He's hoping you'll take him with you to Harlesden.'

(Why am I doing this? she wondered. Why do I always try to help? – But it's true. Kevin has a kind of flair for this, and Ashley could get a job anywhere.)

'Admires me, does he?' She could see he was pleased, concealing it beneath lowering brows.

'He says he's learned all he knows from you.'

Was she overdoing it? Evidently not.

'Really? Surely not . . . *Really*. Hrrumph!' His mood lightened perceptibly. 'It's true Mr Hough is a young man with ideas . . . but I thought he found me a little old-fashioned . . .'

'What do you mean?' Alma asked.

Mr Portico hummed, then came and perched his shapeless bulk on the edge of her desk. An idea was forming in his mind. He spoke, looking at his shoe. 'He wanted me to put tout lines in.'

'Tout lines?' Alma repeated, puzzled.

'Apparently *Garrets'* have got them . . .' He pronounced the name with savage disdain. '. . . The *newer* estate agents tend to use them . . . They ring the competition, pretending to be applicants. That way they get to know about all the others' new instructions . . . One felt – I always felt it was the cowboys' way . . . but perhaps I should think about installing them in Harlesden . . . perhaps Mr Hough would, um, *keep me up to scratch* . . . I might just have a word with him, on Monday.'

Right, thought Alma. That's your lot, Kevin. You're a nice enough boy, but I've got to get on.

– I suppose Kevin and Ashley will never get together . . . But probably they weren't right for each other. I wanted him to be Ashley's way out. I didn't like to think of her stuck with her mother . . . But what do I know? Her mother sounded nice. It just seemed like going backwards, living with your mother . . .

I'll miss these kids. They've been good friends to me. This was a kind of harbour, but nothing lasts . . . In any case, the harbour was – full of sharks. Kevin was a shark, when he was working. I didn't want to think about the things we were doing . . . It was just – *the job*, as Kevin said.

She slipped gratefully into the world of her computer, the world where space and time were really one, where the past could be found at the touch of a button, where you looked back effortlessly, line by line, and finding the truth was a foregone conclusion . . .

She printed out the update and got ready to leave, gathered her clipboard and the mobile phone.

'Bye, Mr Portico.'

'Goodbye, my dear . . .' He smiled at her. Had he ever seen her as a person? 'There's not much point you taking that phone. I shan't be here for much more than half an hour.'

'Oh well. Shan't need it. Just going by the book.'

It was bright, outside the door. They were waiting for her. She stepped over what she thought was a body on the pavement, then saw was two bodies, two small bodies, small round faces, dirty, sculpted eyelids, brown-stained mouths, and the hand that was trying to hide the two faces was pathetically small, a grey-white stone. She tried not to see them, but it didn't feel good. *Get on, Alma*; there were things to be done. Today had a rhythm, urging her on, but her body was always lagging behind, as if it didn't like what it saw of the present, as if it was afraid to go into the future, and it tried to escape, to slip into the past, but the only door to the past was lost. She couldn't be a child. She had to go on. With a vague sense of dread, she began to walk faster. All this was only the remains of the drink. She couldn't let Mr Portico down.

She had to fetch her car and drive to Lilley Road by eleven. The car keys were inside the house. She picked them up, stepped back outside . . . then a sudden pang drove her back into the house, and she shut the door, picked up the phone.

That moment of clarity in the garden. She would ring Paul, ask after his father. See if she could tell him she loved him. If she didn't ring him, one of them might die, and it would never be known, never spoken.

But he wasn't there, and the moment Peeky answered Alma remembered he was lunching with Adam: what lowered her spirits, though, was Peeky's frank dislike, because why should Peeky bother to dislike her if she wasn't having an affair with her husband? – And it's all my fault. I drove him away.

Don't be ridiculous, she told herself, but her fragile good mood was on the rocks. Last night's worries crawled back into the light. His father will die. We're just letting it happen –

It's not even my business any more.

Paul was in the past, like happiness.

And suddenly she was frightened for her mother. Without considering the time of day, she rang her mother. *She is my mother . . .*

'Mother?' she said. It had rung a lot of times.

'Alma?' Her mother did not sound pleased. She was very breathless, or else bad-tempered. 'Is something the matter? Is someone ill?'

'I just wanted to know how you were.'

'I was on my way out, same as always, on Saturday . . . I always go to Pen-y-bont and get some meat for Eileen to eat on Sunday. *I was halfway down to the gate, Alma.* It's not good for me to rush about . . .'

'I didn't know,' said Alma. 'I wanted to hear you.' And she realized it was true; at least Gwen was still there.

'Well you *should* know,' Gwen said. 'I've been doing it for the last fifteen years. Ah well, can't expect you to think about me, you're tearing about with your London life—'

'Mother.' Alma stopped her. She took a deep breath. It was so unfair. She wouldn't put up with it. 'Why do you want to make me feel guilty? Why do you make me feel a bad daughter?'

Alma heard her mother's shocked intake of breath. A pause, then Gwen spoke in a familiar register. 'Are you cross with me, Alma? Have you just rung up to be cross with your mother?'

The old tactic. Poor little me.

Alma thought fast. She didn't have to react. She had to speak from her own true feelings. 'I rang because . . . I love you, Mother. I just wanted to know how you are. I felt a bit lonely. Do you understand?'

'Well,' said her mother, not committing herself, but yielding, no longer pursuing her daughter. 'Well, that's nice. I suppose you're working . . . You'd better get on, dear. Sorry if you thought I snapped . . . But remember, don't ring me on Saturday mornings. Sunday evenings, that's when I miss Daddy.'

'Father,' Alma corrected without thinking. But maybe Jack was the answer to everything.

'Bye, dear.'

'Mam . . . I wish we could have a proper talk one day.'

'You'll have to stay for longer then . . . but don't go wasting your money on the phone.'

It was curious how Gwen liked to do the phoning. But that way, of course, she kept control.

'I *will* try and stay for longer, one day . . . I *shall* come. We'll have time to talk. I'll give you a ring next week, Mam.'

In terms of conversations with Alma's mother, this counted as a victory. Yet Alma felt curiously unsettled by it, curiously reluctant to say goodbye, though normally she couldn't wait to put the phone down. Once it was down in its silent cradle, she felt depression running back, the thing that had hovered above her for days. She felt alone. She felt unloved.

Why the hell did I come back into the house? It has no meaning any more. It's not really a home. No one but ghosts.

She tried to tell herself, at least I'm not homeless, driving to the flat in Lilley Road, seeing from fifty yards away the family standing outside the house, a youngish couple with two small children, a pushchair and a babe in arms. People who expect me. People who need me. She braced herself to meet their needs.

The flat, she could see as she shook hands with them, their acid pastel woollies, their faded anoraks, would be completely beyond their means, and she also knew they would want it, badly. It was what they described as a 'Must Be Seen', an 'excellent three-bed period conversion' with a 'streamlined modernized kitchen-breakfast room.' Even more alluring, it was fully furnished, because the builder who had done the conversion with a view to living there with his new bride, had been jilted at the altar, and had washed his hands of the whole thing, curtains, carpets, three-piece suite in pale, hopeful, youthful colours, their plans, their dreams, their cream-petalled wall-lamps . . . he must have expected to be happy here.

'Lovely,' said the woman, red-nosed from the cold. 'It's lovely, isnit. Oooh, it's lovely. DON'T TOUCH, Hayley. I'm warnin' you . . .'

The husband, thin and strained-looking, with hair already combed over to one side, tried to ask the questions of a man of the world, a confident man with plenty of money, but their need, their hunger was palpable, it hung on the air as they gazed about them, and they touched things, gently, then took their hands away, quickly, as if they were touching what they weren't entitled to, as if someone might think they were stealing.

I hate my job. I'm glad we're closing, Alma thought. I want to *give* them the houses. She was getting increasingly desperate to go, but the Allsops found it impossible to leave, the dream was too powerful while they were still inside it, still playing the part of potential buyers, as long as they were here it might still come true . . . all of them were sniffing, copiously. She hoped their hands were reasonably clean.

'Could I just have another quick peek at the bedroom?' the woman asked. They all trooped back. It was pale blue, with cream curtains and cupboards. She stood and stared. She longed. She yearned.

'And so all fittings would definitely be included?' Mr Allsop asked, trying to sound firm.

'Yes, in the £95,000,' Alma said. She wanted to be kind, and yet stop pretending. 'Remember we have lots of cheaper three-bed flats . . . it's the fittings that make this one expensive. Our two-bed flats start at fifty-five.'

'Well we like this one,' he said obstinately. 'We're thinking about this one . . .' And so they went on thinking, hoping. It was another twenty minutes before she got them out, shuffling downstairs with the grizzling baby who didn't look attractive, caked with yellow grouting where his nose had run and not been wiped.

Their car had one wing a different colour, badly crumpled, thinly painted. The 'Baby on Board!' notice had not saved them. Would anything save them? Alma wondered. Did anyone care about the poor any more? Life went too fast. We pushed on in front of them.

'We'll be in touch,' Mr Allsop said. 'When we've discussed it.' He wanted to leave sounding in control, but his wife's longing forced her to speak. 'We thought it was lovely,' she confided. 'It *is* lovely, isn't it?'

'Yes,' said Alma; they looked at each other. Then the woman turned her head away. Alma knew she would never hear from them again, but she said goodbye extra respectfully. She stood on the pavement and watched them drive off. She thought that she saw them beginning to row.

37

COULD HER SENSE OF grey emptiness be connected to hunger? The hunger that always followed heavy drinking? Alma decided it was.

Lilley Road, as the property particulars mentioned, was 'convenient shops', in this case an adequate delicatessen only fifty yards away. Alma left her car outside the house and walked to the shops. A small ache hovered low in one temple. It was a shabby, friendly little row of shops a little detached from the main high street, no longer quite supporting itself. There was a small bank, which would soon be closing. A greengrocer's with a mean array of fruit; the shopkeeper stood in the window looking worried. It wasn't just in Wales, Alma thought. But the delicatessen was Italian, and quite good. She would buy some Ciabatta bread, some olives . . .

Outside the bank, though, she glimpsed a familiar thin back; a head of red hair; a red and white umbrella. It was Ashley, talking to a tall blonde woman. Ashley had her arm round the woman's waist; they were scanning the exchange rates in the bank's window.

'Ash,' said Alma, touching her shoulder.

'*Alma*,' said Ashley, spinning round. She seemed excessively surprised. Up close, the other woman was elderly, her hair mostly white, her skin fine and lined. She looked like Ashley, didn't she?

'– Is this your mother?' Alma said, and smiled warmly, extending her hand. Gwen's instilled good manners.

But the tall woman laughed. 'I'm Nicky,' she said. 'Are you Alma? We once spoke on the phone.'

– Another Nicky? *The same Nicky*. 'Nicky,' said Alma blankly, thinking fast.

'I hear that you're all out of a job . . .'

'Soon,' said Alma. She looked at Ashley, who wouldn't look at her, playing with her umbrella.

'I've got to draw some money,' Nicky said. 'The queues are dreadful . . .'

'They always are,' Alma said, with an effort.

'Stupid of me to choose this branch, but Ashley had some shoe repairs to pick up . . .'

Alma racked her brains for something to say. 'Kemble Hill is like a village,' she managed. 'I never go out without running into somebody . . .'

'In any case, I'd better go in. See you in a minute, Ashley. Glad to have met you, Alma.'

'Ashley,' said Alma, when she had gone, 'is this *the* Nicky?'

'Yes,' said Ashley. 'I'm sorry, Alma. I live with her. My mother's dead . . . I didn't know you, you see, when I told you that bullshit. And a lot of people . . . well, they're weird. I know *you* wouldn't care. You're a grownup.' She stopped looking at her feet, and smiled at Alma, a pale real smile. She was very pretty. So the scarlet lipstick was just for work.

'I am a fool,' said Alma. 'I really thought that you and Kevin . . . I really thought you liked him.'

'Well I *did*,' said Ashley, earnestly. 'I quite like blokes, as a matter of fact. I was interested . . . I got in a muddle . . . But I mean, I love Nicky. We've been together seven years. *Don't tell Kevin.* He could never understand.'

'I won't,' said Alma. 'Course I won't . . . but if you don't tell people, how can they understand?'

Ashley stared across at the Saturday traffic, dull-backed beetles full of clenched, trapped people. 'Nicky's completely upfront about everything, but I find it hard, I don't know why . . . I've never been able to be myself.'

'Join the clan,' said Alma. 'I've always felt that.'

'But you seem . . . so sure of yourself . . .'

'It's called age,' said Alma. 'It's an illusion . . . but if it helps to know, it does get easier. I think I'm finally getting a bit braver.'

'We're going to Paris for Christmas,' said Ashley.

'I'm jealous,' said Alma. 'I love Paris. We always meant to have a honeymoon in Paris. We put it off. We never did.'

'We're happy,' said Ashley, firmly. She wanted it to be understood.

'You're lucky,' said Alma. 'Not many people are. Have fun. I'll miss seeing you every day.'

'Me too,' said Ashley. 'But I'll see you on Monday.'

They hugged each other briefly, saying goodbye.

Alma walked on towards the delicatessen. It seemed further down the road than she remembered. So Ashley and Nicky were going to Paris. We missed our chance to go to Paris. They were happy together. We were once happy. I didn't value it. I threw it away. The weekend stretched ahead of her; no one was coming. Her head still ached, dully, dimly. She heard her feet dragging and pulled herself erect, shoulders back, speeding up, easing her forehead out of its frown. But she didn't feel right; nothing was right. It was too late for her and Paul. The marriage was over. She knew that, finally. And she was old. Fifty years old.

– *But I don't look fifty. I won't look fifty. Stay upright. Stay alive.*

'Looking lovely, as usual,' a warm voice said. He was standing in front of her, black against the sun, unrecognizable for one split second, blocking her path. 'Where are you going?'

He was very handsome. He wore a black trench-coat and black silk scarf which made his hair look even blonder. His jaw was very slightly too heavy, but his smile was wonderful, his eyes were clear, he was utterly the opposite of poor Mr Allsop with his grey complexion and retreating hairline – he looked young, and fun, and he was looking at her.

'I've been showing someone round a place in Lilley Road.'

'Not the three-bed flat, was it £90,000?'

'The three-bed flat . . . incredible inside. Not my taste, but everyone likes it.'

'I was going to ask to see that flat. I don't suppose . . . Now look. Are you about to have lunch with someone?'

'. . . No . . .'

'I think you work too hard and worry too much. I think you need looking after, Alma. Now this is what we're going to do. I shall take you out to the best lunch that these parts have to offer, and then you can show me Lilley Road. Combines business with . . .' he touched her hand, and she felt the tingle run through her body '. . . pleasure.'

Alma thought, very rapidly, couldn't think. At least it was activity. At least he liked her. At least it might keep the emptiness at bay. And he was attractive; very. 'OK.'

They began to walk along the pavement together, the first time she had ever walked with him, and she liked the feel of his arm, his man's shape, the pleasing height of his broad shoulder . . .

But this is all wrong. This isn't for me. This is another life. Stay away from him, Alma . . .

The little voice worried, but it was too late. Don't be a prig, she told herself. You need to be taken out of yourself. You need some fun. You need a treat. And after all, we ran into each other . . . It must be meant. A lucky break.

'So you weren't working *that* hard,' he said, as they sat in the warmth of the Indian restaurant, which was nearly empty, on Saturday. 'You turned me down. You made me sad.'

That pleasant feeling of anticipation. For the next hour or so, life would be simple, light and warm and unthreatening. She would be amused. She would be fed. For an hour or so, she could play the child. She stroked her hair down over her shoulders. He was big and comforting. He could play Daddy.

'I thought I might have other appointments,' she said. 'That's why I rang to put off our drink.'

'You play hard to get,' he said, looking at her, looking long enough to be sexy, his large light eyes, piercing, definite, as if he thought that he *had* got her now, was about to get her, if he played his cards right. You won't get me, she thought, but the game might be fun. She felt younger, prettier because he wanted her, and the light in the restaurant was the ageless, flattering, rosy light of lunch-time courtship, pretend there is neither day nor night nor work to be done, there is only us . . .

Live in the present, Alma thought. It's what I've been wanting. Live in the present.

She'd had a gin and tonic, and now he ordered wine, without consulting her, telling her. 'They never have any drinkable beer here. So we'll have the Muscadet, and some water.'

Though the restaurant was so empty, the food took for ever, and they drank eagerly and nibbled on a poppadom, finished the poppadom, asked for another. The table was small, and Simon was large.

I must stop thinking of him as Edberg . . . *if only Ashley could see me now.*

He asked her about herself, which was pleasant, though his eyes strayed round the room as she answered. His lips were sensual, slightly undershot. She didn't tell him about Zoe. She wouldn't trust this man with Zoe. Zoe was real, and he was not, he was an actor, a lunch-time distraction . . . She drank the wine. Her bloodstream responded. She didn't feel empty. She felt hungry, but good.

'You're very good-looking,' she told him, frankly. 'Doesn't it make things hard for you? Don't you find men are resentful, sometimes?'

'I'm glad you think I'm good-looking,' he said. 'I used to model sportswear, you know . . . My mother was very good-looking.'

'But how do people react to you?'

He looked at her oddly, his eyes harder. 'Well – sometimes they don't treat me seriously. Sometimes they don't think I mean what I say.'

They were two-thirds through the bottle by the time the food came. She was definitely enjoying herself. He had a tender way of looking at her, of helping her to food, filling her glass . . . filling up her glass when it was only half-empty.

'This is a treat,' she volunteered. 'It's lovely to be looked after.'

'I really enjoy taking care of you.'

That 'taking care' had a definite charge. *He is talking about desire*, she realized. *And his desire is infecting me.* There was a seamless join between the burning food, the exhilarating wine, and his graceful body, leaning towards her, shading her, and the rosy red warmth under her own skin.

She asked him about his family. 'I was lucky,' he said. 'We were always very happy.' Yet the details, when she drew them out, were bleak, though nothing mattered in this restaurant, nothing hurt, that was understood, everything had become incidental to the golden ring which enclosed and tightened. They finished the wine and ordered more by the glass and he told her his mother was beautiful and special, a singer, rarely there when he was little, and later very ill with rheumatoid arthritis, always in pain, always tired, 'and her temper was terrible, poor thing. It was the pain, of course . . .'

'Did she hit you?'

'Oh yes. I'm sure we deserved it. It did us no harm. I mean, I adored her . . . She died in her fifties. I was only fifteen. My brother was younger.'

'That's sad,' Alma said, and he smiled at her, at her voice, which she could hear sounded over-concerned, the slightly maudlin note of drink.

'I was lucky. It didn't really affect me . . . My brother had a breakdown, but I was fine. You have to forget, and get on with life. It's up to you. Live for the present.'

They drank to that. Alma knew this was the answer. Be with someone firm and definite. I've been too introverted . . . This is now. This is great. They had drunk a great deal, by the time they left, and Simon kept his arm around her shoulder after he helped her on with her coat, and she found with dismay that she was slightly confused, for it took her some time to find the key which would take them together into the flat.

38

PAUL WAS SITTING in the Dog and Duck getting increasingly irritated with his son. He had started the day in a good mood. The Education Committee's final decisions about the budget had come through on Friday, and most of the cuts had been cut in half. Perhaps they hadn't liked the sight of voters marching. Perhaps they had achieved something after all. He and Bob had gone and had a taciturn beer on the strength of that, and he'd gone to bed happy.

But today he'd trekked into the centre of town to see his son, and Adam hadn't come. The young were hopeless about time; the children in his school wandered in in the mornings at any time between nine and ten, it was impossible to get anything started . . . and now it was Saturday, his precious Saturday, and he was being messed about again.

He would have to buy a pint for Adam, so he eked out the half he had bought for himself; he would have a proper pint when his son arrived. *If* his son arrived, which looked increasingly unlikely. If he'd known how late Adam was going to be, he would have gone to the bank machine . . .

Here was not where he wanted to be. He was bored, and hungry, and the pub was cold, the weekend shadow of its busy weekday self. It smelled of old beer and sour smoke. It smelled of hangovers and loneliness.

Forty minutes late. He'd eaten two lots of peanuts and his tongue felt shrivelled by all the salt. *Damn you*, he thought. He had plenty to do, but Adam had sounded so queer on the phone, almost desperate to see him –

Then he doesn't bloody show. This place is damp and cold and dead. The barman looks like an aged lizard, pickled by the weekday cigarettes. And Adam *did* sound depressed. I know I didn't imagine it. And I wasn't very nice to him, on the phone, let's face it I was rather taken up with Peeky . . . But Paul didn't feel like being guilty just now.

Feckless bloody youth. I could have been at Dad's. I'd have gone to my parents, if I hadn't been meeting Adam . . . (Well I *might have done*. He knew this wasn't quite fair.) What if Dad dies before I get there. What if I never see him again?

By two o'clock, Paul was incandescent. He emerged from the pub into the bright cold day. The street where Adam lived was to the right, the underground was to the left, but before he decided Paul saw a bus, red and splendid, a number six, thank God some things in this country still work, come sailing down the street in the direction of Ealing, and he ran for the bus-stop, running hell for leather, sprinting, he felt, like a boy of eighteen, he was sure he would beat the bus to the bus-stop, but as he slowed, gasping, slithered to a halt, his right arm waving like a paddle, *Made it, terrific, soon be inside* – he watched the bus sail past the stop. It was completely empty but it wasn't stopping, and he glimpsed the young face of the bus conductor, grinning at him from his solitary splendour, from the bus that he thought was his own private car, as it roared away into the future.

Paul shook his fist. The red oblong sailed on, gay, impervious, not for him. Paul felt old. What was the point? Nothing these days seemed to have a lot of point. Why have buses without any passengers? Why have schools without any funds? Why be a father if you never see your kids? People these days can't communicate. None of us manage to talk to each other. Nobody cares about anyone else. We're all on our own, every one of us . . .

Without making a conscious decision, Paul trudged back along the street towards his son's address, registering complaints from his Achilles' tendon, which hadn't had to flex like that in ages. I can't even run any more. I'm a crock . . .

Paul trudged round the corner, rang the door. If Adam wasn't there, he would leave him a note. He rang again. Someone thumped downstairs. Good, he's there. I shall give him an earful –

But it was a slight girl, with hair pulled back in a single heavy tail behind her shoulders. She looked hurried, or confused, or distressed. Paul stepped back lest his bulk on the doorstep alarmed her. She had serious brown eyes and pale full lips.

'I'm Adam Bennett's father,' he said. 'He lives on the top floor . . .'

'Yes.'

'Is he in?'

'Yes. Come in. I'm worried . . .'

'He was supposed to meet me for lunch.'

'He's ill, I think. There's something wrong. Someone phoned for him an hour or so ago. A girl, his sister –'

'– it couldn't be his sister –'

'– and I went up to fetch him, and music was playing in his room, I thought he couldn't hear me so I looked through the keyhole, and he was still in bed, and I knocked and knocked but he didn't wake up, so I told the girl he was asleep or poorly, but just now I thought I'd better see he's all right, I don't know him well but he seems so nice, and he's just *lying* there, I'm sorry to sound upset but will you come and see . . .'

Paul's heart began to grow, to knock at his chest, to semaphore in wild alarm, and he followed the girl up the dirty stairs which were only carpeted on the first two floors, and then it was bare wood, and their feet were loud, and he wished the thin girl would go faster, faster, and he thought, I shall never forget this climb, I shall never forget the brown plait of hair, intricate, heavy, knocking at her shoulderblades because she's half-running, but not fast enough . . .

He loved his son. He loved his son. He loved his son. Had he ever said so?

And then he was hammering on the door, the big stupid hands thumping beside her small pale ones. Chopin yearned and swelled from within; then a staid man's voice. Must be Radio 3. He thought he heard a groan, then he knew it was the traffic. He knelt down, clumsily, eye to the keyhole, saw nothing, peered, craned, saw something, a bed, blankets. A body on the bed.

'Adam!' he yelled. 'It's Dad, Adam. Open the door! Let me in!'

He had to move away from the door to shout. There was no response. He bent back to the keyhole, banging foreheads with the pale thin girl whose face was taut and blank with fear.

Nothing, then he managed to find the bed. The body. To follow along the body. The body of his beloved son. The hand, the wrist, the shoulder, the side of the head, oh Adam's head, his cheekbone, too sharp, his mouth, gaping. The body of his son lay on that bed, half-covered by a blanket. Adam's body.

As the second split, as time jolted, splintered, Paul lurched upright, he punched the wall, he saw Adam aged six with piercing clarity, learning to ride his first bike in the park – wobbling ecstatic across the green blaze, his straw-blond hair, his shining face, his tremendous pride at being watched and praised – Now Paul was possessed, fists clenched, yelling. 'ADAM! I'LL KICK THE FUCKING DOOR DOWN!'

But someone was pummelling his shoulder. 'Mr . . . sorry, I've forgotten your name, but he moved, he moved, I'm sure he moved!' She had two tiny spots of colour in her cheeks, and her solemn brown eyes were bright with excitement. Hope lurched back; he replaced her at the keyhole, he searched, he found him. But nothing moved. He was utterly still. '*Adam!*' Paul shouted once more, in a fury. He kicked the door, once, twice.

Then the head jerked. Lifted like a tortoise. Fell back again. Adam sat up, slowly. 'Dad?' he croaked. 'Dad. Oh God . . .'

After what seemed like an age, he came to the door. The bolt slid back. Another pause. The key grated in the lock. Paul wanted to burst in, but he waited.

Suddenly Adam stood before him. Tall, rather taller than his father, blond and tangled, completely naked, his tall soft body, his long boy's legs, the darker blond fuzz at his genitals, his pink face heavy and strange with sleep or something more absolute than sleep . . . He was dazed, or confused. He saw the girl, and placed his hands across his penis. His vulnerability, his innocence. He's still a child, Paul thought with wonder, how could I have forgotten that he's still a child?

'What happened?' Paul shouted, realized he was shouting, softened his voice. 'Can I come in? We had a date this lunch-time . . . *Are you all right?*'

Adam walked back inside, leaving the door open, sat down heavily on the bed. Paul followed him into his space. The thin girl hovered like a ghost behind him.

The room was small, and stale, and dark. Only the music shone

301

and yearned, had gone on living as he lay in the shadows. Adam reached out and switched it off.

'Nothing . . . goes right. Nothing works,' he said, thickly. 'I'm no good at anything.'

The girl came in and pulled the curtain. Light poured in on this little space, this little scene of desolation. *How can he live in this miserable box*, thought Paul and then *Thank God it's not a coffin*.

Beside the bed, a whisky bottle, cap off. Paul reached to put it on, automatically, and so he saw the aspirin bottle, and the spill on the floor, the little spill of spent snow, the straggle of pills behind the radio, and so the picture was almost complete, and then Adam handed his father the note.

39

THERE CAN BE LIFE IN EMPTY HOUSES, or things attempting to burst into life. Empty houses can long to be filled, can ring and throb with the strong desire of those outside to come in from the cold.

In Alma's house, the phone was ringing. It rang and rang, and was not answered. The hall table shivered with the force of it; the Michaelmas daisies, the last from the garden, pale mauve and mustard in the afternoon sun, quivered their tassels in the tall glass vase. Alma had forgotten her answering machine. AT HOME, it said; but there was no one at home. Without her decision, it could do nothing. The bell died briefly, and then shrilled on, and the house gathered, the house waited, something would happen – something was flexing, shifting, surely, it had been empty too long, someone must come – but no one answered, the bell grew exhausted, the hall fell back into silence again, and three o'clock passed, and four o'clock passed, and the sunlight left the tops of the flowers, stayed briefly on the walls, on the pictures of the children, two pale watercolours of the children as pretty wraiths, too transparent, too blond – then abandoned the ghosts as the sun went down and the hall grew dark, Alma didn't come home, and now in the dark the phone rang again, impatient, angry, where had she gone?

– For someone is wanting to creep back in. Someone came as the light was dissolving, weakening, bringing the friendly darkness, someone came slowly down the road, someone waited behind the hedge, someone picked berries from the holly tree and dropped them nervously on the pavement, someone, after a thirty-minute pause, crept up the concrete path like a beetle, eyes down, head down, arms round its belly, someone terribly afraid, someone hovered by the porch, shaking, someone stared and stared at the house as if it were a face which could yield an answer – someone stepped forward, and pressed the bell, the heavy brass doorbell which rang loud and pure, not an electronic bully like the telephone, round stones of sound dropped sweetly through water – dropping through water – dropping – falling – rang again, echoed, faded away.

Someone stands in the porch for a second.

A face, a cheek, leans against the glass, wants to touch the house, feel the house, enter the house like a living body, wants to creep in, to come back home.

They want to come in, but the mother is gone.

Alma is somewhere else. Alma doesn't really know what time it is. Alma is sitting with Simon Edwards on the sand-pale sofa of the Lilley Road flat. Alma is flushed and untidy. Alma's long hair coils over her body. Alma has taken off her jacket, and her jumper. Alma's white blouse shows the beginning of her breasts, her small pretty breasts, her long smooth neck. Alma has one hand upon her thigh, her narrow thigh in its lean black skirt. Alma is laughing, and licking her lips. Alma doesn't look at all like a mother.

But Simon looks as he always did, only more so, now he has taken off his coat. The room isn't big, the sofa is quite small, the paleness is dazzling in the low beams of sun, almost blinding on the whites and yellows, the seaside colours, virginal, the unused colours of someone's dreams.

Simon looks very large indeed, his large square head on his thick male neck, his broad shoulders like a rugby player's, his muscular thighs which press out his jeans. He is stroking his body. He is liking his body. He is sure his body is going to be pleased. He is happy with his hunger for Alma's body, with anticipating what they will do, with knowing what she will let him do, with thinking where she will let him go. Into her body, going back home.

As they were walking back to the flat, their bodies touching, their steps unsteady, Alma had confessed she liked cigars.

'Large cigars or small cigars?'

'Oh . . . just the smell of them. The feel of them. Large cigars are more . . . luxurious.' Life hadn't been luxurious, recently.

'Do you like to feel them in your mouth?' he asked. She laughed, they were friends, everything was funny, and he went into the off-licence and came back with two enormous cigars and a bottle wrapped in green tissue paper.

'You said you liked them big,' he said.

'I can't possibly drink any more,' she said.

'It's nearly Christmas. You have to relax . . . I've been looking forward to this for some time. We could . . . take a line . . . if you like it . . . ?'

'Is that drugs?' She heard herself sound ten years old.

He laughed. 'Don't worry, you stick to brandy.'

He was very definite, and very intimate, and somehow all of this was familiar, she had been with him a lifetime before, and the course of events was already determined, and when they got into the cold small flat he said 'Let's pretend, let's be newly-weds' and he dug around till he found a glass and poured a large slug from his bottle of brandy, and then brought the small fan heater from the kitchen and turned it on full in the immaculate front room, where the builder had thought he would live with his fiancée, where real newly-weds had once dreamed of living, and Alma found herself telling him this, and it was somehow sad, and complicated, but Simon didn't understand the sadness, Simon didn't need the complication.

'I'm interested in us,' he said. 'I'm interested in you, Mrs Bennett. You're very slender. You're very light. I bet I could pick you up one-handed. Here, let's try it –'

'Whoa,' she said. He had huge hands, broad fingertips which dug into her arm, leaving five red marks where she pulled away. 'I got to finish my brandy, haven' I. Mustn' spill it. Mustn' make a mess. Got to look after this nice clean flat.'

The sun had gone. It seemed suddenly dark. She hadn't brought the mobile phone. There was no one to call in any case, no one to hear. No one to help her.

'You're a sweet little girl. You're tipsy,' he said. 'Don't worry, I'll put down my overcoat. I can always clean my overcoat . . .'

– So she would be split, smeared, spilled.

He put his hand under her hair at the back with a sudden movement, his fingers diving through it, found her neck, which felt small beneath his fingers, took it in his grasp as if she were a

305

rabbit, squeezed it gently, then not so gently, but his face was tender, his face was excited, the face of a man who would soon be in bliss.

But she didn't want this. It was all a mistake.

'I'm not a little girl,' she said, very quietly. She pulled away from him with an effort, reached across and switched the light on. There was no shade. It was startlingly bright. She froze beneath it; she could not think.

'You're my little girl. Let's get undressed. Here, I'll undo these buttons for you. Or do you want to help me with my trousers. Hey, sit on my lap –' He reached out to grab her, laughing, lazy, a giant cat which pawed its prey, and she didn't know what she ought to do, the present was ending, the playful present, the golden present where she had been safe, she was being pulled into a different game, into the endless past which would be her future, and she clutched her glass, she ducked out of reach, she played for time while she finished her drink, but why was she here, what were they doing, she didn't know who she was looking for . . . a terror began at the back of her throat, this was all very old, she was very small, it had never been what she meant at all, she could not see, the light was blinding, she had lost her shoes, her bag, her coat, she had lost her voice, she had lost her self –

'Come on,' he said, 'don't keep me waiting.' His jeans and underpants were round his knees. 'I know you want it. I know you're hot.' His hair was yellow-white under the light-fitting, a lock flipped forward where he'd pulled off his shirt, and I have to do it, I have to, she thought, he's been nice to me, I owe him it, I can't disappoint him, it's all my fault – she sat for a split second more on the sofa and he reached across and took her hair, a clump of pale curls between his fingers, and tugged at it, held it, pulled her across – 'Beautiful hair,' he said, breathing hard. 'Now come on, darling. It's me. Wake up.'

'Sorry,' she said. *Sorry, sorry*. His needs were huge, she must not let him down, but he was too large, and she was too small, and even her best could not be enough – then he pulled at her hair again, and it hurt.

'Don't give me *sorry*,' he said, lip curling. 'I'm going to make you glad, Alma.' He pulled at her buttons, but his hands were too big, two buttons burst off and fell on the floor and she heard the little sigh of tearing cloth, and then he was so close he was everywhere, he was breathing through her, his hands passed through her, his huge leg pressed her down on the floor, his presence burned her, he combed her like air, his wetness closed over her face and drowned her, and she was an absence, a doll, a nothing . . .

She was half on her back, spread across the sofa, his weight on top of her, dragging at her skirt, licking at her face like a plate of food, gorging like a child who could never be satisfied, tearing at her blouse, eating her breasts – she opened her eyes, and she saw the skylight, and in the skylight, a square of blue sky, the theatrical turquoise of very early evening, unbelievably beautiful, that brilliant sky, the sky at its turning into night, the sky at its margin, where two worlds meet, where colour blooms, where all can be known, and on the edge of the skylight, against the blue but lit up from below by their blaze of electric, a tentacle of ivy shivered, three or four leaves, spectacularly bright, white and green points of absolute precision.

I do exist. I'm part of that.

'Get off,' she tried to say, 'get off,' but nothing audible came out, and she called on her body, gathered her body, *my body, mine, my living self*, it did have walls, it was complete – and with a sudden twist and lift of her body took him by surprise, over-balanced him, she had pushed him off, he fell like a drunk cursing, crashing, 'What?' he shouted, 'what the hell is going on?', thick with anger, rubbing his elbow which had turned beneath him.

She stumbled to her feet, clutching her blouse. 'I'm sorry,' she said. *But you mustn't say sorry.* 'I don't want to do this. *I don't want to.* I'm sorry if you think I led you on—'

'What's the matter?' he shouted. 'You're enjoying yourself,' and his will was stronger, his face was very red, he was ready to burst, he was going to destroy her – 'Come on,' he said. 'Come on, you bitch.'

'I will not be abused. I will not be abused!' She was screaming at him, her voice was hoarse. But the words came out. The words were said. There was silence. Both of them were breathing hard.

307

She became her anger, her lost clear self. She knew she was no longer smaller than him.

'You knew what this was about,' he said. 'You knew I fancied you. Didn't you?'

'That doesn't mean I have to have sex.'

'You wanted me. You wanted it.'

'I'm a grown woman! I changed my mind!'

He stared at her, standing in the middle of the room, screaming at him, her voice tearing. Something slumped in him; something broke or yielded. He stared at her, baffled. He turned away.

'So keep your hair on. You're fucking neurotic. I'm not a rapist. I don't need to be . . . You bloody women don't know your own minds.'

'I know my own mind.'

Her head was aching, she had grains of mascara in her eyes, her blouse was torn, but she knew her own mind. What was the phrase? She had a mind of her own.

And my body . . . my body . . . my poor mute body. It had pushed him away. It had finally spoken.

I didn't let him hurt it. It's here. It's mine.

After he had gone, slamming out without a word, his blond hair askew, sullen, thwarted, she cleared up the mess, tidied the flat. Then she left it to its emptiness.

40

THE EARLY EVENING had closed into night by the time she drove down Arbutus Road. Back, she thought, to another empty house. The missing link in the chain of bright houses. She had learned to orient herself by that gap, the absence among the presences.

But somehow or other she drove straight past it. She realized when she got to the bend in the road that she had somehow managed to miss it. *I must still be tipsy* – but she didn't feel tipsy. She felt sober, and shaken. Exhausted; stirred. She longed to be home, in her own home. She stopped, did a weary U-turn, drove back.

– Which explains it, she thought. It's because I left the lights on. The bay was ablaze, and the upstairs landing. It was as if she had driven into the past, but she realized that she had merely left the lights on. The house looked alive, though it was just an illusion. The house looked better. It looked like a home. The sadness of empty houses, she thought. Of all the empty houses in cities –

She opened the door, and heard voices. Panic. Don't be stupid, it's the television. I must have left the television on – but she never had the TV on in the morning. She stood in the hall irresolute. Go back out and call for help –

Then he came out of the front room and stood before her. 'Alma,' he said. 'Did I make you jump?'

Fear yielded to delight. 'Paul, my love . . . you could have telephoned.'

His familiar big body, his big kind body, his harassed, handsome, uxorious face, worried, tender . . . love welled up in her.

'I telephoned all bloody afternoon. Look, you'd better sit down. Have you been working? You stink of brandy –' his voice sharpened, jealous. 'Oh well, never mind. Better not tell me. This is important. Listen.'

309

She sat on the sofa; the television was on; he switched off the sound, and stared at her.

'I had a long business lunch, that's all.'

'I didn't know that you lunched with clients –'

'Well we're closing down. It's complicated. Mr Portico was there on his own—'

'Oh, Portico. Oh, that old fart.' She let it slide. This would be her secret. He was reassured, had gone on to something else. He probably had secrets; she would have a secret. One day she would be able to tell him.

'I said, sit down.' She saw he was serious.

'Paul – oh Paul – it's Zoe, isn't it . . . ?'

'Adam's upstairs. He's in his room. Look, he's quite all right, or he will be all right, but something happened . . .'

'Quick! Tell me!' She was seized by terror, her stomach squeezed –'

'Alma, he tried to kill himself. Not very efficiently, thank God. Aspirin and whisky. Fifteen tablets, which is far too few. I'm sorry to tell you this, I know it's terrible. I found him in bed, in that house. He was groggy, with a terrible hangover . . .'

'Did you get him to the doctor? Was he stomach-pumped?'

'He didn't want anyone to know. I rang Gerald,' – an old friend of Paul's who was a GP in the East End – 'who said he should be perfectly all right, but he came over and saw him all the same . . . Adam *is* all right. He was shamefaced with Gerald . . . It's *us*, damn it, who should be ashamed . . . I mean, I've been preoccupied . . . It was such a shock – I'd just gone over for lunch. He's sleeping it off in his bedroom. Now don't be upset – *Alma* . . .'

'But I can't believe it . . . He's not been unhappy –'

'– He's been very unhappy. Desperately. There was this girl, another lawyer. He was bringing her here. She let him down –'

'– My God, I forgot to ask him about it – I said he could, I wanted to help – I forget about Adam, that's the awful thing.'

'He still needs us. He's still very young.'

'I'll go up and see him.'

'Yes. But he's asleep . . .'

'Are you *sure* that he's all right?'

'Medically, yes . . . but have you seen his new room? It's a broom cupboard . . . It's no good for him . . . You realize I had to bring him here.'

'Paul, for heaven's sake – of course you did.'

Alma sat there stunned for a moment, staring blindly at the television screen, then realized she was looking at burning tower blocks, at black and orange belching out on to the blue, thick as tar, heavy as death, engulfing the small running bodies who screamed and waved their arms without making a sound, terrified stick men running towards her . . .

'I'll switch that off. There's no point without the sound –'

'Thank you, Paul. I mean, for what you did –' As she passed close by him to go up to Adam they clung to each other without a word.

They were grownups now. They had to be. They had lived together for a quarter of a century. They shared two children. They were Mummy and Daddy. They had grown middle-aged: they had somehow forgotten. Now they remembered. They held each other.

Alma opened the door of Adam's room. They used to do that sometimes when he was little, peep inside to see he was sleeping. He lay in his bed, his head to one side, the duvet askew across his body, one shoulder and half his torso bare. His feet almost overshot the mattress. How could he ever have grown so big? – His arms were spread wide, his feet together. What image was she reminded of?

– Icarus, exhausted. An ash-blond Christ.

That hair, she thought. It's Daddy's hair. The genes for that came down through me. That flop of pale hair across his forehead. Daddy's face, was it; half-remembered . . . ?

But Adam looked perfect, and unwounded. Thank God he hadn't managed to hurt himself. In sleep his profile looked young, relaxed, the deep-set orb of one closed eye, his mouth, nearly as full and soft as Zoe's . . . Why does sleep unlock my tenderness?

And then she thought swiftly, it could be death, death would stretch him out like that, and she crept up closer to feel his warmth, to make sure his shoulder-blades were rising and falling; they were, and he suddenly turned on to his back, the miracle of

311

his living body, the curly blond hairs still fine and scattered, the nipples as naked as a girl's, his generous mouth moving, mumbling, the very faint stubble across his cheek, the little pitting of his skin where teenage acne had left its mark, and she was glad of the imperfection, imperfection was real, was living.

'I'm sorry, Adam,' she whispered, touching him, touching his hand which lay spread out, open, ready to receive whatever she would give. 'I'm really sorry' – but that wasn't it, she realized as she tiptoed away, and she turned and said, slightly louder, 'I love you.'

'Mum,' Adam muttered, and she jumped, bent closer, waited for more, but he was asleep, he had turned on his side, turned his soft cheek.

'Was he awake? Did he say anything?' Paul asked her, when she got downstairs. 'Can we get him something?'

'Sleeping. He's fine. He said "Mum."'

'Well . . .'

'Yes, I know. I'm really going to try. We'll all sit down and talk in the morning . . .'

'May I stay the night?'

'I just assumed . . .'

'But if *I'd* assumed it, you'd have been annoyed.'

'Yes. No. I wouldn't, today. Please stay, Paul. I hope you will.'

'Do you know, I just want to get my head down. I'm happy to see you. But I just want to sleep. If I had my dream, that would be it. Zoe and Adam would both be back, and I would come home and sleep and sleep. We were always so busy, when we were together, we never seemed to get enough sleep . . .'

'Where will you sleep? . . . There's Zoe's room . . .'

They stared at each other, unsure, enquiring. And Alma thought, it's time to be mother. He was her man; she'd look after him. She had chosen him a long time ago; he had never frightened her, or forced her. He was Adam's father. He had saved her son. Now she wanted to look after him.

'Sleep in our bed. You'll be comfortable there. You'll feel at home.'

'What will you do, then?' His voice was unsteady.

'I don't know yet, I'm not ready for bed . . . I've got things to do. I have to think . . . I might come and join you, you never know . . . How long is it since we slept together?' – In another life, another country. For the house felt different; lighter, looser.

'Don't remind me . . . abstinence has been awful . . . I haven't been unfaithful.' That was his gift. He didn't have to say it, but he did.

'No . . . nor have I.' And that was hers. 'Go on, go to bed. I shall put on some washing.'

'Oh sod the washing.'

'I always do the washing . . . Adam must have some. You'll want clean pants. And my clothes feel filthy. I have to get clean.'

'On Saturday night? It's your sodding mother . . . "Duty before pleasure," wasn't that it?'

'Maybe it's her, but it's me as well. You'll wake up in the morning and it will all be done. Then you'll be glad.' But she knew he wouldn't care.

'I won't give a monkey's. I never did.'

'That's what's so maddening about you—'

'That's what people are like, maddening. If you live on your own you'll never be maddened.'

'I think I've had enough of living on my own.'

And yet, she enjoyed it, when he'd gone upstairs, walking about the empty rooms which they hadn't had a chance to untidy yet.

The house felt at ease. It was quiet at last. She could no longer hear the repetitive voices. Perhaps they had gone, had finished with her?

It's me, she thought. I've heard enough. If Zoe came home, perhaps I would be ready . . . Maybe we could move. We could leave at last. Maybe we could find a new place together . . . Already it was just rooms, spaces.

She watered plants, she straightened pictures. She looked into the lit worlds of her pictures. She looked at her print of a Bonnard bedroom, one that she hadn't looked at for months, one she hadn't wanted to look at. The blowing curtains, the glow of the flesh. The little answering flame in her, small and secret, a candle flame. Another print of a child running, running in the middle of a sheet of light, the bright ground going on for ever, the child's face blank, any child's face . . .

– *If she came home.*

313

But I must forget her . . . the tormenting, perpetual presence of her absence . . . it's Adam's turn. I must think about him.

She dipped into the photograph album and found a picture of Adam as a boy, pink-cheeked, English, wholesomely handsome, blond as hay, thick-haired as a Palomino pony, and put it on the mantelpiece, right in the middle, in place of a picture of twelve-year-old Zoe. Nearly every picture in the house was of Zoe. Why had she never noticed it before?

Adam was her son. He was still alive.

I shall have to concentrate on him. Him and Paul. They'll both need time. If the office is closing I'll have a bit of time . . .

And I have to make a life for myself. I'm old enough to be myself.

– I have to settle accounts with Mother. There are no accounts . . . it can't be settled . . . but I have to make her talk to me. Or at the least, I'll make her listen. Maybe then I could love her properly. Maybe we could be close at last. If we could somehow be naked together . . . She sighed. She had never seen her mother naked. No, it was nonsense. She would never listen.

Gwen was encrusted, calcareous. She would never know what lived inside. Exposed, it would be terrible; it *was* terrible, when Alma had tried . . .

But somewhere, thought Alma, she must be hiding. The child that my mother was. The one I could understand and pity. The one who could have been friends with me, when I was a child, when I was lonely.

But her parents forced her to hide away. And she hid so well that she can't be found.

She's somewhere, though, I know she is. If I had more patience. If I were kinder. If I could move outside myself . . .

Even the fathers. Owen, Jack. Were babies once. Needy, not bullies. Everything could have been different for them. They must have been pressed down a narrow path. Then suddenly it was all too late. And now they're dead, and they've done their damage. Whatever the details. Whatever they did. Things they did because they knew no better. Things they did because they could not stop. Things they did because they had been wounded in some deep place that they had forgotten . . . the secret place they could never find. So instead, they repeated. Passed it on.

Never to know. They had never known. The brilliant sand, dissolving, sifting.

They stretched down the beach, the rows of babies, separated by the dazzle of time, by the bands of sand between the generations which meant they could never touch each other. One row were parents, the next were children, and down that division sorrow flowered, the words unheard, the wounds untreated. From the power of the parents, sorrow flowered. From the needs of the children, sorrow flowered. The needs of the children, so new, so naked, crawling to their parents, infinitely hungry. As *they* had once crawled towards their own parents . . .

And then the sand blew across the picture. She could not remember; would never remember. And yet it was common, what had happened to her. She knew that much, that she held it in common. That everyone suffered, in the house of childhood. Perhaps there were further, more terrible rooms, but they interconnected, they were not separate.

And always the children became the parents. Owen and Jack were once those babies. Jack is in Adam's yellow hair. Perhaps that's why I could never love him . . . But he was a child. He was innocent. Adam, bearing the sins of the fathers . . .

I have to love him. Now I can love him. If I can love him, I can break the pattern.

That was the secret. *Love allows* . . . love allows us to be ourselves.

Love might allow him to be himself.

Fade the past into a different future . . .

She tiptoed into the upstairs bedrooms, enjoyed the sleeping shapes of the men, picked up socks, shirts, pants, pulled up the duvets to cover them. It was a cold night now, the house was cooling, creaking, rustling as the temperature dropped, as the moon came up, as the faint stars prickled. She loaded her fouled clothes into the machine. Getting things straight, sorting things out . . .

She was making things decent again, that was it. *Gwen is in me. She's part of me* . . .

Alma went to bed. It was only ten o'clock. Paul didn't wake. She didn't wake him. She didn't feel sexual. She was deeply tired, and almost content. The bed was warm. They curled like commas. Life was peaceful. She swam, she slept . . . Something was missing, but Alma slept, woke briefly to a sense of fear and guilt, it was all her fault, she had led him on, and then realized the man was Paul, curled against him and slept again.

Turned and floated. They were in her arms, they were all in the water, they were holding hands . . . Eileen was telling her Gwen couldn't swim. 'She never could, and she's too old to learn. Leave her alone, she is my sister,' but Alma was begging Gwen to take her clothes off, 'Everyone else has, Mother, you'll drown,' but she mustn't drown, she had something to tell her, and now Gwen was wading out beyond the rocks, she was very large, or Alma was small, her enormous legs somehow reached to the sand, she was wading far out beyond the shallows, 'Mother, come back, I need to talk to you,' but 'I'm looking for Zoe,' her mother called back, 'I have to find her, it's getting cold, I bet she hasn't got her vest on . . . how on earth will she manage in the real winter? She won't come to see me, and I am her grandma –' 'You won't find her,' Alma shouted, 'there are thousands of children stranded out there,' for at last she had seen where her mother was going, there was a long island a hundred yards out, still in the sun, though it had left the mainland, a long broad sandbank of ash-white sand, gleaming like pearl, like wax, like skin, the skin of the thousands of naked children who lay and rested in the last of the sun, and her mother called 'Of course they're not lost, why must you always exaggerate?' but as Alma watched, her lips frozen, she saw it sink, she saw it settle, she saw it struggling, waterlogged, she saw the body of her mother grow darker, she was stifling, suffocating, fighting it off . . .

She woke up sweating, terrified, on a peak between fear and sexual excitement, tangled in the baggy tee-shirt she'd put on, and she pulled it off, shivering a little, pulled the bedclothes over her, and Paul woke up and made love to her, swiftly, tenderly, they knew each other, she came in seconds, on the ebb of the dream, and he followed too, only moments later, lay inside her and slept like a baby.

41

WHEN SHE WOKE UP NEXT, at her habitual time, the pointless time of three a.m., she got up and walked to the window, restless, and Zoe was in the garden again. Alma stared through the curtains and saw her daughter.

She had seen her there a hundred times when anxiety woke her and drove her to the window, when the wind rustled and troubled the leaves, when the bones of the house ached and turned. Zoe would be crouching behind the pillar of darkness which was the cypress whose smell she loved. She would move as the wind moved the cypress, creep through the front garden, never showing her face, the bushes parting as she crawled across, all in black, black as night, surely that hedge concealed a child, but it was rooted, featureless, inhuman, useless, never Zoe, never her daughter, despite the hope that would pierce Alma, hold her at the glass, peering intently, her heart beating, her heart drumming, trying to distinguish between shades of darkness, trying to will the ghost to come back.

If I could touch her. If I could . . . feed her. If she were lying on the lawn after school . . .

Zoe was there, that night, the same shuffling ghost, shivering over the leaves in the moonlight, playing on the edges between moon and clouds and the winter wind which blew from Russia, how can she survive, how can any of them survive . . . ? More solid than usual, for the moon was bright, but still almost vanishing into the bushes. Slower than usual, and more tormenting, stubbornly, slowly coming down the path, long hair rippling like evergreen branches, bigger, sadder, older than usual.

Sighing, Alma went back to bed, praying that Zoe was safe inside, anywhere warm and out of the wind. She was sixteen. She would soon be seventeen. If she was lucky, if she survived.

Alma nosed closer to Paul's warm body.

If she could float. If she could float in time. This was the bed. This is the bed. This is the bed where she lay between us, lies between us, loves us both . . .

Nothing is lost. She cannot be lost. That tiny body still lies between us.

It was six when Alma woke again, too early, the merest line of light at the curtains. Her punishment for yesterday's brandy. But Paul was here. A nugget of comfort. Adam was here. Relief; guilt. She would sleep again. She wasn't ready to face it, the weariness of the winter light . . .

But sleep had gone. She would have to wake up. She went downstairs in her dressing-gown, remembering, as she did every day, the morning she had found the casual little note on the landing, and everything shifted, everything stopped, and when it started again, a light had gone out.

Halfway downstairs, she remembered her slippers, padded back up, came down again, pulled her dressing-gown tightly round her and opened the front door to fetch in the milk. But it was Sunday, of course. Nothing would come; she had lost track of the days; time had no meaning.

The bitter wind. The fresh damp air, smelling of smoke as well as earth, of sour earth, of rain, of petrol, the smell of the city of men in the morning. She breathed it in deep, that raw wild smell. It was not quite dawn; it was not quite dark. Grey streaks of light lit up the sky, painted across the racing clouds. Under her feet no frost. One line of crimson where sky met city.

She saw how the darkness was lifting from the garden. A very faint green leaked back into the leaves. She looked at their familiar winter shapes. All along the road, the shapes of the bushes, the small cold gardens they forgot at night, and yet they were part of them, part of the houses . . . The inbreath of air made her teeth chatter. Alive, she thought. I'm here, and alive . . .

She saw her then, crouched against the porch, half-hidden by the bulk of the creeper, wrapped in something, a sleeping-bag, was it, covered in a coat, in a pile of clothes. But her face, her face. Her real face. Plumper than before, smooth as ice, grey as stone in the flat grey light. Her hair. So much of it, grown so long, so long away to have grown so long, such thick dark hair round her head like a nest. Thank God that something was keeping her warm . . .

'Zoe,' she cried, and she knelt beside her, bare thin knees on the icy concrete, she felt she was kneeling on her bones; she didn't care, she knelt beside her.

But Zoe was tired; perhaps she knew she was home; she went on sleeping as the sun crept up, as the absurdly brilliant pink of our star slipped above the horizon and between the houses, as a little blood, then a little more, returned to her skin, her lips, her cheeks, as she ceased to be a child of stone, as living colour painted her, as her mother knelt beside her and watched, as she took the hands in their cold gloves, saying 'Zoe, Zoe,' over and over, as her mother stroked her cheeks and wept.

When Zoe finally half-woke, confused, she reached out her arms, her hands outstretched, for all the world as if her mother could lift her.

'Mum,' she said. 'Don't get cold . . . I didn't want to wake you. Is Adam all right? The girl at the house said—'

'Yes,' said Alma, 'yes. Yes. Adam is fine. He's here, Zoe . . . You're freezing, darling. Come back inside.'

But she could hardly stand, she was stiff with cold, and they stood on the threshold in the wonderful light, the morning blazing on Zoe's broad clear brow, her gaze on the ground, her lips trembling, and then Zoe managed to look at Alma, facing the shock and the fear of meeting: her eyes can rest in her mother's eyes, green in green, dissolving, living, and all down the road Alma sees the leaves moving, the dark camellias beginning to shine, the sad rhododendrons, the brown hydrangeas with their long-dead flowers are all waking, changing, every dark cone is coming alive; the arms of the children stretch out to the houses, the silent children creep into the sun, touch the light, reach up for more, raise to our eyes the white slopes of their hunger. Their unloved bodies, their unlived lives. Drawn to these homes, these dreams of shelter.

'I lost a baby. I had . . .' stumbles Zoe, but her teeth are chattering too much. Alma will hear her, but not yet. She is deaf with joy; *found, found* . . .

319

42

WHAT IF NOTHING IS LOST, never lost entirely? – If time is a circle? – If love could return. And lack, and need; meek, mute.

If need crept back, and asked to be filled. If fear returned, to collide with courage. If we had time to feel, to listen. The impossible meeting would surely happen. The unimaginable could be imagined.

If only we could slip from the room for a second . . .

Gwen died four days after Zoe came home, knowing she was back, dreaming she had seen her. Alma could never ask the questions that might have unlocked the cupboard of childhood, but look, the child is in her arms. Paul's father lived on for another two years, survived three more strokes, forgot he'd been happy, forgot he'd been sad, forgot, forgotten . . .

– Or is it that he slipped from the room for a second? Maybe he woke with the French windows flung wide and walked out into the landscape we have just dreamed, stretching away in every direction, perspectiveless, dazzling, unbounded, peopled.

Maybe the children are there already. Millions of them. The uncountable lost ones. Loud as life, running, laughing. Sun on the black, the ash-blonde, the auburn.

Myself, yourself, my mother, my father. Still young, still potential. All the lost children.